Twilight of the God

A Dying Gods Tale

Patrick Boal

DEDICATION

To Ginevra and Argia.

FORWARD

This is a story, a work of fiction. Names, characters, businesses, organizations, places, events, locales, and incidents are either the products of the author's imagination or used in a fictitious manner. Any resemblance to actual persons, living or dead, or actual events is purely coincidental.

This story is a sequel to the novel *Dying Gods*. It can be read as a stand-alone story, but I suggest readers may take more from the story if they read *Dying Gods* first. This story is not for children or those of sensitive natures. A few passages might disturb or upset. They are intended to do so.

Patrick Boal, Mississauga, Ontario, Canada

"O, how shall summer's honey breath hold out

Against the wreckful siege of battering days,
When rocks impregnable are not so stout,
Nor gates of steel so strong, but Time decays?"

Sonnet 65 5-8
William Shakespeare

CHAPTER ONE – DINNER IN PARIS

Paris, France

Water on sheet glass. Flowing down like rain on a windowpane. Frothy white soap bubbles, driven from my love's long, dark hair by the shower spray, splashed up and rushed down the lightly tinted glass.

I watched her soap her hair and rinse it clear. And then, as she elegantly soaped her face and body, I smiled. I had not been truly alone with her for half a year, not since May 1st, Beltane. She motioned my gaze away with a flick of her chin, but I could see the smile beneath the frothy lather.

She was still pretty, my Rhiannon. Not beautiful or ravishing or exquisite, but pretty. Her natural figure is wonderfully ample, her skin lightly tanned and her eyes... Her eyes are dark, deep like the eyes of a deer. She was 31 when I met her, six years earlier on that mountainside in the valley. She was still every bit as lovely.

To my pedestrian mind the hotel room was a strange design. The shower was a glass booth fully visible from the rest of the room, as was the whole, glass-enclosed bathroom. It was a tiny room in a retro brutalist style – exposed concrete walls. All oddly late 20th century. Barely a meter from the shower stall, the bed was built into a raised dais, with the length of my forearm between the mattress and the walls. It was comfy, though, the bed.

From where I lay upon the comfy bed, I had a clear view of the shower. Behind my head, real rain rattled against the plate glass window that served as the exterior wall. And beyond that lay Paris in the late fall – on November 1st, Samhain. I was dressed in a grey linen suit with a white cotton shirt and black tie. My black shoes were on my feet, on the bed. If I lived in a noir movie, I would have been smoking pensively. But I didn't. And I wasn't. I was waiting to go out to dinner at a "super" Moroccan restaurant suggested by the concierge. I was looking forward to it. A lot. So was she.

1

Now, you may think it strange, given that I had not been with my love for half a year and she was resting one hand against the glass while cleaning her bottom with a tiny bar of lavender-scented soap and looking me straight in the eyes, that I was thinking about Chicken Bastilla. And, I admit it, a Moroccan pastry with herbed chicken, eggs, raisins, almonds, dusted with powdered sugar and cinnamon cannot hold a candle to a steaming, soapy Rhiannon in a glass box. But our reservation was in less than an hour. And it had been six years since I had been out of the valley and, while The Three Crowns is a fine establishment with wondrous cider, well… Paris, dammit. Moroccan food. And fine French wines. All awaited, just beyond the door.

I watched as she turned beneath the spray from the nozzle, perhaps a few more times than necessary, and stepped away from me into the frosted glass of the bathroom. She emerged moments later wrapped in a fluffy white towel.

"Enjoyed that, you did," said Rhiannon.

"True, it is," said I. "I thank you for it. It was surely one of the best moments of my life."

She looked at me sharply.

"No. I mean it," I said.

"Really?" she asked.

"Yes."

"Well, then."

She crossed the room, edged up the side of the bed and bent down to kiss me, her long, wet hair dripping all over me.

"That will have to do you, 'til after," she said, straightening. "I will just be a moment."

That was a lie, of course. In the end we had to get the concierge to summon a cab to run us from the hotel to the Maison Arabe. Do not ask me how we got there. The Rue de Babylone is a thin, one-way road in front of the three-story Hotel de O'Keefe and the restaurant was the other way. The driver, a stout Gaul, seemed to know where he was going, though. We arrived in one piece and dry.

This may have been her plan all along.

The restaurant was all plate glass, brightly lit and stylishly modern. (I know this, because it seemed to make Rhiannon happy.) From our glass-topped table by the window, we watched the rain come out of the darkness and wash downward. Rhiannon was smiling and lovely in a deep-cut black dress with 3rd century Roman, braided-rope style gold earrings and a simple solid gold torc.

A few moments after we settled in, an older middle-eastern man with a deeply impressive, curled, grey moustache, in a pressed white shirt and black tie, brought our menus and the wine list. He spoke French. Rhiannon replied in the same language and ordered a cabernet franc and merlot blend from Bordeaux. 1998. She was spoiling me.

"Order you should," said Rhiannon.

"Don't speak the language," I said.

"You studied it for eight years!" she said.

"Not a word," I said. "I am Canadian." I smiled as moustache man brought the wine and performed the requisite ritual. Rhiannon tasted it and nodded in approval. He poured. I tasted. Smooth and gentle on the tongue. So good.

"Thank you, my love," I said. "And you are beautiful tonight."

"Thank you," she said. "And handsome you are."

"You are too kind." But I smiled. And so did she. And we drank the wine as the rain splashed down the windows in the dark. I thought of her in the shower. And I drank the wine.

"Slow," she said. "It was expensive, and we need to make our allowance last a year. And, when you drink you get melancholy. Tonight is not the night for melancholy."

More and more she dropped the old language structure. My influence, I am afraid. Six years of exposure to my badly-educated ramblings. I did not mention this as it always made her cross. She was correct, of course, about the melancholy.

"Well…" I opened my two hands in a gesture of futility.

"Understand, I do," she said. "Your young wife is currently seducing the man who will be the next Lord of Summer. You are tossed out of your own house. Your children…" She shrugged. Bare shoulders in a black dress. The Roman gold sparking under the bright restaurant lights.

"I have you," I said. "For one more year, I have you. And, I can accept my wife, your daughter, with that younger man. That was always part of the deal. I knew it, always. What upsets me most is that my best friend will be the one training him to kill me. Bloody hell, that hurts."

"Sucks, it does," she said. Then she looked up, a little startled. We both laughed.

"And, Celyn knows all my tricks and weaknesses," I said.

She looked at me over her wine.

"I know, I am not supposed to win. World ends. All that," I said.

She nodded. "Besides, I love you," she said, softly. "Do you think I will let you die so easily?"

Monsieur Moustache returned just then, clearly overhearing the last comment. He made no sign of it. Rhiannon ordered black olive tapenade with fresh baguette for the appetizer and Chicken Bastilla for two as the main. And another bottle of the Bordeaux.

"I will see you have more training when the time comes," she said. "And, there is our little adventure. Our quest."

I rolled my eyes and she saw it.

"Real it is," she said, firmly. The slight slur to her speech from the wine made me smile. "And find it we will!"

"You are all being terribly kind, and it is an excellent reward and distraction, but it's just an old story," I said, and smiled in what I hoped was a reassuring way. "We are in Paris. You and I are alone in Paris. Let us just be in Paris."

The wine came right then. The ritual was performed once more, and it comforted me.

We had first discussed the idea of our little quest one misty morning on Llyn Dwythsch. This little lake, which lay somewhat south of our hidden Welsh valley, was a favorite fishing place for me in the summer. Calm, fog-shrouded and mystic, surrounded by green mountains: I had it stocked regularly with rainbow trout and I spent countless mornings there with my girls. But, that day, it was only Rhiannon and me – just three days after the three Rowans – Anna, Rhiannon and Clarine – had together told me about the new challenger, Roland Hamstead. This presumptuous toad - a large, fit, young man of twenty-three is just a year older than my wife. And, he is of the valley, from a traditional family. Much more suitable than I am; it is an easy argument. He will be the one to fight me and, if all goes as it should, sever my head from my body.

I had been expecting the conversation as the timing was right – six years had slipped by. But I had not expected the matter-of-factness of it all. Clarine had been distant, distracted. Rhiannon had watched without saying a word. Anna had been stone-faced. It was painful and I barely managed to keep it together.

That day, the fishing day, Rhiannon had picked me up in her old Land Rover and we made our way up the loose-gravel tracks to the old stone boat houses on the east shore of Llyn Dwythsch. We did not mention the conversation on the way up to the lake. When we arrived, I slipped the small skiff from its moorings on the wooden dock and rowed us out onto the water. A light rain hung in the air, more of a heavy mist really, all curtains of white moving faintly across the water in waves. Before that day on the water it was rare for me to be allowed time alone with Rhiannon. Clarine did not like it. So, I knew things were changing. I just did not know how abrupt it would be.

Rhiannon took the oars and I baited my hook – nothing fancy, just a worm on a hook. I placed a bobber about a meter from the hook and cast out over the still water. We sat quietly and listened to the sounds of the lake – the water muttering against the side of the skiff, the harsh cry of the Lesser Black-backed Gull. I was surprised when Rhiannon spoke.

"It is the way," she said. "But, sorry I am."

"We all knew it was coming. It was still hard," I said.

"Cameron, my love, you are an idiot, but you handled it well," she said.

"Barely," I said. "I almost lost it." I sighed and it seemed to echo back across the water. "Me having a breakdown would have made it worse for everyone. She is my wife, after all, and there are the children to consider."

"An idiot, you are," she said, but managed a little smile. "But..." It trailed off. I turned and she was looking down. I did not like the look on her pretty face.

"But?" I asked.

"Asked, I have. We, you and I, can leave the valley for one year to search for a way out." She looked up, straight into my rather confused face. "We must find the Lapis Exillis."

Back then on that misty water, she looked a little crazed, perhaps even dangerous. She trembled a bit as she spoke and dropped one of the oars into the water. But, I knew she loved me dearly and had suffered during the last six years of my marriage to her daughter, so I felt only a quiet peace come upon me.

"My love, my Latin is poor at best, but why would we want to find a small stone?" I asked softly. "And, how could I leave my daughters for my last year of life?"

She turned, noticing the oar in the water. We both watched it float away.

"You must leave the House of The Rowans," she said. "Soon the new Lord will come to the house."

"He's not the new Lord until I am dead," I said, crossly. "Maybe it will be his fucking head on the green meadow. Don't write me off so easily."

"It cannot be." She shook her head. "Idiot." But, she smiled. "This is the Cameron O'Donnel I love."

"But I have to leave the house?" I asked.

She nodded. "And soon. It is best the children get used to the new one..."

"Fuck," I said.

"It is the hardest part," she said. "Always." She cleared her throat, an un-Rhiannon like trait. "Also, the Lapis Exillis is the Grail."

"The Holy Grail?" It wasn't really a question.

"A clue we have," she said seriously, "From the old times. We must go to Paris."

All I could manage was... "Huh." No one likes to learn their love is barking mad.

It was her turn to sigh. She pulled the remaining oar out of the water and poked me with the dripping end. "Look, do you want to spend a year travelling with me in southern Europe, all paid for, or do you want to hang out in the forest like Verspertin-Smythe did before you took his head?"

"When you put it that way..."

And so, despite my confusion and disbelief, we ended up somewhat tipsy at the Maison Arabe in Paris, drinking brilliant wine and watching the arrival of our black olive tapenade and fresh baguette appetizer. The baguette steamed lightly as Monsieur Moustache set it on the table in its linen-lined wicker basket. The tapenade was beautiful. I could make out black cured olives, capers, garlic and parsley. It smelled wonderful.

"Salivating, you are," laughed Rhiannon. "You may begin."

I did. And, around a mouthful of bread and wonder, I said, "I have been making a study of it, the Grail."

"Ha!" she said. She did not laugh. She said "Ha!"

"Ha?"

"Ha! Reading the Graham's Notes one-hundred-and-fifty-page book for high schoolers entitled 'The Quick Grail' is not making a study of anything!" She was a little adamant.

"I have time constraints," I said, maybe a tad petulantly, but, continued, somewhat boldly, I thought. "One-seventy-five-ish, pages wise. But, granted. Anyway, I couldn't help but notice that the general story was heavily based on the Christian mythos. You know, blood of Christ and all that."

"And?" she asked.

"Well, we are not. Aren't we rather heavily pagan, with this whole cycle-of-the-seasons, dying-god thing? So, how does all this reconcile?"

"That is a big word for you, reconcile." She was smiling, her face a little pink. She was not used to so much wine and we were barely into the appetizer. "But, yes, difficult it is. You are correct, sir."

"I am?" This was somewhat startling.

"Storytellers in the middle ages were no different than those today," she said. "Thieves they were. Taking many older tales, pagan tales, and putting a Christian veneer upon them. The cup that caught the blood of Christ? A golden bowl? A gem-encrusted platter that feeds a host? Hogwash!"

She was getting a little drunk, so I was cautious. I motioned for Moustache. "De l'eau s'il vous plait."

She pointed at me. "French that was!"

"I can also ask where the toilet is. It doesn't count."

He brought the water. We both drank some.

"So, do we have these earlier stories?" I asked, tentatively.

"In truth, we have little," she said. "Medieval Welsh stories have some similarities with the Grail legends, but the idea that the Grail is an all-feeding caldron is much debated by scholars. The tales by Chrétien de Troyes, Wolfram von Eschenbach and Geoffrey of Monmouth are really the best sources. And they are heavily corrupted."

This answer was both strangely sober and detailed. I watched as she took an oversized serving of the tapenade. This made me happy.

"You have been making a study, though?" I asked.

"An idiot, in truth you are," she said. "For five years."

I gestured with a piece of bread in a questioning repeating circle.

"Because I love you, you fool," she said. There was no smile.

"I am. And, thank you," I said. "You really believe it, don't you?"

"I do," she said firmly. And soberly.

"Well, then," I said. "You have plan, I am guessing?"

"We do. Some clues I have from the valley. Tomorrow we shall begin our little quest. But, now, tonight, I need you to tell me how beautiful I am, feed me and take me home," she said.

Monsieur Moustache arrived to lay down the cutlery and plates for the main course. He then set the golden Chicken Bastilla between us. I hardly saw it.

"You are beautiful, you know," I said. "I have loved you since the moment I saw you on the mountain."

"Know it I do," she said. "The day I passed your death sentence."

"Tch," I said. "It is a small thing. Had to be done. And I got to be with you." And I meant it. Who back in Canada would believe that? I had changed much in the six years since I had arrived in our valley.

We finished our meal, slowly, not rushing it. The Bastilla was perfect: flaky, rich, spicy but not overwhelming. The chicken was tender. Rhiannon paid. I lost track of things a bit as more Bordeaux flowed. Somehow a black cab was waiting. We ran to the car through the driving rain.

Back at the hotel, well I don't remember much. Rhiannon, naked, on me. Her skin soft and warm, a pleasure to touch. Then later in my arms, her head on my chest, drooling a little. So cute. If I lived in a noir movie, I would have been smoking. But I didn't. And I wasn't. I was just watching her and wondering, was there really a way out?

Eventually, she turned over and put her head on her pillow. I am pretty sure I heard her say, "Let the world end, then." But I may be wrong.

CHAPTER TWO – THE MUSEUM

Paris, France

It is only a few kilometers from the Hotel de O'Keefe to the museum and the rain had eased overnight to a light drizzle, so we decided to walk. Who does not want to walk the streets of Paris, after all? So, we headed down the sidewalk. I was quiet, a little sheepish.

To either side, four-or five-story buildings in traditional neo-classical, restoration, and neo-gothic styles offered shops to the street, with apartments and some offices above. The people we encountered were hurried, eager to get out of the rain. We took our time. One becomes used to the rain living in Wales.

After about five minutes I tried a conversational gambit.

"It was a natural mistake," I said. "You do like him."

She did not look at me. "C-L-U-N-Y," she spelled. "Not C-L-O-O-N-E-Y. You are an idiot!"

"He is a great actor," I said. "You could see them having a museum…"

"No," she interrupted. "The Musée de Cluny. You are a complete moron."

"Granted," I said. "Will you hold my hand?"

"Embarrassed I should be to be seen in public…" she said. But she took my hand.

"I did some research…" I started.

"Reading a pamphlet you found in the hotel lobby on your way out the door is not research!" she said.

The light rain continued to fall. Automobiles moved past us in the street, whooshing as they rolled through the puddles. I realized I had not fed her breakfast. I really am an idiot.

I pointed. "Look! A lovely café. For breakfast."

"It is closer to lunch," she muttered.

"It's art deco…" And it was, too. All plate glass, chrome and black and white marble. "And look at those croissants, all lovingly arranged under that glass dome."

"Where?"

"On the counter, just there." I pointed. "Some of them are artistically drizzled with chocolate…"

We sat at the counter on chrome-rimmed stools below black-and-white photos of Picasso, Hemingway, and F. Scott Fitzgerald. She ordered two chocolate croissants and black coffee. I ordered a full sausage-based breakfast with black tea. The beverages arrived immediately. Bless the French.

"So, my research tells me that…" I began.

"Yes?" she asked.

I continued warily. "That the Musée de Cluny is a medieval building started in 1334, but it was added to throughout the dark ages and became a museum in the mid-1800s."

"And?"

"It is best known for the Unicorn Tapestries?" I suggested.

"La Dame à la Licorne tapestry cycle," she said.

"And we are going to find a clue to the Grail in the tapestries?" I asked. I hoped my breakfast would come soon, because, you know, it was all just kind of silly. And we were a little hung over, after all.

"No," she said.

"In the catacombs?" I asked.

"Pardon?" she asked. But she did not look at me as two, giant, chocolate covered croissants were placed in front of her by the bow-tied, goateed gentleman behind the bar. She took a bite. Chocolate oozed from inside the croissant. For a moment, her pupils contracted.

"In the catacombs below the museum. Are we looking for a clue there?" I asked.

"No. Where did you get that from?" She took another bite. I was salivating just watching her. She spoke with her mouth full. "You are just making stuff up. You are not taking this seriously."

"Not at all," I lied. But, you know, in movies they always look in the catacombs.

"Idiot."

My breakfast arrived: two massive pork sausages, two eggs over-easy and buttered toast. Thank all the gods.

"The museum is built on Gallo-Roman baths from the third century," she said. "We will look there."

"And we will do this because?" I asked around a piece of juicy sausage.

"The Ahnenerbe found something there right before Paris fell to the allies. They were captured but wouldn't talk. My great uncle read the report and confiscated it," she said.

"Bloody Hell," I said. "The Ahnenerbe. The occult bureau. It is only day one and we are jumping right to the freak'n Nazis. You can't be serious? Also, stole is the word you are looking for, not confiscated."

"The Germans spent more on the Ahnenerbe than the Yanks spent on the Manhattan project to develop the bomb. They were deadly serious about the Grail," she said. I could see she wanted to be cross with me, but can one really be angry while eating chocolate croissants in a café in Paris?

"You just want to see the tapestries," I said.

She did that pouty thing she does.

"Well," I said. "Me too. But, why would a Gaulo-Roman bath contain a clue to the whereabouts of a medieval item?"

"Pre-Roman, Celtic or Gaul," she corrected. "And, know of it the Romans did. Caesar mentions it in Commentarii de Bello Gallico when he is describing the druidic religion."

"Commentaries on the Gallic War," I said. "It was the first thing they assigned us in Latin class."

She bestowed her smile upon me. "You are a scholar. Useful this will be."

I pierced an egg yolk with my fork. "I dropped out after two classes."

"Lazy man," she said, but rather fondly. She had finished her first croissant.

"So, what do the evil Nazis tells us?" I asked, by way of distraction. The toast was light-rye and it tasted fantastic with the egg yolk.

"The Ahnenerbe, specifically SS-Standarten Führe Wust, left us a map from 1901, which my great-uncle confiscated with the report," she said. She reached into her black leather bag – too big to be a purse – and, rather dramatically, pulled out a small cardboard tube.

"Which you have," I said.

"Which I have," she agreed.

"You are having a lot of fun, aren't you?" I said.

"I am," she said.

"Excellent. Let us see it then."

She pulled a single page out of the tube and rolled it out onto the table. The document was yellow with age. I could see a floorplan on one side, but she laid that side against the tabletop, revealing the back of the page. There were various handwritten notes in German and Latin.

"Here," she said and pointed.

It read "Lapis Exillis – Aqua therme – Südwesten Ecke Marmor geschnitzt." She looked up a me. "Or, Lapis Exillis, Hot baths - Southwestern corner marble carving."

She flipped the paper over and placed it floorplan up. It curled itself into a cylinder. She spread it out again, using a saltshaker to pin down one side and the pepper to pin down the other. I admit, she managed to intrigue me. I took a closer look.

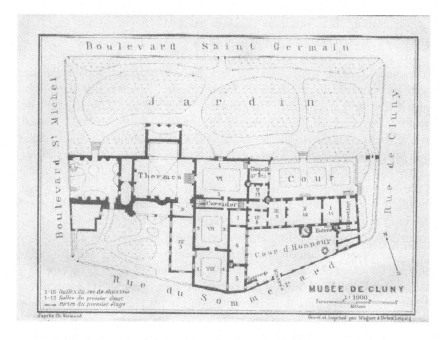

Figure 1. Floorplan, Musée de Cluny, 1901, Lord Summer's Collection

It was my turn to point. "This part to the left, around the Thermen, is ancient. These middle areas, VII, VII and VIII, are nineteenth century add-ons and, to the right, everything else is medieval."

"Thermen is obviously the baths, but you know this how?" she asked.

I pulled the Musée de Cluny pamphlet from my coat pocket and unfolded it onto the table beside the older document. The pamphlet's floorplan was pretty much exactly the same as the one on the shaker-laden document, but when someone has gone to all the trouble of revealing a century-old parchment taken from the Ahnenerbe, it is better not to draw attention to such things.

"I see. Your research," she said.

"Indeed," I said. "So, after breakfast, that's where we go?"

"Yes," she said. She looked down at the plans. "Of course, just because something was there in 1944…"

"That's okay," I said. "I really do want to see the tapestries and I'll bet the gift shop is amazing."

An outstanding survivor of the chaos of the middle ages, the two-and-one-half story Musée de Cluny is sits on its own grounds, including a formal medieval garden. It is a wonderful jumble of pointed gothic arches, crenellations, turrets, and stone gargoyles. We entered the museum through wooden doors and wandered slowly through rooms of medieval statues and one of nothing but luminous, back-lit stained-glass windows, until we entered the darkened room of the tapestries.

Six 500-year-old tapestries, each roughly three-by-three meters in size, are presented along a curved wall. The visitor stands in a loosely circular room and can turn to see them all. Each tapestry depicts a lady flanked by both a lion and a unicorn. The weaving of wool and silk is exquisite. Breathtaking. Five of the tapestries are said to symbolize taste, smell, hearing, sight and touch. The meaning of the sixth, where the lady is either placing or taking a necklace into or from a small chest held by her servant, is a mystery.

On that early November day, only a handful of others were in the room: an elderly couple bundled in grey sweaters, two serious-looking students sketching the tapestries and a young Germanic looking fellow with close-cropped blond hair and John Lennon-style round, wire glasses.

I leaned over Rhiannon's head and quietly whispered, "We are being followed by your evil Nazis."

She glanced toward the you man, then whispered back, "It's been three-and-one-half generations since the war. You cannot blame that young man. Let it go. Now, shush."

I could see she was hypnotized by the workmanship. She herself was a skilled weaver. But, in my mind I could not help but see the burial shroud she had created for that battle, six years before. The moon and comet – picked out in gold thread – hanging in the night sky. The exquisitely detailed oak and beech reaching from the forest floor into the night. And, below the trees, the tops of torches flaring in the night lit the battle. The two contestants swung axes directly toward their adversary's neck. One was me, the other Vespertin-Smythe. A circle of people surrounded us, watching silently.

In the end, Vespertin-Smythe lay wrapped in that shroud upon the smoky pyre. But, still… I had loved that man in my own way. And killed him with an axe. And those wondrous tapestries in that carefully-designed room were all big enough to wrap me in for the flames. I was patient, though. I looked, carefully. And remained silent, even while my mind wandered off – wondering why the Lady and the Unicorn tapestries? Why does the lion get no mention? Poor thing. Eventually, Rhiannon took my hand and led me away from the weaving, down a modern set of stairs into the roman baths, specifically, the frigidarium.

Everyone knows that the roman public baths were divided into three segments: the caldarium (hot water), tepidarium (lukewarm water), and frigidarium (cold water). In the Musée de Cluny, the frigidarium is the best preserved, with the original fourteen-meter high, groin-vaulted ceiling sheltering an impressive collection of era-relevant stone carvings.

"Come," she said. She led me to the southwest corner of the huge room. Before us stood a three-meter-high statue of Neptune, a little beaten by time, but still clearly Neptune and clearly beautiful. The base of the statue showed a faded inscription.

"A clue, perhaps?" said Rhiannon and she bent to examine it.

"It is not marble," I said. "The stone is limestone."

She stood. "Cachu hwch."

"Pardon?" I asked.

"Never mind," she said. "Profanity."

"Perhaps they moved it?" I suggested, not wanting to see her upset. "Let us look around."

So we did. I would like to claim we had a plan or followed some sort of logical methodology, but we just wandered around. There were carved marble sarcophagi, carved marble capitals from pillars, and carved marble statues in all states of disrepair. There was a lot of carved marble.

After about one-half hour we wandered back together.

"See anything?" she asked.

"No 'This way to the Grail' signs." I shrugged. "It could be anything. You?"

She shook her head.

"Time for lunch, then?" I suggested.

She gave me a smile. "Soon. But we need to find out what was where in 1944."

"And we do that by?"

"Asking," she said, looking around her until she spied a tiny, blue-jacketed, kilted, long-haired young woman with a name badge that read Lolita. Rhiannon walked toward the girl. I tagged along.

"Hello. Bonjour," said Rhiannon. "Parlez vous anglais?"

"Mais bien sûr," said Lolita.

"Thank you, kindly," said Rhiannon. She bent her head toward me. "He is a bit of savage. Claims to speak only English."

"Hello," I said, giving her my best smile.

Rhiannon saw it.

"Better watch out for him," she advised the girl. "He is a bit of a lolicon."

The girl laughed. She leaned closer to Rhiannon. "This isn't my real name. I found the badge in a locker when I started. But it is a lot of fun."

"I am not a lolicon!" I said, perhaps a little too loudly for a museum.

Rhiannon said, to the girl, "I see," and to me "You married a teenager."

"That was not my fault!" I said. People were turning to look.

The girl with the Lolita name tag was looking at me questioningly. I could not tell if it was a good or bad look. But she was extremely cute. Instinct told me this was going to end badly if I were not insanely careful.

"Actually," said Rhiannon, "We have a question."

"Ah," said the girl. "Please go ahead."

Rhiannon pointed to the southwest corner of the frigidarium. "What was on display in that corner in 1944?"

"In 1944? In that corner?" I could see the girl was processing it.

"Yes," said Rhiannon. "I know it sounds odd."

"My mother was not even born in 1944," said the girl who was not Lolita.

"Perhaps the museum has some photos of old exhibitions?" I suggested, making sure my voice remained polite but somewhat cold.

The girl looked at me and I could see she was not stupid. She suppressed a smile. "There is a collection, but it is only for researchers. You need to arrange access in advance." She smiled warmly at Rhiannon. "But there is a super, large-format, picture book showing lots of previous exhibitions from days gone by in the gift shop." The girl with the Lolita name tag gestured toward the exit with her right hand, using that inverted-hand motion that models use to draw attention to a product.

Rhiannon nodded. "Thank you. We will look and be back." She headed toward the exit. I smiled at the girl and followed. As we left the room, Rhiannon watched me. I did not look back at the girl.

The gift shop at the Musée de Cluny is modern and, really, well, museum gift shops are the best, aren't they? But this one had posters, replicas of the Lady and the Unicorn tapestries and books, books, books – including the one we wanted. This book was a large coffee-table book with a hard cover. In French. And, it cost 110 euros.

We flipped through black-and-white photographs from the 1930s and 1940s, including images of the frigidarium.

Rhiannon bought the book and we headed back to the frigidarium. The girl smiled when she saw us return and came to meet us.

"And?" she asked.

"Yes," said Rhiannon. She opened the book but struggled to both hold it and turn the pages. "Cameron, hold it you will."

"Of course." I took the book and turned toward her, balancing it on my left forearm. She began to flip through it.

"Hello, Cameron," said the girl. "I am Lolita." Big smile. She extended her hand. I shook it with my right hand.

"This is Rhiannon," I said, nodding toward my lady with my head.

Rhiannon looked up and gave her a quick smile.

"Here," Rhiannon said, pointing at a grainy, black-and-white, full-page photo. "From the 40s this is. The corner was full of stone sarcophagi."

The girl moved in to look over Rhiannon's shoulder, but could not quite reach that high and had to step in and lean over my arm. "Oh, we still have those. They are huge so we do not move them around much. Most of them are in the cour d'honneur."

"The Court of Honor?" I said. "Didn't we come in that way."

"You did," said the girl. She pointed. "Back that way."

"Of course," I said.

Rhiannon turned to the girl who was not Lolita in name. "Thank you for your help."

The girl gave a polite little bow. "Happy to assist." She looked Rhiannon in the eyes, not even glancing at me. "I get off work at three… Perhaps the three of us could meet to have a drink?"

Rhiannon actually smiled at her. "Thank you, no. He is my lover and I want him all to myself, at least for a while."

The girl nodded. "I understand. Sorry if I have offended."

I said, most emphatically, absolutely nothing.

"Not at all," said Rhiannon. "This way, Cameron." I followed in her wake.

On the way up the stairs to the ground level, I said, "The French are not the Welsh."

"Indeed," she said. But she turned and looked me up and down. "A good boy you were."

I felt almost like a dog being praised and patted, a disturbing sensation for a grown man. What a strange creature I had become.

She took my hand and we walked into le cour d'honneur.

The Court of Honor is enclosed on three sides by the museum and on the fourth by a high, stone wall with a large, gated archway that opens onto the traffic of Rue de Sommerard. In medieval times, persons of status would have been formally received there. Lesser souls would have used the side entrances.

The sarcophagi were arranged on stone plinths in a neat row along the wall furthest from the street. I confess, here, that I had not known they were sarcophagi when we first walked past them, as they do look rather like big ancient bathtubs or troughs. But, in my defense, I had not really been paying attention.

Leading me toward the sarcophagi, still holding my hand, Rhiannon was definitely into the whole quest thing. But, please understand that for me, heading toward a line of coffins left me a little less than enthusiastic.

The ten sarcophagi were all clearly labelled in both French and English.

"What do we look for?" I asked.

"Any of the grail symbols," she said. "Cups, obviously, but also doves, pomegranates, olives…"

"Pomegranates, olives?" I asked. "What does a pomegranate even look like?"

"Pomegranates were a symbol of wisdom. Olives were a fertility symbol," she said. "And pomegranates look sort of like an onion but are usually portrayed cut open so you can see the interior. They grow on trees like apples."

"Not a lot of pomegranates in Canada," I said.

"Canada is a long way from Paris," she said.

I thought of the girl who was not named Lolita but said nothing.

"Start at that end, I will," said Rhiannon.

We split up and examined the sarcophagi. I got stuck, hypnotized by the first one in line. Big, maybe three meters long, one wide and one tall, and of white, luminous marble, it was carved in a Greco-Roman style with three panels of relief on each side. The lid was missing, so it really did look like an excessively fancy bath.

Across the panels, a priestess or perhaps goddess performed a ritual near a well – her hair was short and tightly curled, held in place by a laurel wreath or crown, ringlets falling to each side of her pretty face. Her body looked rather like Rhiannon's, round and shapely, well formed in every way. In fact, the resemblance was uncanny. In the reliefs she showed as naked, but for the crown and sandals. Yet hints of color suggested that clothing might, once upon a time, have been painted over her skin.

In each of the carved panels she undertook a different task, in one holding a covered dish, in another, a smoking brazier. I walked slowly around the sarcophagus. Eventually, I noticed Rhiannon standing watching me.

"I found nothing," she said. "And, you, anything besides ancient porn?"

I glanced up sharply. "I found you in stone by a well."

She moved up beside me and bent to examine the panel closest to us. "The face is different, I do not have a straight, classical Greek nose."

"But the body is totally you, absolutely perfect," I said, realizing only after I said it that it was probably not too bad a passing remark.

She took my arm and drew my head down to kiss her.

"Let's go have lunch," she said. "Then a rest?"

"Excellent plan," I said. And I took her arm and steered her toward the gate. Just as we were about to exit the cour d'honneur I said, "Didn't I read something about wells during my Grail research?"

"Reading the Graham's Notes one-hundred-and-fifty-page book for high schoolers entitled '*The Quick Grail*' is not..." She trailed off, turned and headed back to the sarcophagus. I waited for a moment, regretting having spoken, and trailed after her like the dog I am. She waited for me and turned as I arrived.

"You are correct, sir," she said.

"But, lunch," I said. "A rest."

"Lunch will need to wait for a bit," she said. "This is it. Well done."

"Seriously?" I said, entirely appalled.

"Pardon?" she asked, then. "Oh, sorry. That was an accidental pun."

"If you say so…" I replied, but did not forgive her.

She bent down to read the inscription. "It was brought here from the Priory of Ganagobie in Alpes-de-Haute-Provence in 1879."

"Which is where?" I asked.

"South of France, near Marseille," she replied, without taking her eyes away from the inscription.

"But why is it related to the Grail?" I asked. "I may have skimmed the part on the wells."

"May have?" She stood and turned to me. "It is the very beginning of the Grail story, at least in the Elucidation, you see."

"Not really, but please continue," I said, thinking rather of Rhiannon as the priestess in the carvings. It was not much of a mental leap, after all.

"We do not know who wrote it, but it was created to serve as an introduction to Chrétien's Perceval," she explained. "Basically, it is the story of how the wasteland to be redeemed by the Grail was created."

"Not the wasteland, please!" I begged.

"It does not have to be a metaphor or an allegory or whatever," she said. "It is totally acceptable to think of it literally. In fact, in our religion, we do."

"Thank gods," I said. "I was having flashbacks to high school."

She took my arm, quite gently, I noticed.

"I understand," she said. "High school is a time of horror for many, but it passes quickly." She patted my arm. "In the "Elucidation", we learn how the – let me use another word – the desolation was created."

"Much better. Thank you," I said, gratefully.

"In ancient times, in the country of Logres, the following was true," she began. "In those days the earth lost the Song of the Wells and girls who lived within them."

"How did they live in the wells?" I asked.

"Stop interrupting," she said. She let out a little sigh and her shoulders sank a fraction. "It is a translation question. Obviously the original was in quite old French and the word was 'puis', which comes from the Latin and can mean wells, springs, hills, grottos or even fairy mounds. So let it go. It is not an exact science."

"So, in ancient times in the country of Logres, the following was true," I said, quietly. "In those days the earth lost the Song of the Wells and girls who lived within them."

"Yes. In those days travelers could arrive at one of these wells and ask for any food or drink they desired and two beautiful girls would come out of the well, one carrying golden cups of drink, pastries, meats and bread, the other carrying a white napkin with the requested food."

"Unfortunately for all, a new king was crowned in Logres who did not respect the old ways. This King Amangons raped one of the women of the wells and stole her gold cup. At this point, she would no longer emerge from the well, but the well still provided food to travelers."

"So, no desolation yet, then? I asked.

"No. No desolation yet," she said. "But then, the king's barons learned what he had done and did the same, raping the girls of the wells and stealing their golden cups. Then none of the girls would come out and no food or drink was provided."

"Well, you can't blame them," I said.

"Indeed," she said. "Then the desolation fell. Trees lost their greenery. Meadows became wastes. Lakes evaporated. And, none could find the court of the rich fisherman."

"The Fisher King," I said.

"Emm. Then, years later, maybe, the tale of this woe came to the court of Arthur," she said. "The KORT then decided that they should restore the wells and protect the girls."

"Kort?" I asked.

"Knights of the Round Table. Do try to follow along," she said.

"Fine. KORT."

"By the time they got to Logres, however long that took, the king and barons had all died horrid deaths," she said. "But, the KORT, being a thorough lot, hunted down all their descendants who lived near the wells and killed them all by the sword or hanging."

"So much for the child not suffering for the sins of the parent," I said.

"Different times," she said. "But it did not really work. The land remained barren and the court of the rich fisherman could not be found. Then, they realized that only completing the Grail quest would restore the land."

"So all that slaughter for nothing, then?" I asked.

"Maybe," she allowed. "But that is what these carved panels represent. We need to take some photos."

"Give me a minute," I said. "Please wait here."

She nodded. I dashed off to the gift shop and picked up a lovely small book – with excellent color photos – detailing and explaining the collection of sarcophagi. I returned and handed her the book and she flipped through it until she found the sarcophagus with the wells.

"Perfect," she said. She took my arm and steered me toward the archway exiting onto the Rue de Sommerard. "Now we can have lunch and such."

"Excellent," I said. "Most excellent."

We did not eat at the McDonald's across the street from the Musée de Cluny. I mean, seriously, if you had one year left before head-from-body separation, would you eat American fast food in Paris? I mean, I suppose if you are Parisian it would be okay from time to time, but, if you are even visiting Paris without certain knowledge of your time of death? What madness is that?

Half-a-dozen other small cafes sit across the street from the museum, including an intriguing-looking, street-fronting creperie. But Rhiannon had not been focused entirely on researching the Grail myths. She had other ideas.

We turned down Boulevard Saint-Germain, strolled for a short while, entered a hat shop, looked at hats, exited the hat shop, turned down the Rue de l'Eperon (I found the bars on the windows depressing as always – they speak poorly of humans in general), and strolled up to the Ballard Restaurant.

"We have reservations here for eight tonight," said Rhiannon.

The restaurant occupied the entire ground floor of a fairly large, four-story, stone building. Parts of the street level were faced with dark paneled wood – traditional. I peered in one of the windows. White-linen tablecloths, dark wooden chairs, a bar of white, grey and red marble.

"So, expensive?" I asked.

"Maybe," she allowed.

"Also, it is four hours until eight," I said. "Lunch?"

"Show you the restaurant, I would," said Rhiannon. "You wanted traditional French cuisine and this is it."

I had foolishly walked onto dangerous ground. She had obviously spent some time researching and choosing this bistro. And I was complaining.

"It looks wonderful," I said. There was a menu in the window. I drifted toward it. "Oh. Brilliant."

She came up beside me and took my arm. I looked down at her and she smiled. She was going to forgive me.

"Yes. I have pre-ordered the duck with olives for two as our main. I know how you like duck," she said.

"Most excellent," I said.

"But first, lunch," she said.

"Do you have any thoughts on lunch?" I asked, because I am a shameless coward.

"Room service," she said. "I have to cure you of your lolicon fantasies. Or, aren't I young and tiny enough?"

"Oh," I said. Because, even I could see this was one of those questions which cannot possibly be answered without leading to some kind of pain.

Fortunately, she was intentionally tormenting me, and laughed aloud at my suffering. It was a sign of her affection; I am quite certain.

"Make yourself useful for once and get us a taxi," she said.

The restaurant was on the corner, so I stepped forward and raised my right hand. Immediately, a dark blue Volvo taxi pulled up to the curb. I stood there in disbelief. Rhiannon slipped past me and opened the door. Still in my stunned state, I got into the vehicle and she sat beside me.

"Hotel de O'Keefe, s'il vous plait," said Rhiannon.

The driver grunted and set the meter running.

By the time we got back to the hotel, I had recovered from what was clearly divine intervention in the taxi-hailing event. The only question in my mind was... Which Gallic god had intervened? I mean who has dominion over taxi cabs these days? Mullo, god of mules? Cimialcinnus, god of roads? Ratis, goddess of luck? I mean, seriously, how do they divide up the responsibilities when new technologies crop up? Or is it just... "No, no, that's not in my job description."? That would explain a lot about modern society, actually.

When the door to our strangely brutalist, concrete-walled room clicked shut behind me, Rhiannon started dropping her clothes to the floor.

"A shower I need, first," she said. "Watch, you may."

"Um, okay," I said.

I watched her from the bed. She took a long shower, slowly soaping and scrubbing herself with a white washcloth. She did not turn below the falling water. She stood facing me, watching my face the entire time. Eventually I could no longer wait and rose from the bed. She motioned me to stop with her right hand, turned and slipped out of the shower. Moving quickly to me, still soaking wet and somewhat soapy, she kissed me and took my hand. She led me to the bed and lay back, opening her legs.

"That thing you do," she said.

I smiled, knelt on the floor beside the bed, and, ever so slowly started that thing I do. She placed one hand to each side of my head. Eventually, after a variety of sounds – some of which, I fear to report, resembled a cross squirrel – and some twisting and flipping, she commanded, "Inside you must be."

I obeyed, as always.

Later, as we lay side by side beneath sheets and a warm wool blanket, my arm around her, she sighed, deeply.

"Good that was, at last," she said.

"It was," I said.

She tilted her head up to kiss me. "Too long have I heard those sounds coming from your bedroom window. Drove me mad, it did."

"I know it has been hard on you," I said. "I am sorry, I did not know you could hear anything."

"Your fault it is not. She is a frightful whore," said Rhiannon.

"Your daughter is not a whore," I said, but quietly. "And you three Rowans choose her for me, not I."

"I could have slit her throat a dozen times, daughter or no," she said.

"But you didn't," I said.

"No," she said. "But duty that was. Only duty."

There was nothing to say. The Rowans hold the world together. Duty trumps all. I was but a dying god – a lesser being.

"But, in the past that is," she said and lay her head on my chest. In a few minutes she was asleep, drooling. I smiled and held her gently. The resilience of the Rowans is astounding.

Later we rose, dressed (me in my suit, her in a lovely, silk, dark green, off-shoulder dress), moved out through the elegant, concrete and steel hotel lobby, to a waiting Mercedes taxi – courtesy of the concierge. As we rode to the restaurant, where we arrived promptly at eight o'clock, she held my hand, quietly, saying nothing. It was, I think, her turn to be a little melancholy.

As we pushed the double, wooden doors open, our world changed. Rhiannon's face awoke into a bright smile. Before us – well-dressed people, dark-wainscoting, waist-high paneling below cream-colored walls hung with black and white photos from days gone by, white tablecloths sparkling with cutlery and gleaming wineglasses. Immediately to our right, behind a small pulpit of oak, stood the grey-suited maître d'hôtel and, slightly behind him, to his right, a woman in bowtie, pressed white shirt and black trousers. The maître d'hôtel looked over the top of his gold-rimmed glasses and tiny, not quite Hitlerian moustache.

"Bonsoir, monsieur et madame. Avez-vous une réservation?" he said, suggesting strongly that we, clearly tourists, did not have said reservation and were about to be sent packing.

Rhiannon was more than a match for his kind.

"Bonsoir Monsieur. Mais bien sûr. Raul à l'hôtel de O'Keefe était assez aimable pour arranger les choses, comme toujours," said Rhiannon with a small smile.

"Le nom?," he replied, curtly.

"Rowan," I said.

He looked up, as if startled to hear me speak, then consulted his leather-bound book and nodded. He raised his right hand and made an arcane gesture, hardly moving his fingers. The woman stepped forward.

"Table quatorze," he said.

"This way," said the woman.

We followed her through the tables, wending our way toward table fourteen. Our fellow diners seemed to be a mix of locals and tourists – the locals dressed at least in business attire, some of the tourists rather seemed to be letting the team down.

As we got perhaps twenty steps from the door, the woman said, "Do not mind Marcel. He sees himself as manning the walls to keep out the barbarians." She laughed at her own joke. I liked her right away.

"No worries," I said. "We are barbarians, after all."

Rowan gave me a tiny, cute smile.

"Too true," she said.

We arrived at the table. It was set for two but could have seated four. I approved. I pulled out Rhiannon's chair and waited for her to sit. She sat, with a somewhat quizzical look on her face. I moved to my own chair, opposite her.

The woman gave me a smile and said, "Peter will look after you tonight." She backed away a few steps, deftly exiting our little drama.

Rhiannon leaned across the table and said, quietly, "I was not certain you would not pull the chair out from under me."

"This is a classy joint," I said, equally quietly. "Ya gotta have manners."

"Expect it all the time, I shall, going forward," she said.

"Mais bien sûr," I said, making a mental note.

Peter arrived and presented two leather-bound menus – one at a time to each of us in turn, starting with Rhiannon. Peter also wore black bowtie, white shirt and black trousers. It was not entirely clear whether Peter was a boy or a girl or, perhaps, neither.

"Good evening," said Peter. "Madame has pre-arranged for the Canard de Challans aux olives for two?"

"Yes, I have," said Rhiannon. "But I thought I would give my love the illusion of choice by letting him choose his starter."

"Quite right, madam," said Peter. "It is most important we provide them the illusion. Would madam like to see the wine list?"

"Please," said Rhiannon and she favored Peter with a smile.

Peter handed over a parchment-covered wine list, gave an almost imperceptible bow, and departed.

"I often feel as if I am the only one who has no idea what is going on," I said.

She flipped through the wine list.

"They have 366 wines, you know," she said. "A Burgundy? Or, Bordeaux, perhaps? Or something from the Rhone valley?"

"Could you possibly be more pleased with yourself?" I asked.

"This day is shaping up rather nicely for me," she said, not looking up from the wine list. "And for you?"

"Perfect day," I said and turned my attention to the menu.

When Peter returned, I ordered the preserved duck foie gras with toasted country bread to start, which seemed to break some kind of rule as I noticed one of Peter's slender eyebrows twitch a bit. Rhiannon ordered the quinoa, bulgur and beetroot salad with goat's curd, which I thought was a bit of a cheat given the more traditional choices available.

Peter queried whether madam had had enough time to consider the wine and madam chose a burgundy. I watched as Peter departed.

"A bob haircut actually does bob as one walks," I observed.

"He is very cute," said Rhiannon.

"She, I think," I countered. "And, yes, very cute. And don't call me a lolicon."

"You really are the only one who has no idea what is going on sometimes," she said.

Fortunately, at that moment, Peter's gender seemed irrelevant as Peter was an excellent waiter. The wine appeared almost immediately, and Peter performed the wine-opening and tasting ritual in an elegant, unrushed manner that was a joy to watch. Rhiannon sipped and approved; Peter filled our glasses and bobbed away.

"Cheers," said Rhiannon.

"Indeed," I said.

We lightly touched glasses with a slight ring from the thin and fragile crystal.

I sipped. Excellent.

"You are smiling again," said Rhiannon.

"It is a taste of Shangri-La," I said. "I am loving our meals here. Can we find an excuse to stay for a few more days?"

"Because we are going to starve in the south of France?" she asked.

"Valid point, but still…"

She laughed and took a deep sniff of her wine. "We should do a little research on the Priory of Ganagobie in Alpes-de-Haute-Provence and on the sarcophagus, I suppose. Is that a good enough reason to hang out in Paris?"

"An excellent reason," I said. "Where did the sarcophagus originate? Was it always at the priory? Was the priory always a priory? If not, what was it before? How does it all tie in with the sacred wells? It will take days to uncover these mysteries."

"Days?" she asked.

"Possibly weeks," I said, admiring her over the top of my wineglass. "And many lunches and dinners. And naps."

"And where shall we undertake this research?" she asked, serious once more.

"Um. Perhaps I should check the lobby brochures when we get back to the hotel?" I asked, unfortunately just as Peter arrived with the appetizers. I was treated to another raised eyebrow.

He, or perhaps she, presented the starters.

"La pâté de canard," said Peter placing the lovely platter before me with a sliding motion. "Et la salade." It was duly set before my love.

"Lovely," said Rhiannon, but I could see her eying my pâté and toasts.

Peter turned to Rhiannon. "Pardon, madam, but I could not help but overhear. Perhaps madam might consider the Bibliothèque Mazarine for research into the medieval issues, it is not far from here, or the Bibliothèque Richelieu-Louvois for the ancient period. Also quite close."

"How very kind, Peter," said Rhiannon. "That is most helpful."

"I spent hours in both when I was undertaking my Masters," said Peter.

"What did you study?" asked Rhiannon.

"Ah. Feminism in ancient times, mostly," said Peter. "Not so useful, perhaps, but dear to me nevertheless, madam."

Rhiannon bestowed her greatest smile upon our waiter. I guessed his gratuity would exceed the included amount significantly.

"Good for you, dear," said Rhiannon. "I admire you tremendously."

Peter turned a little pink at this and laughed in a girlish way. But, then, Peter leaned in closer to her.

"Also, madam, you may choose to wonder why the older German couple appeared to pass the maître d'hôtel an envelope to switch tables. They may have an interest in your conversation," said Peter. The bobbed head nodded imperceptibly toward an older, well-dressed couple seated about three meters away.

"Perhaps they just wanted different table?" suggested Rhiannon, equally quietly.

"Perhaps, madam," said Peter. Another slight bow and Peter departed.

I spread my foie gras on one of the little toasts with the tiny knife provided.

"I swear, it is almost like I am not here. By the way, I'm with Peter on the you-know-whos," I said, because they were behind Rhiannon. I could see them clearly trying to eavesdrop.

She leaned forward and hissed. "We are not being followed by Nazis! There are lots of Germans in Europe. Nine high-speed trains a day travel between Berlin and Paris. It only takes eight hours and change to make the trip."

"And you know this how?" I asked.

She looked down at her salad. "Brochure in the hotel lobby."

"Ah ha!" I said a little too loudly. Heads did turn toward our table.

I took a crunchy bite of toast and pâté.

"Oh, so good," I said. "Buttery almost. Maybe paprika? A little? Onion?"

"Let me taste," she said.

I considered arguing based on the fact that she had ordered a salad, but survival instinct kicked in.

"Please help yourself," I said. And she did, rather too much I thought.

"Seriously," she said. "Why would Nazis be following us? It has been more than three generations since the demise of National Socialism. Do you think that if they knew something, they really would have waited three generations to follow up?"

"Well, at least you are not trying to argue that they are not around anymore," I said. "Also, maybe they did not have your little piece of paper with the floorplan? Maybe they did not know where it went after the war?"

"Well, it is true that SS-Standarten Führe Wust, whom you will recall was the source of our little paper, did not survive the war. He died in an 'accidental shooting' at a Dutch prison camp," she said.

"You know how I feel about air quotes," I complained.

"Sorry," she said. She started to reach for the wine to pour me a top up, but Peter appeared instantly beside her to take up the task, quickly adding to both of our glasses then fading away without a word.

"Hands off the wine bottle, my love," I said.

"Taboo, clearly," she said.

"Indeed," I said. "But, accidental shooting?"

"Yes. The SS were kept in separate camps and in the Netherlands. They were guarded by former members of the Dutch underground armed with Sten submachine guns. Apparently, the Sten was prone to accidental discharges," she said.

"So, scores being settled, and all that?" I said.

"Live by the sword, die by the sword," she offered.

"Tell me about it," I said. "Though, in my case it would be the axe."

She reached across the table to take my hand. "Melancholy," was all she said.

"I apologize," I said. "But..." The wine with so little food was beginning to threaten my logic. We had ended up missing lunch entirely.

"But the entire evil Nazi thing is just so unlikely, especially as believe in the Grail you do not?" she said with a slight smile.

I took the hand that lay upon mine own and kissed it on the palm. Then I placed it back on the table and released it.

"You are attempting to negate point A, the Nazis chasing the Grail, as unlikely by saying that that point B, the existence of the Grail, is unlikely. You do this because you know I think that B is unlikely, but you are not allowed to use this argument as you do not accept point B yourself," I said.

She offered up her cute little pout again, which, by the way, is totally cheating in any argument with a man. There exists no counterargument.

"But I am not trying to convince me, I am trying to convince you," she said. "I do not need convincing."

"That is so illogical..." It was at that point she took the last snippet of foie gras and the last toast from my plate. I realized then it had all been a clever distraction. Her salad remained untouched. She looked me right in the eyes as she took a crunchy bite.

At that moment, a rare and unforeseen event occurred, much to my amazement and delight. Peter's delicate left hand swept in to remove my plate, followed immediately by the right hand, which inserted a new platter of preserved duck foie gras and little toasts. I looked up into Peter's pretty eyes and smiled my gratitude.

"Mais bien sûr," said Peter with a lovely lilt.

I could not tell if it was serious or in jest, so I responded with an even broader smile. Peter stepped away, displaying an unnerving ability to appear and disappear at will.

"You are being honored, my lord," said Rhiannon, bowing her head, just a fraction. She smiled, but at the same time seemed serious. I really am the only one who does not understand what the heck is going on – at least some of the time.

"Apparently, touching your appetizer is also taboo," she said. "Foresee I do how this meal will end."

She was no longer smiling.

Now, please understand that this was more than a little creepy. The Rowans, you see, do at times see the future or, at least, possible futures. And, it is usually a warning of some kind – a call to action, as it were. I had seen more than enough during my time in the valley – rituals, dreams, animal sacrifices – to immediately focus on her remark.

"Foresee as in see. Or, foresee as in guess?" I asked quietly. Sometimes when she has seen things, Rhiannon can become frightening.

She took my hand again. "Oh, Cameron, so sorry I am. Guess. Totally, guess."

I sighed. "Don't do that, please. Or next thing I know it will be rituals in the forest and dreams of my mother as a tree. Terrifying."

"Watch my language, I shall," said Rhiannon. "It is the wine, I suspect."

She took another sip of Bordeaux. I am pretty sure I could see her smiling, again, around the lip of the glass. That woman can be scary.

"So, might I make a small and insignificant suggestion?" I asked.

"You may," she said.

"Assume that we are being followed by whomever; can we act accordingly?" I asked. "Just because I do not believe in the Grail does not mean that crazy people do not believe."

"Include me in that group, you do," she said.

"No. No. Not at all," I said hastily and, I thought, sincerely.

"Hmm," she said. "Let us try to be aware of our surroundings. We should do that regardless. And mind what we say when we speak in public."

"Prudent," I said.

She did not touch my pâté again, and instead focused on her salad. When the main course arrived at the appropriate time naturally, I actually gave out a little gasp of joy. My Rhiannon knows me all too well.

26

Peter cleared space in the center of the table and set down the Canard de Challans aux olives for two. The oval, white platter presented a golden, roasted duck set on a bed of plump green olives. The smell of the crisped skin intoxicated. An empty round plate accompanied the platter.

"Ah," was all I could manage.

Peter responded with a slight tilt of the bobbed head. "Shall I carve, monsieur?"

"S'il vous plait," I said.

Peter carved the beast with a two-pronged steel serving fork and a long, thin blade, gently setting a slice of breast on both of our plates. He efficiently carved the rest of the beast, arranging it in layers on the empty plate. Carving meat well really is a skill, one I did not have, having suffered so many years as a vegetarian. I admired Peter's handiwork tremendously.

I waited until Peter performed the ritual departure until I took my first bite. Often duck is overcooked, dry. That was not this duck. The flesh was moist and tremulous. The glazed skin was perfectly crisped, not burnt. I looked up to see Rhiannon's eyes close as she slowly chewed.

Peter, possibly a mind reader, brought a plate of oven-roasted new potatoes – we had not known to order this separately – and, after a confirming nod from my love, another bottle of wine.

Some Christians believe that the Rapture is when true believers will be kicked upward from earth to heaven on the Second Coming of Christ. I now understand that the Rapture is eating Canard de Challans aux olives for two at an insanely traditional restaurant in Paris with your love, an exquisite bottle of Bordeaux, and Peter as your priest. We both declined dessert, finding it hard to move past perfection.

As we completed our meal and Rhiannon paid the ridiculous bill, Peter advised, "I asked Marcel to call you a taxi. A light, but chill, rain is falling."

"Very kind," said Rhiannon.

As we put on our coats, I noticed Peter had not departed. After a moment, the bobbed head leaned in close to Rhiannon.

"Madam," said Peter, most quietly. "My shift runs quite late, but perhaps afterward… A drink at your hotel? The three of us?" And, just in case she had not understood. "Together?"

She gave a small sigh, but then showed Peter a true smile.

"My dear, he is my lover and we have limited time," she answered equally quietly. "I do want him for myself. All to myself. I apologize."

Peter nodded. "I understand." But Peter took my hand, walked us to the taxi, and stood waving in the rain as we drove away.

"That was kind of sad," I said as the Mercedes' windshield wipers clack-clacked in what was now a strong rain.

"Yes," said Rhiannon. "Peter is a delicate soul."

"Umm?" I asked.

"Yes?" she said.

"Does this sort of thing happen to you all the time? Because, I promise you, it never happens to me. And this is the second time this trip," I said.

She was quiet for a while, then took my arm and rested her head on my shoulder. "It is not happening to me, my dear," she said. "It is happening to you."

"Please explain," I asked.

"You are a god, now. A dying god, granted, but still a god. Women and, I suppose, those who are like-or-as women, sense this instinctively. They are attracted to you and to your consort," she said.

"That is nonsense," I said. "This never happened in the valley."

"Feared are the Rowans in the valley," said Rhiannon.

"Huh. And none of you Rowans thought to mention this at any time during the last six years?" I asked.

"That would have been stupid from my perspective and from Clarine's" said Rhiannon. "Obviously. Idiot."

Bibliothèque Richelieu-Louvois is one of seven sites that house the national library of France – fourteen million books, maps and manuscripts. Centuries old, parts of its collection, including the Royal Library, wandered throughout France before finally finding a home at Richelieu-Louvois in the early 1700s.

The caramel-colored stone buildings are two or three stories in a variety of styles, the library having been organically rebuilt and refurbished numerous times. The structures inside are works of art, both architecturally and literally as frescos and murals adorn walls and ceilings.

The ballroom-sized main reading room is the diamond of the library. Three gallery levels of books line the outer walls. Slender wrought iron pillars support a soaring ceiling of multiple domes, each capped with a circular skylight. Wooden reading desks in straight rows line the floor. Were these desks swept away, one could easily play three games of basketball simultaneously in the vast space.

The next morning, Rhiannon and I entered this holy space through a three-story, glassed-in arch. I froze, both enraptured and confused.

"Good gods! Where do we start?" I asked.

Rhiannon quickly glanced around and said, "Well, perhaps with a librarian? At the librarians' desk."

She pointed toward the center of room where a bar-like desk surrounded a work area for the librarians. A short line of people led to three rather grumpy looking middle-aged women manning the counter. We took our place in the line.

It took a while, maybe a half an hour, to reach the counter. These librarians were seriously helping people and it took time. The woman who addressed us wore a formal, high-collared, black-and-white print dress.

"Oui?" she said.

"Hello. Bonjour," said Rhiannon. "Parlez vous anglais?"

"Yes," she said. Eyeing me up and down through her half-moon glasses, she added. "We do not have Wilbur Smith!"

I opened my mouth to speak, then abruptly closed it. She had pegged me correctly, after all.

Rhiannon laughed which I thought was a bit much.

"We are looking for any information about a sarcophagus now on display at the Musée de Cluny. It was moved there from the Priory of Ganagobie in Alpes-de-Haute-Provence in 1879," said Rhiannon. "Might you be able to help?"

"Almost guaranteed," said the librarian. "It is certainly a part of the Cardinal Richelieu collection. They were meticulous in his day, the church. Now, of course... Phttt! It will be in Latin of course?"

"That's fine," said Rhiannon.

I smiled supportively, though I could not see how this would be true.

"You will need to look," said the librarian. "The Latin manuscripts were re-cataloged in the General Catalog of Latin Manuscripts between 1939 and 1991. There are seven volumes to the catalog."

"Seven volumes..." I said.

"The Old Latin Collection began in 1740," said the librarian. "It includes material from the most ancient collections of the Library of the King and many more collections absorbed in the seventeenth and eighteenth centuries. It is one of the finest collections in the world!"

"Seven volumes is fine," said Rhiannon. "Could you point us in the right direction, please?"

The librarian took this literally. She pointed. "Third level up, beneath the second mural of the tree from the right."

Rhiannon thanked her and we headed toward the stairs to the upper levels. Before we got there, we heard a familiar voice from one of the reading desks.

"Madam!"

We turned. Peter from the Ballard restaurant sat in a snappy, blue blazer, a white shirt, black pants and wing-tipped loafers, beaming up from one of the long, wooden reading desks. A large, hard-cover book lay open beneath Peter's delicate hands. Two more exactly the same size were piled beside the first.

"I have it here!" said Peter.

Rhiannon changed course and headed toward Peter, ignoring glares from the other patrons. Tagging sheepishly after her, I carefully avoided making eye contact with anyone. It was a library, after all.

Peter rose and came toward us, meeting us in an open space at the end of one of the long reading desks. Rhiannon leaned forward and kissed one, then the other of Peter's lightly rouged cheeks.

"Dear one, thank you" said Rhiannon.

"Tut," said Peter. "Of course I came. Here, you would be dear lost lambs by yourselves." He nodded toward the reference desk. "Those harridans would eat you alive."

"True enough," I said, extending my right hand toward Peter.

"And tut again," said Peter, slipping past my extended hand and kissing me lightly on both cheeks. "This is France not the U.S.A.!"

"Canada, not America, please," I said, yet again.

"Same thing," said Peter.

I opened my mouth, but Peter covered it with his hand.

"Teasing," said Peter. "I apologize deeply and sincerely for my error and will strive to do better in the future."

They were both laughing at me, though, so I did not pursue any of the obvious questions. Why was Peter there? For his knowledge of the library or of ancient languages? Had they arranged it in advance? Was Rhiannon messing with my mind for amusement, again? I decided to be the non-hysterical Lord of the Valley. The Tao advises that we do not fight the unfightable, after all.

"So, what have you found?" I asked, using a fractionally deeper, alpha male voice. Rhiannon showed me two raised eyebrows.

"Oh, I have totally found them," said Peter. "If you know your way around the indexes, it does not take long. The church records from the time are good, where they still exist."

"Cameron," said Peter, giving me a small, cute smile, "A quick and painless history of the priory. Created in the 10th century by the Bishops of Sisteron, ceded to the Abbey of Cluny in 956, and the Benedictines raised up the church and Romanesque cloisters in the 12th century. And, here is an important bit, the monks of Iles de Lérins transported their relics to the priory for safekeeping from coastal raiders in the 15th century..."

"Ah," I said. "Including our sarcophagus?" And do not think I did not notice that Peter had joined the long list of people who explain things to me as if I have a short attention span.

"Perhaps. We will need to check the actual manuscripts to see if it is true," said Peter. "The monastery was looted repeatedly during the French Revolution, by both sides, but the sarcophagi were likely too heavy to cart away. The Priory of Ganagobie sent them to the museum in 1879."

"As for the manuscripts, we should examine three. One is an account of the move. Apparently, it happened only with the assistance of God: the sarcophagi must have been a bitch to move in 1879. The other two documents essentially inventory the move. I think."

"You think?" asked Rhiannon.

"We will not know until we actually look at the documents," said Peter. "Which, I suggest, should be our next step."

"And they are to be found where?" I asked.

Peter laughed. "Oh! They will not actually let you see them. You are both uncredentialed foreigners. And, you might even be American! But we can get them to make archive-level, photographic copies. Just give me a moment. Please wait."

Peter headed toward a nearby exit. Rhiannon turned to give me kiss.

"Well done," she said.

"Emm," I said, determined, for once not to respond like a golden retriever.

"Peter is taking a week off to help us," she said.

"Emm," I said.

"He is coming with us to Alpes-de-Haute-Provence on, as Peter says, a bit of an adventure," she said, watching me carefully. "But that is all the time he could get off on short notice."

"Most kind of Peter," I said.

"We are paying for his hotel and such," said Rhiannon.

"Of course," I said.

"You are taking this well," said Rhiannon.

"Not at all," I said, in my own mind claiming a victory. "Peter will be brilliant at choosing the right restaurants."

"He will be," said Rhiannon, looking at me with a degree of caution.

"She, I think," I said.

"Actually, I prefer he," said Peter. "I prefer to identify as a man."

He had appeared, ninja-like, beside us.

"Indeed," I said.

"Most days," said Peter.

"Of course, I am sure it is hard to resist an LBD with your slender figure," said Rhiannon.

"Exactly!" said Peter. He cleared his throat. "Also, the copies will be ready late tomorrow," said Peter.

"Which really leaves only one question," I said. "Where do we go for dinner?"

Peter took my arm and guided me toward the great, glassed-in, arched entrance way. "I know a lovely little Bistro, right near your hotel, nowhere near as expensive as la Ballard, but good food and brilliant, I mean truly brilliant wines…"

Rhiannon trailed after us. I caught her reflection in the glass as we approached the doors. She looked perplexed.

After we exited the library onto a busy sidewalk, I stopped and offered her my other arm. She took it. The three of us headed off together, with Peter chattering happily, into the mystic.

CHAPTER THREE – THE SOUTH

The Countryside, France

Outside the windows, vineyards and forest slipped by kilometer after kilometer, the trees dark green and the vineyards light brown in the early evening November light, all rendered indistinct by the smooth motion of the train.

"I love this," I said.

"Average speed of more than 260 kilometers per hour on the Paris to Marseille run," said Peter, proudly. "Top speed of over 300 kph. Totally electric. We will travel 783 kilometers in just over three hours."

"France has more than 2,500 kilometers of high-speed rail track and is building 600 plus more. Is there a better way to travel? These trains are thirty years old, for goodness sake, and they are just perfect!"

"Actually, I meant the wine," I said. "But, no, there is no better way to travel."

Rhiannon, Peter, and I took up three of a four-seat grouping. Rhiannon and Peter faced toward the front of the train. I sat on the other side of the small table of indeterminate material, facing them. Between us lay a 750 ml bottle of cold, white, bubbly wine from the Limoux area of Languedoc, three glasses and a small, wicker basket of smoked salmon and cucumber sandwiches (no crusts). The wine originated from the small snack bar at one end of the car; the sandwiches from Peter's carryon. The rail car was lightly populated with a collection of tourists and business travelers.

It is, indeed, a civilized way to travel.

"The wine is lovely," said Rhiannon. "And so are the sandwiches. Thank you, dear." She placed her hand on Peter's arm. He turned pink. He did that a lot.

I took another half sandwich and took a bite. "Very good," I said, nodding.

Today, we all sported blue jeans and tee-shirts, travel attire. Peter managed to look stylish. Rhiannon looked shapely and desirable. I looked like a castaway, but my shirt had a drawing of a long-haired, breaded, man in sunglasses, and a message… "Abide", so I was pretty darned proud of myself.

Peter was on a roll. "So how many kilometers of track for the most civilized way to travel does Canada have?"

"None," I said. "We are useless."

"Well, Great Britain has almost none," said Rhiannon, supportively.

"It is not permitted to make fun of the English," said Peter. "Too easy. Also, you know, we have fought you for too long already. We must have peace."

"And Canada?" I asked.

"A proper, modern country," said Peter. "You are supposed to know better."

"Fair enough," I said.

"Argue, you will not?" asked Rhiannon. "You are so protective of your country."

I took a sip of the wine, which paired perfectly with the sandwiches. "Well two things," I said. "Peter made these wonderful sandwiches and it is embarrassing for a country like mine – where it would make perfect sense – not to have high-speed rail. We have been debating it for decades. The French system is thirty-years old for gods' sake. So, no; no argument. Peter, do I detect a hint of dill?"

"A touch," said Peter. "Just a pinch."

I took another bite.

"So, if you are so proud of your country, why are you travelling under a British passport?" asked Peter. "I saw it when we booked the train. I'm simply curious…"

"Well, Rhiannon said it would be easier to travel in Europe with an EU passport," I said. "So, she got me one."

"Just like that?" asked Peter.

"She knows people," I said.

"Hmmm," said Peter. He made a few little circles on the table in a small puddle of spilled wine. This was not a good sign.

"And, why are you shown as nobility in that document?" asked Peter. "The Lord of Summer? France is a republic, you understand… And that is an ancient title. Mythic, really…"

"Ah," I said. "That is a long, long story. And one I am not so keen to dwell upon."

"Do you know the story of the Dying God?" asked Rhiannon, quietly. She took his hand.

"Of course," said Peter. "*The Golden Bough* was part of my studies. A

33

small part, but still."

Rhiannon turned to me. "My love, why do you not go to find the bar car. You may have two, double Irish whiskies."

I gave her a smile, but not a real one. And they both knew it.

The bar car was modern, stylish in an everything-must-be-fireproof sort of way. I got my whiskey, just one, and found a seat by the window. The evening light turned the countryside shades of purple and blue as it washed by the train windows. I sipped my drink extremely slowly. It was smooth and peaceful.

When I returned, Rhiannon and Peter were side-by-side holding all four hands. I could see that Peter had been crying, but when I sat down with a flump, he looked up and gave me a genuine, bright smile.

"So, are you heading home?" I asked.

"Tut," he said. "I am a Laurent, and we Laurents are made of sterner stuff."

"So, you don't think we are crazy?" I asked.

"Oh, you are clearly mad," said Peter. "But that is a small thing, after all. At least, now, I understand what we are looking for, however mad you may be."

"You are a kind soul," I said.

He turned pink, again.

"Wait 'til you see the hotel I have booked! It is in the forest and the restaurant is four stars," said Peter.

The mid-nineteenth century Gare de Marseille Saint Charles train station is surprisingly charming. It sits high on a hill overlooking the city and is of stone, magnificent wrought-iron, and glass. One can easily feel the romantic stories of the millions of passengers who have used the station down through the years.

Or, at least that is what I thought until Peter motioned for me to lower my head so he could whisper right into my ear.

"It is haunted. A total nightmare. They built the whole thing on the Saint Charles graveyard," said Peter.

"No way," I said.

"It was more than 100 years before that movie," said Peter.

"Still, who does that?" I asked.

"The French," whispered Peter.

"What are you two talking about?" asked Rhiannon from a few feet behind as we headed toward the car rentals. She was struggling with a wobbly wheel on her suitcase.

"Nothing," said Peter and I in unison.

We picked up our vehicle from the ubiquitous O'Keefe car rental booth without issue. Rhiannon was a little quieted by my pre-booked choice of a white 1983 Citroën Méhari compact, two-door, 4x4 SUV. It looked a little like a small, open-topped Land Rover and had a soft, tent-style top.

Peter scooped up the car keys and announced, "I will drive our little dromedary."

When we got to the carpark, we found that even though the Méhari I reserved was a four-seater, as the agency had promised, the vehicle was really designed as a two-seater, with little room for luggage.

"There is no room for luggage," said Rhiannon. She turned to me. "You will sit in the back, with the bags."

I climbed in and they loaded the bags in beside me and then on top of me. The Hello Kitty on Peter's hard-plastic carryon glared up at me. Given the situation, I passed the Michelin map to Rhiannon. They seemed to have lots of room up front, after all.

Peter drove in a style that could be described only charitably as energetic. In truth, I closed my eyes before we exited the car park and did not open them again until the motion stilled somewhat and the anguished cries of pedestrians faded. He was Parisian, after all.

When I opened my eyes to the red-tiled rooves of the Marseille suburbs, the traffic signs advised we were on the A7. Rather quickly, we found ourselves on the mostly four-lane A51 rolling up into the forested rocky foothills of the Alps, often tracking alongside the broad valley of the dark, gleaming, and ferociously meandering Durance River in the gloaming of the evening.

I could see Rhiannon's smile in the rear-view mirror and realized that I was feeling rather fine myself. Paris is a wonder, but it felt good to be back amongst the hills and trees. And, I must confess, seeing Peter's transformation was an additional wonder. At first, I thought our cute and rather pretty young man with the matching set of Hello Kitty luggage became another creature entirely behind the wheel, flicking his headlights with great vigor, gearing down and up in rapid succession with great confidence and surety whilst passing tarp-covered trucks of goats or hay by mere centimeters, and teaching Rhiannon an entirely new French vocabulary based on the agricultural sector. But then, shifting my head slightly and seeing Peter's devilish little grin in the mirror, I realized it was merely a physical manifestation of the great courage it must take him to be himself every day. And, he both spoke and read archaic Latin.

I was pretty darned impressed by the boy, especially as I understood his motivation for our onward rush – dinner reservations at the hotel d'Pinus Nigra.

We exited the four-lane A51 at the D48, decelerating rapidly on the exit ramp, more rapidly on the overpass above the A51, and even more rapidly as we turned right and approached the toll booths. All of this is even more impressive in a thirty-odd years old vehicle with an ABS body.

Rhiannon handed Peter a note to feed into the toll machine. He handed her back a few coins. She held her hand there for a moment before realizing she had the change in its entirety.

Peter made the universal gesture of two open hands with a shrug, interesting as he was accelerating rapidly away from the toll gates. In the town, he took a sharp left, a right, did not deign to slow for the climb up a switchback, and turned right onto the D4096. In moments, we blasted around a traffic circle and were out of the town.

To either side of the two-lane, paved road – farmland. We were higher now and could still see the Durance River valley to our right.

Peter glanced over his shoulder. "We will be there soon!"

"This is exciting!" I said. He had done the run in just more than an hour. I had estimated it would take more than an hour and a half.

"We will make our reservation!" said Peter.

In a few moments, the farmland to the left of was replaced by hills rising above the road and forest. A few moments later a small black-and-white sign pointed us onto a gravel road to the left. Peter geared down, took the corner cautiously, and began our climb up the seven switchbacks to hotel d'Pinus Nigra.

The hotel d'Pinus Nigra is surrounded by a five-meter-high, 13th century wall of cream-colored ashlar sandstone. A square, roofed gatehouse protects the main entranceway, while four round towers, also roofed, guard the corners of the chateau's courtyard.

The reason for all these roofs is that, within the hotel courtyard, the four walls – each roughly 100 meters long – are lined with sandstone buildings that look rather like stables. Two sides of the quadrangle are a producing winery; the fourth side is a covered car park for guests' automobiles.

Once the home of a ne'er-do-well aristocrat, the hotel stands against the rear of the walled area. It is an organic looking place, not at all grandiose, but, rather simple in style as matches its 13th to 15th century origins. Again of squared, cream-colored sandstone, it consists of four, linked, rectangular blocks of two large stories and one of four stories.

The entire chateau is surrounded by a forest of eponymous black pine, mountain pine and silver fir, which rise from the chateau into rocky, limestone hills.

Peter drove slowly, much like a completely sane person, up the graveled drive, through gates beneath the gatehouse, and pulled gracefully into an open parking space within the well-lit covered park. A man moved in from behind our vehicle and opened Peter's door.

"Bonjour, hello," he said. "Welcome to the hotel d'Pinus Nigra."

Peter jumped in his seat. "Mon dieu, monsieur, vous m'avez effrayé!"

The man, a roundish Gaul with restrained mutton-chop sideburns, in black pants, white shirt with black tie and a paisley patterned vest, looked crestfallen. "Désolé, monsieur, mon erreur."

"You really cannot sneak up on people like that!" said Peter, which I thought a bit rich, but said nothing.

"Again, my pardon, sir," said the man. "We have a camera at the bottom of the drive so we may be here when guests arrive. Êtes-vous le groupe de Lord Summer?"

Rhiannon leaned over so he could see her. "That is correct."

"Excellent," said the man. "I am Claude. I understand you have a reservation at the restaurant. Please allow me to take your bags to your room, the chef is a little particular about timeliness…"

Rhiannon and Peter got out of the car and Claude started to reach in for the bags.

"Oh monsieur!" said Claude. "The Citroën Méhari is a fine classic, but maybe not for three people. Please let me help you!"

Claude extricated me from beneath the luggage. Peter gave him the vehicle keys and we three headed for the front door of the chateau.

After we were out of earshot, I said, "You booked us under Lord Summer?"

"Such things are useful when making reservations, my dear," said Peter.

"Indeed," said Rhiannon.

"I thought we were travelling under the radar?" I asked.

"Not for accommodation and food!" said Rhiannon. "I am starving."

"Fair enough," I agreed.

We passed through the glass doors into a sparse, white, vaguely art-deco lobby. This must have taken some work as the stonework behind the paint was clearly early medieval. A middle-aged woman clad identically to Claude waved to us from behind a black-marble counter.

"Bonjour, hello," she said. "If you leave me your passports, I will check you in while you freshen up for dinner. Your table is ready!"

"Are we late?" I asked. She seemed a little agitated.

"No, Monsieur, but you will be in 10 minutes!" she said. "The restaurant is to your left!"

Rhiannon handed over our passports and we headed into the restaurant – all soft light, glass tables, and light wood paneling. The elderly maître d'hôtel waited at the entrance and took our coats to hang in the alcove. He nodded toward an empty table where a young woman stood. There was, apparently, no time to speak. We moved as one to the table. Rhiannon waited for me to pull out her chair, which I dutifully did. As she sat to my right, I noticed that Peter also waited for me to pull out his chair, which I did. He sat to my left, giving me a lovely smile.

The thin, young blonde woman, said, "Welcome. Thank you for being on time," giving us all a grateful smile.

"Is there a problem?" I asked.

"No Monsieur, not at all, but the chef, he has a bit of a thing…" she said.

"About timeliness?" I asked.

"Indeed, Monsieur. Indeed," she said.

"It does seem a little odd, that is all," said Rhiannon.

Peter put his hand on her arm, then on mine. "But it is worth it. My chef de cuisine recommended it strongly. Strongly."

I nodded and Rhiannon patted his hand.

"Your chef de cuisine?" asked the blonde, reservedly.

Peter smiled, but Rhiannon answered.

"Monsieur D'Laurent has your job at la Ballard," she said.

The woman turned a little pale. "À Paris?"

Peter broadened his smile.

"Please allow me to get your menus right away," said the blonde. She departed at speed.

"Peter. Does that happen all the time?" I asked.

"My mistake, I usually do not let on," he said.

We did not see the blonde again that evening. Rather, a short while later a thin, grey-haired, bearded man approached our table. He also wore what appeared to be the hotel uniform of black pants and tie, white shirt and paisley vest, but his shirt was adorned with black cufflinks.

"Good evening," he said. "Please forgive us, but Mademoiselle became faint and needed to lie down. I am Montague and I will be looking after you this evening."

"I apologize," said Peter.

"Not at all, sir," said Montague. "Not at all. It is my pleasure."

Montague handed us the burgundy, cloth-covered menus.

"Peter, perhaps you could order for me? I am a little tired," I said. In fact, I was still trembling from the drive to the hotel.

"Of course," said Peter.

I handed Montague my menu and Rhiannon followed suit. Peter nodded.

Montague handed Peter the wine list. I relaxed. It was all going to be fine.

Peter took his time examining the menu whilst Montague waited quietly. After only a few moments, Peter ordered, "Amuse bouche."

"Of course, Monsieur," said Montague, a little offended.

"To start, the blue lobster, marbled foie gras & smoked eel. For the main, turbot fillet with herbed butter, followed by pigeon from Louargat roasted in woodcock, with buttered vegetables. The cheese plate…" Peter looked up to Montague. "I am sure you can improve upon what is noted here."

"Of course, sir," said Montague.

"And for dessert, the chocolate cake, clementine and chestnut sorbet," finished Peter.

Montague looked to Rhiannon and me. "The same for all?" he asked.

"Sounds great," I said. Rhiannon nodded.

Peter glanced briefly at the wine list. "We will start with Sylvain Loichet Les Gréchons Ladoix 1er Cru 2013," he said firmly.

"Oui, Monsieur," said Montague. "Immédiatement." He backed away two steps from the table, turned, and headed off to the kitchen.

Rhiannon looked first at Peter then at me. "You two, we cannot do this every night."

"Tut," said Peter. "Or course not, but this will be wonderful. And we can have as much wine as we like. No more driving today!"

He put his hand on mine. "Did I not order without hesitation? Was that not manly?"

It was my turn to turn a little pink. "Very. Most certainly."

"We would be lost without you," said Rhiannon.

A young, brush-cut shorn, possibly Germanic man brought two clear bottles of water to the table and backed carefully away. Neither Peter nor I said a word while he was near the table.

Rhiannon sighed. "You two. The Nazis are not following us."

We two looked at each other.

"I would ask you boys to please grow up," said Rhiannon. "But that would be a) pointless and b) no fun."

I looked at Peter and whispered. "Could you please explain the water?"

The two bottles of water were both of thick glass with a stopper held in place by a fixed contraption of hinged wire.

"This is naturally carbonated water from the estate's spring," said Peter. He turned to Rhiannon. "It really is like North Americans are barbarians. Have they completely lost touch with the simplest aspects of culture?"

"Well, Cameron, truly a savage is," said Rhiannon. "Did you know he used to hunt moose before he became a vegetarian?"

Peter covered his mouth with his fingers. "No!"

"Hunt, he did," said Rhiannon. "With a rifle. Can you imagine he was allowed a rifle?" She thought this most amusing and giggled to herself. And, we had not even seen wine yet.

"No. I meant he was a vegetarian?" asked Peter.

"Don't you start," I said.

"Why did you end it?" asked Peter.

"What with the animal and, I suppose, human sacrifice and all, it seemed rather hypocritical," I said. "It is kind of disrespectful to sacrifice a bull and then say you won't eat it because it is cruel."

"I guess that makes some kind of sense..." said Peter.

"Also, rare sirloin with peppercorn sauce," I allowed.

"Ah. Indeed," said Peter. "But, in truth, I am still a little, um, focused on the sacrifice portion."

"It is a small thing," said Rhiannon. She waved her right hand in regal dismissal.

Montague arrived with the white wine, confirmed the choice with Peter and performed a successful wine-tasting ritual. After Peter's nod of approval, Montague poured the wine, we all tasted it, and saw that it was good.

The amuse bouche arrived shortly thereafter. While it was beautifully presented in the form or shape of a rose flower on green spinach leaves and may have been fashioned from raw or smoked salmon, I could not say anything about the taste. Rhiannon, you see, quite liked hers and it vanished in a moment. Then, taking her fork in her left hand, she quickly scooped my amuse bouche over onto her plate.

Peter looked at her, eyes wide open.

"It is ok," I told him. "Not an issue."

"Well," he said. "As long as I know the rules…" As he nodded his head, his bob bobbed in a rather cute way.

Rules. I should mention that, at that time, I felt most uncertain about how the universe was unfolding, rules-wise, partially because of the stranger-in-a-strange-land aspect of travel in France and partially because of being on a quest for the Grail to avoid death. But mostly, just then, because I could not get out of my head that Claude, the bag man, had said, "Please allow me to take your bags to your room." One room. Not two.

I tried to work it through. Rhiannon is my lover, not my wife, okay only because my wife is currently seducing the man who will likely kill me and become the next Lord of Summer, and I love her – Rhiannon that is. But, that is still two layers.

Because I am just a dog, I suppose, I found myself attracted to Peter, who was neither my lover, nor my wife. And my lover was not a sharing person, bringing us to three layers.

Peter identified as a man, but his anatomical gender was, at the time, still a mystery to me – though I guessed he was not male, anatomically speaking. And, I had no idea whatsoever about the rules of etiquette for such things. I really did not want to hurt his feelings, or Rhiannon's. Bringing us up to four, or maybe five, layers.

What would you have done? It was all beyond me. I chose to 'sip' my wine and radically change the topic to something more reasonable, something I could handle – the quest for a mythic object.

"So, did we ever get a chance to look at those copies from the museum," I asked, which turned out to be an excellent thing to have said.

"Good boy," said Rhiannon, which rather reinforced my belief that she could sometimes read my mind. "That is perfect."

I saw Peter smiling his cute little smile at the "good boy" but, nevertheless, he reached into his bag, pulled out some rolled papers, slipped them out of the elastic, and unrolled them on the table holding the edges down with his hands.

"On the train, when the two of you weren't causing me to burst into tears, I did take some time to study these documents," said Peter. "The content is mostly lists of artifacts transferred to the Musée de Cluny from the Priory of Ganagobie in the late 1800s. And, yes, the sarcophagus is included in the list, having come allegedly from the monks of Iles de Lérins in the 15th century. It is also noted that some artifacts remained at the Priory because of their holy nature."

"It confirms what we knew," said Rhiannon.

"So how long a drive to this Iles de Lérins?" I asked.

Peter looked at me with his head tilted, which was, yes, quite cute.

"Quite a long one, I should think," said Peter, quietly.

Rhiannon put her hand on mine. "My love. They are islands."

"Sometimes one can drive to an…" I gave up. "Oh."

"They are just a bit off the coast of Cannes," said Peter. He put his hand on my other hand. "It is okay, my dear. All will be well."

"Please excuse me, I want to freshen up before the appetizer." He stood, smiled at Rhiannon, and slipped away.

After he was out of earshot, Rhiannon said, quietly, "It will be well. He is going to the girls' room."

"And?" I asked.

"Because a girl he is, anatomically speaking," said Rhiannon.

"But, just because he uses that washroom doesn't mean he is that, um, way," I said.

She leaned in even closer. "I have heard him pee," she said. "A sound not from a pidyn."

"Pidyn?" I asked.

She started to flush. "πέος," she said.

I just looked at her.

"陰茎," she said.

This did not help.

"A walrus," she hissed. "He does not have one."

In truth, I had understood at "pidyn", but she had turned bright red, so I no longer felt the need to draw attention away from my islands gaffe.

"And why is that important?" I asked, by way of demonstrating my modern sensibilities.

"Because, like him you do," said Rhiannon. "And if he is a girl then you are not a homosexual."

"And that matters because?" I asked.

"I am your lover," she said. "It might bear on that matter."

"So closed minded," I said.

"But that is not why," she said. "If you are gay it might disrupt the ritual combat."

"Oh. Back to me losing my head. Super," I said.

"It is a fertility ritual!" she hissed, quite loudly. Heads turned. "Responsibilities we Rowans have."

"Could we skip the whole Cameron's death theme for one night?" I asked.

"Indeed," said Peter from behind me. He leaned against the back of my chair and put a hand on each of my shoulders. "Let the poor dear be."

I did not start. I was getting used to his ninja ways.

Rhiannon closed her eyes and bowed her head. "So sorry I am. Sometimes I think I am too hardened to it all."

Peter kissed me on the top of the head and sidled into his chair.

Montague brought the appetizer just then, thank goodness: blue lobster, marbled foie gras and smoked eel, all lovingly arranged on a bed of late-season greens upon a dark blue stoneware platter. Peter clapped his hands in joy. I saw Montague suppress a smile as he set the platter in the center of the table.

"Dear gods," said Rhiannon. But I saw she was swallowing saliva.

"Beautiful," was all I could manage.

"Thank you, sir," said Montague. He withdrew.

Peter picked up the serving tongs. "Shall I be mother? Is that not what you Britishers say?"

"Neither one of us is British," I said. "But, please do."

Peter served, dividing the portions equally with almost socialist precision. This worked for me, but I could see Rhiannon glancing longingly at the lobster tail on my plate. Peter was a useful soul.

We managed to proceed through the rest of dinner – the turbot with herbed butter set out, the entire flatfish, on a huge round platter in the center; the golden, stuffed pigeons; the cheese plate and the chocolate cake – without discussing anything inappropriate or upsetting. Peter told us about growing up on a small farm near Montpellier. Rhiannon shared tales of the valley – gently edited. I listened.

Montague brought another bottle, or maybe two, of Sylvain Loichet Les Gréchons Ladoix 1er Cru 2013 during the meal at appropriate moments.

I was not chastised for any of my thoughts or behavior throughout the remainder of the meal. I wondered if Rhiannon's inherent tsundere nature was mollified by the environment or perhaps just by Peter's oh-so-cute manners and kindness. But I am usually wrong about such things, so I shut down such unnecessary reflection and let it all wash over me.

A fine, pleasant evening, indeed.

I did not touch my chocolate cake. I just looked at it, smiling like a peasant fool.

"You do not like it?" asked Peter. "I thought you would."

"I cannot," I said. "I have reached my limit. I will just look. Rhiannon?"

She set down her fork. "No thank you, my love. I, too, have had more than enough." She had taken one bite.

Peter laughed, but also set down his cutlery. "Very well. I shall have them send it to our room with a bottle of Laurent-Perrier Ultra Brut." He looked at me and patted my hand. "Dry champagne, my love."

I tensed a little at that. I had been "my loved" from both sides of the table. But Rhiannon patted my other hand and smiled, so I relaxed.

Peter made several arcane gestures in the air with his right hand, made sure that Montague saw it, and stood. Rhiannon took my hand and pulled me to my feet.

"Just like that?" I asked.

"Just like that," said Peter.

Our room was on the third floor, overlooking the walls at the back of the chateau toward the dark of the varied pine forest. Original medieval, dark wooden paneling covered the walls. The furniture, clearly antique, looked to be perhaps 300 years old. The king sized, four-poster bed with red-velvet drapes that could be drawn closed to limit drafts – not an antique but done it the same style – dominated the room. To the left of the bed, a sitting area with a modern, leather couch and chair. To the right, a separate room for the bath and toilet.

Our bags had been set to the side of the room. I moved toward them. Rhiannon stopped in the doorway.

"Understand, you both will," she said. "I will sleep in the middle. Rules there are."

"Tut," said Peter. He looked down, quite shyly and diffidently to his left.

"Of course," I said.

The bags were empty. They had already been unpacked into the armoire and the dresser.

"I am not used to this," I said.

"Do not get used to it," said Rhiannon. "Peter, will you please watch our expenditures?"

"I will be more careful," he said.

"Thank you," said Rhiannon.

A short while later, Montague and two henchmen arrived to set out a service for the deserts on the low table in the sitting area. The champagne was set in a free-standing, silver ice bucket. Champagne flutes were set on the table with great care.

"I will pour," said Peter. Montague nodded and he and his minions departed.

Peter opened the bottle with a slight pop and poured, but only for Rhiannon and me.

"If you do not mind, I am going to take a quick shower and change into my jammies," said Peter. He searched through the dressers, scooped out some clothing and vanished into the bathroom. My eyes followed him, but only until I noticed Rhiannon watching me.

"Total lolicon," she said.

We clinked glasses. The champagne was dry as sand and velvety. Amazing.

"This must cost?" I asked.

"All of it?" she said. "Insane. Do not ask. But you have earned it."

When Peter came out of the bathroom, Rhiannon was sitting in my lap kissing me.

For the record, Peter's jammies were a baggy, blue-flannel shirt and matching loose trousers highlighted with small and varied images of Hello Kitty. That night Rhiannon wore a transparent, blue, floor length negligee on her goddess-like body. I wore a t-shirt and boxers in the Cameron plaid. On the bed, the sheets and heavy duvet were of pure white cotton.

Rhiannon slept in the middle. Honest.

The cult center of Ganagobie has had its ups and downs throughout history. Pope Stephen VIII issued a papal bull in 939 recognizing that Cluny Abbey possessed the Priory at Ganagobie, but that does not mean that the various Catholic sub-cults acknowledged the bull. In fact, in 1491, while other Europeans were off confirming North America's existence, the Abbey of Cluny laid siege to the priory to regain it. Various political and religious entities vied for the land until, finally, the Ancien Régime had had enough and shut it down in 1789. During the French revolution only a few years later, the property was sold and many of the early medieval buildings destroyed.

By 1891 the Comte de Malijay owned the place. Rumor had it that the poor count had, in addition to his wife and official lover, a mistress. This may have damned his immortal soul, so, to balance things out, he gave Ganagobie to the Marseilles Priory. Much rebuilding and restoration was needed, during which early medieval mosaics were rediscovered.

Peace for Ganagobie, however, was short lived. The Marseilles cult was driven into exile in Italy by the Association Laws -- whatever they were -- in 1901 and were not able to return until 1922. But, even then, they did not return to Ganagobie, instead taking up residence in the much swankier Hautecombe Abbey. It was not until 1992 that they decided to move to a restored and rebuilt Ganagobie – there were too many tourists at Hautecombe Abbey.

I kept this little bit of history to myself during the short drive from the hotel d'Pinus Nigra to what was now the Benedictine Abbey of Ganagobie. Because, after all, my research document was in fact a nicely printed, four-color brochure from the hotel lobby and apparently that does not count as valid research when one is on a quest for a mythic religious object. I could not then, and still do not, understand why this is so, as where would one expect to find the key touchstones of myth? In some lost and dirty tome? Of course not. More likely it would be distilled by the culture, up front and staring you in the face in a glossy pamphlet! But this is only the wisdom of a god, after all. And peace with one's lover and companion must come above all – except, obviously, for peace with one's wife. Normally.

Without baggage the vehicle was quite roomy enough for three, and, as it was a lovely sunny day, Peter insisted we drive with the top down. On the highway this was, according to Peter, "blustery". On the climb up the multiple switchbacks from the valley to the abbey, it was fresh, but most pleasant. On either side of the D30, the open forest of bright green oaks and yellow-green Aleppo pines covered the steep red-brown marl and sandstone hillside. The scent of the forest, the sharpness of pine, and the dryness of the air contrasted strongly with the rich loamy aroma of the sisal oak forests of our Welsh valley. But still, being among the trees calmed me.

Peter handled the endless shifting of the manual transmission with alacrity – all the more impressive as the beast has four normal speeds and an additional three-speed transfer gearbox for climbing severe slopes. I could see that both he and Rhiannon were bubbly, happily eager to reach the abbey. Rhiannon was keen to learn the origin of the sarcophagus, but Peter was on a quest of his own. Beside me in the back seat sat an empty Styrofoam cooler he had wrangled from the kitchen staff at the hotel. He was determined to fill it with Banon à la feuille, a small, unpasteurized, unpressed goat cheese wrapped in softened chestnut leaves and tied with a raffia palm.

I now knew more about Banon than anyone really should know about a cheese. Fortunately, whilst driving on the highway, the rushing wind precluded speech. Not so on the way up the switchbacks.

"They have made these cheeses here in the hills of Provence since Roman times," said Peter. "The affinage…" He looked back at me. "The curing takes only two weeks, then it is dipped in Eau de vie, a fermented, double-distilled fruit brandy with neither color nor opacity. The water of life if you will. It can be stored in an earthen container and will last for years. Years! It can become most strong in flavor. My chef de cuisine was quite keen that I return with a bounty of this treasure."

Rhiannon patted his knee. "I am sure we will find some," she said. "We will not leave without filling your box."

Rhiannon was rewarded with a heart-melting smile.

The Méhari made it to the top of the grade without trouble and we found ourselves on a broad, mostly treed plateau. In a few short minutes we were at the abbey.

The abbey perches on the edge of a cliff overlooking the broad, green Durance river valley. Approaching the retreat, one sees only a long, high, stone wall with an adjoining chapel to the left – a plain, simple, red-tiled, peak-roofed building, perhaps twelve meters high, and built of light-colored stone in the Provencal Romanesque style. Only the five progressively smaller arches surrounding the wooden double front doors of this building and the stone panel above the doors are carved. In the Arabic-looking Mozarabic style, the carvings show Christ hobnobbing with an angel and various mythical beasties – apparently representing the four evangelists. The twelve apostles are cut into the stone of the lintel below the panel, above the door. The three apostles to the right appear to be doing the conga.

Peter parked our vehicle in the allotted, grass parking lot and we headed toward the entrance to the chapel – the only obvious approach. We left the Méhari's top down.

We were the only people in sight. November is clearly not the priory's peak season. As we approached the entrance, Peter stopped and clapped his hands.

"This is a national treasure," said Peter.

"It is pretty impressive," I allowed.

"Impressive it is," said Rhiannon.

"Tut," said Peter. "You must be more accepting of other people's religions. After all…" Peter winked at me. "He really is just another dying god, you know."

"Eh?" I said.

"True it is," said Rhiannon. "Better PR he had than you."

They both found this terribly amusing and were still laughing as Rhiannon pushed open the right-hand door and we entered the chapel. I pushed through after them and found them frozen beneath the scowl of a tall, black-robed monk.

"C'est un lieu sacré," said the monk. "Vous allez déranger nos autres invités."

I ignored the fact that there were no other guests in sight for us to disturb and said, "Please forgive us. Sometimes they are like children." It felt really good not to be the one messing up.

He eyeballed Peter. "S'il vous plaît avoir un decorum, monsieur."

Peter turned bright red and put his hands to his checks. "Un million de pardons, monsieur. Je suis vraiment désolé."

"Me too," was all Rhiannon could manage.

"Humph," said the monk. "Well, you best see the mosaics, then." He pointed at Peter's face. "And then visit the gift shop!"

"Or course," I said. "Absolutely."

"Actually," said Rhiannon. "We are not here for the mosaics. We are here trying to get a bit of history on something."

"Not here for the mosaics?" said the monk. "Everyone comes for the mosaics. They are a national treasure."

"We will be delighted to see the mosaics," I said. I glanced around the spacious, stone-arched chamber. Rows of pews ranked either side of the main central aisleway leading to the choir area and beyond to the table that served as a pulpit. "Will you walk with us?"

"Of course, monsieur," said the monk. He led us toward the front of the church.

"This place has quite the history," I said. "Siege, war, plague, revolution."

"So true, monsieur." He gestured around him, cartwheeling both arms. "All of this, almost totally destroyed several times."

"But rebuilt so conscientiously. So true to the original," I said.

"Indeed. One truly sees the hand of God," said the monk.

"Indeed," I said. "I also understand there are some ancient sarcophagi the public may see?"

"So you are here to see those things?" said the monk. "Pre-Christian and nowhere near as impressive as the mosaics. But you may see them. The rest of the abbey is closed to visitors, of course. Ah, and here we are." He gestured, again with both arms. We had arrived at the altar, an area cordoned off with velvet ropes.

"The beautifully colored mosaics on this floor show lions and griffins and so forth, as shown in the medieval alphabet. The motifs are in the oriental style. We are told that the images represent the fight between the vices and the virtues."

"And they are how old?" asked Peter.

"Perhaps 12th century," said the monk. "They were originally commissioned by the Prior Bertrand."

He had clearly given this speech a thousand times but was also clearly proud of the place.

Peter, I could see, was intrigued. But, Rhiannon stood, stunned, her mouth actually hanging open a fraction.

"My love?" I asked.

"I have..." she started then looked down and began to rummage through her bag. She pulled out a cardboard tube and handed it to me. It was open at one end, so I put my middle finger in and pulled out a yellowed paper. I unrolled it. It was a pencil sketch of the mosaics.

Figure 2. Sketch of Mosaics at Ganagobie Abbey, Lord Summer's collection.

"This was taken from SS-Standarten Führe Wust," said Rhiannon.

The mosaic of the elephant with castle was clearly circled.

"What could it mean?" I asked. "Is it under the mosaics?"

"Is what under the mosaics?" demanded the monk. "What nonsense is this? Nothing is under the mosaics. They were removed for restoration and only returned to the abbey in the early nineteen eighties. Why are you here?"

Peter put his hand on the monk's arm. "We had no idea that this drawing was of your mosaics, did we?"

"No, not at all," said Rhiannon. "It is a shock. I had no clue what this was…"

"Some of us had no clue we had the drawing," I observed.

"Actually, we are trying to find out where a certain sarcophagus came from," said Peter, quietly. "A variety of objects were moved to the Musée de Cluny in the late 1800s. One of them was a sarcophagus showing a priestess at a well? We understand that it originally came from the Iles de Lérins?"

Peter's manner seemed to sooth the monk.

"Then what is this talk of the SS?" he asked.

"It is a small thing," said Peter. "Some of our research documents on the sarcophagus were repossessed from the SS by this woman's relatives in the closing days of the war. It does not really bear on anything at all."

Peter gave the monk what is quite possibly the cutest smile imaginable, complete with dimple.

"Hmm. I see," said the monk. "Very well. Many objects were moved here from Iles de Lérins in the old times, but I know the sarcophagus of which you speak. It is local. It came from one of the troglodyte caves on the edge of the plateau." He motioned, with only one hand this time, toward the north.

"Could we go to the cave?" asked Rhiannon.

"There is not much to see," said the monk. "A few inscriptions and carvings on the wall. Post-troglodyte, of course." He perked up. "It is a lovely walk up through the forest, though."

"Is there a spring or well nearby?" I asked.

Rhiannon looked at me with clear approval and I felt that dog-like joy of happiness.

"Of course," said the monk. "If you follow the walking trail to the caves. Many people used to refresh themselves at the Well of Saint Nemetona. You may purchase a brochure with a good map in the gift shop."

"Is it far? Could we go today?" asked Rhiannon.

"Or course," said the monk. "It is only a short walk."

"But what of the drawing?" asked Peter.

I handed the sketch to the monk. He examined it.

"A dubious talent, your SS man, but I cannot imagine the connection to the sarcophagus of the wells," said the monk. "Perhaps your SS man just liked elephants?"

He thought this quite funny and chuckled to himself as we headed out through the chapel's front door toward the gift shop. At the entrance he took his leave. We thanked him profusely.

The gift shop, you should know, at Ganagobie Abbey is worth attending. In addition to the expected religious artifacts, one may purchase balms, soaps, essential oils, fragrances, honey, jams, olive oil, and incense, all crafted by the holy order.

Peter bought a tin of Shea Butter to sooth his hands. Rhiannon bought two, 12 milliliter glass bottles of essential oils – eucalyptus and pine. I bought the brochure with the map.

At the cash register, Peter queried the young monk who took our euros about locating Banon à la feuille. The youngster gave elaborate directions in French to a local farm. I assumed that later in the day we would be getting lost.

The name of the trail worried me a touch, as a walking route with the nom de guerre "The Cliff" does not imply a gentle assent. However, the trail rose from the abbey at a reasonable rate, climbing about one-hundred meters over two-and-one-half kilometers up through rocky terrain with an open forest of green oaks and pine to either side. High above the valley floor, the air became clear and fresh, flavored with dry pine needles.

The three of us made an easy assent. Rhiannon and I were more than accustomed to climbing from our hikes in the valley, and Peter proved to be fit as a fiddle, climbing readily with firm, sound strides. I tried not to watch him, so as to avoid further lolicon accusations you will understand, but saw Rhiannon laughing at me for my efforts and just gave in.

The more we climbed, the more I became fascinated by the green oaks. I had not seen this type of oak before coming to southern France, but had read of it – having developed a bit of a thing for oak trees during my time as Lord of Summer. The green oak grows from five to twenty meters in height and can be two-thousand years old. Its leaves resemble holly and appear somewhat leathery. It looks like the tougher, more resilient, sister of the sessile oak so prevalent in our valley. Its trunk is often twisted with age.

The path was clearly old and much used through the centuries. At one point, after perhaps half-an-hour, Peter jumped toward me and slipped his arm through mine.

"We are walking on a Roman road," he said, with a wide smile.

"We are not?" I asked.

"Totally we are," he said.

And it was true. That section of the path was uneven, rectangular, well-worn, grey stone blocks. Only parts of the road had survived over the centuries, but it was still recognizable.

Rhiannon took my other arm. "Impressive work, to be sure," she said.

"My people were Roman," said Peter. "Way back. It's from the Roman surname Laurentius, which was understood to mean 'from Laurentum'."

I laughed, happy to be deep in the forest and wandering through history. "Well, your people built well, to be sure," I said.

"Did your family name used to be D'Laurent?" asked Rhiannon.

"Laurent, it is now," said Peter. "There is no place for aristocrats in my France!"

"You hate them so," I said.

"Not you, mon Seigneur. You are both loved and useful," said Peter.

Peter let go my arm and bounced ahead of us. Rhiannon leaned close and said, "The boy loves you. Be kind and gentle."

But he heard it and turned and pointed at me.

"You better be!" he said and turned away with the flash of smile.

"Also," said Rhiannon. "He just called you his lord."

"Ah," I said. I could think of nothing else to say. It was a little overwhelming.

As we climbed higher, the trail began to run parallel to the edge of the cliff, sometimes wandering perilously close to the edge. I worked hard to keep the consternation from my face, but in the end, Peter took hold of my right arm and Rhiannon grabbed my left as we navigated the trickiest bits.

It was a long way down to the forest and rocks below; but beyond, the Durance River valley spread out in a verdure vista. The meandering river found its way over the scattered, grey stone of its own bed. Farms hid, scattered in amongst the forest. Small, white towns gathered at old bridges over the river. And, today, a cerulean sky scattered tendrils of white cloud.

As we drew closer to the top of the plateau, the trail graduated away from the cliff face and we started to see hints of a large cream-colored, stone wall through the trees.

"That is the Oppidum barré," I said. "It is about one hundred and fifty meters long and completely protected the medieval town. It is now about five meters high in most places, but used to be much higher. The ruins of a circular tower are at the far side. In the center should be a small keep or gatehouse. The wall is only on this side as the other sides of the town are protected by the steep cliffs."

"A town, up here?" said Rhiannon.

"Not much left, apparently," I said. "The town was never permanently inhabited. Mostly it is just tumbled stones. It was first used about 1000 A.D. during the bloody chaos of the collapse of the Carolingian Empire, though it was populated in the twelfth and thirteenth centuries, the monastery's glory days. They guess there were issues with water supply. And, the plague."

"Though, also apparently..." I waved the brochure, "the caves should be just ahead on the right, before we get to the wall."

Peter snatched the brochure from my hand and turned to Rhiannon.

"Is he always so insufferable?" said Peter.

"Insufferable, he is," said Rhiannon. "But it is cute."

By then, I knew better than to comment. I congratulated myself on my skills.

About forty meters before we reached the wall, a small trail led off to the right and down, back toward the cliff edge. It opened onto a large sandstone shelf. To the right, the abyss. To the left lay the three caves. Or, as it had said in the brochure the 'grottes'.

The caves appeared to be natural, large openings in the rock, two to three meters high below giant stone slabs, a most natural habitat for early humans. Here and there, the remains of piled stone walls at the cave entrances showed they had been used in more recent times as homes or for storage.

Peter cleared his throat dramatically. "Ahem. According to the brochure…" He held it before him with both hands. "These caves have been occupied since at least Neolithic times." He looked over the brochure. "Cameron, that is about four thousand years ago or earlier."

"I know that," I said. "It is the last bit of the stone age."

"Nice," said Peter. "Well done."

"He watched a BBC special after a night at The Three Crowns with his wife," said Rhiannon. "While I watched his first daughter next door."

"I thought he had two daughters" asked Peter.

"Believe, I do, the second one was created that night, on the sofa," said Rhiannon.

"So, not so well done?" asked Peter.

"No," said Rhiannon.

"It was a most interesting spec…" I began.

"Cameron, I suggest you not speak for a while," said Peter. "You really need to learn to think before you share your wisdom."

"Hmm," I said. A degree of coolness had clearly manifest. My skills were apparently useless.

"So," said Peter. He folded up the brochure. "This is as far as Cameron's research treatise takes us."

"See, I do not, a well or fountain," said Rhiannon.

I started to open my mouth, but Peter covered it with his hand.

"My dear, you are having a time out," said Peter.

He did not remove his hand until I nodded. Then, he turned to Rhiannon. "Nor do I. Let us explore the caves."

We each took one of the three caves. Mine was not huge, being about the size of a small shop. The ceiling was high and I could easily stand with no danger of hitting my head. The sandstone walls were dry.

In the middle of the cave, an old fire pit had seen recent use. The broken, green beer bottles suggested teenagers. It certainly would have kept the troglodytes warm and dry, but I cannot say it appealed much to me.

To the right, a basin had been hollowed out of the rock. Above the basin, a stone pipe about five centimeters in diameter emerged from the stone. Both basin and pipe were completely dry.

After about ten minutes, I met the others back outside on the shelf.

"You may speak, Cameron," said Peter.

I looked at Rhiannon.

"Yes, you may speak, but you will pay later," said Rhiannon.

All of this was deeply unfair, you must be thinking; but the Fairness Fairy was nowhere to be seen so, for me, discretion was the better part of valor. One always pays a price for love, after all.

"A dry basin. No sign of water," I said.

"Nor in mine," said Peter. "No sign of Saint Nemetona."

"Hmm," said Rhiannon. "Let's try further on."

We followed the side-path back to the main trail and turned toward the medieval town ruins. We climbed the path through the open forest and came out into the sunlight. Ahead of us the stone wall stretched far to the left, but right before us a high, arched gate led into the town. The stone arch or, rather, arches were still in place – first a pointed arch, then a classic Roman-style arch within the pointed arch's recess.

Through the arches, we could see the overgrown ruins of the old town, moss and scrub over tumbledown stones. Before the gate, however, something much more distracting sat. A stunningly beautiful woman with short, tightly-curled black hair with ringlets falling to either side of her face, a generous figure, and a mesmerizing smile looked up at us from her perch on a squared chunk of stone. She wore an off-the-shoulder, dark green, peasant-style dress and held a large sketch pad in her lap.

There was some discussion later about what actually happened next, but I will now share the true, completely innocent version of events.

Welcomed by her smile, I stepped forward and said, in a perfectly normal voice (not in a deep low, oh-you-are-talking-to-a-pretty-woman voice), "Hello, bonjour, how are you?"

Nothing more than a simple, pleasant greeting was suggested or implied.

The woman stood and her smile grew brighter, revealing attractive dimples. Her face flushed. At this point the following happened, though I am not certain of the exact order of events.

Something hit me in the back of the head, in retrospect likely Rhiannon's bag. I bent forward away from the impact. Then, something hit me in the stomach, in retrospect likely Peter's foot. And I fell down onto the dirt and gravel, somehow getting sand all over my tongue. I remember it as somewhat salty. I started to spit it out. I also remember thinking that Peter must be pursuant of the martial arts as the kick had been finely placed.

The woman stepped back alarmed, as evidenced by the O shape her lips assumed.

Peter stepped toward the woman, turned and said to Rhiannon, "I will get this one."

Rhiannon nodded, but she glared down at me with devil eyes.

"Ignore him, please," Peter said to the woman with the lovely shoulders. "That was his third strike today."

I was pretty sure this was not true, but my tongue was covered with sand and I was already on the ground. The ground was not uncomfortable, so I rolled onto my back in the dirt. The November sun shone still warm enough to be pleasant, so I relaxed.

"Uh, hello," said the woman in strongly accented English. She stepped forward and offered Peter her hand. "Claudette de Memoir."

Peter shook her hand politely, yet distantly.

"Please allow me to introduce, Rhiannon Rowan," said Peter. He gestured to me with his other hand. "She is his maîtresse-en-titre. I am Peter D'Laurent, their, um, companion."

"I see," said Claudette. She took a few paces forward and looked down at me. "You have a name? Are you hurt?"

"He is having another time out," said Peter. "He has no name."

"I am fine," I said. "I have been trained for this sort of thing."

"You are trained for kicks to your stomach?" asked Claudette.

"More or less," I said.

Claudette took a step back. "Well, nice to meet you. Please have a nice day."

"Thank you," said Peter. "But before we go can you direct us to the Well of Saint Nemetona?"

"Saint?" said Claudette. "Hardly. She is no saint; she is one of the old ones."

"Indeed," said Rhiannon. "Of the forest, I believe?"

"Of the Holy Grove, indeed," said Claudette. "Are you pagans?"

Rhiannon said "Yes," and Peter said "No" at the same time.

Then, Peter sighed and said, "Fine, yes. Yes, we are pagans."

Claudette looked down at me, "And you?"

"Very much a pagan he is," said Rhiannon.

"Very much?" asked Claudette of the short curly black hair.

Rhiannon and Peter smiled vacantly at her.

"I see," said Claudette. "Well, do not follow the monks' document. The last thing they want is a pagan holy site. I would show you the way, but I think that might offend."

Rhiannon said "No" and Peter said "Yes" at the same time.

I closed my eyes.

"Perhaps, I will just point the way, no?" asked Claudette. And, I could see, in my mind's eye, a cute, very southern European pout.

"Please," said Peter, nudging me gently with his boot.

"Perhaps I should just stay here? On the ground?" I asked.

Rhiannon said "No" and Peter said "No" at the same time.

"That way," said Claudette. She must have pointed. "A trail leads down the cliff, just before you find the abbey. It is the old way."

"Back at the abbey?" I said.

"Yes," said Claudette. "Walk to the church and follow the path to the left. You will see a group of graves cut in the rock. Take the trail down to what they call the washhouse because the monks cleaned their clothes there. This is the sacred well."

"Seriously?" said Peter.

"Mais bien sûr!" said Claudette.

Peter nudged me with his foot again. As I opened my eyes, he offered me his hand. I took it and he pulled me to my feet. For a small person, he is strong.

Rhiannon sighed. "Let us go. At least it was a lovely walk."

"Forgive me," said Claudette. "Why do you seek the well?"

"We saw a sarcophagus at the Musée de Cluny," said Peter. "We believe it came from here, from near the well."

"I know it," said Claudette. "The sarcophagus of the Lady by the Well."

"That's the one," I said.

"They say it did come from this place," said Claudette. "And in the old times, there was a temple there. They say it is not really a sarcophagus at all, but that it caught the water from the sacred spring. You will see the replacement when you arrive there."

"You are well informed," said Peter. He tried to sound polite but failed.

"I have lived here for a long time," said Claudette. "I spend much time in these forests. The people talk to me and they tell me things. But tell me, please, why are you interested in the sarcophagus?" asked Claudette.

"We should go or we will lose the light," said Rhiannon.

Claudette smiled what I took to be a kind smile, though, during my chastisement later that evening, I learned that others took a different view.

"Ah oui, we do not wish you to lose the light," said Claudette.

"Come, mon Seigneur," said Peter and he took my hand and started to lead me back down the path toward the abbey. Rhiannon trailed after.

I turned and waved goodbye to Claudette. She raised her hand.

"Mon Seigneur. Merci pour votre service," said Claudette.

I turned to Rhiannon for a translation.

"She thanks you for your service," said Peter.

"Eh?" I asked. When I turned back, Claudette was gone, perhaps having stepped through the gateway.

"She is gone," I said.

Neither of the other two turned back to see.

"Good riddance," said Peter. "Sitting up here sketching in an off-the-shoulder dress. No jacket when it is this cool. That cute salon cut. Those big, bouncy…"

"Too true," said Rhiannon.

At this point, I did not remark that I thought she had been nice or lovely, but I did feel it safe to say, "Her directions were helpful?"

I received no response.

The walk back was uneventful. If the lack of conversation suggested a degree of chill, that was acceptable. The forest in early November was still. A light wind rattled and rustled the leaves of the oaks and the scent of fallen pine needles erased all memory of the Paris diesel and ozone, setting my addled mind to rest. No further violence was done to my person. That was enough. I had learned not to judge the fury of the women in my life. Having an exceptionally limited life expectancy puts stress on everyone. And, despite what we learn in kindergarten, sharing is hard in adult relationships and rarely ends well. I am sure that Clarine, Rhiannon and, indeed, Peter would have never tolerated me if I, well, you know, weren't doomed to die a spectacularly gruesome death in a sacrificial combat required to sustain all life on Earth, giving me a certain utility and, apparently, some kind of strange attraction for certain women – though I am reasonably certain Rhiannon made that last part up to boost my sagging spirits.

As so often is the case, descending the rocky path took more care and time than the ascent. We arrived back at the abbey as the sun neared the horizon and took the path to the left, as instructed by Mademoiselle D'Memoir. The path descended gently through open, oak forest, paralleling the sand-colored cliff face to the left with a steep drop off to the right. One could see that centuries before this path had been a road, as here and there cobbled stone surfacing or steps showed through the forest litter of leaves, twigs, earth and gravel.

In a short while, we came upon small caves and overhangs in the cliff to the left. A few moments later...

"There..." said Peter, pointing ahead.

This was completely unnecessary as most obviously the entire cliff face just a little ahead was covered in lush, verdant vines, while, at the base of the cliff, a bright emerald of grasses and small forest plants reached toward the pathway.

"I hear running water!" said Peter, bounding ahead.

"He is such a dear child," said Rhiannon, softly.

"A cute, homicidal, ninja child," I thought, but obviously did not say as she gazed fondly after him.

"Here!" said Peter. He crouched at the base of the cliff.

As we approached him, I saw a thin rivulet, perhaps as wide as my forearm. It sprang, frothing, directly from the rock, running along the cliff's base, beneath an overhang, heading downhill alongside the path. We followed.

"Ah," I said. "Now this is a place of considerable beauty."

Peter came up and hooked my left arm. "Indeed."

At the base of the cliff all was green. And green of vine and mosses rose up the cliff to merge with the leaves of the trees overhead. We stood, sheltered, breathing in the chapel of forest, stone and water.

The rivulet ran into a large, unadorned, grey stone trough that once must have appeared much like an industrial wash basin. Jade green moss and running vines had reclaimed the stone and water to absorb the basin back into the chapel landscape.

Rhiannon stepped forward and lowered her head to the water. She stopped just short of touching it.

"Cold it is, and smells clean," she said.

"You can see they must have really used this trough to do their washing once," I said. "It is divided into two sections, one to wash, one to rinse."

"This is a sacred space," said Rhiannon. She looked around. "But there is no sign of the ancient temple."

"No," said Peter. "They would have removed all trace. The stone was likely reused in the foundations of the monastery."

He sighed. Deeply. "There is nothing. No carvings, no writings. It is a dead end."

"Perhaps we can find some fragment at the abbey?" said Rhiannon.

"It is a wonderful place," I said.

"It is," said Peter sadly, somehow.

"No. I mean it is full of wonders," I said. "You know, the original meaning." He looked at me and found me smiling like a lunatic.

The ruby, early evening light slanted down through the trees striking the cliff and washing it red. The running water refracted the sunlight, throwing a flickering, stained-glass window on the rock and vines of the cliff. At that moment, all was perfectly still. No sound rose from the highway far below. No jet plane coursed above.

"Perfect," I said.

Rhiannon came up and took my other arm.

"There it is, then," she said. "In the right place we are."

"But there are no clues!" said Peter. Water welled up in the corners of his eyes.

"Cameron, our Lord of Summer, will sleep here tonight and dream," said Rhiannon.

"I will?" I asked, not only because we were staying in the nicest hotel that I was ever likely to see.

"You will," said Rhiannon. "And I will forgive you your trespasses."

"Fuck!" said Peter.

We both turned to him.

"Fuck. Fuck. Fuck. Fuck," he said, stamping his right foot in a cross and manifestly cute manner. "She looked exactly fucking like the woman on the sarcophagus."

"Oh dear," said Rhiannon, letting go of my arm. "She did, did she not?"

And, it was true. Mademoiselle D'Memoir had looked exactly like the woman in the carved panels, even right to the nose.

"It did not seem safe to mention it at the time," I said quietly.

"You did not notice!" said Rhiannon. "You are just looking for an excuse."

This may or may not have been true.

"Well, she probably just styles her hair that way out of respect to the original goddess," I said.

"There you go," said Peter. "That does not mean she could have helped us…" He did not seem to have convinced himself.

In the end, Peter insisted on running back up to the top of the plateau to look for Mademoiselle D'Memoir. Whilst he did, Rhiannon, having no faith in his adventure, returned to the hotel d'Pinus Nigra in our mechanical dromedary to fetch some bedding. I wondered how she would explain her request.

I found a fallen log near the basin upon which to perch.

Though I had been surprised by the notion of spending the night in the woods, I was not averse to it. My time in the valley had made me quite familiar with the process of mystic dreaming. I was no stranger to the Land of Nod.

"But, here?" I asked out loud.

Whom was I asking, I wondered? I walked over to the spring, put my face down and drank from the running stream. I need not note what a stupid thing this was to do, but, well, time was short and it seemed the right approach. The chill water tasted of salts and minerals. I splashed it on my face and it felt good in the November air.

"What a place," I said aloud. When no one else is about, it is fine to speak to oneself, is it not?

I explored further down the trail. It looked much as it had above the spring. I returned to the water just in time to see Peter jogging toward me. He had actually run all the way up and back down the trail. He panted, but only lightly.

"Anything?" I asked.

He shook his head.

"Worth a try," I said.

"You knew she would be gone," said Peter.

"I have lived in the house of the Rowans for almost seven years. Even someone as thick as myself picks up a few things," I said. "Also, don't drink the water. It is a little too minerally."

"That is not a real word," said Peter. "Also, you must have drunk it to know it has too many minerals."

"I am a god, remember," I said.

"Hmmm," he said.

But we both laughed at our collective folly. And it felt good to laugh with him there in that chapel of green.

I found a soft place to sit on some moss, leaning up against the side of a twisted old oak. Peter perched on the edge of the basin, running his fingers through the water.

"So, you are really going to sleep here tonight?" he asked.

"You heard Rhiannon," I said.

"Aren't you The Lord of Summer?" he asked. "Does that not make you the ruler or something?" He could not even say it straight without needing to cover his mouth with his right hand to suppress a giggle.

"I will give you the real answer to that question," I said. "I realized a long time ago that the Three Rowans endure. They keep the whole shebang going. They bear the weight of it all. We glory boys, the Lords of Summer, are just passing through. We are meteors across the dark sky above a still lake. That is all."

"But you really fight and kill and die?" he said, only half a question.

"Too true," I said. "But that is nothing compared to the horrors The Rowans must endure, generation after generation. You must see that it will be far easier for me than for her. She will have to carry on. And her daughter, too. Again. And again."

"And you really believe it all?" asked Peter.

"I have to, don't I?" I said. "Imagine if I just got on a plane back to Canada and I was wrong? Besides, promises have been made."

He smiled at me then. A dangerous smile.

"You are the Lord of Summer, after all," he said. "I guess you really are."

"That doesn't mean I am not a fool," I said.

"You always say that, but I think you must have been the last to know," he said, the dangerous smile still there. "And the dreaming, tell me about that?"

"Well. It has helped me find my way before," I said.

"How so?" he asked.

"I see things, talk to people, or dream a narrative. There is always something to learn, even if I don't always get it," I said. "Dreaming isn't really the right word. It seems real."

"And where do these dreams come from?" asked Peter.

I laughed. "A few theories there!" I said. "From the old gods? From supportive spirits? Or, just the unconscious mind processing what it already knows?"

"I can guess Rhiannon's view," he said. "What is yours?"

I stopped laughing. "I don't actually know anymore. Things have changed since I became, well, me."

"Hmm," he said.

"Well, of course, there are the potions," I allowed. "That may have something to do with it. Rhiannon says they just open the gate, though."

"Drugs?" he asked.

"Herbal stuff," I said.

"Drugs," he said. "You really are a fool."

"True. True," I said. "But, as noted…"

He nodded. "Promises have been made. Responsibilities have been assumed."

"Indeed," I said.

"Indeed," he said.

There followed a short pause where we heard only the running water and the light wind through the oaks.

"I will stay with you tonight," he said finally, not looking up.

"That is very kind," I said. "But I have to do this alone. Completely alone. No one on overwatch."

"No one in the bed?" he asked.

"Indeed," I said. "One must be completely solitary. As one is when one exits the world."

"Are you not afraid?" he asked. "Alone in the forest? Alone in your dreams?"

"Yes," I said. "But that is part of the deal, I suppose. Part of what is taken on." I did not say the rest. What more was there for me to fear, after all? Back then, I saw my future as fixed.

Peter came and sat by me on the moss, beneath the bole of the ancient and twisted oak. I put my arm around him and we stayed thus, in the silence until Rhiannon's return.

Rhiannon appeared first, strolling down the trail toward us. Behind her followed Claude, the roundish Gaul from the hotel who had helped with our luggage. He, and the six who followed after him, large men of muscle, wore the black pants, white shirts with black ties, and the paisley patterned vests of the hotel staff. These men were laden.

Rhiannon came up to us and looked down.

"I promise you," she said. "I just asked for a mattress from one of the poolside lounges and a sleeping bag."

Claude stepped up beside her. "Impossible, madam. Quite impossible."

First, they set up a folding wooden dining table and three folding chairs. Next, beside the fountain basin, they set up a white canvas cabana of the type one might find at the beach – four poles supporting a tent-style roof with white curtains drawn open on all four sides. Inside, they unfolded a large, wide cot and made it up with white pillows, linen, and a white comforter.

Claude erected an iron brazier and lit the self-starting coals with a long, wooden match. He looked up.

"The self-lighting coals is cheating a bit. My apologies, monsieur," said Claude.

"It is a matter of no concern," I assured.

I watched in awe as they laid a white tablecloth over the dining table and set it for three with the same china from the restaurant. Dinner was removed from insulated carryalls and set out on the table. Watching, I realized I was famished.

Claude gestured with a wave. "I apologize, once again, monsieur. On such short notice, we must go with what is on hand. A small roast turkey, a kale salad, les petites pommes de terre – in a lovely red-pepper cream sauce, though – and a few small mince pies for afterward. Oh! Mon Dieu! I nearly forgot the wine."

But Claude's bearers had not forgotten the wine, nor the silver wine bucket for the ice, and all was duly arranged upon the white tablecloth.

Peter rose and gave Claude a quick kiss on the cheek.

"How very kind you are," said Peter. "I will serve here tonight."

Claude remained unfazed. He nodded and motioned for his crew to depart. "We will return tomorrow morning to clear away."

"Thank you, all," I said.

Claude tilted his head in recognition and followed after his bearers.

"Well," I said, after Claude disappeared behind the cliff face. "Imagine that."

Peter turned to Rhiannon. "Can I stay with him? He says it will not work if I do."

"You may not," said Rhiannon.

He started to pout.

"But, worry not," she said. "We can linger until late…"

And linger they did. The turkey was slow-roasted with olive-oil and fresh garlic glaze. The kale salad was simple, but sharp and balanced the turkey well. And Claude was correct, the red-pepper cream sauce on the baby potatoes was indeed lovely.

Peter made a few more conversational sorties toward the notion of staying with me in the forest that night, until Rhiannon, somewhat under the influence of wine and worry snapped, "The gods have rules, dammit!"

This surprised me as I had rather thought they were Rhiannon's rules. But she is a goddess to me, after all.

Peter pouted and it was all I could do to refrain from taking his side. Because, you will understand, Peter pouting…

By the time they headed back up the path, the sky was lit only by the reflection from the waxing gibbous moon. The two could not wave goodbye as they were laden with the dirty dishes. Peter had insisted there were no bears in southern France, but I am Canadian and certain habits can never be broken. Also, I had read in a brochure at the hotel that there are in fact bears, but, after the-well-at-the-top-of-the-mountain fiasco earlier in the day, it seemed imprudent to argue based on said documentation.

A light breeze washed up to my little camp site from the valley below, bringing familiar farm smells. Cattle. The semi-sour scent of goats or sheep. The sweet smell of hay and mown fields. And, of course, the dry, pine taste of the forest itself.

A simple, clay cup remained on the table. I knew it held a bitter, thick, amber-colored liquid. I smiled. I had walked this road many times, but always in the misty forests of the Welsh mountains. There, the air smelled of loam, still pools and the breathing of the trees that blocked the stars. Here, this was a different forest, indeed: different oaks and pines, thin soil, open and airy. And, in November, cool, fresh. I walked to the table and drank the mixture, best done quickly. Rhiannon claims the chances of death from it are slight, but it is best not to dwell upon it.

My t-shirt and boxers lay upon one of the pillows. I changed into them, leaving my clothes on the table, and slid beneath the sheets and comforter. I did not close the cabana's curtains. Better to see the forest all around. I lay still, my head propped up on the pillows and it did not take long for the forest creatures to come back into their own. Small rustlings, at first distant, then, slowly, closer and closer. Snuffling near the table, then near the bed. A tiny, curious face poking up over the foot of the bed. Groundhog-like. A marmot?

"Boo," I said, oh so quietly. The face vanished. Little feet scurried. I giggled.

"Ah," I said, closing my eyes.

I could still see the forest, but it appeared rather like a line drawing, silver-white ink on black with fine details, moving, of course, in the light wind. I raised my arm and it radiated the same silver white, while the comforter and sheets showed pitch black.

"Huh," I said. "That is new." I looked around. "Puck, are you about?"

"Thou speak'st aright; I am that merry wanderer of the night." The voice came from behind me, small and musical.

"I can't see you," I said.

"You could turn around," said Puck.

"The bed is so comfy," I countered.

"Fine," said Puck. He flitted over my head and turned to face me in his classic fairy form.

"Hey, Puck. Thanks for coming along," I said. "This always works out better when you are here."

"What about that time we ended up in the goblin bordello in Hong Kong?" asked Puck.

"I thought we agreed never to mention that," I chided.

"True," said Puck. "Hey." He motioned to his attire. "Check it out."

His tiny form seemed to be clothed in a small black uniform.

"Are you wearing an SS uniform?" I asked. "It is hard to make out, it being so tiny and all."

"SS Obersturmbannführer Puck reporting for duty," shouted Puck, saluting with the British-style salute, not the infamous one. I did not point it out, not wanting to encourage him.

"Some people might find that disturbing," I offered. "The fairy SS?"

"Obersturmbannführer Otto Rahn," said Puck. "The Grail researcher."

"I am confused. We are having an actual conversation, with words," I said. "No metaphor? Allegories? Whatevers?"

"Have patience!" said Puck. "All will be revealed."

"You are such a liar!" I said.

We both laughed.

"SS Obersturmbannführer Otto Rahn," said Puck. "The Grail researcher."

"Please, do continue," I said.

"In 1933, he published *Kreuzzug gegen den Gral* – Crusade Toward the Grail – and in 1937, *Luzifers Hofgesind* – Lucifer's Court. Both books link the fall of the mountain fortress Montségur and Cathars with the Holy Grail," said Puck. "The basic gist was that Esclarmonde of Foix and the Cathars were the guardians of the Grail. You may have heard the theory? There was that book in the 1980s and that popular novel early in the 2000s?"

"The movie had Tom Hanks?" I asked. "He is a really fine actor."

"That's the one," said Puck. "You know, it is hard to talk to you when you are stoned out of your mind."

"I only see you when I am stoned," I countered.

"We both know that is not true, don't we?" said Puck.

"Eh?" I asked, then shook my head to try and clear it. "So, we should go to Montségur?"

"No," said Puck. "It is all absolute nonsense."

"Please explain," I said.

"Otto Rahn had it all wrong, the poor dear," said Puck. "Completely and totally wrong."

"Poor dear?" I said. "You can't poor dear the SS."

"Because of his writings, he joined the SS in 1936 at the request of one Heinrich Himmler. In 1937 he was assigned to be a guard at Dachau as punishment for a drunken homosexual escapade and resigned from the SS in 1939."

"I see," I said.

"The Gestapo advised him to commit suicide. He froze to death on a mountainside in Austria and was found in March 1939."

"Suicide?" I asked.

"It was ruled suicide," said Puck. He shrugged, then snapped his fingers. The uniform misted away, revealing a Roman toga.

"So, poor dear," I said. "But why do you tell me all this?"

"Because, poor dear, you are in the realm of the Cathars," said Puck. "You would have come across all this silliness soon enough. I don't want you wasting your time on all this Cathar Grail poutine. You are on the clock."

"Don't I know it," I said. But I giggled, again. "Why are you in a toga?"

"Ah, you are paying attention for a change," said Puck. "Open your eyes."

"My eyes are open," I said. "Else how could I see all this silvery, ghostly forest, which is manifestly cool by the way?"

"First, thank you," said Puck. "Second, just open your freak'n eyes." Puck always tried not to swear, one of his more endearing traits. He flew forward and placed a tiny palm on each of my eyes.

The silvery forest shifted sideways and returned as a new forest or, maybe, an old forest. The terrain remained the same, but the trees had changed. And, sunlight speared down from a bright, clear, light-blue summer sky.

I found myself lying on a cold, marble dais in the center of a small classical Roman temple. The base of the temple looked to be roughly seven by fourteen meters, all in white, blue-veined marble, while the fluted pure-white, Doric columns rose up five meters to a stone-framed roof with white-painted wooden boards forming the base of the roof itself. The forest sat close on all sides of the temple, green and scented moist. I could hear running water behind me, toward the cliff.

I rose and sat on the dais, my legs dangling over the side. Seated, I could see the sarcophagus of the Lady by the Well from the Musée de Cluny, spring water sluicing down a small, marble aqueduct to fill the sarcophagus with swirling waters. The details appeared as if they had just been carved.

The top of the dais was stained red.

In front of me, an older man, balding with a grey beard, knelt facing the dais, his head bent in prayer. He wore a short cape, a tunic, and checked trousers. Behind him, approaching us, a small procession neared the temple. An older woman, perhaps forty, led two younger women. All wore green, transparent, silk robes that exposed their right breast and folded up over their heads to form a simple hood.

The women appeared not to see us. The youngest carried a simple clay bowl.

"I don't think they can see us," said Puck.

I looked down. Puck's fairy form now sat beside me on the dais, his feet dangling.

"No, looks not," I said.

"Same location, different date?" asked Puck.

"Looks like," I said.

"Fascinating," said Puck. "And those babes are hot."

"Priestesses, I suspect," I said. "And the altar looks to be stained with blood, so maybe tone down the puckishness."

"Just watch, boyo," said Puck. So I did.

The three women moved slowly to what clearly was not a sarcophagus after all. The youngest bent to fill the clay bowl with clear, cool water. Then, still in stately procession, they approached the older man who knelt before Puck and me.

He rose, turned to them, bowed, then straightened. The young one held the bowl up for him to drink and he did so, deeply. The older woman smiled, gave him a slight bow, and the three priestesses turned to depart, making their way back up the path.

"Could that be the Grail?" I murmured.

"Beats me, boyo," said Puck. "But, if it is, then there it goes."

The man turned and faced the dais and knelt on one knee. He looked up, first at Puck, then at me.

"Oops," said Puck.

"What gods are you?" said the man.

"Ah, we are not gods," said Puck. Then he looked at me. "Well, he is, sort of. It's complicated."

"Hmm," said the man. He stood.

"Sorry to interrupt your ritual, sir," I said. "We do not mean to be rude."

"That is fine," said the man. "One only rarely sees divine beings. And, so I should tell you in a shameless attempt to curry favor, you will understand, if by the Grail you mean the Small Stone, then that is not it."

"Oh," said Puck. "You sure? And what language are we speaking, anyway?"

"Yes, and Latin, obviously," said the man.

"Your dress is not Roman," observed Puck.

"British," said the man. He placed one hand on his chest and gave a slight bow. "I am Lestinus of Glevum, a simple travelling healer on my way to study at the Asklepion."

"The Asklepion?" I asked.

"Hippocrates?" asked Lestinus.

"Draws a blank, I'm afraid," said Puck.

"Founded by Hippocrates? Major medical school? On the fair isle of Kos?" said Lestinus.

"Doesn't ring a bell," I said.

Lestinus sighed.

"People do that a lot around you," said Puck.

"You didn't know either," I said.

"I only know what you know," said Puck. "Obviously."

"Um, back to the Small Stone," I said, not wanting to completely wander from my way. "How do you know it is not that bowl?" I gestured after the departed priestesses.

"Everyone knows the Small Stone is kept safe at the Asklepion," said

Lestinus. "Obviously. Everyone."

"A stupid question," said Puck. "Who is the current emperor?"

"Valentinian the Great," said Lestinus. "May he reign forever."

Puck turned to me. "All you need to do is remember that name and tell a grown up."

"Fine," I said. "I will remember."

Lestinus sighed, again.

"I was praying for an intervention, but apparently I got the idiot god," he said. "Do you have a name?"

"This is Puck," I said. "I am Cameron."

"Not a god I know," said Lestinus. He looked disappointed.

"A dying god," I said.

"Ah," said Lestinus. "Running out of time?"

"Indeed," I said.

"Hence the interest in the Small Stone?" asked Lestinus.

I nodded.

"Well, I was going to ask you for the favor of the high priestess, but why not travel with me?" he said, pointing down the path away from the temple. "It is in Kos. Also, I hear the beaches are wonderful in Greece."

"Can we do that, Puck?" I asked.

Puck shook his head.

"Why not? Bending time, space and all?" I said.

"Because your time on this excursion is up, boyo," said Puck. "Look at me."

Puck was starting to fade, as were the temple and forest.

"Crap," I said.

"Language, please," said Puck.

"Thank you, Lestinus," I said. "Time for me to go."

Lestinus waved his right hand slightly.

"What am I, chopped liver?" said Puck.

"And you, too, of course," I said and smiled. "Always good to see you, my friend."

Puck turned a bit pink at that. And I found myself back in the bed, in the cabana, propped up on my pillows, looking down across my white comforter, toward my legs, where a small wolf lay curled up against either side of me, fast asleep.

I lay still and quiet for a long time, eventually drifting off to sleep. When I woke, the beasts were gone and the morning sun touched the top of the cabana.

I dressed, washed my face and mouth in the spring and waited in a spot of sunlight by the table. Rhiannon's brew left me a little disassociated from the normal perception of time, so I was a little startled when she appeared before me arm-in-arm with Peter, followed by Claude and his companions.

After the requisite hugs and kisses with my lover and my companion, I turned to Claude.

"Claude, you might have mentioned the wolves," I said. "The wolves were not in the brochure."

Peter and Rhiannon looked at each other knowingly.

"Ahem," said Claude. "Wolves, monsieur?"

"I woke in the morning to find two grey wolves sleeping on the bed," I said. "I am not blaming you, of course, but some forewarning…"

"Perhaps, the wine…" began Claude.

"I wondered myself," I said. "But there is wolf hair on the lovely, white comforter."

Claude walked over to the bed and ran his hand across the bedding. I had the satisfaction of seeing his eyes open the smallest margin in surprise.

"Ahem. Well, they are quite rare…" said Claude.

"You slept with wolves?" said Peter, quite excited by the notion. He skipped over to the bed and examined the comforter.

"Mon Seigneur is a bit of a dog, after all," said Rhiannon.

"It is not funny…" I began. "But before I forget, wolves aside, I am supposed to tell the grownups: first the Asklepieion, founded by Hippocrates on the isle of Kos in Greece and, second, Valentinian the Great, may he reign forever. It was there, then."

"Well done, my love," said Rhiannon. She took my head in her hands and kissed me on the lips. I kissed her back.

"Also, all that stuff by the SS Obersturmbannführer Otto Rahn, forget it. It is rubbish," I said.

"Do I need to understand that part?" asked Rhiannon.

"No," I said. "It is now a known, false unknown."

"Okay, it is," said Rhiannon. "Anything else?"

"Maybe some guy stuff," I said. "I will share with Peter, later."

Peter took my right arm. "Guy stuff," he said, and stuck out his tongue at Rhiannon. She opened her mouth to speak, but, in the end, just shook her head.

"Oh!" said Peter. "We got the Banon à la feuille. Enough to fill the entire box. And, it is breakfast time. We can order into the room after…" He sniffed my arm. "After you shower. You do smell a little, um, doggy."

Peter turned toward Claude. "Could you please take care of the tidying up?"

"Of course, monsieur," said Claude. He turned to me. "Mon Seigneur, so sorry about the wolves."

"That's okay," I said. "It was just a little startling."

Claude took control and the work began.

We headed back to the vehicle. Halfway up the cliff-side path, Peter, who still had a firm grasp of my arm, turned to Rhiannon and said, "Sorry about the wolves."

They both thought this was terribly funny. Somehow, by the time we got back to the hotel, Peter had decided to express-ship his cheese to Paris and accompany us to Greece. I am uncertain whose idea this was, Rhiannon's or Peter's, but in the end, it kept me from being gutted like a fish.

I never did get to taste the cheese.

CHAPTER FOUR – THE ISLAND
ARRIVALS

Apparently, one cannot fly from Marseilles to Athens. Rather, one must fly from Paris to Athens. So we did. Marseilles to Paris. Paris to Athens. Athens to Kos. Somewhat startled by the hotel bill, Rhiannon booked us in economy class with a four-hour layover in Athens.

Here is the thing, however. Just on the other side of security, Athens' Eleftherios Venizelos International Airport has a wine and cheese bar serving an excellent variety of quality local Greek cheeses and wines. Time passed tastily.

Four hours later our Aegean Airlines fifty-two-seat, ATR 42-600 turboprop lifted off, climbed for thirty minutes, then descended. We landed to emerge onto an open tarmac, taking the cool, embracing night wind full in the face. A three-quarters moon rode high above a mountain peak.

An hour later we exited the small, aging terminal, luggage in hand. Rhiannon pointed to an old, blue Mercedes bus with Olympic emblazoned on the side in faded white lettering.

"All expenses paid," I reminded her.

We grabbed a taxi, spurted out of the airport parking lot and onto a traffic circle.

"Where you go?" asked the driver. In the half light of the dashboard I glimpsed a balding head and dark Stalinesque moustache.

"Kos town," said Peter. "The Hotel Starry Blue Skies."

"Endaksi," said the driver.

Peter slid into me as we exited the circle. The taxi accelerated rapidly down a hard-topped highway, into a tunnel of night.

"This is a fine car," I said. "A Mercedes, isn't it?"

"Ne, a Mercedes," said the driver. The car swung out and passed an old Citreon.

"It would certainly be a shame to damage it," I offered. "Perhaps you might want to go a bit slower?"

"No problem, is finished," said the driver. "I get new one next month."

But he glanced in the mirror, saw my face, a ghostly circle against the darkness beyond the rear window, and eased his foot off the accelerator.

"Where you from?" he asked.

"Canada, Wales, Paris," I said.

"How long you on vacation?" he asked.

"On business we are here," said Rhiannon. "We do not yet know how long it will take."

"What you do?" asked the driver.

She hesitated.

"We are looking into the market for vinyl siding," said Peter. "Just to see if there's an interest, you know."

"Ah, plastico," said the driver. He nodded sagely. "Is good."

The taxi crested a low hill and began a long descent from the highlands, toward the lowland, coastal plain. A string of colored sparks lined the glittering black of the moon-lit Mediterranean, ran off to the right and linked with a large splash of lights in the distance.

"Kos town," said the driver. "Is very beautiful."

"Yes," I said.

We swept down onto the plain and the main highway swelled into a broad, two-lane, expanse of new blacktop. Our driver accelerated again, rushing us through the darkness, past fields, white villages, and stretches of glass-fronted concrete stores.

"So much looks new," said Rhiannon.

"Yes," said the driver. "The tourist money. Much, much money; very quick. Too quick, maybe. Then, crash."

"A lot of development?" I asked.

"Before, yes, many new places to sell your sidings, now..." said the driver. "Maybe big hotels by the beach, up in the mountains. Maybe is good."

The Hotel Starry Blue Skies lies just outside of Kos town, surrounded by open market-garden fields, a few hostelries, and a few young palms. That night, the front drive was empty. November is post-season.

The taxi pulled in front of the glass doors and the driver handed Rhiannon his card.

"You call me," he said. "I born here. I know Kos."

Rhiannon looked at the card. "Thank you, Nikos. Perhaps we shall."

We unloaded our suitcases and Nikos pulled away. I turned to Peter.

"Plastic siding?" I asked.

"I panicked," said Peter, pouting.

I sighed. "Plastic siding it is."

Rhiannon stood staring at the Hotel Starry Blue Skies. Glass doors opened into a large, two-story, modern poured-cement structure, all painted – inside and out – bright white with traditional Greek-blue highlights. Inside, the light-colored marble floors shone to perfection. Large plate-glass windows, everywhere. Furniture was of light wood, all modern and vaguely northern-European in style.

"Been here before, I have," said Rhiannon.

"In a previous life?" asked Peter, eagerly. Clearly he was well on his way to joining Rhiannon's little coven.

She smiled, somewhat wistfully. "In a way. When I was a teenager. On summer holidays. Now, in winter we are."

"In so many ways," I said.

She took my hand and led toward the doors. "No going back to those times. Never changing is the past."

"This same hotel?" asked Peter, trailing after.

"No, but one stamped from the same pattern," said Rhiannon. "They are built for the Scandinavians."

"No beach activity this time of year," I said.

"But there is a heated pool!" said Peter. He caught up and took my other hand. "I booked the hotel."

We approached the front desk, a chest-high construction of light teak with clean lines and insets of white, blue-veined marble. I stopped about three paces from the desk.

"Peter, any chance that Claude from Hotel d'Pinus Nigra recommended this establishment?" I asked.

Peter looked toward the reception desk, then down at his feet.

"Maybe," said Peter.

"Any chance you had Claude make the booking?"

"Maybe," he said. He started tapping his right toe. "Claude said it would be fine."

"Excellent," I said.

Imagine Claude, the roundish Gaul with thinning hair and restrained mutton-chop sideburns, but older and with a little less hair – completely grey – and dressed in a floral, loose Hawaiian shirt. This person awaited us behind the registration desk.

Rhiannon looked from Peter to me, then back again.

"I swear..." she said, but gave up and approached the gentleman.

"Hello," she said, and tried on a tired smile. "We probably have reservations."

"Madam, you are the party of Lord Summer?" asked the man.

"We are," said Rhiannon.

"Then, in truth, everything will be fine, far better than fine. Claude called and explained all your needs," he said. He spoke quickly, looking

Rhiannon directly in the eyes. "I am the manager, Claude's brother, Yiani Papadopolous. I have arranged a lovely room, one large bed, of course." He waved at the three of us. "A lovely large veranda with a lovely view of the sea. Of course, it is a little cool this time of year, but you have a hot tub. A lovely hot tub. Everything is prepared. Absolutely prepared. Champagne will be sent to your room."

He hung his head a little, then. "But, I apologize, this is a small island. It is not France. The champagne…"

"I am sure it is lovely," said Peter. He stepped forward, took Rhiannon's right arm, and looked up to her. "Hot tub?"

"Fine," she said. "But we cannot live like this all the time!"

"No, no, madam," said Yiani. "All is fine. It is off season. We have few guests. All is reasonable. Very reasonable. Claude really is most apologetic about the wolves. Very apologetic. Also, there are no wolves in southern Greece. None, sir. Zero. In the north, a few, yes. But here. No wolves."

Peter began giggling. Rhiannon passed our passports and her credit card across the desk to Yiani. Yiani smiled.

A few moments later, the paperwork complete, Yiani rang the desk bell soundly, then stilled it with his hand.

"I am crestfallen to advise you must carry your own bags," said Yiani. "We are a reduced staff in off season. Also, our restaurant…" He looked at Peter, then down to his paperwork. "Our chef is seasonal. Our cook is fine, but, local home-style dishes only."

Peter grasped Yiani's hand in his own. "I am sure it will be perfect," said Peter. "We love traditional Greek cuisine."

Yiani turned bright pink. "Thank you, so much," he said. "But. But, I have made reservations for you tomorrow evening at Petrino in town." He looked at Peter. "Not like Paris, of course, but excellent." He opened his two hands in a motion to include all three of us. "And very romantic, all stone with a lovely fireplace. Just lovely. A car is arranged, of course!"

Rhiannon began to open her mouth to speak, but I stepped forward.

"Thank you, most kindly," I said. "You have been generous and understanding. Please tell Claude not to trouble himself over the wolves. It was a small thing. A small thing."

I turned to the others. "Shall we just have a nice Greek salad and an appetizer tray in the room? A little champagne and a soak in the hot tub before bed? It has been a long, long day."

"Please," said Peter.

Rhiannon gave me a quick kiss on the cheek. "Good boy," she said.

I turned to Yiani.

"I will arrange it," he said. He placed three key cards in a folding envelope, wrote 201 on the front, and passed it to Rhiannon.

"Welcome to the Hotel Starry Blue Skies."

We wended our way toward room 201, trundling our luggage behind us. The Hotel Starry Blue Skies is a two-story, rectangular structure arranged around a large central courtyard with a generous pool – steam rising from the warm water into the cool evening air – and a shuttered, frond-roofed pool bar. At intervals, steps climbed from pool level to the second level where a balcony ran around the courtyard. At the far end of the courtyard, on the ground level, an archway opened into the darkness. One could hear the sea crashing against the shore beyond the archway.

Above, the sky was neither starry, nor blue. A grey mist began to fall.

Room 201 was on the second level at the far end of the courtyard. We thumped our bags up the marble steps, Rhiannon swiped her card and Peter entered the room. A short moment later, Rhiannon and I heard a low sound, an odd combination of oh and ahh.

"Oooaah," said Peter, quietly.

We pushed into the room behind him. Or, rather, into a small sitting room with a sofa and two stuffed chairs set around a small coffee table of light-colored wood. To the rear of this room, Peter had opened twin leaded-glass doors to reveal an enormous bedroom. He stood there, frozen, arms akimbo having just pushed open the doors.

Rhiannon moved to stand directly behind him and placed one of her hands on each of his shoulders.

"You may have a different idea of reasonable than most people," she said.

I stepped forward and stood beside her.

"Well," I encouraged. "We won't be cramped."

The room measured easily fifteen by fifteen meters. Broad, plate-glass windows lined the exterior wall and opened onto a large patio. Beyond that, a stormy, wave-tossed grey sea churned against the beach.

Inside, a large bed, at least king-sized, dominated one end of the room. Two more sofas and three stuffed chairs formed a seating area around another small table. A glassed-in shower and large bathtub stood in this room and a white, paneled door led into a separate washroom. Near the bed, mirrored doors concealed a large, walk-in closet.

To one side, close to the main doors, a small teak bar appeared to be fully stocked with various shiny and colorful beverage bottles.

As before, all was gleaming teak and white, blue-green veined marble.

"There is a shower," I said. "And a bar. Both things there are."

Peter released the doors and pointed. "And a large hot tub. On the patio. As promised."

And there was, too, although the heavy, iron patio furniture was set off to the side and wired together. Off season.

Rhiannon was glancing from Peter to the glass shower stall. Back and forth. Back and forth. He eventually noticed this repetition.

"Oh," said Peter. "He likes to watch."

"He does," said Rhiannon. But, despite herself, she started to giggle.

"Well," said Peter. "We are well beyond that, one suggests. I am a little body-conscious, though. You must be kind."

"Indeed," I said. "But you have nothing to be concerned about. You are lovely."

"Completely lovely," agreed Rhiannon.

He turned a light shade of pink.

"Well, thank you," he said. "Let's unpack."

And so we navigated yet another shoal without injury. And unpacked.

The Greek salad and appetizer tray did not arrive promptly.

"Shall I call the front desk?" I asked, reaching for the light-blue telephone.

"Be still," said Rhiannon. "So North American you must not be here, on a Greek island. It will come in good time. And, Peter?"

"Yes, my love?" he said, meeting her eyes.

"Paris, this is not," she said. "No looking down your pretty nose on the cuisine, understood?"

"It will be good," said Peter. "Claude promised. He would not sent us into the wilderness! He is not a savage."

"Well," I said. Knowing well my roles and functions, I headed to the bar. "Who would like a pre-champagne drink?"

I saw Peter cast a quick glance at the shower stall.

"Dry martini, please, mon Seigneur," said Peter. "And please do make it dry. You get a little excited with the vermouth."

I nodded and looked to Rhiannon.

"Hmmm," she said. "Jumping right in, are we?"

Peter smiled his cute little smile and cast his eyes downward.

"Very well," she said. "The same then, please."

I made three – dry as the Sahara – vodka with just the slightest touch of vermouth and delivered two before taking up mine own.

"À ta santé," said Peter.

"Cheers," I said.

"Indeed," said Rhiannon. And they both giggled, again.

We drank, just a small sip. Peter smiled.

"Good boy," he said, and kissed me on the cheek.

"Thank you," I said. I looked down at him and then over to Rhiannon. They looked as bedraggled as I felt. It had, in truth, been a long day. Modern air travel is a nightmare for all but the wealthy.

"You were both very patient today," I said. "I know it was a long day for you."

"It was," said Rhiannon. "I really am exhausted. There is no air in those things. I hate it."

"Indeed," I said. And they both giggled again. Seriously. I cannot help it, you know. It is just the way I talk.

Rhiannon tossed back her martini and said, "Another, please," holding out her glass.

Fortunately, a knock on the door signaled the arrival of food and drink. Peter leapt to the door. Again, seriously, he bounded, easily rising a half-meter from the marble floor, and opened the door to the suite.

A young Nordic man in pressed, black trousers and Hawaiian shirt stood behind a small cart laden with food and drink. Peter took care of it, making all necessary conversation, having the young man arrange the two, large platters and the champagne within reach of the hot tub and discretely handed the young man some rolled up euros.

I smiled at Peter fondly the entire time.

After he closed the door behind the young man he turned with a smile. "Hot tub?" he asked.

I turned to Rhiannon. "He is a wonder. Which of the tapestries do you think gave birth to him? Smell, hearing, sight or touch?"

"Oh, touch, I think," she said. "And you?

"Hmmm. Sight, maybe?" I said, but looked to him.

"Ha!" he said. "Obviously the last one, the enigmatic unknown. Mystery. Obviously."

"Obviously," I agreed.

"Hot tub," said Rhiannon.

Peter pranced to the sliding glass door, shedding clothing as he went. As he turned to close the door behind him, I could see his cheeks turn red with the cold. He fled to the safety of the tub.

I looked at Rhiannon with a raised, right eyebrow, then undressed and clothed myself in a fluffy, white, hotel bathrobe. Rhiannon did the same. Together we ventured out onto the patio. A steady, brisk wind from the sea brought the scent of salt and seaweed. It was cool, certainly, but not freezing.

"Quite manageable," said Rhiannon. She dropped her robe and elegantly slipped over the edge of the tub into the water. I never tired of seeing her voluptuousness. And seeing them both, just their heads above the steaming water seemed, suddenly, quite mythic, reminding me of the hot spring pool of the Rowans in the oak forest just beyond the town. I joined them.

Rhiannon opened the champagne with an excessively theatrical pop and filled three delicate flutes. I accepted mine gratefully with a nod, as did Peter. We drank and it was good.

I turned my attention to the platters. You may think this odd. You might ask why I was looking at appetizers when I was in a hot tub with two beautiful, unclad women? Well, it had been a long day, of course, and we were all tired. Also, in a complex relationship, social rules and forms of etiquette prevail and I have never been good at either, even in simple situations. At least half the time, I really did not know how I was meant to behave with my lover and companion. So, I mostly left things up to them, as they both seemed to have evolved an understanding – whatever it might be.

"Can someone please explain the food?" I asked.

This appeared to have been the correct thing to say, as they each rewarded me with bright smiles. Peter stood and leaned over me to point out the dishes one by one.

"Greek salad with tomatoes, cucumbers, onion, feta cheese. Olives seasoned with salt, oregano and olive oil. Taramosalata fish roe, with breadcrumbs, olive oil, lemon. Tirokafteri feta cheese spread, with roasted red peppers." He said and looked down at me. "It is spicy."

"Tzatziki you know. Skordalia is a potato, garlic, olive oil and vinegar spread. Grilled squid, done over charcoal. Loukaniko lamb sausage. Grilled octopus. And grilled pita bread, with which we eat it all."

He used a wedge-shaped pita slice to scoop up some skordalia and shoved it in his mouth, the white goo dripping down his chin. He sank back into the water. I lifted the platter and held it for Rhiannon.

She began with the octopus, as did I.

"So," said Peter, sipping some more champagne. "While we eat, and before we get to the inevitable and one of us takes our boy…"

"Fine," said Rhiannon. "I acknowledge it is your turn, first."

I said nothing but looked back and forth between the two of them, somewhat startled by this direct communication and understanding. I became rather fearful.

"But before that," said Peter. "I do have some questions and or thoughts, because, while I do love you both, I fear you may be quite mad. And I thought that, as we are all here together, soaking and eating without a layer, so to speak, between us, now might be the time for a conversation."

I tried the skordalia. It tasted strongly of garlic. Wonderful.

"Please do go on," said Rhiannon. Her voice, I could tell, sounded of vodka and champagne.

"First, to summarize, we are looking for the holy grail so that Cameron does not die in a brutal battle in less than a year, correct?" said Peter.

"Correct," said Rhiannon, biting into some of the grilled squid.

"But he has to die or the cycle of the seasons ends and the world collapses?" said Peter.

"As we have discussed," said Rhiannon.

"So, how exactly are these two things possible at the same time?" asked Peter.

I took some more skordalia and added, "I admit, I have rather been wondering the same thing."

Rhiannon closed her eyes for a moment then looked at me with a sad smile.

"I understand that for you this is all mostly a lark, a fun trip with you lover in your last days," she said. "And, now, with Peter, of course. Am I correct?"

"Mostly," I admitted.

"And, then, you expect to go and fight your wife's new lover and die, correct?" she said.

"I hope to cause him some pain, at least, the bastard," I said. Peter sidled over and took my arm. I could see he was trying not to weep.

"But, yes, correct," I said.

"And you, Peter," said Rhiannon. "What do you believe? Is it just a lark for you as well?

I cannot imagine what errant demon possessed Rhiannon to say such a thing as even I knew what would happen next. And it did.

Peter started sobbing loudly and rested his head against my shoulder. Tears streamed down his face into the steaming water.

"Seriously?" I asked, looking at Rhiannon.

"Sorry I am, but it needs to be stated," said Rhiannon.

"It was," said Peter through his tears. "But, now, I do not know!"

More sobbing, followed by, "I do not know what to believe! You both may be crazy and this may be some sort of weird cult thing and you are starting to suck out my mind!"

I put my arm around Peter and said, "Fair enough. I'd say it is all true and it is not a funky cult, but I would say that either way, I suppose."

"Yes!" said Peter in a near wail.

Rhiannon floated forward and sat across my lap, facing Peter. She took him in her arms and held him against her chest to let him cry. This continued for some time. Determining that continuing to snack would be bad form, I kept one arm around Peter and held Rhiannon with the other.

Eventually, the sobbing subsided, and Peter said, "You never answered the question."

Rhiannon kissed his forehead and said, "I do not know how both are possible at the same time. It is a mystery of the Grail. I hope to discover both how and why. The only other alternative is that my true love will die and I will be heartbroken for the rest of my life."

Peter hugged her then and they both cried. This too went on for some time. And, I admit it, I was thinking, "Seriously? I'm the one who is going to die. I can't even see my own kids. Am I crying? Am I falling apart?" But, really, I knew better than to speak. Which proves, by the way, that old dogs can be retrained.

Eventually the tears and hugging ebbed.

Sniffing, Peter said, "I have more questions…"

Rhiannon took his head in her hands, kissed him full on the lips, and he responded. And I loved her for it, as it very nearly distracted him. But after a moment, he pulled away.

"Are we really here just because Cameron saw it in a dream, because that really is crazy," said Peter.

"Why?" asked Rhiannon.

"Because if we follow his dreams you and I will eventually end up in maids' outfits, wearing cats' ears and ending every sentence with 'meow' for God's sake!" said Peter.

"It's a valid point," I allowed.

"He is not a completely sane man," said Peter.

Rhiannon sighed.

"Is he?" asked Peter.

"No. But all dying gods break somewhat near the end," she said. "Think what they go through as the Lord of Summer. Think of the responsibility and the killing, of the cruelty of the last year when you lose your family and are cast out of your home. Then, a painful death. At least Cameron gets to be with the one he loves." She kissed me and I loved her even more.

And, when she was done, I said, "Most of that is true for anyone with any kind of a life, of course. I am not so different. It is just a matter of degree." But I knew it was true. I did not like the word break, but I did sometimes feel like I was falling apart a little, inside, especially if we were far from a forest.

"Oh, aren't we the wise one?" said Peter. This was apparently funny as they both started laughing. I like to think it was stress relief, but that is likely my ego.

"But," said Peter. "Seriously, why are we in Kos? I mean it is wonderful, but?"

"Because, as the Lord of Summer, Cameron has a connection to the gods, to the mystic, if you like," said Rhiannon. "The gods and spirits speak to him with the help of his spirit guide."

"Spirit guide?" I asked.

"Puck," she said.

"I don't think so!" I said. "He is more of a companion. A friend."

"Now he is, after nearly seven years," said Rhiannon.

"They speak to him? Why?" asked Peter.

"Because he exists in the realm between worlds. He is both a deity and a human mortal," said Rhiannon.

"I do?" I asked. "In the realm between worlds?"

"Try to follow along, Cameron," said Peter. Then, to Rhiannon, "Why him?"

"Because I fell in love with him at first sight," said Rhiannon. "And, yes,

I know, it was selfish as I doomed him to an early death."

"Bitch," said Peter.

"I know," said Rhiannon.

"It was worth it," I said. "I have told you before. I will tell you again. It was worth it. I love you."

"And me?" asked Peter.

I froze in fear. But Rhiannon saved me. She kissed him again and said, "Of course he does. Who would love you not?"

"It is true," I said.

"Cameron, food," commanded Rhiannon.

I reached for one of the trays and held it between them with one hand. Peter poured more champagne.

Around a bite of lamb sausage, Rhiannon said, "Tomorrow we will head to the Asklepion."

"We will need some help," said Peter. "Rome and Latin I am good with. Greece and Ancient Greek will be a challenge. And we should find someone with a good understanding of the place and its history."

"Do we mention the Grail?" I asked.

"I think we have to, so it will need to be someone with an interest in myth and the other world," said Rhiannon.

"Tomorrow morning, I can make some calls to my old professors," said Peter.

"Excellent," I said.

"Also, one last thing," said Peter.

"For goodness sake," I said.

"Be good," said Rhiannon, patting my head. "What is it dear?"

"Um. I want to have..." he began. "I want to be..." He looked at Rhiannon. "I am 33."

"You are not!" said Rhiannon. "I am only four years older than you? Impossible!"

"Impossible or not, it is the truth," said Peter.

"What?" I asked.

Rhiannon slid off my lap. "Well," she said. "He is a fertility god, after all."

She took the tray from my hand and set it aside. Then she took my champagne and drained it and set the glass behind her.

"You will need both hands," she said.

Peter rose up out of the water and straddled my lap, setting himself down lightly. He did not weigh much at all. He turned to Rhiannon.

"Hold my hand," he said. "This is important. And, I am a little scared."

"It is a sacred act," said Rhiannon. "To take the child of a god."

But she laughed and took Peter's hand with her own right hand. With her left hand she placed my hand between her legs.

"You don't get him all to yourself," said Rhiannon.

"But, I won't be here, later," I said, quietly.

Peter heard neither of us, I think, being distracted by the act of mounting me. I held him loosely around his back with my left hand. Being an excitable soul, he bit my shoulder. I tried to focus on my handiwork with Rhiannon. Blood trickled from my shoulder into the steam on my chest and dissolved.

"Then will two at once woo one;

That must needs be sport alone;

And those things do best please me

That befall preposterously," said Puck, from behind me.

"Quiet, you." I said.

"Um," said Rhiannon. "What is that my love?"

"Puck is making fun of me," I said.

"Away, Puck," said Rhiannon. "Now is not your time. It is not yet your time."

She was beginning to lose focus. I knew her well.

"What?" gasped Peter.

"Never you mind," said Rhiannon. "Focus. Take what you need."

It began to rain heavily, the cold water lashing the surface of the water in the hot tub. I slipped my left hand between Peter's legs and began to massage him as he rode me. He began to twist.

"Oh, mon Dieu," he said.

Rhiannon moved her hand to hold his back and keep him in place.

"Up and down, up and down,

I will lead them up and down:

I am feared in field and town:

Goblin, lead them up and down.

Here comes one," said Puck.

"Not funny, Puck," I murmured.

"Marie, mère de Dieu," gasped Peter.

I could hear Puck laughing.

"Puck!" I said.

"What?" he replied. "Cannot Robbin Goodfellow have a bit of fun when the boundaries are blurred?"

"But we are spirits of another sort:

I with the morning's love have oft made sport,

And, like a forester, the groves may tread,

Even till the eastern gate, all fiery-red,

Opening on Neptune with fair blessed beams,

Turns into yellow gold his salt green streams.

But, notwithstanding, haste; make no delay:

We may effect this business yet ere day," said I, and laughed.

"Oh, well done," said Puck. "But, my fairy lord, this must be done with haste, For night's swift dragons cut the clouds full fast."

Peter paused for a moment, thank goodness.

"Puck, why does it have to be done with haste, seriously?" said Peter.

"Thunder and lightning, could be very, very frightening," said Puck. And, indeed, out across the wave-whipped Mediterranean, forked lightning split the darkness.

Rhiannon looked at Peter with both shock and admiration. She reached between my legs and held me tight at the base and began to move up and down as Peter resumed his motion. It did not take long after that before Peter achieved his immediate goal, because, well, really, seriously, I did not stand a chance.

He began kissing my face in the pouring rain. Rhiannon sat back and exhaled deeply.

"Hearing Puck," she said. "That is no small thing. He is an amazing boy."

Peter slid off my lap and into Rhiannon's. "She is an amazing girl. Tonight. Obviously," said Peter.

"Seriously," I said, taking deep breaths.

Rhiannon smiled and kissed her.

"And tomorrow?" I asked.

Peter poked me in the forehead with his finger and pouted.

"Cameron," said Rhiannon. "Tomorrow is a new day. Please do try to follow along."

"Seriously," said Puck, fading away into the storm.

We managed to save the remaining bottle of champagne, but, alas, the driving rain destroyed the food.

We took the champagne to bed.

CHAPTER FIVE – THE ISLAND
SANCTUARY

Kos, Greece

"Vassilia Traka, professor emeritus of the University of Alban in Scotland," said Peter. "Born and retired on Kos. Apparently, not entirely sane, according to my doctoral advisor."

"Perfect," I allowed.

"A PhD.? This is a confession?" asked Rhiannon.

"It is true, I fear," said Peter.

"And your thesis?" asked Rhiannon.

Peter pouted. "In retrospect, it may have been a stretch," said Peter. "Roman Eunuchs' Influence on Roman Emperors in the Late Empire."

He turned to me and placed his hand on my knee. "Cameron, dear. I am through that phase. No worries."

We three sat at a small, round, wrought-iron table, in a tiny, somewhat rundown café overlooking beautiful Eleftherias Square, the focal point of Kos town. It was lovely, even in a light November rain. Created by the Italian overlords during the rebuilding after the 1933 earthquake, the square is a wonder of light-colored stone and open air. Sitting with our hot beverages, we looked out onto an 18th century Ottoman Defterdar Mosque, the archaeological museum, and the market hall, the latter two still serving as named and both in the style of the Italian colonial period.

The remaining towered structure, with a history best overlooked, was originally called Casa del Fascio and once served as the command center for Mussolini's Fascist Party on Kos. Now, the ground floor housed a restaurant.

On the far side of the square, a medieval gated wall led to a street of restaurants and bars, all shuttered for the off season.

Peter looked quite elegant in a blue blazer and pressed grey flannel pants. Rhiannon wore a short, black dress with a black jacket and I sported a blue wool, pin-striped suit. We awaited the professor emeritus' arrival.

The day had started well with everyone cheerful. I woke with Rhiannon's head on my chest, drooling as was proper. Peter lay curled up against her in his blue-flannel, Hello-Kitty jammies. After we roused, Peter sang quietly to himself as he dressed. Rhiannon sang in the shower.

I looked at her quizzically as she emerged and started drying herself with a large, fluffy white towel.

"Peter is 33. I am only four years older," said Rhiannon.

But Peter was not to be distracted from his good humor and merely stuck out his tongue at her whilst buttoning up his pressed, white shirt.

It took Peter only a few calls from the hotel room telephone to get hold of Vassilia Traka's contact information and only one more to get her to agree to meet us for coffee.

After a light breakfast of fruit and toasts at the hotel, Nikos the cabbie drove us into Kos town.

"Doctor D'Laurent?" asked a hooded woman, her face barely visible in the shadows cast by her bright-yellow, knee-length, rubberized Mackintosh.

Peter stood. "Professor, Doctor Traka?" asked Peter.

She stepped into the shelter of the café and reached across the table to shake his hand, dripping, I must add, all over my lovely wool suit.

"Vassiliki, please," she said.

She stepped back and unzipped her raincoat, stepping aside to hang it on one of the hooks next to the small bar. Beneath the Mackintosh she wore a heavy wool sweater and black trousers. Her grey hair was held back tightly in a ponytail. Deep wrinkles crisscrossed her face.

"Peter, please," said Peter. He motioned for her to take the empty seat at our little round table.

"Thank you," she said. She started to pull the chair toward her but stopped. "This is not the siege périlleux, by any chance?" laughing at what was apparently a little joke.

Peter returned a perfectly natural smile. "No, not at all," he said. "That seat is reserved for me."

Her laughter dissolved into confusion, but she took her seat.

Rhiannon stared at Peter with some dismay.

"Um?" I said.

Still standing, Peter motioned elegantly toward both Rhiannon and me.

"Please allow me to introduce Cameron and Rhiannon," said Peter.

"Good to meet you," she said. "Peter, they are your grad students?"

Another perfectly natural smile from Peter. "Not at all. Cameron is mon Seigneur and Rhiannon is his lover, amongst other things."

Peter sat. He even managed to do that elegantly.

"Your lord?" asked Traka.

"Indeed," said Peter. "I am their companion."

"Companion?" asked Traka. "In arms?"

"If need be," said Peter.

I looked beseechingly at Rhiannon. She smiled at me kindly and patted my knee.

"Perhaps," she said, "We have gone astray, conversationally, at least." She motioned to Peter, me and herself. "We are together, that is all."

"Together?" asked Traka.

It was nice to see that someone else had trouble following along from time to time.

"In all things," said Peter.

"Including our area of research," said Rhiannon, segueing boldly.

"Ah," I said, and raised a finger. "The Grail."

She looked at me, really for the first time. "The Grail. That is a rather wide-ranging topic for research. I have been studying aspects of the Grail legends my entire life. And your area of research is The Grail, is it?"

Peter cleared his throat, gently. "Hence the telephone call."

She turned back to him, only to be met by his most disarming smile.

"We are really here following up on a tidbit we discovered during our rather broadly-based readings," said Peter. "We really focus on ancient, pre-medieval precursors of the Grail stories. And, apparently, the Grail was here on Kos during Roman times."

"And you came to that ridiculous conclusion how?" asked Traka.

Fortunately, at that juncture the café owner brought her a double expresso, apparently her usual. She took a small sip.

"Ah, that's better," she said.

"Well," said Peter, "We do not mind sharing, I think?" He looked to Rhiannon.

"We do not mind sharing," said Rhiannon.

"Based on some unpublished research notes," said Peter, "We examined a certain sarcophagus at the Musée de Cluny, which led us to a certain monastery in the south of France. An inscription there indicated the Grail was believed to have been on Kos in Roman times," said Peter.

"I am not sure that was entirely in the spirit of sharing," I said.

"I know the sarcophagus," said Traka. "And the monastery was the Priory of Ganagobie, correct?"

Peter gave a slight nod.

"There are no such inscriptions there," said Traka. "I spent an entire month going over both the priory and a few shreds of the ruined temple. No inscriptions."

There then began a long pause. It stretched out. Peter and Rhiannon smiled vacantly. I could not believe they were leaving it to me.

I sighed. "My fault, I'm afraid. I am not always well behaved," I said.

"How so?" she asked, focusing on me now with an intent, aggressive gaze.

"You will recall the caves?" I said.

"Yes," she said.

"And the remnants of plaster?" I asked.

"You didn't!" she said.

"I may have," I allowed, looking down at my tea, then my fingertips. "But, either way, behind the plaster…"

"I see," said Traka. She turned to Peter. "You could lose your tenure for this. Which institution are you from, exactly?"

"Oh," said Peter with an ungentle smile, "I left all that foolishness behind and took up a higher calling."

"You are with the Church?" she said, clearly alarmed. She turned to Rhiannon and me. "And you two?"

"We are truly connected to the gods," said Rhiannon."

"You are being most annoyingly vague!" said Traka.

"I apologize, deeply and sincerely," I said. "You must understand that we are sharing what we feel is wise. Some of the research materials we have, um, acquired are of dubious moral origin. As a professional you would not want to be tainted by either our sources or our actions."

"Oh! Well explained, Cameron!" said Peter. He patted my knee. I fought down the happy golden retriever feeling.

"That is strangely well phrased," said Rhiannon. She looked at me fondly.

Traka watched these exchanges intently. A few moments of silence followed. She sipped her expresso. I sipped my tea. Peter kept his hand on my knee. Rhiannon touched my cheek with her fingertips.

"What a strange crew you are, indeed," said Traka, finally. "A lost-looking fellow, a woman clearly his lover, in the truest sense of the word, and a young, um, man…"

"Obviously," I said.

"Indeed," said Rhiannon.

Traka nodded. "Young man who is the dear companion of both. And you are doing what? Following breadcrumbs to learn of the Grail? You must admit it is absurd. All of it. You three, your foolish research. All of it. Absurd."

A cold quiet settled on the table. I saw Peter's other hand start to slide toward a set of cutlery that lay still wrapped in a paper napkin. I rested my hand on his.

"And, why exactly absurd?" I asked quietly.

"First, this threesome," said Traka with distaste, "It cannot last. You are fools living in a fantasy world. Second..." She stopped as she saw tears begin to trickle down Peter's stony face. Her mouth worked up and down, but no sound was produced. She also noticed that, despite my efforts at restraint, Peter had managed to get hold of a butter knife.

"It is true," I said, "Our relationship does have a best-before date. It is a tiny miracle for me and all the more precious for its ephemeral nature. As, indeed, are the many wonders of this world."

"Cameron..." said Rhiannon. But she hung her head.

Peter stood to move and sit in my lap, resting his head on my shoulder with one arm around my neck. I noticed he retained the butter knife in his other hand.

"However," I said, "I would suggest that this unfortunate reality does not excuse your rudeness in the least."

The proprietor stepped up and quietly and slowly took the butter knife from Peter's hand. He set down another expresso, more hot water for my tea, and two Caffè Americanos for Peter and Rhiannon. He surveyed the table then turned to Traka.

"Good professor, please treat our guests with respect," said the proprietor. "You have crossed a line, I think, which your position, age and crankiness cannot excuse."

Traka deflated, her shoulders falling with a sigh.

"Yes. Yes." She looked up to the proprietor. "Thank you, nephew. You are entirely correct. I forget myself, sometimes."

He nodded and returned to behind the small bar where he began flipping through the pages of his newspaper.

Traka looked at both Peter and Rhiannon. "I apologize for my remarks. They were unkind and insensitive. Please forgive my stupidity. I clearly tread where I know not."

"Excellent apology," I said. "And, I promise you, I know my apologies."

"Apology accepted," said Rhiannon. Peter nodded, but did not leave my lap, unintentionally keeping me from my tea. Rhiannon, ever vigilant and aware, passed me my cup.

"And, second?" I asked.

"Second?" asked Traka. "Ah, yes. Well, let me say it this way, perhaps. You say that you are interested in ancient, pre-medieval precursors of the Grail stories?"

"Indeed," I agreed.

"The Celtic legends, for instance," said Rhiannon.

Traka nodded. "Of course, but also eastern Christian, perhaps the Byzantine mass, Phoenician vegetation rituals..."

She saw Peter hug me tighter then.

"Pure legend, such as that whole idea that Joseph of Arimathea brought the Grail to Glastonbury," she continued. "The English stories put the

Grail Castle in England, French stories in France, Spanish stories in Spain. But these are all stories, myths, legends. And. And. Please forgive me for saying so, second, it seems to me that you three actually are seeking the physical Grail?"

"Possibly," said Peter.

"Well, you know there is no such thing. There never was," said Traka.

"Please explain," said Rhiannon.

"Well obviously," said Traka. "As Emma Jung and Marie-Lousie von Franz explained in Die Graalslegend in psychologischer Sicht all those years ago, the Grail poems were written to embrace a two-part psychic need."

"A two-part psychic need?" I managed.

"Cameron, the first need was to expound upon and elaborate the core symbols of the Christian religion. The second need was to creatively develop certain unresolved problems, for example..."

"Sexuality, the shadow and the unconscious," said Peter. He kissed my cheek. "I had an elderly German professor. It was required reading. Sorry, Cameron, you are not going to like what comes next."

"Why?" I asked warily. Because, you will understand, I believed the conversation had moved into a much safer zone.

"Obviously," said Traka. "The Grail is not real. It is an archetype. Some say the ultimate archetype."

I began to feel the blood drain from my face.

"It is," continued Traka, becoming animated, "The sub-specie aeternitatis, the primal image of the mother, the wondrous vessel. Yes, the ultimate symbol of the feminine. It receives, contains, supports, holds the foundations of life – water, food, wine. It heals. It transforms. It is Jung's anima. The feminine, which manifests as a woman or goddess in dreams. It is real, but invisible; its existence transcends all actual experiences..."

She paused, noting that both Rhiannon and Peter were hugging me tightly.

"It is fine," said Peter. "You could not have known. He was horribly frightened by archetypes as a child in secondary school."

"Ah," said Traka. "Sadly, that is not uncommon. But, Cameron, there is really nothing of which to be frightened. And archetypes are part of the foundation of Jung's work. Perhaps you could let me try to dispel the horror with a simple, gentle explanation?"

"Jung. Archetypes," I whispered, frozen in the headlights of amok academia. "Please don't."

But Traka, clearly a true believer if ever there was one, could not be stopped.

"According to Jung..." said Traka.

"Which Jung?" asked Peter. "Carl or Emma?"

"Carl," said Traka. "According to Jung, and I am paraphrasing a touch here, an archetype is a preconscious psychic disposition that enables a person to react in a human manner."

It was my turn to mouth soundless, wordless, disconnected thoughts.

"For goodness sake," said Peter. "Are you actually trying to kill the poor dear?"

"No. No. I am terribly sorry," said Traka. "It just came out. Let me try again?"

"Fine," I said, regretting it immediately.

"Think of it this way. Stories often have heroes, right?" said Traka.

"Yes," I acknowledged.

"The hero is an ancient archetype that has been around nearly forever. In this case, it is an archetypal model for us, a cultural prototype of behavior for when we want to do things to try and make the world a better place. When we need to be a hero, we know how to think and behave. And because everyone in our culture is familiar with the archetype, they know how to respond. Because, we all know the hero archetype."

"So, Cameron, you can think of an archetype as a common way of behaving or thinking about things," said Traka. "That is not so scary, right?

"Maybe," I allowed. "A set formula for behavior?"

"You may think of it that way," said Traka. "In fact, Plato called archetypes…" She did air quotes. "Forms."

"Please do not do that," said Peter.

She looked to him, startled. "I am so sorry. It just slipped out."

Peter gave her his reassuring smile. She carefully put her hands in her lap.

"For Plato, they were an ideal blueprint for behavior," said Traka.

"So can we call them forms, instead of the A-word?" I asked.

"No," said Traka. "Because there is more."

"I knew that," I said.

"Cameron, she is doing very well. Be patient," said Peter.

Rhiannon petted my hand, reassuringly.

"So, in all of us, both individually and as a culture, archetypes pre-exist, waiting for us to need them, if you will," said Traka.

"That sounds like mysticism," I said. "Not really true."

Peter got off my lap and sat back in his seat.

"Seriously?" he said. "I do not think, my love, that you get to say that."

I lowered my eyes. "Fair enough."

"That is fine, my dear," said Peter. He focused on Traka. "That sounds like mysticism. Not really true."

"Not at all," said Traka. "There are many ways of thinking of this from a psychological standpoint. Jung, Carl not Emma, held that archetypes exist in the collective unconscious of a culture, based on thoughts and images in stories, myths, religious rituals, and such. And – here is a key in the case of the Grail – that they emerge or, as he would have said, are actualized when a person or society needs them."

"Actualized?" I said.

"Sorry. Pretend I did not say that, it is just jargon," said Traka. She plucked nothing out of the air and threw it aside. "Look. Nasty actualized gone."

"I am not a child," I said.

"Most of the time," said Rhiannon.

"True," said Peter.

But Traka had acclimatized to our little tribe and moved ahead.

"Think of it this way," she said, "At a simple level, everything we do is based on a role, almost always. Father. Mother. Child. Maiden. These are all roles and archetypes. They show us how to behave and think in an acceptable way."

"For example," said Peter, pointing at Traka. "The Wise Old Sage."

She looked at him. "I am reminded of the old part every morning as I awake, young man, I do not need to be reminded by you!"

He gave a slight, seated bow. "My turn to apologize, I think."

"But, nevertheless, true," said Traka. "Cultures rely on archetypes. The boss. The sergeant. The Wise Old Sage. Whatever. But what if the culture or person needs an archetype that does not yet exist for that entity?"

"Yes!" she said. "It emerges. It is created from the unconscious of the culture. That Grail was, at the time of the middle ages, just such an archetype. It emerged to fill a need. It emerged in the Grail poems and stories. King Arthur. Perceval. Galahad. Gawain. Their puzzles and adventures. The Grail Castle. The Fisher King. All of that. It illuminated a new way of thinking, of seeing the world."

"But," said Rhiannon, "these stories were evolutions of older Celtic stories. Other Grail-like objects." She enumerated them on her fingers. "Dagda's caldron – fed the hordes. Bran's magic caldron – restored life. Caldron of Caridwen – poured the drink of wisdom. Caldron of Tyrnog – only cooked meat for a brave soul. Basket of Gahanhir – multiplied food from one to one hundred. So how could it be an archetype created in the middle ages?"

"Indeed," said Traka. "These symbols, these deep, universal motifs are slow to evolve. Slow to emerge. It is possible the Grail stories are even based on an ancient story of Alexander at the temple of Dionysus. But emerge it did, in full force, in the middle ages."

"So," I asked, knowing full well that I should not, "What does the Grail symbolize? What form of behavior? What way of thinking about things?"

"Ah! That depends on the story," she said. "And there are many Grail adventures!"

"I freak'n knew it!" I said. "These types of conversations should only happen in a bar."

"Cameron, it is not even eleven," said Peter.

"Not even lunch," said Rhiannon.

"But it will be soon," said Peter. I leaned over and kissed his cheek. He squeezed my hand.

"The Grail," said Traka, "helped medieval people find new ways of thinking about things. Jung, Carl, said that God needs renewal from time to time, so the collective conscious and collective unconscious meld and a new symbol emerges."

"Meld?" said Peter.

"Fine. He did not say meld," said Traka. "But it is close enough. And I'm trying to keep Cameron from bursting into tears."

"Thank you," I said.

"Let me give a pre-medieval example, as that is your area of interest," said Traka. "This was the ancient idea of the king, which transitioned into a new, broader archetype in the latter middle ages. Jung, Emma this time, tells us that – and again, I paraphrase badly, I'm seventy-five for God's sake – in ancient times they believed the king contained the divine spirit of the tribe or nation. On him depended the psychic and physical wellbeing of the tribe. The rain, the fertility of the women and livestock, the fruitfulness of the fields; it was all on him."

"If he grew sick or was wounded, the king was ritually killed. Too much depended upon him."

She noticed that Rhiannon and Peter had become somewhat still.

"Am I being unclear?" asked Traka. "Not making sense?"

"Not at all," I said. "We are particularly familiar with this myth. You have our undivided attention."

"Very well. I shall continue," said Traka. "In the stories, Perceval, Galahad or Gawain, depending on the version, finds his way to the Grail Castle in the blighted realm of Logres where the Fisher King – the keeper of the Grail – lies wounded, bleeding, but unable to either die or heal. So, the land remains blighted."

"In these stories, the problem is either resolved or not from a story perspective and, here is the key, from a psychological perspective. The Grail emerges first as an image in these stories and is slowly resolved through the stories into a tool for understanding and, really, enlightenment."

"So," said Peter, "you believe the king absolutely must die? That is the only way the story can be resolved?"

Traka laughed. "You ask that question so seriously. But, yes; in the Grail stories, the Fisher King must die or the land will not be restored. In all versions, he dies three days after he is healed and ascends into the heavens. It is a condition from the time before the written word. When a child comes of age, the father hands all over to his son, the mother to her daughter. Knowledge is passed on. It is the continuation of human consciousness. It is central to human mental and cultural development. And personal psychic development."

"From Emma Jung's perspective, in the Fisher King we find, depending on the version of the story and the way you look at it, something that must be redeemed from a condition of unconsciousness, or something that is old and needs to be replaced, or something ailing that must be redeemed, or even knowledge which can be learned to help redeem us all."

"That's a lot of options," I said.

"It is complicated," allowed Traka. "There is a lot of room for interpretation."

"But, it seems to me," said Rhiannon, "that these interpretations support the old idea of sacrificing the king, rather than helping people think differently?"

"It is true," said Traka. "The stories helped to raise the issue, but not necessarily solve the problem. But people could see that there was a problem and that the problem was unresolved."

"Perhaps we are just too close to this myth," I said. "We have studied it a good deal. And really, I still don't get it. Is there a simpler example?"

"Well," said Traka. She hesitated. "First I will need to touch on two simple terms from Jungian psychology?"

I closed my eyes in an attempt to suppress the mental anguish.

"Please," said Rhiannon.

"Very well. Anima and animus. It is simple really. Anima is the feminine side of the personality. Animus is the male side," said Traka.

"Anima is your girly side," said Peter. "You know you have one. I've seen it."

"Well, maybe," I allowed. "But so do you, young man. I, too, have seen yours."

Now, I will admit that I was simply trying to be annoying. But, for some reason this got me a hug from both Peter and Rhiannon. I just do not understand sometimes.

"And," continued Traka, with a resolve I had to admire, "In the middle ages, it was all about knightly virtues like valor, fortitude, constancy, loyalty, things like that. No recognition of the anima at all! The Grail stories, however, constantly introduced female figures which clearly represented the anima, anima which normally aided the adventurer by forcing him to adopt a more feminine perspective. It was a way of starting to bring this feminine side into the light in a way the audience could embrace."

"So, totally all about archetypes then?" I asked, having delved quite far enough into this badger hole for one day. "Not real at all then, the Grail?"

"No," said Traka. "It is quite impossible."

"I see," I said. "Well, join us for lunch, professor?"

"First, beg your pardon, I must," said Rhiannon.

"Yes?" said Traka.

"So, why, then, did you spend a month at the Priory of Ganagobie in Alpes-de-Haute-Provence looking for clues?" asked Rhiannon.

I loved her, of course, but at that moment admired her so. She missed nothing.

Traka stared across the small, round, wrought iron table at Rhiannon, her grey eyes sinking back into the massed wrinkles of her face. But she said nothing.

"It is all fine," said Peter. "Nothing is amiss. Rhiannon and Cameron are, of course, quite mad. And, I suppose I have joined them in that fine madness. But your significant academic reputation is at no risk in any way. We will publish nothing. In fact, we will say nothing. Nothing. Were we ever to find anything at all, it would never be mentioned anywhere, ever."

Traka remained quiet. Peter watched her, then turned to me suddenly.

"Oh, by the way, Cameron, Rhiannon and I have agreed that I will not return to my work for at least a year or so," said Peter. "I should have mentioned this yesterday."

I turned to Rhiannon. She smiled and merely nodded.

"Ah," I said. "That is incredibly kind." I took both their hands and held them. I felt the tears begin.

"Forgive me," I said. "I am much too fragile these days. I apologize."

Traka watched us in silence.

The proprietor brought me a small box of tissues and I dabbed at my eyes.

Finally, Traka took a deep breath, not quite a sigh, and said, "Why do you seek the Grail?"

I was too upset to respond – it was all desperate foolishness anyway. Rhiannon took over the task of wiping my tears with the tissues.

Peter looked over at us and said, "Mon Seigneur is The Lord of Summer. We are looking for a solution to that particular challenge."

She looked at us, one at a time, me with tears streaming down my face, Rhiannon mothering me shamelessly, and Peter watching with calm certainty.

"Well," she said, finally. "You should probably take some time to change before lunch – into something less formal. I will feed you luncheon at my house at one. It is just outside of town, a little up the mountain. We can talk further. I will share my unpublished notes. I am seventy-five, after all."

"You are correct, there are a few mentions of it being here in ancient Greek fragments and in some Latin documents. All unpublished, of course. You may take no photographs or anything from my library. Agreed?"

"It is," said Rhiannon.

"Hmph," said Traka. "I am not saying you are not insane, of course?"

"Of course," said Peter.

"You also must agree to share nothing you learn from or about us," said Rhiannon.

"Tut," said Traka. "Of course."

"I saw Nikos waiting around the corner as I came here. He waits for you, I think? He is my nephew and knows my house. He will bring you."

The proprietor brought the bill rolled up in a small shot glass. He placed it before me.

"She has twenty-seven nephews and grand-nephews on this island," said the proprietor. "It will be good for you to remember this."

Vassilia Traka, professor emeritus of the University of Alban, apparently did not do too badly as an academic in the damp and misty hills of Scotland. About a ten-minute drive outside of Kos town, her villa sat upon a small hill within a series of hills rising in steps toward the low mountains lining the southern coast of Kos like a rough spine.

As Nikos's Mercedes pulled up in front of Traka's entranceway, he turned to the three of us in the back seat and said, "Do not break things. Auntie has many old bits and bites. Do not break."

"Cameron," said Rhiannon.

"Do not break anything," said Peter.

Nikos laughed. "Okay. All is good. You pay when I get you, later."

My feelings were a bit hurt by that, but I decided they were just amusing themselves, so I said nothing. Goodness knows we needed some light amongst the grey of that rainy day. We slid out of the back seat and Nikos rolled away.

The double wooden door to Traka's villa stood before us, three steps up from a gravel drive. The door divided the light-brown, windowless, stucco wall, that rose to about five meters high and ran straight for ten meters to either side of the doorway. The roof was red, ceramic tiles.

"It looks," said Peter, "like a Roman villa. Fascinating."

"Unlikely," I suggested. "Though I was reading in one of the lobby brochures that there is one here; second century, restored as a museum, definitely worth checking out."

"Well," said Peter, "The brochure would say that, would it not?"

The left-hand door swung open just then and Traka moved out onto the front step. She looked tiny and frail beside the large doors.

"I cannot," she said, "believe I invited you three to my house. I must be senile."

Peter bounded up the three steps, taking both of her hands in his.

"Tū benignissima es!," he said.

Her eyes opened wide. Big. Like the charming older women in Hayao

Miyazaki films.

"You will speak Latin with me?" asked Traka. "Can you keep up?"

"Scilicet!" said Peter.

She looked, down the steps, to me. I shook my head.

"Non loquetur," I said. Rhiannon stared rather adoringly at Peter.

Traka took Peter's arm and led him into the house. Rhiannon and I followed through a short, high-ceilinged entranceway into an open courtyard surrounded by a covered colonnade. The courtyard measured perhaps seven meters wide by fifteen long. Raised beds of herbs surrounded a waterlily-clad pool in the center of the garden. The light rain hissed gently on the water.

"Wow," I said. "Outstanding."

Rhiannon walked out into the rain and began to fondle a meter-high bush.

"This is Rosemary," she said, "Huge, it is!"

She turned to Traka.

"So jealous am I," said Rhiannon. "How wonderful to live here."

Traka gestured at courtyard with two hands. "This, all of this, would be impossible in Scotland."

"Well, except for the rain," I said.

She laughed at that. Peter pouted.

"This house was built by one of the Italian governors in the 1930s," said Traka. "I have completely restored it, of course, but I tried to keep the original sensibility. For example, you may find it a bit dark, especially on a dreary day like today. I added no external windows."

A quick look around the courtyard showed that all the villa's rooms opened onto the courtyard with either large windows or glass doors. The windowless portions of the walls were stucco with painted geometric designs. Beneath our feet, large, auburn, terracotta tiles covered the floors.

Traka followed my gaze.

"To get the handmade tiles I wanted, I had to order from Mexico," she said. "Can you believe it?"

I bent down to feel the rough undulations within the clay tiles.

"Cameron," said Rhiannon. "Be good."

Traka laughed. "Very tactile, is he?"

Peter giggled.

Rhiannon came out of the rain and reached down to take my hand. She pulled me up. "Do not be in such a hurry to leave me. The forest will wait. Stay with me, please."

"I was just feeling the tiles, for goodness sake," I said. But I was lying, of course. In that courtyard, in that gentle rain, the scent of vegetation – rosemary, thyme, an orange tree, basil and more – lay heavy and intoxicating, held in by the surrounding walls. If I closed my eyes, I knew I would slip away to the forest above the House of the Rowans where the sound of the rain on the sacred pool matched, note for note, the pattern of this rain upon the courtyard pool.

Traka started off along the colonnade toward the far end of house.

"Lunch is through here," said Traka. "I had it laid out in the library so we could talk."

We all trailed after her. But then, I stopped.

"Does anyone mind terribly it I stay in the courtyard for a while?" I asked. "I could join you later?"

Peter took my arm.

"No, Peter," said Rhiannon. "I need you."

Traka nodded. "Stay out of the pool. You will frighten the fish."

I nodded, but thought, "spooky," because I had just been thinking how inviting the smooth water of the pool looked.

They exited the courtyard through double, paned-glass doors. Peter looked back at me questioningly as the door closed behind him.

Around and about the garden lay carefully placed, fragments of Roman and Ancient Greek architecture. I took a seat on the capital of a Corinthian column and closed my eyes, turning my face up into the rain.

The tiny mist-like droplets fell unendingly, washing my cheeks, soaking my hair, running in rivulets down my neck and chest.

"It might as well be spring in the valley," I said.

"Tut," said Puck. "You are going to catch a cold." The voice came from behind me. I did not turn or open my eyes.

"You know I don't get sick anymore," I said.

"True, true," said Puck. "But only a fool sits in November rain."

I smiled at that.

"Do you remember, Puck, this far back, to the time when the Romans came to Britain?" I asked.

"I do," said Puck. "They brought much blood and sorrow. But then again, much blood and sorrow prevailed before they came, and of much the same kind. Then, for 350 odd years things were better. But alas, returned to sorrow once more."

"Did you see many of them?" I asked. "What were they like?"

Puck laughed. "Practical. They honored the gods. But, they mostly kept away from the mountains. Not stupid were the Romans."

"Imagine if you were a Roman in about 300 A.D. and you were transferred from Kos to Hadrian's wall," I said. "Boy would you have been pissed."

Puck thought this terribly amusing. We laughed together.

And the rain fell lightly against my face.

After a while, some period of time, Puck said, "You are weary."

"I am," I said. "From time to time. Weary is the perfect word for it.

Awake; not tired but worn out. Earlier today I became excessively emotional."

"Weary. From the old German through to old English," said Puck. "Werig, which is basically tired or sad; but is related to worian, which is to wander or totter."

"You make this stuff up," I said.

"Which is basically what you are doing now," said Puck.

"Wandering?" I asked.

"Um. No. Tottering," said Puck.

Indeed, I was. I felt my back slide down the rough, carved side of the Corinthian capital until my behind hit the tiles. I leaned back and rested my head on the marble.

"It is fine," I said to Puck. "Alles gut."

"I am going to miss you, when the time comes," said Puck. "But, for now, do you mind if I get your young man to put you to bed?"

"Ah, I am good here," I said. "Let them play."

The cool rain felt good on the warmth of my cheeks.

"Stultus es," said Puck.

I awoke in a small, old, wooden bed in a tiny, white-washed room, beneath a comforter stitched in bright, colorful, abstract patterns. A small fire provided shifting, orange light and shadows. A voice from the shadows said, "Your creatures sleep. I said I would watch over you." Traka.

"I would be the creature," I said. "They are quite human, I promise you."

"And Puck?" asked Traka.

"Um. Puck?" I said.

"Who came to fetch Peter for you?" asked Traka. "Is he quite human as well?"

"I've always rather viewed him as a projection from my unconscious," I said.

"I think you might see that theory does not quite work in this context," said Traka.

"It is a puzzle," I allowed.

"I must admit, it is," said Traka. She moved forward out of the darkness and came close to the bed, looking intently at my face. "I am intrigued. I only wish I were younger."

"Don't we all," I said.

I heard the legs of an old, wooden chair scrape across the tile, a hollow, rough sound. She set the chair beside the bed and sat. In the firelight, her face showed orange and shadow.

"Apparently, you do," said Traka. "They told me quite a fantasy."

"There was crying, I warrant?" I asked.

"Some, yes," said Traka.

"I wish they would let it go," I said. "Then we could just enjoy the year."

"As best you can," said Traka.

"Indeed," I said.

"And the Grail? What of that?" asked Traka.

"Well…" I said.

"It is just a story?" said Traka.

"Yes. It is kind of fun, though," I said. "Occasionally, it gives me hope. But, even if true, there is a paradox."

"Yes. It seems that saving you destroys the world, so why find the Grail?" Traka chuckled, a deep throaty laugh that really should not have surfaced from a woman that tiny.

"Ah," I said. "Rhiannon has faith. What can one do?"

Her laugh trickled to an end.

"After we found you and put you to bed, then the tears really fell," said Traka. "In the end, they may have cried themselves to sleep."

"Together, I hope?" I asked.

"Yes, together," said Traka. "In a bed this size, can you imagine?"

"Easily," I said. "They are quite fond of each other."

"You are quite open-minded for an American," said Traka.

I was going to explain about not being an evil American, but the weariness still sat heavily upon me, so I just smiled.

"It will be nice for Rhiannon to have a nice, young man to keep her company after I am gone, don't you think?" I said.

"Open. Minded," said Traka.

"It will be nice for Peter to have a woman like Rhiannon, don't you think?" I said.

"You really are a practical person," said Traka.

"Just really, really tired," I said.

"Humph," she said, followed by a pause so long I almost drifted back into sleep.

"You know," she said. "They told me all about you. All of it. Down to the children. I guess it is something about being grandmotherly."

"Sorry," I said.

"That is okay. From an anthropological point of view, it is fascinating," said Traka.

"I have heard that before," I said.

"I'll bet," said Traka. "But from a human perspective…"

"Indeed," I said.

"Let me tell you a story," said Traka.

"Do you mind if I drift off?" I asked.

"Not at all," said Traka. "Please do."

"When I was very, very young, here on this island, I had a baby. I won't say I was in love with the father, but he was exceedingly handsome, a tall, strong, deeply tanned, Greek farmer. So, there it is. And they took her away, my baby. And, because my father was well-to-do, the boy was sent away as well, to another island, I think. They never would tell me. And, later, they sent me away to school and I never did see my child again."

"I am sorry," I said.

"Those were the old times," said Traka. "It was not that unusual. Worse things happened in those days, in this place. I never returned until I had my doctorate. I couldn't, somehow. And I never married. Oh, I had boys and later men, of course. But something was broken inside. I never got over it. And, I see the same in you now. Something is breaking inside."

"Rhiannon says it happens to all the dying gods near the end," I said. "It is the way of things."

"That is what they said when they took my baby, all those years ago. *It is the way of things*," said Traka. "They never even let me name her."

"Flora, Morgan, and Andrew," I said.

She patted me on the head, like a dog.

"I know," she said. "So, anyway, I am going to help you three, lost souls as you are, to search for something that most likely does not exist. What do you think of that, young man?"

"I think," I said. "We missed our dinner reservation at Petrino."

She bent and kissed me on the forehead.

"Welcome to my house, oh thou errant god," she said. "Let this be your sanctuary in times of troubles."

I really did not know what to say to that, so I smiled at her in thanks, and closed my eyes.

When I awoke, before I opened my eyes, I felt Peter's weight pressed up against me through the comforter. I smiled and stretched out my arm to rest it over him, then stopped. Peter did not have long, wiry fur. I opened my eyes. A giant beast lay on the bed beside me; stockier than an Irish Wolf hound, not as thick as a mastiff, but huge nevertheless. The creature's face lay about a hand-span from mine. It watched me. The dying light of the fire flickered in its eyes. It did not look happy. I smelt dog breath.

"I wonder," I thought, "if this is your bed?"

Fortunately, I had recently woken up with wolves, and I slept with both Rhiannon and Peter, so I knew exactly what to do. I stayed exceptionally still, closed my eyes and slept.

The next morning the grey clouds had moved off to Africa and a lovely warm sun beamed down from a perfect blue sky. I awoke with Rhiannon sitting on the side of my bed smiling down at me.

"I called the hotel," she said. "Yiani will rearrange Petrino for this evening and have breakfast sent to our room at the hotel in about an hour. Nikos is on his way to fetch us. You are going to have a long soak in a hot bath."

"Did I miss a lot?" I asked.

"Not in the scheme of things," said Rhiannon. "The good professor is going to join us for supper this evening."

"So not a drunken bacchanal, then?" I asked.

"A drunken bacchanal it is not," she said.

"Hmm," I said. "Does the professor have a gargantuan dog?"

"Several," said Rhiannon.

"Thank goodness," I said. "Also, did Puck get you guys last night?"

"Peter said he did," said Rhiannon.

"I see," I said.

"You do not need to worry," said Rhiannon. "You have just been away from the forest for too long. It happens, you know…"

"With dying gods, I know," I said.

"Traka says there is a cypress forest above the Asklepion," said Rhiannon. "Let us talk about it tonight. Today, for you, is a rest day. Get dressed."

She stood and turned to leave. At the door, she paused and looked back.

"Wait until you see the good professor's library," she said.

We passed the day in languorous idle. I did take that hot bath, with lavender scented bubbles, if you must know, and Peter scrubbed my back. Indeed, throughout the day the two treated me with extraordinary kindness. I slept most of the day and awoke late afternoon feeling both well and content.

Nikos drove us into town, leaving us at Petrino Restaurant. Apparently, we had initiated an arrangement where we no longer paid on a ride-by-ride basis. I find it is best not to ask about such things.

Petrino Restaurant occupies a space in a mixed residential and retail part of Kos town – small apartment buildings, shops, and houses. In the summer season, a lovely, rambling outdoor garden patio for alfresco dining leads to a beautifully renovated, two-story, 19th century, stone building. In November the patio is vibrant green with plantings and an overhead entanglement of vines, growing in profusion. The tables and chairs are stacked away or under covers. Dining is indoors.

Indoors a fire crackled happily, though, granted, I may be anthropomorphizing. At least its crackling made me happy. Peter smiled broadly as we were led to our table near the fire by our waiter-to-be, a handsome young man named Aris. Natural-colored wooden tables and chairs were complemented by similarly hued beams supporting the ceiling. Walls were white stucco and undressed, natural stone, the floor a mix of terra cotta tiles in a pattern of shades.

The firelight shed a lovely glow across the entire space.

"Lovely," said Peter, as I slid out his chair and slipped it in behind him. He was dressed to the nines, as my grandmother would have said, in a slim-fitting black tuxedo with plain white, button-down shirt and black bowtie.

Rhiannon waited for me to pull out her chair, then bounced gently and exquisitely into it. She sat to my right in her all-purpose LBD and pearls. I wore my standard, the aforementioned wool suit. The good professor had yet to appear.

"All the gods, you two look wonderful tonight," I said.

"Thank you, Cameron," said Peter. I got a tiny kiss, more of a dab really, on my cheek from Rhiannon.

"And, I must say," said I, "Those are lovely pearls?"

"Indeed," said Rhiannon. She fingered the necklace. "Peter bought them for me this afternoon. We went shopping in town while you rested. There are several small jewelry shops in the old town shopping streets."

"Did you, indeed?" I asked Peter.

"Indeed, I did!" said Peter. "You do not approve?"

"Hmm. I confess to suppressing pangs of jealousy," I admitted. "But, yes, I approve."

Rhiannon rested her hand on my knee.

"Complicated it is, in truth," she said.

"Em," I said, but I was watching Peter realign his cutlery at exact ninety-degree angles to the edge of the table. It was as if a switch had been thrown in his Peterian mind. His slight smile was that of Satan.

"You," he said, "Have bought Rhiannon presents without buying me a thing yet." He looked down off to the side, way too coyly.

"Nothing," he said.

I felt Rhiannon's hand tighten on my knee. I looked over at her to find her smiling vacantly. Clearly, this was some kind of cunning trap, but by whom and for whom? And what was the goal? And how could I surrender and concede without hurting anyone's feelings?

"Have I?" I asked lightly, starting to examine the menu.

"Yes," said Peter. "At the airport in Paris, you bought her an expensive raincoat."

"You already had one?" I suggested. I began to look around Petrino. "Isn't the professor late?"

"Not for Greece," said Peter. "And, at the airport in Athens, you bought her the cutest little gold earrings. And I was standing right there. Right there."

Rhiannon's hand once again tightened on my knee.

This was dangerous ground, indeed. At that time, I had considered buying an appropriately different pair for Peter, but feared it might offend his masculine temperament. Obviously, I had been wrong. Equally obviously, it would be poor judgement to mention it. I froze.

"And," said Peter. Then he leaned forward and said it again in a quiet hiss. "And, right before dinner I started my period. I am not pregnant. It is your fault. Your fault. You are supposed to be a fertility god for fuck's sake."

Rhiannon gave my leg a squeeze. I looked at her to see her suppressing a laugh.

"Just so you know," said Rhiannon, looking me dead in the eyes. "Seppuku is your only viable option."

"Totally," said Peter.

I bowed my head slightly.

"I apologize deeply and sincerely and will strive to do better in the future," I said. "But it has only been a few days."

"Peter!" said Rhiannon. "Look at me."

He did.

"Two things," said Rhiannon. "One, you will just have to try harder. And, two, this means you can drink tonight."

"Oh!" said Peter.

"And," I said, "Tomorrow I will lend you both my credit card and you can go shopping."

"No," said Rhiannon.

"You must come with us and use your own credit card," said Peter.

"Yes," said Rhiannon.

"Shopping?" I said. "For jewelry?"

No response.

"And clothing?" It was a guess.

"Yes." In stereo.

This was clearly no time for me lecture on how sexist and stereotypical their behavior appeared or how they were more than capable of paying for their own purchases. My view was too North American. This was clearly intended to be some sort of strange southern European tribal bonding ritual.

"I would be happy to join you on this excursion," I said. "I would beg you to remember, however, that I am not a wealthy man, having no income as it were."

"Of course," said Peter.

"Actually," said Rhiannon. "Not entirely true is that. A salary you do have, as Lord of the Valley."

"I do?" I asked.

"What do you think Clarine and your children have been living on?" asked Rhiannon. "You do pretty well, actually."

"And exactly how long have I had this income?" I asked.

"About six years," said Rhiannon. "Your wife said not to mention it."

"I see," I said. "You know that I, personally, have been living quite frugally off of my savings?"

"And most appreciated it is," said Rhiannon. "Your children will have access to it, later."

"I see," I said. "You really might have mentioned it."

"And go against my own daughter?" asked Rhiannon.

"Actually," said Peter, perking up. "Am I not more fertile close to my period? How does that work, exactly?"

"Your guest is here, sir," said Aris, from behind me.

"Yia sou!" said Traka, from behind him. The Greek Kissing Ritual followed, with everyone standing and Traka kissing and being kissed on both cheeks. Traka settled into the seat beside Peter.

"What a lovely day," said Traka. "I do so love the sunshine."

Aris cleared away our menus and looked to Traka.

"Aris will choose our food tonight," said Traka. "Does anyone have allergies?"

"We do not," said Rhiannon.

"Alright. Off you go, Aris," said Traka, followed by a short exchange in Greek. Aris slightly bowed to Traka and departed.

"He wanted to know who was paying before choosing the food and wine," said Traka. "I said you were."

Peter laughed.

"Aris is a good man," said Traka. "If only he weren't dating that Greek-American girl. Those girls are a bad influence." She shook her head.

"A nephew?" asked Rhiannon.

"Great nephew," said Traka.

"Well, I hope he brings the wine soon," I said.

"Now, don't be peevish, Cameron," said Traka. "I bear good news. I have arranged access to the Asklepion for tomorrow, after it closes at 2:30 – winter hours. It should be fun to ramble around on our own!"

"How exciting!" said Peter, suggesting that the switch had returned to its original setting.

"Thank you, kindly," said Rhiannon.

"So, where do you think we should begin?" asked Traka. "Do you have a plan?"

Aris brought the first bottle of white wine just then, showing it to his great-aunt.

"This is the Dikaios from Triantafillopoulos winery, auntie," said Aris. "I think you liked it last time? It should go well with the fishes."

"Open it, dear boy. Open away," said Traka.

Aris performed the traditional wine-tasting ritual: Traka tasted and approved. I could not help but smile as I watched Aris pour our glasses.

The light, golden wine spiraled and swished into the large wineglasses, catching the fluttering light of the wood fire.

"Beauty," I said, quietly.

"Yiamas!" said Traka, raising her glass. The clinking of glasses ritual followed. I tasted the wine carefully – light and slightly floral. Excellently chilled.

"Perfect," I said.

Traka drained half her glass. "Adequate," she said. "But back to the plan. Is there one or are you just casting about in the dark, like the Fisher King?"

She chuckled at her own joke.

"Well, actually," said Rhiannon. "We have a bit of a clue."

I was about to ask "we do"? but thought better of it.

"In the infamous bag?" asked Peter.

Rhiannon gave a broad smile. "Yes!" she said. "An old postcard from the, er, collection."

She dug into the depths of her bag of holding and drew out a battered, black and white, cellophane-wrapped card and passed it to Traka.

Figure 3. Postcard, the Asklepion, early 20th century, Lord Summer's Collection

"Hmm," said Traka. "Early 1900s. Obviously the Asklepion." She flipped it to examine the back. "German handwriting. Looks like it has been through the wars."

She looked across the table at Rhiannon. "Literally. The collection, eh?

Ahnenerbe records?"

"Originally," allowed Rhiannon.

"I believe, Cameron, you said your sources were of dubious moral origin," said Traka. "You were correct, sir. Difficult to publish anything based on this material."

She frowned, then smiled broadly.

"But you do not intend to publish so you do not care," said Traka. She finished her glass in one swallow. "How insanely liberating. Not giving a flying fig about peer review or codes of conduct. This is going to be so much fun!"

"Aris!" She waved her glass randomly in the air.

Aris appeared with another bottle. He spoke Greek while twisting in the corkscrew.

Traka laughed. "Aris reminds me of my manners. He tells his auntie not to yell in the restaurant."

Aris smiled fondly, set the opened bottle in a bucket of ice near the table, bowed slightly to his aunt, and departed.

Traka returned her attention to the text on the card.

"A rough translation would be from the springs or maybe pools?" said Traka.

"Wells?" I suggested.

"Ah," said Traka. "As in the women of the wells? Nicely done. The Asklepion was originally founded around a sacred well. Even today, one small pool lingers, which never runs dry, not even in the hottest summers. I have seen frogs there even in mid-August. It is near the lowest of the three tiers. I guess we could start there. But, what are we hoping to find?"

Traka passed the card to Peter, who studied it intently.

"Inscriptions? Drawings? Carvings?" suggested Peter.

"It is an ancient monument, blasted by the sun of two hundred thousand summer days," said Traka. "It is mostly exposed stone in our time, I fear. Any other thoughts? And, Cameron, do not touch the surviving plasters! The Asklepion is an internationally significant monument. In ancient times it was eclipsed only by Epidaurus as a center of healing. So, hands off."

"Also, wish you do not to upset the owner, Asclepius," said Rhiannon.

"Do you have any thoughts, professor?" asked Peter.

"Well, according to Jung and, before you ask, both Jungs, the Grail serves as a symbol of the self. It serves a transcendent function, a psychic function, if you will, to bring about the synthesis of the conscious and unconscious ultimately into the realized self."

"It represents psychic man in his entirety as, quote, 'divinity reaching right down into matter'. And, yes, I may be paraphrasing. Cameron, please pour me some more of the Dikaios, which, by the way is named after our island's little mountain."

I did so, giving her a good, full glass of amber.

"Interesting, of course," said Peter. "But – Cameron, you may pour for both of us – I am not sure how it is helpful?"

Rhiannon smiled as she observed me fill, first her glass, then Peter's.

"Good boy," she said.

I raised my right eyebrow at her, archly.

Both Peter and Rhiannon began to giggle.

"Tut," I said. "I tut you both. You have only had one glass of wine and you already giggle."

"Cameron, dear," said Peter. "We do have private conversations to which you are not party. This giggling is an extension of one such conversation."

"Do I get to know?" I asked.

"No," said Rhiannon.

"Fine," I said. "Professor, any other thoughts?"

"Logically, if we are to have a meaningful discussion, we should start by summarizing what we know about the Grail," said Traka. "Please allow me to start, as I have been researching the Grail for almost half a century."

Rhiannon smiled her benediction.

"First, we do not know what it looks like," said Traka. "It could be a golden goblet or platter, a simple clay cup or a stone, a meteor fallen from heaven."

"Or a caldron," said Rhiannon.

"Yes, or a caldron," said Traka. "So, again, it really could be any sort of vessel. We just do not know."

"So what do we know? We know the qualities it possesses, at least according to the tales. I'll just run through them, shall I?"

"Indeed," said Peter. "Please do." He swirled his wine and sipped, his bob bobbing just a touch, delightfully.

"It provides food to taste. Whatever you want, it supplies," said Traka.

"Speaking of which… Do you think the food will come soon?" I asked. They ignored me.

"It provides spiritual solace. It preserves youth and life," said Traka.

"Heals wounded knights," said Peter. "And emits light and a sweet fragrance."

"Yes," said Traka, looking at him askance. "Rejoices the heart – one cannot sin on the day one sees it. And it can tell good versus evil."

"No comment, Cameron," said Rhiannon.

"If you are unbaptized, then you cannot see it," said Traka.

"Ha!" said Rhiannon.

"Sorry," said Traka. "This is the Christian version."

"Writing may appear on the Grail allowing the faithful to know the will of God," said Peter.

"One of the more obscure stories, but well done," said Traka. "Only those who are predestined can find it."

"He is a god, totally predestined," said Peter, pointing to me. By now, Peter had a rosy pink glow to his cheeks.

"The defender of the Grail can have only the one love prescribed by the Grail," said Traka. "Ah. Oops. Sorry."

"We don't want to defend it, just borrow it for a bit," I said. "Mostly for the healing wounded knights part. Not so much for the snacking part."

"Snacking?" asked Traka. "Somehow I never thought of it that way."

"Nevertheless," said Rhiannon. "The healing part is our focus. Any mention of reattaching severed heads?"

"In Sir Gawain and the Green Knight, yes," said Traka. "And Gawain is the protagonist of many of the Grail stories instead of Perceval or Galahad. So, maybe?"

"Perhaps a change of conversational direction?" said Peter. "Or I may end up in Cameron's lap crying again."

"Indeed," I said. "My love, do you have anything else in your magic bag that might be relevant at this point in our tale?"

"Maybe," said Rhiannon. "Sure you are that you wish to see it now?"

"Only if you are sure it will not ruin your evil plans," I said.

"It should be safe," said Rhiannon. She reached into her bag and withdrew two more cellophane-wrapped cards. Traka reached across the table and took both.

Aris started bringing creations from the kitchen, carrying three dishes on his left arm and holding one in his right hand. He set them, one-by-one, on the table between us.

Grilled octopus artfully arranged with lemon and greens. Flamed saganaki cheese with herbs and olive oil. Village salad, which smelled of olive oil and spices. And, grilled ribs presented on a wooden cutting board.

"Lovely," said both Peter and I in unison.

Traka stared up at Aris, saying nothing. Aris stared back confidently. Then he started, turned and hurried away, returning moments later with a basket of bread, olive oil, vinegar and a plate bearing a rather large slice of feta.

"Thank you, Aris," said Traka. He departed.

"One must have the basics, after all," said Traka. "We are not here to starve!"

The postcards were set aside. Traka served each of us from the central dishes as though her duty and right, which perhaps it was. The flavors? Exquisite. The vegetables existed an order of magnitude of freshness and wonder above anything ever available in Canada. The grilled octopus? Tender, with just a hint of charcoal from the grill. After a few moments,

Aris returned with a large platter of grilled vegetables and another of grilled, thin sliced, rare beef. He rearranged the dishes to make room for the additions, then turned quizzically to his great aunt.

"I approve," said Traka.

Aris smiled and his teeth were perfect white.

"It is the old quote," said Aris. "The recipe does not put the soul in the chef. The chef puts the soul in the recipe." He stepped away.

"I am totally going to use that," said Peter.

We ate. We drank. Traka told us about her island – of hiking in the mountains when she was young, of beaches where bouncy Scandinavians play badminton naked in the summer surf (there was general agreement, then, I would never visit said beaches), and of ruins wandered alone in full moonlight. We told her of our valley – of steaming sacred pools, of bull sacrifices with gushing blood, and of fishing in pure mountain lakes. Peter quizzed Traka on local Greek wisdom on achieving pregnancy. Eventually, through a bit of a haze, I saw Traka once again examining the cards.

"This one is from the Italian occupation – our local museum," she said, turning it over to examine the back. "German. What did you do, loot the Nazi archives?"

Figure 4. Postcard, The Archeological Museum of Kos, Lord Summer's Collection

For some reason, she was looking at me.

"What's it say, what's it say?" asked Peter.

"Roughly, 'check the museum collection for item'," said Traka. She passed the card to Peter. "Rather obvious, one would have thought."

"The other one?" asked Traka, to herself. "The castle by the harbor.

Also from the Italian occupation."

"There's a castle?" I asked.

"You must have driven past it to get here," said Traka.

"Oh!" I said.

She flipped the card, looking once more at Rhiannon.

"German, again. One word. 'Inschrift'," said Traka. "Inscription. Well, that narrows it right down."

"The owner of that card, SS-Standarten Führe Wust, wanted to return to Kos, but his notes suggest he was unable to do so because of the war," said Rhiannon. "He may not have completed his investigation. I like to think we might."

Peter began to laugh. I could see him swaying.

"Perhaps," said Traka. "That is enough for one night. But please bear in mind the qualities of the Grail. Even if we do not know its form, we can look for an item with any of those qualities. Tomorrow we visit the Asklepion and should be awake, at least."

"And shopping!" said Peter.

Figure 5. Postcard, The Castle of the Knights, Lord Summer's Collection

"Oh," said Traka. "Are we going shopping?"

Rhiannon leaned over and kissed me strongly.

"Yes, Professor Traka," she said, after she wiped her face with her napkin. "We are going shopping. I trust you will join us?"

Somehow, it was all good. Calm, with just a hint of woodsmoke from the fire and herbs wafting from the kitchen. And quiet. At that moment, I noticed no one else sat in our part of the restaurant.

Traka saw me examining the room.

"Well, we really could not have had a good chat with prying ears all around. Could we?" she said. "I told you Aris is a good man."

Nikos drove us home to the Hotel Starry Blue Skies. Claiming emotional exhaustion, Peter dropped his fine clothes all about the floors of our room, rinsed himself in the shower, and collapsed on the bed. Rhiannon kissed him goodnight and headed out onto the terrace, into the cool of the evening. Peter looked at me inquisitively, so I walked over and sat on the edge of the bed. I kissed him goodnight as well.

"C'est bon," he said, and closed his eyes.

I sat with him for a few minutes until his breathing evened, then moved quietly to join Rhiannon in the hot tub. The heat from the water worked its way slowly into my bones. Above, the stars radiated light, crystal sharp and terrifying. Rhiannon reached over with her feet and rested them in my lap.

"A good father you would have made," she said, quietly.

"I have made a good father, I think," I said, equally quietly.

"I meant for my children, idiot," said Rhiannon.

"Well, too late for that for that, I suspect," I said. "As George Elliot said: 'We must find our duties in what comes to us, not in what might have been.' But, I guess you need no words about duty."

"As in Middlemarch's George Elliot? And, no, I do not," said Rhiannon.

"Yes, as in Middlemarch," I said.

"Ooh, I love it when you get literary," she said. And she poked me with her toe.

"Don't tease," I said. "Even I have read Middlemarch."

"He was a she, you know," said Rhiannon. "Mary Anne Evans."

"I did not know that," I allowed.

"And, a married man's lover, she was," said Rhiannon. "Created a terrible scandal when it came out. 19th century it was, after all."

"This seems a common theme," I said.

"Well. Peter is giving me ideas," said Rhiannon. "And, know I do, that you will not be here."

"We both have our duty," I said. "This would be outside of custom and religious practice for the valley."

"I think it is more of a guideline," she said, edging closer.

"Just because you are a Rowan does not mean you can make stuff up," I said.

"You know, do you not?" asked Rhiannon. "You do know?"

"That you love me?" I whispered.

"That I would murder for you, just to keep you. That I would have them bind a man tight and I would cut his heart from his body with a flint knife. I would eat the raw heart in the old way," said Rhiannon. "I would build a Wicker Man and fill it with souls and burn them, not even hearing their screams. If it would work, then it would be so."

"I know," I said, lightly. "But I would rather you not, 'cause, you know, it would be mass murder and all." I reached out to pull her close, but she dodged away.

"I am serious," she said. "I love Peter dearly, but I would come up behind him while he rides you and makes his cute little sounds and I would place a rope around his pretty neck and strangle him slowly to death – as it was done in the old times. I would do anything to keep you. Anything. Sometimes I even think, let the world end."

Sometimes she frightened me. Sometimes I forgot that she had indeed killed before, back when I had first come to the valley.

"I know," I said. "I do know. But it will not work. And, it would be wrong, morally. I would not have it."

"As if you would have a say," Rhiannon said. She stood and started moving slowly toward me through the water, walking as the steaming dark water grazed her waist. She looked down at me, both beautiful and terrifying. All was silent, but for the crash of waves from the beach.

"You will give me a child so I may hold onto a small part of you. This I have seen. This is how it shall be."

"If you get with child before Peter, he may well strangle *you* with a hempen rope," I said as I held up my hand.

"I have foreseen," said Rhiannon.

She took my hand and laid in on her belly.

"I have seen it," she said.

CHAPTER SIX – THE ISLAND
RUINS

Kos, Greece

According to the Christian mythos, when in the beginning God created the heavens and the earth, the earth being untamed and shapeless, God said, let there be dress shops! Or it must have been so, because otherwise why else would there be so many? Specifically, why would there be so many on a small Greek island in the middle of the Aegean Sea?

I did not say this out loud, nor would I ever. It might upset people.

Old town Kos has lovely public squares in the Italian fashion and pretty, narrow, winding cobblestone streets. In the summer season, lightly clad people throng the streets and alleyways, the shops and restaurants, all bubbling and bustling with holiday good humor and, perhaps, a thin haze of alcohol. In November, the streets are mostly clear and quiet, even on a bright, sunny, clement morning.

We met a short walk from the main square on Xanthou, a pedestrian-only street lined with small boutiques set around a charming square. The good professor waited for us at an outdoor café, bundled in a heavy, wool cardigan and sipping her morning espresso.

Peter bounded forward to indulge in the Greek Kissing Ritual. Traka rose to meet him with a broad smile.

I must confess here that I do not understand the GKR. Think about it, each of we three kisses Traka twice. That means she receives six kisses. She kisses each of us twice, dispensing six kisses. And this is entirely social. Think of the viruses and bacteria exchanged. Is it any wonder the Mediterranean civilizations were plagued with plagues?

Additionally, Peter holds that the GKR is completely and entirely different from the French Kissing Ritual. I have asked him to explain the differences many times, but in the end, he claims it touches upon qualities of the soul that a cold, venial, North American barbarian could never understand.

It is best not to argue. And, as they say, when in Rome…

I embraced Traka gently so as not to damage her frail frame, kissing her cheeks delicately. Returning two, equally gentle kisses, she combined with her hug a surreptitious grope of my left buttock, then stepped back.

"Privilege of age," she said, with a shameless grin.

Peter and Rhiannon both found this highly amusing – snickering unpleasantly – partly because they enjoyed my discomfort at being groped, but mostly because they understood my predicament. There is no way a large, fit man can respond negatively or harshly to a slight, seventy-five-year-old woman, without being a complete cad.

In the end, I just stared at her for a moment, then bowed slightly.

"Good man," said Peter. He took my arm and kissed me lightly on my cheek.

Rhiannon, still laughing, shook her finger at Traka.

"Those buttocks are not for general consumption!" said Rhiannon.

"So! You are not as modern minded as all that," said Traka.

"No," said Peter. "We are not." He had stopped laughing.

"Ah," said Traka. "As long as I understand."

"Shopping?" I asked.

"Yes," said Traka. "I will suggest a shop, but first a bit of history for Cameron, so he may understand what is about to happen."

"Oh good!" said Peter. I could not help but smile. He is so adorable.

"Kos is mentioned in the Iliad," said Traka. "A band from Kos fought for the Greeks in the Trojan war. The Greeks have been on Kos since the 11th century B.C.E. – over three-thousand years. The original Carian colonists were defeated by the Dorians from Epidaurus who worshipped Asclepius. Over time the sanatoria and industry created by the Dorians became famous, so despite multiple invasions and changes of the aristocracy, the foundations of the economy did not change overly."

"And how does this touch on the shopping challenge?" I asked.

"Shopping is not a challenge," said Rhiannon.

"Bad man," said Peter.

"The industry is the touchstone, vis-à-vis our shopping excursion," said Traka. "Kos is, obviously, at the far end of the Mediterranean. It then had first access to silk thread from the east. Aristotle tells us of the large, silk-weaving factories on the island – all the labor performed by female slaves, of course."

"Fucking aristocrats," said Peter. "I hate them so." He looked up to me. "Except you, my love."

"Yes, the guillotine did prove useful," said Traka. "But, pushing boldly on, even during the Roman period – and the Koans got on quite well with the Romans as they declared Kos a free city in 53 A.C.E. – Kos was famous for its silk, semi-transparent light dresses."

"So, I thought, with your interest in pre-medieval civilizations and with her body, Rhiannon might be interested in something similar?"

I felt Peter twitch slightly on my arm. I looked to see him with a vacant smile stitched to his pretty face.

"Peter," I said, "Perhaps you, too, would be interested in such an item?"

"I, too, would be interested," said Peter.

"Excellent," said Rhiannon. "What do you think, Cameron?"

"I am seeing both of you in long, flowing, soft, silk, semi-transparent robes," I said. "I am not thinking."

Traka laughed at that.

"Good boy," she said.

"Not her, too," I thought, but smiled inanely.

"Cameron," continued Traka. "I embarked on this little historical recap for you. I mentioned that the Greeks have been here for three thousand years. The Egyptian kings valued Kos as an ally and stationed ships here to patrol the Aegean. We even held a branch of the library of Alexandria. Herod paid an annual award to the winners of our athletic games. People who have been in one place for a while have their own way of doing things."

"Yes?" I asked.

"So, you must be patient when we are shopping," said Traka. "Very patient. Not one word about the passage of time."

"Yes, ma'am," I said.

Traka pointed across the small square.

"The first boutique!" she said.

And so, it began.

Now, if you have spent any time shopping for clothing with a group of European women, then you may choose to skim quickly through this next part. Otherwise, enlightenment has been found in stranger places.

The first shop appeared innocent enough and the proprietor, who knew Traka through some complicated family connection, appeared to be a perfectly nice, ordinary middle-aged woman with a moon-shaped face, dark eyes, and a healthy figure clad in a simple blue skirt and white blouse. All of this was but one of Loki's many illusions.

The shop's interior was a simple, white-walled, well-lit, open space filled with chrome racks of women's clothing – dresses, pants, shirts, jackets, all in a myriad of fabrics, patterns and colors. Nothing apparently sinister, until you do the math.

A quick appraisal as I walked through the open plate-glass door, revealed roughly ten meters of two-level clothes racks along the longest wall to the right. Closer examination showed an average of two clothing items per centimeter. The terrifying math shows 2 x 100 x 10 x 2 = 4,000. Four thousand items of clothing on just one wall of the shop. The racks along the front and window side of the store stood only one-level high, as did those arrayed in the center of the shop. Altogether these added roughly nineteen more meters of racking. That is seven-thousand, six-hundred more pieces of apparel.

We are talking eleven-thousand, six-hundred items in one small store. Earlier, I had counted five women's clothing boutiques within the square.

Traka was an intelligent woman. She knew the terrain and I had been forewarned. But I was about to see further evidence of our wise woman's wits.

As we entered the shop, the proprietor rose from her chrome-legged, black-vinyl topped stool and set aside her newspaper. An exchange in Greek passed between Traka and Loki's minion, with three or four volleys fired each way, until the proprietor smiled and turned to Rhiannon and Peter.

"Welcome, I am Hestia, I am married to Traka's nephew's wife's brother. I have several very nice examples of what you seek," said Hestia.

Only then did I see Traka's wisdom. She told us a tale with a bit of history, which she knew we loved. From that, she had given us a goal we could all embrace: the semi-transparent dresses.

I leaned over and spoke quietly into Traka's ear.

"Well played," I said. "You narrowed us down from eleven-thousand, six-hundred potential items to several very nice examples. Impressive."

"I have been down this path before," said Traka. "You are welcome. You may pay for lunch."

"Happily," I said.

In the end, we visited three boutiques, tried on fewer than thirty items – each item needing to be examined, discussed and judged by all – and bought three semi-transparent dresses. Rhiannon chose an ankle-length, emerald-green silk flowing wonder that defied the physics of light and reflection entirely to flutter about her form, both revealing and hiding it simultaneously. Seeing the look on my face when Rhiannon emerged from the change room, Peter insisted she buy two just in case. She chose a second in iridescent white. It stopped my heart.

Peter settled on a knee-length, light blue, shimmering illusion of silk and sequins that floated about his slender shape, concealing all. Rhiannon noted he would need only one as he 'pranced about naked half the time anyway'.

Traka watched us interact in wonder and not without considerable amusement. In my mind, I gave her credit for dispelling Loki's handiwork so painlessly. I paid with no sorrow.

Lunch was savory crepes from an open-air café down by the small harbor. The crisp, cool air came over the water smelling of salt and seaweed, with a hint of diesel. As we sat on a bench overlooking the water, Peter hummed happily to himself as he nibbled the edges of his crepe. Rhiannon watched him with a wistful smile.

Traka had been correct; a medieval castle dominated the waterfront. Tour boats, battened down for the winter season, bobbed gently at rest along the harbor edge.

"A perfect moment," I said. "I could not be happier. Nice choice for lunch, professor."

She looked up. Unlike the three of us, she had rejected a savory crepe. Nutella marked the corners of her mouth. A piece of banana stuck to her cheek.

"Thank you," said Traka. "You know, Cameron, after observing you three this morning, I feel I should share another historical tidbit."

"Hmm?" I said, my mouth full of chicken and melted gouda.

"In addition to various names in Ottoman, Kos was known by other names in ancient times including Meropis, Cea, and Nymphaea," said Traka.

"Nymphaea, eh?" I said.

"Nymphaea," said Rhiannon smiling at Peter.

"Indeed," I said.

"Thought you might like that," said Traka.

After lunch, Traka headed home to her villa, and we returned to the hotel. The dresses needed to be tried on and showcased once more, with a hurtful no-touching rule for me – something about greasy crepe hands.

At that moment when Rhiannon stood, white and shimmering in silk and Peter stood barefoot in sequins, both holding each of the other's two hands, staring and smiling at each other, I said, "Perhaps it is time for me to soak in the hot tub?"

"Yes, Cameron. Thank you," said Rhiannon.

"Please," said Peter.

So, I did. And the water was welcoming, hot, restorative. I looked out over the dunes, the beach and the curling waves, hearing the gulls cry from the open, cerulean sky. And, I did not peek. Not once.

The Asklepion sits on the eastern slope of Mount Dikaios overlooking the azure Gulf of Keramos in the middle distance. Back in the day, the ancients hacked three giant terraces, roughly one-hundred meters wide, out of the rock in the middle of a sacred cypress forest. While much of the Aegean is deforested, the Asklepion is still surrounded by that same ancient cypress forest.

As we walked up the path from the parking lot toward the main gates of the Asklepion complex, the fresh, rain-washed, cedar-like scent of the forest stopped me.

"Ah," I said.

Rhiannon stopped beside me and took my hand.

"Is there a problem?" asked Traka, moving up to Rhiannon's right.

"Now this," I said, "is the smell of a woodland."

"Stay with us, please, Cameron," said Rhiannon.

"Indeed," I said.

Traka waited for Peter to come abreast of her, then took his arm.

"There are lots of steps," said Traka. "I hope you do not mind."

"Not at all," said Peter. "I shall be your escort."

We walked up through a small grove of tall cypress toward the front gate.

"Not that way, please," said Traka. She nodded to the right. "A little detour."

On her direction, we skirted the tall fence, cutting through the grove to what was clearly a maintenance entrance – a double, metal-rod gate large enough to admit a good-sized truck into the grounds. A daunting padlock and chain bound shut the two gates.

Traka handed me a single, brass key.

"Isn't this illegal?" I asked.

"We have permission," said Traka. "All will be fine, Cameron."

"Oh, for goodness sake," said Rhiannon. She took the key from my hand and stepped up to the gate, releasing the padlock and pushing one side open about two meters. "Come along, then."

We entered. Rhiannon locked the gate behind us and returned the key to Traka. We stood on a broad gravel path. Directly ahead of us a set of steps more than ten meters wide led up to the first terrace.

"This is known as the Lower Level," said Traka. "Up the twenty-five or so steps is the First Terrace, followed by the Second Terrace, followed, obviously, by the Third Terrace. Over to our left is the remains of the Roman baths – the frigidarium still is in pretty good shape. But mostly, this level was used for athletic competitions in honor of the god. Oh. And music, too. We Greeks are not barbarians. So, what would you like to see first?" asked Traka.

"Perhaps," said Peter, "we could just take each level in turn? We all love ancient history. I would not wish to miss anything."

"Very well," said Traka. "Let us ramble."

We followed the earthen paths through tall, green grasses to the Roman baths. The light-colored stone walls still stood well over our heads – it has oft been noted that the Romans built well. We poked our noses in all

116

manner of nooks and crannies as Traka pattered on with a solid monologue. Here stood the frigidarium, here the tepidarium. Lepers may have been cared for in this underground room.

I could see that Rhiannon and Peter were immersed, both happy and content amongst the weathered stone. Peter, indeed, balanced precariously atop one of the frigidarium walls. He can be a bad boy. Seeing my smile, Traka winked. She came and took my arm.

"Afterward," she said, "We can climb the hill above the temple of Asklepios, into the forest. You will like it there, I think. In the summer the scent is of sunbaked needles from the forest floor, but this time of year it smells like life. And the cypresses sway gently overhead, rustling."

I nodded.

"You have spent time there?" I asked.

"When I was younger and fewer rules were enforced, my friends and I would spend the night up there, camping with a fire," said Traka. "Legend promised that a portal up there opened to another world."

"Another world?" I asked.

"The specifics were somewhat vague," said Traka. "But this is an old legend, going back through many generations."

"Did you ever see it?" I asked.

"Don't be daft," said Traka. "Come on. Let us get started up those steps. It is going to take me a while."

We walked slowly past the high stone wall retaining the first terrace to the stairs. By the time we began our ascent, Peter awaited at the top, looking down with one hand on each hip.

"Your friend is very agile," said Traka.

"He is," I agreed.

Rhiannon hurried up from behind and took Traka's other arm.

"Thank you, dear," said Traka. "One tumble on these steps at my age and it would be curtains. You will note that these steps, while uneven, do not look too poorly. Much of what you are walking on now is restoration by the Italians in the 1930s."

We worked our way slowly to the top of the marble stairs, arriving on the First Terrace to see, along with Peter, a broad, open, rectangular, green field. At the far side of the terrace, a retaining wall of monumental, ashlar, grey stone rose about six meters to the Second Terrace. Unlike the wall supporting the First Terrace, this wall featured twenty-two large, arched niches. Another set of ten-meter-wide stairs led to the Second Terrace.

Traka pointed to a squared, stone block that – given its smooth polished top – had been used as a bench by many a weary soul.

"A bit of a rest, I think," she said.

Rhiannon and I supported her as she walked to the stone and sat with a sigh.

"I am ok on the flat, but stairs do me in," said Traka. "Now, if you look around, you will not see too much." She pointed to the left. "There you can see a fine jumble of stone – a continuation of the Roman baths from the Lower Level. Some mosaics survive, if you are so inclined. But, back in the day, well, you must imagine it."

"Imagine a U of classical Roman buildings, with the base here by us, along the edge of the First Terrace. The arms of the U would have enclosed the space to the right and left. All the buildings opened onto the First Terrace."

"Obviously, these structures grew and changed over the centuries. I will not bore you with the details, but generally speaking, these buildings were the functioning rooms of the hospital – which, remember, was both a temple and a clinic."

"Now, there." She pointed over toward the arches in the wall on the other side of the field. "Those arches used to contain statues, fountains and pools. The fountains and pools were fed by natural springs and sulfurous waters brought from the base of Mount Dikaios. These were a key part of the therapies here, as you can imagine."

"Rhiannon, child, do you still have that postcard?"

Rhiannon dug deep into her bag and withdrew the requested item, handing it to Traka. Traka held it up between herself and the arched wall.

"Good lord," said Traka. "The view has hardly changed in one hundred years." She passed the image to me and I compared the views.

"Cameron, look at the third arch to the left of the stairs," said Traka. "In the image it is quite dark, almost as if he is hiding, but you can see the water flow."

"Who is he?" asked Peter.

"Cameron's kindred spirit, Pan!" said Traka with delight. "The small statue still remains. And the water still flows. It really is quite wonderful. Shall we?" She offered her arm and Peter stepped forward to ease her to her feet.

As we crossed the field, I could see Peter restraining himself. He clearly wanted to bound ahead to the fountain but felt duty-bound to support Traka. Rhiannon stepped next to me and took my hand.

"You are *both* good boys," said Rhiannon quietly.

As we approached the massive retaining wall, I saw that the third arch to the left of the stairs was slightly larger than the others. And, whereas the other arches were classic Roman with a flat wall to the rear of the niches, the arch of Pan's niche started the same, but possessed a second, deeper, arched recess topped with a semi-dome. Within that recess, a small statue of Pan, worn by time, sat cross legged, carved into a marble grotto. Clear, spring water flowed abundantly from beneath Pan, across a jumbled mass of green foliage, splashing into a sizeable pool.

"Say hello to Pan, Cameron," said Traka. "Theologically, you and he are rather similar. What with both of you being nature-based and all."

"Hi Pan," I said. "Lovely fountain."

Pan did not reply.

"He was a fertility god in his own way," Peter observed.

"No," said Traka.

"He wasn't?" I asked. "I thought he was?"

"No, Peter," said Traka. "You may not have Cameron fertilize you in the fountain. It is an important, culturally significant artifact."

Rhiannon giggled. "Professor, really, I am sure that is not what he was thinking."

"It totally was," said Peter.

"Seriously?" I asked. "Peter you have to be more patient. Please."

"Fine," said Peter, pouting. "I was thinking, two fertility gods…"

"It would be cold and extremely unpleasant," I said. "Rhiannon, he is trying to kill me. Please make him behave. You know I have no natural defenses against pouting."

"No sex on the ancient monuments," said Traka. "Peter, you are from a proud, self-respecting culture. It is not like you hail from Wolverhampton for Christ's sake."

"Fine," said Peter, without the pout.

"Well, professor, quite correct you were," said Rhiannon, ignoring the ancient monuments and fertilization theme. "There is no sign of any kind of inscription, at least not here. Everything is too worn by time and the seasons."

"It is beautiful, though," I said. "Look at the clarity of the water. I love how the whole wall beneath Pan is covered with green moss and vines. This is a real fertility god."

"So are you, my love," said Rhiannon.

"That is most kind," I replied and kissed her, gently.

"Shall we continue the tour?" asked Traka.

"I see standing pillars on the next level!" said Peter.

"Then up we go," said Traka.

So, we did, taking the thirty, broad, marble steps one at a time.

"Goodness," said Traka, upon reaching the top. "And we are only at the Second Level."

"It is technically the third level," said Peter. "You are doing really well."

Traka glared it him, then sighed.

"I guess we all do become children again as we age," she said. "Cannot say I like it, though."

"I retract my remark," said Peter. He pointed to the left. "Pillars. Big pillars."

"Aha," said Traka. "That would be what people call the Roman Temple.

2nd century C.E. A late comer to this sacred space. We guess it was for the worship of Apollo, Asclepius' father, and for the imperial cult of Nero. Just a guess, though. Those seven pillars were reset by the Italians in the 1930s."

The mid-sized temple to Apollo stood a stone's throw to our left, five columns standing elegantly side-by-side, bright white against the blue sky, along the temple's longer side, with one base empty and forlorn at the far end, and two more pillars forming the base of an L on the side closest to us.

Directly ahead of us lay a roped-off scattering of large, squared masonry; to the right, another temple with two large, standing pillars.

"This level focused less on treatment, per se," said Traka.

"The pile of rocks was the altar for Asclepius. And the temple to the right was built to show off the treasures pilgrims and patients donated to the temple."

"Cameron, please walk me to the next set of steps. We can sit while they play."

She looked to Peter.

"You two may ramble, young man," said Traka.

Rhiannon and Peter headed off to the temple of Apollo. I took Traka's arm firmly in grasp, as she looked a little shaky, and headed toward the steps to the Third Level.

The ancients constructed both the steps to and the retaining wall for the Third Level in two separate design elements, one above the other. The first element of the retaining wall did not cross the entire hillside; rather, it had been cut into the hillside. To the left of the steps, this retaining wall stood in a semi-circle. Stylistically similar to the arch containing Pan's fountain, it held five empty arches. To the right of the stairs, a straight, roughly ten-meter wide wall disappeared into the hillside.

The second element lay behind the first, a continuation of the steps and a retaining wall of monumental ashlar stones running the full width of the sanctuary.

Traka and I took our place on the first step.

"Thank you, Cameron," said Traka. She tilted her head a bit backwards. "There are sixty steps to get to the third level. And I do not need to hear that I am doing very well!"

"No, ma'am," I said.

"It is nice here this time of year," said Traka. "In August sitting here this time of day would be like sitting in a furnace. Also, it is nice to be the only people here."

"It is," I said. I closed my eyes and tilted my face toward the sun.

"You are bored, Cameron," she said. "Perhaps you are less enamored of ancient life than your lover and companion?"

"Not really. I am quite excited to see it all," I said. "And being here like this, on a cool November afternoon…" I opened my hands, outward, in a gesture of benediction. "But, for me, it is no longer all that ancient. It almost counts as new stuff. Bobbles."

"Your mumblings interest me, young man," said Traka. "Please continue."

"I will attempt to do so, madam," I said. "In the last seven odd years I have come to see things, not in annual cycles, but in seven-year cycles."

"That is still quite a few cycles," said Traka. "Three-thousand years dived by seven years is still quite a few."

"Roughly four-hundred and twenty-five," I said.

"Show off," said Traka.

"I know, eh?" I said and laughed. "But that is not the whole deal. You may find this strange, but as the years have passed, I have been spending more time in the forests above our little valley in Wales. I have been rather losing touch with the passage of time. Sometimes I can sit watching a deer browse amongst the bushes for a few moments and it will seem an eternity. Sometimes a whole night with Puck passes in an instant. And, with Puck, I have seen countless thousands of cycles. You know, humans really haven't been around that long. Just a blink of an eye."

"Easy to intellectualize," said Traka. "Harder to feel."

"Indeed," I said.

"Tell me more about Puck," said Traka. "You can imagine my disbelief when Peter claimed he heard a Shakespearian sprite!"

"Well, Puck and I have been together since I came to the valley," I said. "I see him mostly in my dreams. Though, as of late... He comes more at his own behest."

"At inopportune times?" asked Traka.

"You have no idea," I said. "Seriously."

"In the beginning, though," said Traka. "Did he really come only in your dreams? And were these dreams drug induced?"

"I sense the anthropological mind at work," I said. "But yes, the answer is to both questions. Rhiannon always prepares a mixture of goodness-knows-what in the same clay bowl. It is a tradition of the Rowans from as far back as they know."

"So, Puck could be a delusion solidified by long-term drug use?" asked Traka.

"Totally," I agreed. "That has been my theory for the longest time."

"And Peter could share your delusion because he loves you so," said Traka.

"Absolutely," I said.

"Except..." said Traka. "Except..."

"Indeed," I said. "But to go too far down that path leads to either acceptance or madness. And you have a respected career and all."

"And you have chosen acceptance," said Traka.

"Well, I get the babes," I said, giving her my best smile.

She leaned in close.

"Don't play the fool with me, young man," said Traka in a whisper.

"No ma'am," I said.

"You know, even though you are an idiot and a buffoon, you are taking a stand, sticking with your commitment." she said. "Jung holds that this is even more important to the creation of a true self than consciousness. It is a shame *your* self has to be so…"

She leaned away and straightened her back.

"But here come your lover and companion, so enough talk for now, eh?" she said.

They arrived hand-in-hand, arms swinging back and forth like high schoolers. So cute.

"Up?" asked Peter.

Traka stood, with small tremors migrating up her legs. She took Peter's arm in both hands.

"I will be your mule," said Peter.

Traka looked to Rhiannon. "Is that safe?"

"Entirely," said Rhiannon. "Peter is insanely strong. But Cameron will walk behind the two of you, just in case."

Peter crouched to the ground before Traka. "Mount up, my lady."

Traka chuckled and murmured to herself as she set herself astride his back and he took hold of her legs.

"Ready?" asked Peter.

"Ready, aye ready!" said Traka. "Up! Up!"

He stood, smiling.

"Peter," I said. "Do *not* run up the stairs."

"Oui mon Seigneur," said Peter. He did pout a little, though.

We headed slowly up the sixty stairs. Rhiannon took my hand and we followed behind Peter and Traka, pacing ourselves to remain directly behind. By the time we reached the top of the second set of stairs – which is nine meters wide rather than the nineteen-meter-wide first set – Traka had dozed off on Peter's back.

"Now what?" I whispered.

The main feature of the Third Level – the Temple of Asklepios – lay directly before us, at least fifteen meters wide and thirty deep. Only the base of thick squared stones reached by three steps and interspaced with bright green foliage remained. To the right, a handful of trees broke the view of scattered masonry. To the left, two lonely-looking cypress trees stood in a desolate field of squared, grey stone. Around the edge of the Third Level one could easily make out the ruins of a covered portico or colonnade, but beyond the ruins the entire level was surrounded by mature pine woods, bright green in the November sun.

"Perhaps we can find a comfortable place amongst the pine needles of the forest floor," I said, quietly.

Peter nodded and we headed past the temple toward the small set of stairs that led into the sacred grove. At the back of the Third Level, a gravel path headed up the thirty-odd-degree slope into the forest.

"Cameron, here you lead," whispered Rhiannon. So, I did. Peter followed with Traka, and Rhiannon brought up the rear.

We reached the ancient steps in only a few moments. I led to the left, up a gradual slope, through the trees, over twisted roots into a small clearing. Selecting a comfortable spot in sunlight, I removed my light coat and laid it on the ground. Rhiannon gently took Traka from Peter's back and lay her carefully on my coat.

A quiet breeze rustled the pine needles gently, pulling the grove's scent from its depths to smother all perception, but for the pulsing buzz of cicadas from the cypress above. Traka remained firmly in the depths of sleep.

"What now?" I whispered.

Peter took my hand and turned to Rhiannon.

"It is a sacred grove," he whispered.

"Tsk, serious you are?" said Rhiannon. She lowered her voice. "Fine."

Peter smiled up at me. "Well?"

"I will watch over the good professor," said Rhiannon.

I looked down at Traka.

"I am a little worried about her," I said. "Maybe we made her overdo it?"

"Okay, she is," said Rhiannon. "Do not break the poor boy's heart."

"Well, okay," I said, looking to Peter. "Maybe let us just go into the forest?"

"Fine," said Peter, pulling me away toward the cypress trees where a small path led from the clearing. "Into the forest."

He led me through the trees, the pine needles tugging at the fabric of my shirt with a rough, scratching sound, until the path opened enough to let in filtered sunlight from above. We then moved completely silently, the soft pine needles beneath our feet hushing each footstep.

Peter still led me by the hand, turning at times to give me a sweet, joyful smile. When we broke into the full sunlight of a small, circular glade, perhaps five meters in diameter, we stopped. A squared stone, much worn by sunlight and weather, stood at the center of the glade.

"That is an altar stone," said Peter.

"Perhaps," I allowed.

"A sacred altar stone," said Peter.

"Perhaps. Perhaps not," I said.

"It totally is," said Peter. "Look at the carvings on the sides. Are those not most like the ones on the sarcophagus?"

Sure enough, carvings which may have been most similar covered the stone. But the detail had been blasted by time, making imagination the ruler of perception.

"Perhaps," I allowed.

Peter turned to me, pulled me closer, and kissed me full upon the lips. I took him in my arms.

"You will let me have my way," he said. "Because you adore me."

"I do adore you," I said and kissed him again.

"You on the stone, I think," said Peter. "Me on you."

"Why me on the stone?" I asked. "I was thinking you on the altar…"

"I wouldn't mind, with you, but do you really want to bring me back to Rhiannon with my back all scratched from you flinging me about the altar in your animal lust?" said Peter. He said this in all apparent seriousness. No little smile. No little pout.

"Very well," I said.

He began to pull me toward the stone.

"This is where we will make our baby," said Peter.

He stopped before the stone, bowed to it, and turned to me.

"Undress me," he said.

"Usually," I observed, "it is impossible to get you to keep your clothing on."

"Think of it as a ritual," he said. "I am your Saturnalia present."

I swallowed. First, I removed his zip-up jacket, folded it, and placed it across the altar. Next, I unbuttoned his button-down shirt, and caressed his left breast. He stepped closer and I leaned down to breathe in his scent. I smelled the forest, fresh hair, and a hint of floral perfume. I pulled my head back and looked to see him quivering, just a little.

"Peter, are you wearing perfume?" I asked.

"You know I do not wear perfume," said Peter.

"Peter, my love, I do not think we are alone," I said. I began to slowly button his shirt. The quivering ceased and he became completely still.

"Can you hear them?" I said, quietly. "Moving stealthily?"

"I can, now," he said. "I apologize. I was a little distracted before."

"I was more than a little distracted, myself," I said. I finished buttoning his shirt and held his jacket for him while he slipped in his arms.

"Well, their movement was disguised by the rustling of the cypress," said Peter. "And you were focusing on me, which is only right and proper in the circumstance, so I forgive you."

"Thank you," I said. "Let us head back to Rhiannon. Nice and slow."

As we turned toward the exit from the clearing, a large man in a grey, hooded sweatshirt with a flower logo over the heart, blue jeans and sneakers stepped from behind a cypress into the path. The hood was up. A checked, blue bandana covered his lower face. In his right hand he held a curved sickle.

"Can I help you?" I asked.

No reply. The man slipped into a half crouch and moved toward us, placing each foot carefully, the reaping tool held out slightly to his right. He had training. Two more people stepped into the path behind him, both with covered faces and hooded sweatshirts. Each also held curved blades.

I pushed Peter back and leapt toward the first man. He cut toward me with the sickle. I twisted away, but the blade grazed my chest, just below my left breast. Ignoring the sting, I caught his weapon arm and spun my body, inverting and straightening his arm. I pressed down and heard muscles and tendons tear. He howled and dropped the blade but grabbed me with his left hand and tackled me, pulling me to the ground.

The other two jumped forward, sickles raised. The slighter of the two – likely a woman – sliced down toward me as my face hit the dirt, blinding me with the dust. The blade whistled above my head.

From directly above I heard a cry of anger; Peter's voice, followed by a meaty thud and wet gurgling. The man holding me went limp. Then, the sharp snap of bone breaking. Another scream of pain.

I raised myself to a crouch, blinking the grit from my eyes. The first attacker lay still on his side. The woman stood, holding her arm, an arm that now dangled at an unnatural angle from the elbow. The bandana had fallen from her face to reveal blue-grey eyes, blond hair, and a square chin. The third attacker began to move forward cautiously toward Peter, who stood in a half crouch, feet in a classic L stance, arms by his side.

"Peter…" I began.

He turned, flashed me a manic grin, then moved too fast to see, just a blur. Another cry of pain and the sickle spun away; the hand dangled from the wrist, sideways. Peter bounced back, returning to my side.

"I can kill you, easily," said Peter. "Go."

The two walking wounded looked at each other, then moved cautiously to their comrade. While they tried to raise him, Peter pointed to the path and took my hand. We fled.

We were back with Rhiannon and Traka in minutes. Traka was awake and Rhiannon jogged toward the forest.

"You are bleeding!" said Rhiannon.

I looked down. Blood soaked my shirt.

"Peter, please take the good professor," I said. "We need to get out of here."

"What happened?" asked Traka, staring at the blood.

"Fucking Nazis," said Peter. "Fucking Nazis happened."

"Maybe not," I said. "One wore a logo, a cross within a heart within a flower. They might have been Lutherans."

"Fucking Nazi Lutherans, then," said Peter.

"For goodness sake," said Rhiannon. "Later!"

I learned three new things in the next, pre-dinner, segment of that day.

One, Nikos has a sense of humor. "So, plastico siding is dangerous business?"

Two, Greek doctors require the envelope – that is an unmarked envelope of cash – before they will stitch your wound, even one that is less than ten centimeters long and "really just a scratch."

And, three, as a young person Peter served in the French navy. "I cannot tell you about it. It is not permitted." A man of mystery is our Peter.

The sickle wound was not much – I had taken worse hits during training with Celyn. But, upon seeing the blood, Traka insisted that Nikos take us to her villa. A few telephone calls summoned a doctor, a taciturn older gentleman who made a point of letting us know he was missing dinner and who sewed me up with considerable skill. He would not use pain killers, though. "If you stupid enough to fight…" He did supply antibiotics.

After the hubbub subsided later that evening, we gathered in Traka's library.

The library is long and slender, running the entire width of the rear of Traka's villa, perhaps twenty-three meters from side-to-side and about four meters deep. The ceiling of large, exposed, dark-wooden beams is topped by planking and stands at least five meters high. There are no windows on the external walls, but, in the center of the interior wall, a large, plate-glass pane opens onto the central courtyard garden, letting in a warm, indirect, golden light. To either side of the window, double, beveled-glass doors of old oak, with true divided lights, open into the sheltered colonnade.

Built-in, light-oak, floor-to-ceiling, tome-laden bookshelves cover the three exterior walls. That evening I did a rough calculation, noting that this creates more than one-hundred and fifty square meters of space for shelving books in that one room. I also noted this was not enough shelf space for our wise woman.

In the middle of the room, books and scrolls covered a heavy pine table large enough to seat twelve for supper. Two large candelabras stood in the middle where beeswax had dripped from the tapered candles onto the pine. The six chairs around the table appeared, at first glance, to be occupied by severed heads. At each end of the room, a sitting area of leather sofas and chairs in the old-English club style could theoretically seat a half-dozen people. The sitting area to the right had become impromptu book bins, with volumes not so much stacked as jumbled into disordered masses upon each chair and sofa. The sitting area to the left lay open for actual human occupation. One sofa and four lightly-colored, leather wing chairs were arranged around a cold, stone fireplace set into the bookshelves. The terracotta tile floor of the library gleamed, spotless. Not a scrap of paper or spiral of dog hair could be seen.

We had entered the room via the left-side doors, and Traka immediately herded us toward the sitting area. As no one else seemed disturbed by the severed heads, I followed.

The others began to take their seats but Traka held up her hand toward me – a stop gesture in any language.

"Cameron, there is wood in a small shed out behind the villa. Could you please make a fire? I am a little chilled," said Traka.

Rhiannon smiled at me in a vaguely menacing way.

"Of course," I said.

There is no back door to Traka's villa. It is designed like a fortress. I made my way through the home, out the front door, through the olive orchard, and found the woodshed. I gathered small bits for kindling, medium-sized sticks, some larger split logs, and a few sheets of old newspaper. The wood all appeared to be from the olive trees. The paper was *The International Herald Tribune.*

As I headed back through the orchard, laden despite my wound, I mused on this unfortunate bit of stereotyping. Just because I was a husky, Canadian male, Traka had assumed that I possessed the necessary skills to lay and light a fire. It is true, of course, that all Canadian men are terribly manly, but not all of us grew up spending time in the wilderness. Not every Canadian male can pitch a tent, canoe, hunt, fish and light fires.

Through pure random chance, this stereotype did apply to me – perfectly. I had the necessary skill sets. But, I thought, I would wager seven monkeys to a sausage that Peter could do it better – despite being a stylish Frenchman. Also, I knew he would be watching and judging me; such is the tragedy of stereotypes.

Returning to the library, I headed for the fireplace. In my absence, a low coffee table had been pulled close to the fireplace and the seats had been arranged in a semi-circle around the table. A meal lay upon the table. Plates, cutlery, a large earthenware bowl of stifado beef stew, wineglasses and three bottles of red wine. Fresh bread, a large chunk of feta, and a bottle of olive oil completed the setup.

I squatted by the fireplace and began my task, completely ignoring the beautiful, ruby hue of the wine. I crumpled one piece of newspaper into a loose ball and set it on the stone fireplace floor.

I heard a suppressed 'tch' from behind. Definitely French. I ignored it. It is true that a purest would start with wood chips, bark, or dried leaves, but paper is easier and works better. I then constructed a loose cone shape of small, dry twigs over the wadded paper. Around this, I slowly and carefully built a log cabin-style structure of slightly larger sticks, about twenty centimeters high.

"Professor, do you have a lighter?" I asked, earning me a second 'tch' from behind, which I also ignored. One should use the best tools available, after all. At least I was not stooping to liquid fire starter.

"On the table. By the candelabra," said Traka. "Also, please try not to leave any wood on the floor. My housekeeper, Mrs. Krillia, refuses to clean the room if I leave things on the floor. She is quite firm about it. There was an incident, once."

"Yes ma'am," I said.

The lighter, a nice Zippo with a death's head image on the side, stood upright beside one of the candelabras. I returned to the fireplace with it, having also confirmed that the severed heads were models of some kind, not real. This was somewhat reassuring.

I adjusted the Zippo to give maximum flame and lit the paper. It began to burn eagerly. Within seconds, the small, inverted cone caught the flame and the log cabin structure started to smoke. As the outer work began to flame, I added a small stick at an angle over the top of the fire.

I continued with this method, slowly and patiently adding larger and larger pieces of wood until a good size blaze snapped and popped in the fireplace.

Only then did I turn my attention back to our little tribe. Peter raised one of his perfectly maintained eyebrows slightly.

"Your wine has been poured," he said. He used his chin to point to a glass on the low table. The wine stood before an open space on the couch, between Peter and Rhiannon. I stood and moved to my assigned seat, settling in between them and sinking down into the soft leather.

I held up the wineglass inspecting the color. The flickering flames in the hearth refracted, blended and flickered from the glass and the red of the wine. Hypnotizing, fluttering flames.

Rhiannon, to my left, set her hand on my knee.

"Cameron," she said. "Are you with us at all?"

"Yes, of course," I said.

Peter leaned in close from the right.

"Liar," he whispered.

"It is a lovely fire, Cameron," said Traka. "I feel better already. Thank you, kindly."

"Now, shall I serve?" She looked to Rhiannon.

"Please," said Rhiannon.

Traka served us each in turn, starting with Rhiannon, ladling the stifado – stewing beef in small pieces, baby onions, ripe tomatoes, garlic and bay leaves all in a spicy tomato sauce – onto our plates. Peter broke chunks from the baguette and passed them around the table. He placed the feta within Traka's reach.

"Thank you for the meal," I said. "It is wonderful."

"You are welcome, Cameron," said Traka, "Though my housekeeper deserves all the credit."

"Thank you to your invisible housekeeper then," I said.

"Pardon?" asked Traka.

"I have never seen her," I said.

"Ah. She does not like large men," said Traka.

I knew from bitter experience that there was no point pursuing this statement, so I said, "Please thank her on my behalf."

"I will," said Traka.

The food absorbed us all. When prepared correctly, Stifado offers many layers of flavor. The baguette served as a dipping tool. The wine, gentle and deep, slipped easily over the palate. All was going to be fine after all.

But, inevitably, inquiring minds needed to know.

"I have to say," said Traka, "None of you seems terribly surprised by your little adventure this afternoon."

"Surprised, I was!" said Rhiannon.

"But Peter and Cameron were not even remotely shocked," said Traka. "You were expecting this?"

"Fucking Nazis," said Peter.

"Peter, language, please," said Rhiannon.

"My apologies," said Peter. "We did warn you, however, and you insisted it was our imagination."

"That is because you are both twelve-year olds and someone needs to be the grownup," said Rhiannon.

Peter focused on Traka. "They have been shadowing us since Paris."

"Maybe," said Rhiannon. "I have to admit someone is up to a little something."

"Maybe not Nazis. Maybe not Lutherans," I said. "Sickles are a traditional druidic ritual device."

"Nazi-Lutheran-druids, then?" asked Peter.

"It is also an old Soviet symbol, the sickle," said Traka.

"The flower could have been a rose, so maybe Christian. The heart is absolutely a Christian symbol, as is the cross. Not so much the sickle, though."

"Ahem," said Peter. We all looked to him.

"Revelation 14:14. 'And I looked, and behold a white cloud, and upon the cloud one sat like unto the Son of man, having on his head a golden crown, and in his hand a sharp sickle.' It refers to the second coming of Christ... Christ coming to harvest souls," said Peter.

"Oh. Good boy," I said, patting his knee.

He rested his head briefly on my shoulder.

"Thank you, kindly, good sir," he said.

"So, born again Christians?" I asked.

"A guessing game, it is," said Rhiannon. "No idea do we have."

"That is true," I said.

"Good professor, do you have any way of checking to see if somebody visited a doctor here on the island to have broken bones set?"

"Oh. Good boy," said Peter, patting my knee.

I rested my head briefly on his shoulder.

"Thank you, kindly, good sir," I said.

He looked up at me.

"Just so you know," he said. "I could not possibly love you more than at this very moment."

"Ahem," said Traka. "Could we, just for a while, try to stay on topic, please? Seriously, Rhiannon, I don't know how you manage these two boys."

"I know, eh?" said Peter. But he started giggling. "Thank goodness the two boys are both highly trained combatants!"

I started laughing, holding my stitches in pain.

"Well, there is that," said Traka. "And, yes, I will call my nephew, a police lieutenant, so he can ask around."

"It would be nice to know who shares our area of interest," said Rhiannon.

"Indeed," I said.

"Indeed, indeed," said Peter. "But, you know, evil Lutherans aside, we are now in a bit of quandary regarding next steps, hunt-for-the-Grail wise. Rhiannon, I will not permit him to dream up on the mountain alone so do not even think to suggest it."

"I was not even considering it," said Rhiannon, firmly. She is a poor liar.

"Let's all have a little more wine," said Traka. She rose and exited the room.

I waited for the door to swing closed.

"You two, please stop worrying about me," I said. "I am fine, really. I am not falling apart for goodness sake."

"Cameron, my love," said Rhiannon, quietly. "Sometimes, when you are lying on your back, falling asleep at night, tears flow from the corners of your eyes, down your cheeks, and into your ears. You never make a sound, but do you think we do not notice?'

"Sometimes, when I am sleeping with my head on your shoulder, I awake with the top of my head wet from your tears," said Peter, equally quietly. "So. Do not claim that everything is fine."

"Well, I am a little tired, sometimes," I admitted. "And, sometimes, I get sad for no real reason. But it passes. It is nothing to worry about."

"I let you get hurt," said Peter. "I was not fast enough."

One tear ran down each of his cheeks.

"Peter, no crying, please," I said. "I have never seen anyone move faster."

I turned to Rhiannon. "Seriously, he is insanely fast. You can't even see him move."

But Rhiannon's tears had already started. "I was not even there!"

"At least I am honest about my tears!" said Peter.

Inevitably, this was when Traka returned.

"Cameron?" she said.

"It is not my fault," I said.

"Cameron, come and open the wine," Traka said, somewhat bemused. "There is a corkscrew on the table."

I went to open the wine, an award-winning Triantafyllopoulous shiraz. Traka sat between Rhiannon and Peter, placing one arm around each.

"There. There," she said. "Cameron. Come pour some more wine."

"Yes, ma'am," I said, doing as commanded.

I sat in Traka's chair. We drank. I had seconds of the stifado. Traka put a dent in the feta. Traka poured. We drank. I waited for it. I was ready when it came.

"So, let us talk a little bit about this notion of Cameron dreaming on the mountain," said Traka. "Shall we?"

"There is not a terrible lot to say," I said. "It is a passing fancy of Rhiannon's, nothing more."

"Except for the wolves, of course," said Peter. He sniggered to himself, emptied his wineglass, and held it out to be refilled. Traka passed me an unopened bottle. I opened it with a pop and passed it back. Traka poured.

"Peter," I said. "Be good."

"Well, if I were pregnant, then I would not be drinking. So, I am thinking that this is your fault," said Peter.

"Fine, I apologize. But try to be good," I said.

"You are talking about ritual mystic dreaming, aren't you?" asked Traka.

"Not at all," I said. "I don't even know what that might be."

"And that is how you first contacted Puck, your spirit guide?" asked Traka.

"Puck is not my freak'n spirit guide," I said.

"Give it up, my love," said Rhiannon.

"Merely sticking to the script," I said.

"Yes, thank you," said Rhiannon. "You may stop now."

"Okay, then," I said.

"And that is how you first contacted Puck, who is not your spirit guide?" asked Traka.

"Fine, yes," I said. "That is also how we traced the Grail to the Asklepion in the reign of Emperor Valentinian the Great. Not to mention how I ended up sleeping with wolves in the old temple by the priory."

"Real wolves or mythic wolves?" asked Traka.

"That would be real wolves, but they weren't that big," I said.

"You seem to have taken it well," said Traka.

"In the scheme of things, as far as surprises and oddities go…" I said.

"I suppose," said Traka. "And the whole story about the plaster and inscriptions?"

"I thought he did rather well with that tale," said Rhiannon.

"I see," said Traka.

"Are you angry?" asked Peter, trotting out his cutest pout – a wasted effort. Traka did not look to him, shifting her gaze to Rhiannon.

"I am not angry at them, but disappointed in you," said Traka. "Assuming Cameron is in fact the Lord of Summer, or even if this is a reality you have created for yourselves, how could you be so irresponsible? What if that sickle up there on the hill above the Asklepion had cut into his liver? What if he had been savaged by the wolves? Hell, what if he had run away with this pretty little boy? Where would your cycle of the seasons be then, eh?"

"I am not a pretty little boy!" said Peter.

"You are, you know," I said.

"Really? You are so sweet," said Peter. He struggled up out of the deep, comfortable couch to sit in my lap. Putting my wineglass on the table and wrapping both arms around me, he lay his head on my shoulder and I began to pet his hair.

Rhiannon smiled at us with a certain degree of fondness.

"Good professor," she said. "Look at those two."

"I understand," said Traka. "But still, you are being selfish. Unconscionably so."

"I acknowledge it," said Rhiannon. "I am not a good person. You cannot imagine the things I have done to be with him. I love him so."

She said it so matter-of-factly that Traka froze, just for a moment. Then, she scowled.

Peter's breathing settled into a quiet, slow, steady rhythm.

"He is asleep," I whispered.

They both looked over. Traka's scowl slipped away.

"Fine," she said. "You may put him in the room where you convalesced."

I nodded.

"But do not tarry," said Traka. "I require your presence."

I carried Peter to the bedroom, keeping his head upon my shoulder, and lay him gently on the bed. The night air was cool, so I took the neatly folded comforter from the foot of the bed and spread it over him. He lay there, peaceful, his pretty face framed in the bob of his hair, breathing almost silently through his perfect nose. I left, quietly.

When I returned to the library, both occupants and the seating arrangements had changed. Traka sat in her original chair. She no longer scowled. Rhiannon remained in place on the sofa. Beside her on the sofa sat my sleeping companion from our earlier visit to Villa Traka, the largeish, shaggy, grey doggie.

"You have met Chaney, I believe," said Traka.

"Indeed. We are old friends," I said. "Is he a specific breed?"

"Good heavens, no!" said Traka. "His parentage is a mystery at best."

I sat on the couch beside him and scratched under his snout.

"Hello again, Chaney," I said.

Chaney allowed me to pet him for a few minutes, then circled three times on the sofa before settling into a curl and placing his head on Rhiannon's lap. Rhiannon scratched him slowly with one finger between his eyes. Gradually, his eyes closed and his breathing became quiet.

"Dare we talk?" I whispered.

"He is not sleeping," said Traka. "He is just pretending. He does not like you in the house. You stole his bed."

"Not intentionally," I said.

"He is a dog," said Rhiannon. "He cares not about intent."

"Fine," I said.

"He likes Rhiannon, though," said Traka.

"How could he not?" I asked. Unfortunately, a beast now lay between us. I could not kiss my one-third of the Rowans.

"Your young man is asleep?" asked Traka.

"Peacefully so," I said. "Just like an angel."

"Was he really so fierce this afternoon?" asked Rhiannon.

"I swear to all the gods, you have never seen anyone move so fast," I said. "He chose to snap some bones, but I am sure he could have killed just as easily. He really is amazing. I should have guessed from the way he moves. He is trained, at a minimum."

"At minimum?" asked Traka.

"He almost certainly has advanced training and on-the-job experience," I said. "He did say he served in the navy and the French navy has several commando units. It is just a guess, though."

"Gourmet, scholar, soldier. A renaissance man is your Peter," said Traka.

"Indeed," I said. "And, still, cute as a button."

"As a button," said Rhiannon. She raised her glass to me in salute.

"So, is that it?" asked Traka. "Do you just sail off across the Aegean with your oh-so-cute Peter, never to be seen again on this fair isle of Kos? Or, do you pursue the Grail?"

She clearly was not asking me, as she had one hand raised, one finger extended, trembling, toward Rhiannon – looking too much like one of the three hags in Macbeth for anyone's comfort. I turned to my love, my face in a neutral smile. It was not because I feared either of them at that moment, even though Traka was losing her temper and Rhiannon…

"You call me out?" asked Rhiannon. "Who are you to question me?"

"You question me, in my own home?" asked Traka. "You do not frighten me, young lady. You think you have a history. You are nothing more than a pup! A pup!"

"Cameron!" she barked.

"Yes ma'am," I said, but kept my eyes on Rhiannon.

"Go to the far corner of the library and, on the third shelf, you will find three wooden boxes. Bring them here. Do not drop them," commanded Traka.

Rhiannon nodded. I made my way past the table, past the books jumbled on the chairs and the other couch to the far corner of the room. Sure enough, there on the shelf lay three plain, wooden boxes, each perhaps large enough to hold a softball or two. I took them from the shelf one at a time and held them against my chest. As I returned to Rhiannon and Traka, I noticed that the doors to the library sat slightly ajar. A ninja-like figure lurked in the shadows beyond. Voices had been raised, after all. I smiled into the darkness.

"Bring them to me, Cameron," said Traka. "Set them here on the table."

She pushed the remains of the meal away from her, creating space. I set the boxes, one by one, on the table, and returned to my spot on the sofa. Chaney raised his head, examined me, then turned his attention to the boxes. He silently exposed his fangs.

"You think you are the only ones destined to seek the Grail?" said Traka. "People have sought the Grail for centuries! In some cases, families have been on the trail for generations. I have been seeking it for fifty years! That is longer than you two have been alive."

She pointed to each box in turn.

"Each of these boxes contains what might legitimately have been the Grail," said Traka. "I researched each of them meticulously and at length before acquiring them."

"There is that *acquiring* word again," I said. "How useful it is."

"It was not easy to *acquire* any of them," said Traka. "In some cases significant financial and, well, shall we call it *moral*, cost was involved."

She touched the box closest to her and looked at Rhiannon.

"I admit you have my attention," said Rhiannon.

"Hmph. Let us start with this one. Chaney does not like it as it smells of human blood," said Traka.

The wooden box appeared to be pine and resembled one my father had that held his microscope. The lid lay in two grooves and slid out to the side. Traka set her hand on the lid and pushed it open.

Inside, grey foam held a multi-part goblet in a cutout shaped to fit.

"You can see this goblet is gold. The style is late Roman. The gems look like rubies, but are in fact garnets," said Traka.

She gingerly removed the cup from its cradling foam.

"If you look carefully, you can see the goblet is constructed around a small, olive-wood drinking bowl," said Traka. "Considerable provenance showed that this may have been the bowl used to catch the blood of Christ."

"It smells of Christ's blood?" I asked. "Seriously?"

"Don't be an idiot, Cameron," said Traka. "Two-thousand-year-old blood has no smell."

"Sorry," I said.

"This goblet holds a bit of a history," said Traka. "An unpleasant cult in Iran used it during the reign of Shah Mohammad Reza Pahlavi. They believed that filled with the blood of a virgin the goblet had the power to heal."

"When was this?" I asked.

"The Shah was dethroned in 1979! Have you never opened a history book?" said Traka.

"There is a lot of history, you know," I said, rather pathetically.

"Why is it always the blood of a virgin?" asked Rhiannon.

"I am going to assume that is rhetorical," said Traka. "May I continue?"

"Please do," said Rhiannon.

"At any rate, this goblet passed into the private sector during the collapse of the regime," said Traka. "I managed to find it in Cairo in the possession of one of the descendants of the Shah's first wife – who was of the Egyptian royal family. Said descendant did not wish to part with it, initially." She paused. "But my representative was convincing."

"Acquired it, did he?" asked Rhiannon.

"How did you determine that it is not the Grail?" I asked.

"It did not work?" said Traka.

A short silence followed.

"More wine?" I asked.

Both Rhiannon and Traka held out their glasses. I poured.

Traka took a small sip, then returned the goblet to its case. She slid the lid closed.

"Did we not say that only those who are predestined can find it?" I asked. "So maybe it is the Grail and it won't work for you. Perhaps you are not pure enough in the god's eyes."

"Dangerous ground, there, my love," said Rhiannon.

"Hmm, annoying," said Traka. "Valid, though."

She slid open the box again.

"Take it, Cameron," said Traka.

I nodded and painfully removed the goblet from its case, but fearing to drop it, I lifted it only a few centimeters above the foam.

"Anything?" asked Rhiannon.

"A sense of radiance, light, or perhaps a sweet smell?" asked Traka.

"Nothing," I said. "Perhaps I am too burdened by my history."

"Unlikely," said Rhiannon.

"Peter!" I called out.

He slipped into the room.

"Could you hold it, please. You are the purest soul amongst us," I said. "Sorry, Rhiannon."

"No. It is true," said Rhiannon. "Peter, please take it."

He came forward and cautiously took it from my hands. He raised it and smelled it slowly.

"Not a thing," he said. He placed it back in its case. "Maybe you need to reenact the ritual?"

"You mean the Grail Procession?" asked Traka. "You think I haven't tried that? And it wasn't easy. Do you have any idea how hard it is to find a virgin Grail bearer on an island in southern Greece?"

"My turn to assume that is rhetorical," said Rhiannon.

"Um…" I began.

"Cameron, you do not get to comment," said Rhiannon.

"Okay, fine," I said.

"Peter, perhaps you could put that one back on the self so Chaney can settle himself," said Traka.

Peter returned the golden not-Grail to its case and returned the case to the shelf in the far corner of the room. He returned to sit on Rhiannon's lap. This put out Chaney, who stood, again circled three times, and resettled.

"Box number two?" Peter asked.

"Rhiannon, you will like box number two," said Traka, passing it to her across the table of leftovers.

As Rhiannon took it, she said, "And, Cameron, do not think for a minute I did not notice that you did not let me hold the first Grail."

"Um, you have done too many horri…" I started.

"That's enough, Cameron," said Peter.

"Right, sorry," I said.

"True it is," said Rhiannon.

The second box matched the first in construction. Rhiannon easily slid back the lid. Within, a fragile, lightly hued, aqua glass bowl caught the light from the fireplace. It lay amongst a packing of straw.

"Ooh," said Rhiannon. "Roman? First century B.C.? May I take it out?"

"Of course. It is quiet sturdy," said Traka. "But one would have rather thought that you would prefer B.C.E., rather than the Christian B.C."

Rhiannon removed the bowl from its bed of straw and held it up to the light.

"Beauty," I said.

She turned to smile at me.

"I use B.C. as I am not really into all these modern ideas," said Rhiannon. "A Rowan cannot jump into every modern fad. Obviously."

"Common Era was in use in the early 1700s," said Traka. "It was broadly adopted by Jewish scholars in the 1800s."

"It is new compared to this bowl," countered Rhiannon.

"Hmm. This type of bowl is made with a mold. They took a flat sheet of glass and set it upon the upside-down mold. They then added the ribs radiating from the center like the rays of the sun. Simple, but truly beautiful," said Traka.

"And *this* bowl was used ritually here at the Asklepion. Perhaps we will have just Peter test this one?"

"Seriously?" I said.

"It is rather fragile, my love," said Rhiannon.

"Fine," I muttered.

Peter took the objet d'art from Rhiannon's two hands using only his left hand. He examined the bowl closely, holding it again to the light, bringing it close to his face, inhaling deeply.

"I do feel a warm glow, but I think it is the wine," said Peter.

"Perhaps I will take that," said Rhiannon. And she did, resting it back in its bed of straw and closing the lid.

"Any story behind this one?" I asked. "No human blood, I trust."

"No," said Traka. "But the story of acquisition is quite complicated."

"How so?" asked Peter.

"Let us just say that I spoke from experience when I told you that three-person relationships do not end well," said Traka.

"Oh ho!" said Peter.

"I was not always seventy-five years old, young man," said Traka.

"Point taken," said Peter. "Please accept my sincere apology."

"Accepted," said Traka.

I returned the glass bowl in its case to the shelf, then returned to sit beside Chaney.

"Box number three?" asked Rhiannon.

"Oh, box number three is right up your alley, Cameron," said Traka. She lifted it from the table and passed it into my hands.

"This is a bit like Christmas, when I was a kid," I said.

This box, too, was like the first, only slightly larger. I slid open the lid. Within a bedding of straw lay a shallow, copper bowl, perhaps twenty-five centimeters in diameter. I removed it from the case and held it up to the light. All around the bowl's exterior, relief images adorned the copper. Six separate panels depicted early Celtic scenes.

"You will note the style is the same as that of the Gundestrup cauldron," said Traka. "Though this piece is in copper, not silver."

"Into my hands with that!" commanded Rhiannon.

Now, you may consider this command a touch rude or ill mannered, but one must respect a person's significant areas of interest. And, in the case of my beloved, ancient Celtic artifacts were more than an area of interest. The word obsession vaults into mind.

I passed her the bowl.

Rhiannon held it up so she could see the underside clearly. She turned the bowl slowly, identifying each panel as she did so.

"Cernunnos, obviously," said Rhiannon. "The horns on his head and the way he sits cross-legged are almost identical to the caldron. The three carnyx players. The woman with sword riding a bull. Naked warriors with shields. Deer and boars. Ah, and the sacrifice of a bull. Fascinating."

"This one came to me as a gift," said Traka. "A dear, old gentleman friend from my youth left it to me in his will. The bowl traces back through his family-line in northern France. His roots sprung from the Belgae, you see."

"And the link to the Grail?" asked Peter, taking the bowl from Rhiannon.

"Just family legend," said Traka. "But I include it amongst the three for sentimental reasons."

"Well done," I said.

"Thank you, dear," said Traka. "I have often thought that it is just a bit too close to the Gundestrup caldron, if you know what I mean. But I have never had the heart to get the metal properly dated."

"A forgery, you mean?" I asked.

"One likes to think not," said Traka.

"Indeed," I said.

Peter passed the bowl back to me so I could examine it. As I held it up to catch the light, I noticed that Cernunnos' eyes sparkled.

"Cernunnos' eyes are glinting," I said.

"Well done, Cameron," said Traka. "They are inset glass."

"Far out," I said.

"Back to me, please," said Rhiannon.

I passed it back, via Peter.

"No, you cannot keep it," I said.

"I'm afraid that I have already promised these to the local archeological museum," said Traka. "But not till I am gone! More wine, Cameron!"

"Yes, ma'am," I said. I poured.

"No special vibes," said Peter. "I feel I should note it."

"Thank you, dear," said Traka.

Rhiannon returned the bowl to its case and slid the lid shut. She handed it back to Traka.

"An impressive reminder of how long you have been seeking the Grail," said Rhiannon. "I apologize for making assumptions about your life."

"Not at all," said Traka. "I apologize for my tone."

"Cameron," said Peter. "I believe we find ourselves in the rare circumstance where you have nothing to apologize for."

Traka cackled at this, sounding rather too much like a character from Macbeth.

"Which rather does bring us back to the question: what are we going to do now?" I said. "I mean, personally, I am happy to go sailing off into the Aegean with Rhiannon and Peter; but, you know, if there is a chance to find the actual Grail…"

"Obviously, you need to go and spend the night in the sacred grove above the Asklepion," said Traka.

"Obviously," said Rhiannon.

"Obviously not!" said Peter. "Not when there are nasty Nazi wannabes out there roaming the woods!"

"I am afraid I have to side with Peter on this one," I said. "Wolves, fine. Psychos with scythes, no."

"Perhaps, yes, but perhaps not quite yet yes," said Traka. "Perhaps you need to set yourselves a longer timeframe. You do have eleven months, after all."

"Not really," I said. "I will need to get back sooner, rather than later to get back into my training regimen. The Lord of Summer can't be a cake walk, after all. You will remember that if I don't put in my best effort, win or lose, the ritual fails. And time does have a way of slipping away."

"Tut," said Peter.

"You tut me, sir?" I said.

He giggled at that.

"Tut, I say. We will stay here on Kos," he said. "And I will train you. I am far more qualified than your drinking buddy."

"I can't question that," I said. "But…"

"I am not going to go back to your valley and share you with your wife for God's sake," said Peter. "Especially when she is shagging a stranger under your own roof!"

"Peter, it is possible that you have had too much wine," said Traka.

"Indeed. We do seem to have crossed a certain Rubicon, however," I said.

"A heavy, rain-swollen and tumultuous Rubicon," said Rhiannon.

"My apologies, once again," said Peter. "But, seriously…"

"Seriously," cut in Rhiannon. "I am forced to agree with Peter. No good will it do me to return to the valley. At a minimum, the mother-daughter relationship would not benefit."

"It is settled then," said Traka.

"Do I get a say?" I asked.

Peter stood, slipped past Chaney, and settled in my lap, kissing my forehead.

"No," he said.

Traka snorted at this, spraying lovely shiraz onto her sweater. "I have to say, I haven't had this much fun in years! Besides, you still have your remaining postcards to explore and, scant as the clues are, I suggest that you will need to research them thoroughly – not the way they are now, but how they were during the time of the Italian occupation. And the best place to do that is here in my library."

"That is tremendously kind," said Rhiannon.

"Not at all," said Traka. "I would invite you to stay here, but I don't have a bed big enough for the three of you."

"Stay for too much longer at the Hotel Starry Blue Skies we shall not," said Rhiannon.

"You will need to rent a place," said Traka.

"You have a nephew?" I asked.

Traka looked at me like I was the slow child, not unkindly, but still…

"I will call him tomorrow," she said. "I will explain your specific requirements."

"Hot tub," said Peter.

"Trees," I said.

"Rhiannon?" asked Traka.

"Fine," said Rhiannon. "And walking distance from your villa?"

"Understood," said Traka. "And later, after we make certain no scythed and hooded folks are about, Cameron can dream in the grove – ideally on a rainy night with lightning and thunder."

"Yes," said Rhiannon.

"Acceptable," said Peter.

"Good professor, you seem a little too fascinated by the whole mythic dreaming thing," I said. "Perhaps you should be the one drinking the bitter dregs from the unsanitary clay cup."

"Certainly not," said Traka. "I promise you, though, I will be taking notes. Because you are quite correct, dear boy. I am utterly fascinated. Utterly."

CHAPTER SEVEN – THE ISLAND
INTERLUDE

Kos, Greece

Rhiannon allowed us stay within the warm and fuzzy womb of the Hotel Starry Blue Skies for three more weeks. I remember this time – pampered and watched over by the hotel staff, with no immediate responsibilities or duties – as a golden time, seemingly without barriers of time delineation or cause and effect. Peter, Rhiannon and I settled into a harmonious languor, unmoved by external influences, untouched by disharmony.

Rain or shine, mornings began – not too early, I assure you – with Peter and I taking a run along the beach. These runs in the cool November salt air along the packed, wet sand, the Mediterranean waves playing tag with our feet, ended with a shower and light breakfast in the hotel restaurant.

Who would not want to start the day with fresh pastries and buns, soft local cheese, sliced peaches or melon, yoghurt with honey, local traditional lemon or orange marmalade, olives, boiled eggs, fresh orange juice, and tea or strong, dark coffee? As most people do, we quickly staked out our spot, a table for six by the expanse of plate glass windows overlooking the dunes and sea. In the morning, only a few other transient tribes, families or business folk, passed through the restaurant. We watched them come and go, playing the guessing game – what was the nature of their relationships, where were they bound? We shared the *International Herald Tribune*, spreading it out across the table and squabbling good naturedly over the crossword.

Our improbable relationship solidified. I loved and adored Rhiannon, of course. And Peter? Is there anyone on the entire globe who could resist falling deeply in love with him? I sincerely doubt it.

And for reasons inexplicable, they both adored me.

I understood that Rhiannon had to be the boss – there always must be a boss and no one would ever be Rhiannon's. Being the ruler is a role she knows all too well, and she does it well. Everyone is recognized and everyone has a say. At the end of the day, everyone is content. Peter may or may not have accepted this reality, but at least he pretended to and that was good enough. As we all acknowledged, I was transient. With Rhiannon as the boss, Peter and I could be twelve years old – embracing food, wine, the sea, love, all with child-like joy and wonder.

We began to learn our way around Traka's library. Peter did most of the heavy lifting: Latin, Italian and Ancient Greek are opaque to me. Books and scrolls flowed through his hands like sand. I honed Traka's axe to a guillotine sharpness and laid in a winter store of olive wood.

Everyone has a time in their lives where they say, "I wish it could have gone on forever". Our time at the Hotel Starry Blue Skies is that time for me.

By the time we bid goodbye to Yiani Papadopolous with much hugging and cheek kissing, my wound had healed cleanly, leaving only a thin scar. Somehow, we had managed to acquire a new suitcase and fill it with new clothing. And our new home awaited.

In the end, Peter and Rhiannon pooled their funds and, I rather suspect, mine as well, and bought a masionette up in amongst the silver-green of the olive groves in the countryside above Traka's villa. They made the purchase during the first day of the first week of our idyll at the Hotel Starry Blue Skies.

This three-story, whitewashed building of reinforced poured concrete finished with lime plaster inside and out is traditionally squared in design with a flat roof, reflecting both local style choices, climate, and regulation earthquake-resistant engineering. The ground floor features a shiny, new, open-concept kitchen, living room and dining room. The first floor offers two bedrooms and a utilitarian washroom. The second floor boasts one oversized master bedroom – with its own large, luxurious bathroom. Floors are of terracotta tile. Stairs and entrance ways are of white marble. All the medium-sized, sliding windows include exterior, louvered, white, metal shutters to keep out the summer heat.

There is no hot tub. The bathtub in the master bedroom is a massive, kidney-shaped whirlpool.

Sliding doors open from the living room onto a large, squared-stone paved patio surrounded by a waist-high, rough sandstone wall. The patio surrounds a solar-heated swimming pool sparkling ostentatiously in the sun. Apparently, this pool mitigated the lack of a hot tub.

An olive grove surrounds the house, rolling down toward Traka's villa, and up toward Mount Dikaios. A small, single vehicle garage lay twenty meters beyond the house.

This house was the first we looked at, initially with a view to renting it. However, during that first visit to the new and empty house, Peter made the following remarks, in this order.

"The ground floor is all open!"

"Oh, I love the kitchen."

"There is *so* much light, from all sides."

"There is a patio. I could grow herbs."

"There is a pool!"

"Cameron, do you know how to pick olives? I will teach you."

"These bedrooms are way too small."

"Oh, *this* bedroom is perfect! The bathroom is perfect. You can see everywhere!"

"Where do these stairs go? Oh. My. God. A roof deck for sunbathing."

And, the clincher, revisiting the second level, quietly...

"This will be the nursery."

At that, Rhiannon, looked at him and smiled, saying, "Cameron?"

There was nothing to be done.

"Lao Tzu said: Life is a series of natural and spontaneous changes. Don't resist them; that only creates sorrow. Let reality be reality. Let things flow naturally forward in whatever way they like. How could I argue with that?" I said.

So, they bought the house.

It stood empty, devoid of furnishings. Peter anointed the second day of our idle at the Hotel Starry Blue Skies a furnishing quest. He did not require my presence.

There are many furniture stores on the island of Kos, filled with lovely furniture -- antiques, modern Euro-pop, Scandinavian styles, even build-to-design. At the end of the day, upon returning to soak in the tub, Peter only pouted. Rhiannon advised that none of the shops met Peter's needs.

"I will make some calls," said Peter.

You likely already know this but, apparently, there are different styles of furniture. One of these is the Arts and Crafts style of the early 1900s, which, admittedly, sounds like something plopped together by a three-year-old. When I learned that Peter's Paris apartment leaned in the direction of Arts and Crafts I came to understand that such a thing could not be so. Think of William Morris and Frank Lloyd Wright, hand-crafted, anti-industrial, oak and mahogany, marble, tile inlays, and straight, simple, lines.

Calls were made.

Shipping was arranged.

Rhiannon said it was bad luck to buy the baby furniture yet.

More calls were made. Shipping was rearranged. Two weeks passed. A shipping container arrived in the port. Peter took care of everything. All of it.

When we walked out of the pouring rain through the door of our new home, all was ready, roomy and beautiful. In the end, Peter had shipped the entire contents of his apartment and a few other select items. One could not claim he lacked commitment.

"Do you like it?" he asked. "Do you?"

"Peter, in my case, it is pearls cast before swine, but, yes, it is amazing," I said. "Stylish. Homey. Warm. All at the same time."

"All true," said Rhiannon. "Amazing."

I put my arm around him. "Well done, my boy."

His face turned bright pink.

"Well, now that Nikos is gone, I am going for a swim!" said Peter.

"It is cold and rainy…" I began, but he had already started flinging off his attire and heading toward the sliding glass doors.

"Apparently clothing optional is our pool," said Rhiannon.

"Inevitable, I suppose," I said.

Peter opened the sliding glass door and posed in the doorway.

"Cameron, I bought you a present," he said. "You will find it in the garage behind our house."

He exited. We heard a splash as he entered the water.

I turned to Rhiannon.

"In the garage," she said.

We found three umbrellas in a wicker stand near the front door. I took the largest and Rhiannon and I shared it as we crunched up the gravel drive to the garage. I grabbed the handle and raised the blue, metal garage door. Inside we found a brightly polished, white, 1983 Citroën Méhari compact, two-door, 4x4 SUV.

"He truly loves you," said Rhiannon.

"It is beautiful," I said.

"You are starting to cry," observed Rhiannon.

"I am not," I said. "Dust was thrown into the air when I opened the door."

"Uh-huh," she said.

Establishing any new family relationship is bound to come with a few ups and downs as roles, duties and acceptable behaviors evolve. Our little tribe was no different, I suppose.

I wanted to do the grocery shopping and cook our meals. Peter laughed at this idea, which hurt a little. He assumed the role, being an admittedly brilliant cook. I was permitted to grill outside on charcoal and make salads, but Peter insisted on making the dressing.

Rhiannon assigned me the house cleaning and laundry, and Peter responsibility for all things related to the olive grove and the pool. Rhiannon assumed all of the grownup tasks – paying bills, banking, and interacting with outsiders on business matters.

After an unfortunate event involving a wonderful bouillabaisse Peter had created for dinner, we all agreed on two new rules: no sex during meals and that a first aid kit must be fully stocked and available on all three levels of the house.

Rhiannon and Peter endured a few days of coolness during their debate over whether we would celebrate Christmas or Saturnalia. In the end, Peter's pout carried the day and Rhiannon agreed we would celebrate Christmas.

Peter and I ran every morning, rain or shine, up into the hills above our home. Three days a week, we sparred in the olive orchard. Peter began to train me in corps-à-corps, a mix of funky French Savate boxing and judo. This is the brutal, practical martial art used by the French military.

Two days a week, we practiced with weighted staves to simulate axe fighting. I did a little better with the staves, getting my butt kicked less severely.

Rhiannon sometimes came to watch the corps-à-corps training, but refused to come near us when we practiced with staves. Sometimes she stopped our training until my bruises healed.

In the mornings when I awoke, I would still find Rhiannon with her head on my chest, drooling, and Peter snuggled up against her back, always in his blue, Hello Kitty pajamas.

Thus, we migrated from our vacation trio into a family.

December 20. I remember the date.

Just a little before dinner time, after a morning sparring with Peter and an afternoon on my own, I arrived home from the hot mineral spring Aqua Therme in Agios Fokas. There, at the base of the cliffs, in the pool formed by a circle of rock in the sea, I had soaked away the aches of my muscles and joints, alternating 20 minutes of soaking with plunges into the chill Aegean.

The house showed no lights, only quiet darkness. Normally, Peter would be well into preparing supper and the house would smell of fresh basil and garlic and sizzling olive oil. He would turn, flashing a smile from the kitchen and point to the chosen wine. I would open it and pour three glasses.

But that day the house lay empty. I did a quick tour, calling out for them. No answer. Feeling a strange sense of dread, I jogged from our home to Traka's villa. The front door opened easily. Inside, I could hear quiet voices from the library. I made my way stealthily through the courtyard to the back of the house and listened at the door. I could hear Traka, Rhiannon and Peter. I slowly opened the door only to see the three of them gathered around one end of the large table. Peter stood, leaning forward, his right hand splayed over a large, aged leather tome. Traka sat to his left, holding open an unrolled scroll on the table. Rhiannon sat to Peter's left, leaning back, her arms crossed.

Traka jerked her head up and looked to the door.

"Do not skulk, Cameron," she said. "For goodness sake, you will give an old lady a stroke."

"Sorry," I said. "No one was home. I got worried."

Peter and Rhiannon turned as one toward me. Rhiannon glanced down at her watch, a lovely 1930s art-deco Bulova with a black-rope band. I do love buying them jewelry.

"Oh, Cameron," said Rhiannon. "I am so sorry."

Peter gave a slight bow. "Sorry to have worried you," he said.

I headed toward the table, whilst Rhiannon pushed back her chair and stepped forward to put her arms around me, kissing my cheek and petting my hair.

"You must have been so worried to arrive here in ninja mode," said Rhiannon. "Alright, are you?"

I looked over at Peter.

"You heard me at the front door, didn't you?" I asked.

He nodded. "A ninja you are not."

I kissed Rhiannon on the lips. "I think we will let Peter do all our ninjaing."

"Also, don't think for a minute that I haven't noticed that you two are treating me more and more like a child every day, eh? I can withstand a little worry. So, you really don't have to, you know?"

"We are not," said Rhiannon.

"Ahem," said Traka. "You certainly are."

"Well, he must be our petit chou-fleur," said Peter. "At least until he fulfills his responsibilities."

"Ahem, again," said Traka. "Not in the library. Or, at least, not in my library."

"Of course," said Peter.

"Excellent," I said. Which I have found serves as a fine transition to new, more desirable topics.

"So, what's up?"

"We have something," said Peter with a huge grin.

"We do not," said Traka with the anti-grin.

"We may have something," said Rhiannon. "It is too soon to tell."

She sniffed my chest.

"You smell like Satan," she said.

"Cameron, the sulfur will ruin your clothes," said Traka. "Go and shower and throw your clothing in the wash."

"We can discuss this…" she gestured to the scroll in front of her, "over dinner."

"Good idea," said Rhiannon. "Peter can begin dinner. I will set the table for four."

"I think Cameron needs someone to clean his back," said Peter.

Rhiannon sighed.

"Peter," said Traka, kindly. "You may have better luck getting a bun in the oven if you relax, just a little."

"It is not *all* about getting pregnant," said Peter.

"I understand," said Traka. "But, now that I have successfully invited myself to your home to enjoy your wonderful cooking, I suggest you head for the kitchen."

"Barefoot, not pregnant and in the kitchen," said Peter. "It seems so incomplete."

"Peter, you have a tendency to collapse one hundred years of feminism in an instant," said Traka.

"He tends to collapse most ideologies," said Rhiannon.

"Ideologies are the opium of the chattering classes. And, I do not like to be put in someone else's box," said Peter.

Rhiannon kissed me and pushed me away. "Go. De-sulfur."

I went home and showered, by myself. In half an hour, Peter had prepared a dinner of baked salmon, rubbed with olive oil, garlic and rosemary, and rice, and salad. For the wine, Peter chose Deipnos, a blend of Merlot and Cabernet Sauvignon grapes from the Triantafillopoulos winery. Remembering that Traka would join us, I dressed in a flowery Hawaiian-style shirt and shorts.

As I came down the stairs, I saw the table set with a white tablecloth, Peter's 1950s French Navy dinnerware – white crockery with a small, blue fouled anchor design and crisp blue nautical rope motif around the edges. The tapered, beeswax candles flipped and flickered in their silver candelabra.

Rhiannon blew out the long, wooden match in her hand and turned to see me on the stairs. Smoke curled up from the match. She wore her long, white, semi-transparent dress with a gold torc. Peter, in the kitchen, wore his light blue, sequined, knee-length dress and an apron. He was barefoot.

"You are both more than lovely," I said.

Peter turned to me and smiled.

Rhiannon looked me up and down and said, "Change. The good professor will be here soon."

"But Traka will be wearing her usual heavy-wool sweater and trousers," I said.

"My love, please change," said Peter.

I went back upstairs and put on a pressed, short-sleeve, white shirt and grey trousers. I tried again.

"Do I pass?" I asked.

"Mais bien sûr," said Peter.

A nod from Rhiannon. "Now, you may open the wine."

I found the corkscrew in the kitchen, stopped to give Peter a kiss on the top of his head, opened the wine and set it on the table to air.

"Anything I can do?" I asked.

"The good professor will be cold. Could you light a fire, please?" said Peter.

I watched him for a few moments as he used a copper funnel to pour dried chives, olive oil and balsamic vinegar into a glass bottle. He shook it vigorously.

"You know, everything you do in the kitchen is infused with a deep sense of purpose," I said.

"No. All that I do in the kitchen is infused with a deep sense of love," said Peter. "Idiot."

"My mistake," I said.

By the time Traka knocked on our front door, the fire tripped the light fantastic in the fireplace. After a count of about thirty, she opened the door and came in.

"Yes, I have learned to knock," she said. "Though, sometimes I am tempted not to, just for fun!"

The kissing ritual materialized again, even though less than an hour had passed since we last saw her. I do not understand this ritual at all.

"Peter, it smells wonderful," said Traka.

"Thank you kindly," said Peter. "All is ready."

He waved us to our seats and set a platter laden with a goodly-sized salmon fillet, elegantly dressed in fresh rosemary, in the center of the table. The village salad and a covered dish of rice already waited at either side.

"Cameron," he said. "You may pour."

I poured and, as I returned to my seat, I wondered why they were being so kind. Laying and lighting the fire. Pouring the swirling red wine. Pretty translucent dresses. The light and scent from the beeswax candles. All amongst my favorite things.

I decided not to question my good fortune and enjoy the moment.

"A toast, please, Cameron," said Rhiannon. "No pressure."

"I revisited one of my favorites this afternoon at the hot springs," I said. "Will a quote do?"

"We shall see," said Traka.

"Being deeply loved by someone gives you strength, while loving someone deeply gives you courage," I said.

"Lao Tzu?" asked Traka.

"Obviously," said Peter. "Either that or a Thor comic."

"Well chosen, Cameron," said Rhiannon. "And I am sure something from one of your Thor graphic novels would also have been perfect."

"Um, thank you," I said.

We clinked our glasses. Peter served the salmon with his large-bladed, excessively floral-decorated, white-handled fish server and matching fish fork.

"Peter," said Traka. "Are those handles ivory?"

"Narwhal," said Peter. "Circa 1910."

"Hmm," said Traka.

"It was dead before my mother was born," said Peter.

I lifted the lid from the rice. Steam rose up catching the candlelight.

"Peter, do I smell saffron and garlic?" I asked.

"You do!" said Peter. "Well done."

"Oh!" said Traka. "Rice please."

Rhiannon served the village salad – tomato and cucumber, thinly sliced sweet onion and tender kalamata olives.

"Peter, there is no feta on the salad," said Traka.

"Professor. It is simply not possible to add enough feta to a salad to sate your needs," said Peter. "Please lift the napkin off the dish to your left."

The removal of the napkin revealed a large block of feta and a large Santoku knife with hollows in the blade. Traka leaned forward and sniffed the cheese. She smiled.

"The same cheese you serve at your home," said Peter. "I had your housekeeper buy me a large crock of it. I will never *not* have it when you visit. The inadequate feta cheese issue is resolved."

"I never commented on your feta," said Traka. "Ever."

"You sniffed at my feta, negatively," said Peter.

"I would never have done such a thing!" said Traka.

"Lunch on the 17th, I believe," I said. "Definite negative sniffing."

"Oh dear," said Traka. "I do apologize. Peter, can you forgive me?"

"Try this feta," said Peter.

She did, cutting herself a good-sized slice and using her fingers to break off a chunk for tasting.

"Creamy, dry, perfect," said Traka.

"I forgive you," said Peter.

Traka broke the feta over her salad.

"Excellent salmon," I said.

"Thank you, kindly," said Peter.

"Ποτήριον," said Traka.

"Potérion?" I asked.

"Close enough," said Traka.

"Cup, Cameron," said Rhiannon. "It means cup."

"Oh," I said. "And?"

"It is our little hint," said Peter. "We found a discussion of the potérion being transferred to Nerantzia, the castle, from a monastery in the early 1500s."

"It could mean anything," said Traka. "It could be referring to part of the religious service for the host."

"It spoke of the Knights of Saint John, the cup's guardians, who were transferred with the cup," said Peter. "Why would a normal church cup require guardians?"

"Guardians is only one possible translation," said Traka.

"Forgive me," I said. "Let us imagine for a moment that this potérion was the Grail. Let us say we know where it was in the early 1500s. Didn't the Ottoman Turks invade in 1566? And didn't the Turk part of the castle blow up in 1816? And didn't they stay until 1912 when the Italians took over? Wasn't all lost during the invasion and occupation?"

"Pas nécessairement," said Peter. "The castle did not fall to siege. It was surrendered by the knights after the fall of Rhodos. They made an orderly withdrawal, ultimately to Malta."

"So, they took it with them?" I asked.

"That is where it gets interesting," said Rhiannon. "Not necessarily so. They may have hidden it here, on the island."

"According to our text," said Rhiannon, "they were afraid of losing it to the sea."

"And what is this text, anyway?" I asked.

"Well, that is where it all gets a touch dubious," said Peter.

"A touch?" said Traka.

"The book we found it in is the work of a rather questionable Oslo scholar named Professor Saknussemm. It appears to be part of a small, limited edition series of his work produced by Oxford University Press in the late 1800s," said Peter.

"He was a whack job," said Traka. "Totally off his rocker. He was here on Kos researching the Templars and the Templars were never even here!"

"Was he researching the Grail?" I asked.

"He was more of a geologist," said Peter. "But he did have an interest in lost civilizations, so did delve into history."

"He was likely here as a spy," said Rhiannon. "It was quite common for the British to use academics as agents in those days."

"Hence his work being published by Oxford?" said Peter. "Nice work, my dear."

"Any suggestion as to where the cup was kept?" I asked.

"Allegedly in a domed room near the gatehouse of the inner ward," said Rhiannon.

"Oh, I have been there!" I said.

"You have been to the castle?" said Peter. "Without me?"

"Um. Maybe," I said. "I do wander around a bit when you two are spending the afternoon in Traka's den of iniquity."

"If only!" said Traka.

"So, you have been to the castle," said Peter.

"Yes," I said.

"On your own," said Peter.

"Yes," I said.

"Without me or Rhiannon," said Peter.

"Yes," I said.

"Even though we three agreed we would go together?" said Peter.

"We can still go together," I said. "That I went by myself does not mean that we all cannot go."

"It was implied that we would all go together the first time," said Peter.

"I was walking past. The entrance has a beautiful stone bridge. It was open..." I said.

"There was a pretty girl walking in. You followed her," said Rhiannon.

"There was a pretty girl walking in, but I did not follow her," I said. "Really."

"Cameron's countless moral lapses aside," said Traka. "There is a large, domed room atop one of the towers near the gate to the inner ward. With no record of its use, most assume it was a gunpowder store. But that never made sense, as it is at the top of a tower."

"It is all bare stone," I said. "Except for the ancient Greek inscriptions, of course. And I don't have countless moral lapses."

"Why are there ancient inscriptions in a medieval fortification?" asked Peter.

"The castle was built largely by pilfering stone from the ancient Roman town, which in turn had absorbed many older Greek constructions," said Traka. "There are bits of ancient Rome and Greece sticking out all over the castle."

"It is pretty cool, actually," I said.

"Peter, we can all go together," said Rhiannon.

"Fine," said Peter.

"And, Cameron?" she said.

"Yes?" I asked.

"It was implied that we would go together," said Rhiannon. "Bad dog."

"I apologize," I said.

Traka started laughing.

"You three, seriously," she said. "Cameron, pour me some more wine!"

I poured for the four of us, silently thanking Traka.

"Did Professor Saknussemm have anything else to add?" I asked.

"He claims to have read some church documents suggesting that the cup was hidden in the castle in the time when Fabrizio del Carretto was Grand Master of the order," said Peter.

151

"But he cannot be trusted!" said Traka. "He is an unreliable narrator of his own adventures. It is well known."

"Rhiannon, if he were spying on the Turks for the British, then might there not be something in the intelligence archives back home?" I asked.

"Oh, good boy," said Peter. "But even if there is something..."

"Check it I will," said Rhiannon. "Tomorrow, I will telephone."

"You can do that?" asked Traka.

Rhiannon smiled and nodded.

"Rhiannon's family goes way back, apparently," said Peter. "She got Cameron a British passport with a wave of her hand."

"Not quite," said Rhiannon.

"Pretty much," I said.

"Silence is golden," said Rhiannon.

"My error," said Peter.

"I see," said Traka.

"So, tomorrow the castle?" I asked.

"Only if it is not raining," said Traka. "The worn, stone steps are treacherous when wet."

"The next dry day, then," said Rhiannon.

"It will close over Christmas," said Traka.

"The next dry day it is open then," said Peter.

"You are always rushing," said Traka. "Slow down, enjoy the journey."

Peter and Rhiannon looked down to their plates.

"Oh, Cameron, I am sorry," said Traka.

"That is okay," I said. "Your advice is still good. Ten months is still quite a while. If only we could slow down time itself."

"If only," said Rhiannon.

"I will make it up to you," said Traka. "I promise. You would think that by my age I would have learnt to think before I speak."

"No worries, professor, really," I said.

"No, you all struggle so to remain upbeat. I must be more careful," said Traka. "Rhiannon, may I give him his Christmas gift now?"

"Now?" asked Peter.

"You are trying to get pregnant, after all," said Traka.

"That is true..." allowed Peter.

"Um?" I said.

Rhiannon stood. "Please give us a few moments. Come with me, Peter." She took him by the hand and led him upstairs.

"Good professor?" I asked.

"Patience, my child. All will be revealed," said Traka. 'Make yourself useful and pour me a little more wine."

"It is a good thing you live downhill," I said, topping up her glass.

"It is, isn't it?" said Traka. And she cackled.

"What have you done?" I asked.

The electric lights flickered, came back on, then died, leaving the room in candle and firelight.

"Not again," said Traka.

"Indeed," I said.

"Can you light another candelabra?" asked Traka.

"Of course," I said.

It took me a few minutes to find the second silver candelabra, set the candles and light them. Five candles put off quite a bit of heat, so I held it at arms' length as I carried it to the table.

"There, that is plenty of light," said Traka. "And very pretty, too."

"It is," I agreed.

"Cameron," said Traka. She pointed to the stairs.

Rhiannon and Peter stood on the stairs, each holding a single candle. Peter stood two steps behind Rhiannon.

"Oh, thanks to all the gods," I said and took one step toward them.

Rhiannon and Peter both posed, barefoot, in perfectly fitting maids' outfits, black, knee-length dresses with little white aprons and white ruffles, well, everywhere, and little white caps. And, yes, cats' ears. I inhaled, deeply.

"Takes the breath away," I said.

"So, you like it then?" said Rhiannon.

"So, you like it then, meow?" corrected Peter. He gave a little curtsey.

"Must I?" said Rhiannon.

"In for a penny…" said Traka.

"So, you like it then, *meow*?" said Rhiannon.

"I do. I do very much," I said. "You are so insanely kind."

I took another step toward them.

"Come into the light so I can see you," I said.

Rhiannon took one step forward. Peter blew out his candle with an air kiss and bounded toward me, recoiling at the last second, only stopping himself by placing his open hand against my chest.

"Cameron, your shirt. You are bleeding, meow," he said.

He held up his hand. Blood covered his palm and fingers, like finger-paint. I looked down to see that my white shirt would be ruined.

"Take off your shirt," said Rhiannon. She descended the stairs and walked forward.

I did so, passing it to Peter.

"Your wound has opened," said Rhiannon. She took the apron from her outfit and wiped away the blood.

"Almost the entire cut has opened," she said.

"It had completely healed," I said, and sighed.

"Rhiannon, prepare the envelope. I will call the doctor," said Traka.

She made the call, but by the time the doctor arrived an hour later, Peter and Rhiannon had bandaged the wound to stem the flow and the bleeding had stopped. The doctor examined the wound carefully, then rebandaged it.

"What have you been up to?" asked the doctor. He did not look at Rhiannon and Peter.

"Physical training, meow," said Peter.

The doctor looked over to him.

"Judo, meow," said Peter.

"Well, no value in stitching it again," said the doctor. "But, no more physical training for a month."

"Doctor?" asked Traka.

"It should not have opened, auntie," said the doctor. "I will prescribe antibiotics and return in a week to check the wound."

"Cameron, you need to take it easy," said the doctor. "No heavy lifting or strenuous exercise."

"Sex, meow?" asked Peter.

The doctor's shoulders sank.

"He can go on the bottom," said the doctor. Then, he perked up and smiled.

He turned to Peter and wagged his finger. "But be gentle with him, meow?"

"Yes, doctor, meow," said Peter.

The good doctor refused the envelope and departed.

I sat at the table and slumped forward.

"Cameron, you will be fine," said Rhiannon.

"I know," I said. "But the maids' outfits are covered in blood, just ruined!"

"Not if we soak them in cold water immediately, meow!" said Peter.

He began to strip.

"Quick, Rhiannon. Give me your outfit, meow," said Peter.

Rhiannon looked over to Traka. Traka took a deep sip of wine.

"Don't look at me," said Traka. "I'm staying to finish my dinner."

"And to watch," I said.

"Damn straight," said Traka.

I changed into my original outfit, the flowery Hawaiian shirt and shorts. Rhiannon pulled on an old sweatshirt and jeans. Peter chose a dress shirt, slacks and blue blazer. We regrouped at the table.

"Well done," said Traka. "No reason to let a little blood disturb a fine dinner."

"Quite right," said Peter.

"Does it hurt?" asked Rhiannon.

"Not really," I said. "It more tingles, really."

"I didn't know that the good doctor was your nephew?"

"He is," said Traka. "But on the wrong side of the sheets, as it were. He is one of my brother's adventures."

"Oh!" said Peter. "How exciting."

"His wife didn't think so at the time," said Traka. "She finds the boy useful enough these days, though."

"Never hurts to have a doctor in the family," said Peter.

"Indeed," I said.

"Cameron?" said Rhiannon.

"I admit to feeling a little down," I said. "I thought we were past that particular hurdle. And our most recent clue is rather weak. No offence, Peter."

"None taken, my love," said Peter.

"Do not be concerned," said Traka. "We will visit the castle and have a time of it. And I will arrange for you to have a night in the sacred grove by the Asklepion. You can take the dogs for security."

"Interesting," said Rhiannon. "Two paths forward we have."

"And, I am feeling really fertile," said Peter. "I am having positive thoughts."

"How can you feel…" I began.

"Cameron!" said Traka and Rhiannon, simultaneously.

"Right," I said. "Also, you know the museum at the castle is pretty good, eh? I remembered Grand Master Fabrizio del Carretto when you mentioned him. He did quite a bit to bring the castle on Kos up to snuff with new weapons and provisions. He was the last grand master to die on Rhodes."

"So, if he was the dude in charge when the Grail was hidden, then maybe we need to dig a little deeper into him?"

"Not bad, Cameron," said Traka. "You can become quite lucid when you are drinking and not playing the fool."

"I do not play the fool!" I said.

Peter stood.

"Cameron, I did mention that I am feeling fertile," he said.

"Bleeding he is," said Rhiannon.

"Care not I do," said Peter.

He came around the table and took my hand.

"Come on, then," he said. "I will go on top. It will not be strenuous."

I followed him up the stairs. I waited until he closed the bedroom door.

"Peter, you are just trying to get out of doing the dishes," I said.

"Not just," said he.

It drizzled. It deluged. Christmas came and vanished in a pop of ribbons and glitter, the way it always does.

The doctor came. He took blood and sent it for testing. The wound healed, slowly. The test results came back. I had no autoimmune disorder.

Peter planted a vast herb garden in the rain, whilst naked. He planted one dozen giant white plastic pots: parsley, sage, rosemary, thyme, garlic, marjoram, oregano, lavender, basil, tarragon, and mint in five different flavors. I watched him through the glass doors as he planted. I don't think I have ever seen him happier. How he did not catch his death in the chill rain, I will never know.

Finally, in the second week of January, the sun returned, bright and warm in a clear cerulean sky. In truth, by then my mind had wandered away from our quest. I had taken to hiking in the rain, up through the olive groves onto the lower, cypress-clad slopes of Mount Dikaios to a small, stone, barrel-vault chapel set in the forest by a spring-fed fountain. There, each time I dropped a euro into a slot in a tin box and lit a thin taper to the dying gods who came before.

When it poured, I sheltered in the chapel, taking a seat off to the side and read Thoreau's *The Maine Woods* by candlelight. When it drizzled, I wandered and hunted for mushrooms. I cut them from rotten logs or mossy green slopes with a knife and put them in my wicker basket. Traka reviewed my finds when I returned, keeping the edible and lecturing me sternly over the poisonous.

Peter and Rhiannon continued to delve deep into the mysteries within Traka's library. Sometimes they would come home excited and share their finds and theories. I could see that Rhiannon spotted my feigned interest, and one evening after dinner, I found her crying alone in our room. When I told her that she would always have Peter, it only made the tears worse.

Peter's quest for motherhood continued unabated. All I can say is that it is a good thing a healthy human male produces fifteen-hundred sperm per second. That is several million sperm each day. To optimize the number of sperm reaching the egg, it is best to wait two to three days between ejaculations. I know all this because Peter researched more than just the Grail.

Rhiannon might have lost it with him once, hypothetically.

Imagine coupling with your love, quietly, so as not to disturb your companion, in the dark of the night. You move slowly, up and down, maximizing your contact at the end of each thrust. You creep slowly and steadily toward nirvana, your ample left breast in your lover's mouth. You drool on you lover's head. You are almost there. You feel a tap on your shoulder. You turn. Your companion kneels there in his blue Hello Kitty flannel pajamas.

He speaks, politely, inquisitively.

"Sorry, but he looks like he is about to burst. Can I have the liquid?"

You might reply, "No Peter you cannot have the fucking liquid! The fucking liquid is mine!"

It is just a hypothetical story because, you will understand, were that ever to have happened to anyone, theoretically, one might have to promise never to share the tale. Also, as the provider of said liquids, one absolutely should not remember and laugh quietly to oneself during dinner the next day. Or, if one does one should at least not admit what one is laughing about. One should lie.

The lie is a useful tool in relationships. And so, when Peter, who seemed somewhat subdued, said, over breakfast, "It is beautiful, bright and sunny. The good professor thinks today might be a good day to visit the castle. What do you think, Cameron?"

I said, "Excellent idea."

The castle of Neratzia is a strange, grey, massive jumble of old stones. Large ashlar blocks of sandstone, marble and granite seem tossed together in haste to create the massive presence dominating the old harbor of Kos town. The outer fortress wall stands more than five times the height of a man. Designed to defend in the early gunpowder era, this thick wall encloses a rough rectangle about one hundred by three hundred meters, surrounding a smaller, older, purely medieval castle.

Today, the front of the fortress is gentled by a beautiful avenue of towering palm trees, a broad, flagstone promenade, and vibrant flowering shrubs. Until the Italians filled it, this avenue was a wide, deep ditch flooded with sea water, the castle isolated upon its own island.

We approached the front gates across an arched stone bridge, over the flow of vehicles along the avenue below, through the open double doors and into the darkness of the long, curved, arched-ceilinged tunnel that pierces the massive wall. The bright sun blinded as we emerged once again into the morning. Pausing to let my eyes adjust, I turned to watch the others emerge into the light.

Peter, impeccably dressed in grey trousers, pressed white shirt and a blue blazer, blinked once, flipped open his 1960s-style, cat-eye-framed, tortoiseshell sunglasses and set them on his perfect nose.

Rhiannon and Traka stepped out of the darkness arm-in-arm, both dressed in blue jeans, Traka with her ever-present wool sweater and Rhiannon in a loose-fitting hooded sweatshirt, the front of which offered a drawing of a long-haired, bearded man in sunglasses and the message... "Abide".

I pointed at her.

"That," I said, "is my hoodie."

Traka and Rhiannon both smiled.

"You seem confused, my love," said Rhiannon. She pointed to the colorful drawing. "This *was* your hoodie."

Peter stepped forward to take my arm. "Now it is *ours*."

"I understand," I said, always a safe reply when one is treading new ground.

"When did hoodie become a word?" asked Traka. "When I was young it was a 'hooded sweatshirt'."

"Ahem, fashion question," said Peter. "The hooded sweatshirt was introduced in the 1930s for athletes and laborers – especially laborers in cold-storage warehouses – by Champion Products, née Knickerbocker Knitting Company. It entered popular fashion as athletes gifted their sweatshirts to their girlfriends. It began to get a bad reputation in the 1970s when graffiti sprayers, thieves and skateboarders adopted the fashion."

"Those evil skateboarders," I said.

"I know, eh?" said Peter. "Back in the day, there were no skateboard parks, so they did a lot of trespassing."

"Which does not answer my question," said Traka. "Which, by the way, was rhetorical."

"The word hoodie entered popular parlance in the 1990s," said Peter. "It is still a hooded sweatshirt, but hoodie is in the OED. It is obviously based on the Middle English hood, in turn from Old English hōd; related to the Old High German huot head covering, and huota guard."

"Fine," said Traka.

"That's enough, Peter," said Rhiannon.

"Tee-hee," said Peter.

"Grail, anybody?" I asked.

"No," said Peter. "Some of us have a legitimate, professional interest in military architecture and this fortress combines both advanced medieval and early gunpowder features. All in really good shape, relatively speaking. Let us do the grand circumnavigation of the outer walls first, then do the older works and Cameron's domed Grail room."

"Tut," said Traka.

"You tut me, madam?" said Peter.

"I do, young man. I am not circumnavigating anything," said Traka. "You and Rhiannon go ahead. Cameron will walk with me to the inner ward."

"Of course," said Peter. "I apologize, madam. Also, some of us have been here before..."

"Shouldn't we pay first?" I asked, gesturing to the small booth, occupied by a pretty, young Greek woman.

Traka smiled at the woman and waved.

"My grand-nephew's wife's sister," said Traka.

Peter waved at the woman and smiled.

Inside, the walls comprised the same jumble of massive, squared, ancient and medieval stones as the outside. To our right, a wide, gradual slope lead up to the top of the outer wall. Peter took Rhiannon's arm and headed up the slope.

"They built these slopes instead of stairs so they could move the cannons around," said Peter. "They did not have enough cannons for all of the walls."

"Poor Rhiannon," said Traka. "By the end of today she will know more about transitional military architecture than she cares to."

But as they reached the top of the broad wall, Rhiannon turned to grin at us and wave.

"Ah, she loves him so," I said. "She likes to see him happy."

"If you say so," said Traka.

"I do," I said. "Shall we?" I offered her my arm and she grasped it firmly.

Before us, broad, stone steps led down into an open, green field. Beyond the field lay the medieval inner castle. To our left, a half-buried bridge crossed the field to the castle gates.

"I know you don't really care, Cameron," said Traka, "but that ditch used to be much, much deeper."

"I do care," I said. "I came here on my own, remember."

"You were following a pretty girl," said Traka.

"Slander!" I said.

She chuckled.

"Come on," I said.

We wended our way through the scattered antiquities -- column capitals, frieze fragments, and a curious carved-marble well cap with slots worn into the stone by century upon centuries of rope lowered into and raised from a long-lost well – crossed the bridge, passed under the carved coats-of-arms of past Grand Masters, and entered the inner castle through its main gate. Halfway through the passage into the inner courtyard, Traka stopped and pointed upward.

"For me, this is the niftiest part of the fortifications," she said.

Above us, the passage roof was built from ten ancient grey columns laid crossways along the top of the tunnel.

"The knights took these columns from the basilica of the ancient port. That poor dear dated from the fifth century, but was destroyed by the 469 and 554 earthquakes," said Traka.

"They really did take anything they could get their hands on," I said. "You'd think they would have at least respected the Christian monuments."

"But this leads us to the archeologist's puzzle," said Traka. "Which do we respect, the medieval castle or the ancient basilica? When we attempt a reconstruction, do we damage one at the expense of the other? So, usually, we just leave things where we find them."

"I suppose that is the right thing to do?" I asked.

"Now you are just being polite," said Traka. "Don't worry, Cameron, I rather foresaw the day unfolding as it has. I brought a lovely Italian Chianti and some glasses."

"You didn't!" I said

"I did," said Traka. "Let us get up to the top of the wall, find a place in the sun, and pop her open."

"Because the top of a crumbling stone wall is the obvious place to drink a bottle of wine?" I asked.

"The obvious place?" she asked. "Clearly!"

She again took my arm and we exited the passageway into a lush field of green and bright yellow flowers, surrounded on four sides by the familiar rough-hewn stone walls. To our left, a gentle slope led up to the wall above the gate.

"I believe your domed room is directly at the top of that ramp," said Traka.

"Been there, done that," I said.

"I, too, have been there, you great savage," said Traka. "Try to show a little interest, at least for your harem's sake."

"They are not my harem," I said. "Two does not a harem make. A minimum of three is required. Also, if anything, Peter and I are Rhiannon's harem"

"You really are an idiot, aren't you?" said Traka.

"Rhetorical?" I asked.

"Help me up the slope, Cameron," said Traka. "There will be a nice spot in the sun where we can wait for your not-harem. Be careful, these walls are pre-gunpowder, nowhere near as wide as the outer walls. And there are no railings."

"Yes ma'am," I said. "But please do not use that word in front of them."

"I am not an idiot, child," said Traka. "Now, hold my arm firmly, this is rough going."

We slowly made our way up the broken and shattered stone surface of the ramp to the top of the castle wall. To our right, a round tower about 10 meters in diameter presented a small, dark doorway. Within, I knew, lay a large room with a domed roof of fitted stone. To the right of the door, part of a pillar lay against the wall.

"The perfect bench," said Traka. "Go check for scorpions."

"That would not be my favorite activity," I said.

"Do not be a panty-waisted Nancy boy," said Traka. "For God's sake, how do those two put up with you?"

"Maybe expendable old people should check for scorpions," I said.

But I did it, carefully too. Then I led her over and did not let go until she was comfortably seated with her back against the wall. She handed me her bag.

"Chianti is in there, idiot," she said. "Do you have your Swiss Army knife?"

"I do," I said.

"Get to work, then," she said. She closed her eyes. The rough surfaces and the climb had clearly worn her.

I opened the wine, delved into her bag to find the wineglasses wrapped in newspaper, and poured.

"That is a happy sound," she said.

I looked up to see her eyes open. I passed her a glass and sat beside her.

"Cheers," I said.

"Yiamas, savage," said Traka. She clinked my raised glass.

We tasted.

"Nice," I said.

It was my turn to close my eyes. I leaned back against the castle wall and enjoyed the sun against my eyelids.

"When you are about to go into darkness, Cameron," said Traka, "remember these precious moments."

I looked to her.

"I know, eh?" I said.

"Have you thought about what comes next? I know I have," said Traka.

"Haven't we all?" I asked. "I am hoping I get a break, 'cause of the whole dying god thing."

"Sort of like frequent flyer status?" asked Traka.

"More like business class," I said.

She chuckled. "Well, I hope you do. As for me, I sure hope there is no judge and jury."

"Been a bad girl?" I asked. "Ever hacked anyone's head off with an axe?"

She spit out her wine.

"That was a spit take," I said. "I've never seen one in real life before."

"You make a valid point," said Traka. "No, your sins are far greater than mine, mine being limited to the slimy weaseling and backstabbing of academia. Perhaps if we go at the same time, they will be distracted by you."

"You would rat me out?" I asked.

"And slip through the pearly gates in the confusion," said Traka.

I poured more wine.

"Can't fault you, I suppose," I said.

"It is the ultimate mystery," she said. "Logically, there will be only oblivion."

"I know," I said. "But Puck tells me there's babes. Like the maidens of the wells."

"Babes?" said Traka. "No way that is coming out of your subconscious, your chthonic pagan nature."

161

I laughed.

"You know, Cameron, if you want to take a Christian slant on the Grail, Wolfram said that the Grail was left here on Earth by angels who remained neutral during the tiff between God and Satan," said Traka. "These neutral angels, known as zwivelaere or doubters, opposed the divine opposites breaking apart so they guarded the Grail to help maintain balance. Who does that bring to mind, balance of the seasons man?"

"That's a bit of a stretch," I said. "I ain't no angel."

"Goodness knows," said Traka. "But the situations are thematically related, from a Jungian perspective."

"Are you going to explain it?" I asked.

She patted my knee. "No, dear. Just top up my glass and enjoy your wine."

The fortress walls sheltered us entirely from the January breezes. The sun-soaked stone radiated warmth. The Chianti gentled our collective consciousness. Silence settled, lightly. Again, I closed my eyes. Time slipped.

In time, feeling a sense of being hunted, I opened one eye. Rhiannon and Peter stood looking down at us. Peter pointed to Traka.

"Fast asleep," he whispered.

I set my wineglass down on the stones, extended my hand, and Peter pulled me up. I motioned for them to follow me and stepped through the nearby door into the darkness of the domed room. They followed.

I stopped immediately upon entering the room as the floor is broken and uneven. Peter and Rhiannon pushed up behind me.

"Careful," I said. "The floor is a little tricky."

"It stinks," said Peter.

"Rather musty," agreed Rhiannon.

Peter pulled out a flashlight and began to flick the beam around the room. The room measured about eight meters wide by four high. Both the wall and the dome were of fitted stone blocks.

"Nice workmanship, mon Seigneur," said Peter.

He began to search the room, first working his way around the edges, then circling toward the middle. Finally, he stopped dead center and shone the light up to the apex of the dome.

"Nothing," he said. "No inscriptions at all."

"The Turks would have removed anything Christian," said Rhiannon.

"Indeed," I said. "So, another dead end?"

"Maybe," said Peter, in that 'I am so much cuter than anyone else you ever have or ever will meet' way that he has. *Maaaybe.* "On the way in, did anyone else notice the three coats-of-arms in the marble carving set into the wall on the outside of this very tower?"

I raised my hand. Rhiannon shook her head.

"I do believe that the one with the two crosses and slashy things belonged to Grand Master Fabrizio del Carretto," I said.

"Yes, Cameron," said Peter. "The slashy things. Though some might say quartered with two crosses and three bends doubled."

"Some might," said Rhiannon.

"Anyway, Peter?" I asked.

"Yes, Cameron, the Fabrizio del Carretto whom, you may recall, Professor Saknussemm suggested hid the Grail," said Peter. "Though, likely the old GM would not have undertaken the task personally, of course – but his coat-of-arms, nevertheless. If you were thinking of hiding something, might you not hide it behind a big, hard-to-reach slab of marble set way up on a tower?"

"I might, granted," I said. "Shall we have a look behind it?"

"The good professor would have a fit," said Rhiannon.

"Only if we mention it," said Peter.

"Tonight? Peter and I?" I asked.

"I do not like breaking the law, and the chance of success seems slim, but I will regret it always if we do not. So, fine," said Rhiannon. "But like it, I do not. So, do not get caught. And no wine at dinner. And make sure you put the marble slab back."

Peter bounced over and took my arm, looking up into my eyes.

"An adventure," he said. "You know the most important question?"

"How are we going to move and reset that heavy slab seven odd meters above the ground?" I asked.

"No, silly god. Obviously not," said Peter.

"How to avoid the security cameras?" I asked.

"There are no security cameras," said Peter. "I looked."

"Peter, my love," said Rhiannon. "What is the most important question?"

"What are we going to wear!" said Peter.

"How foolish of me," I said. "Of course. I apologize."

"You apologize?" asked Rhiannon. "Because that is what he is worrying about? I am worrying about you sitting in a Greek jail!"

"I would never dream of diminishing our beloved's joy," I said. "And, even though I understand it not, fashion is something that gives him joy. So, I apologize."

"I understand," said Rhiannon. "But he still needs a smack on the bottom from time to time."

"I do not!" said Peter.

"That is a bit harsh," I said.

"Peter?" asked Rhiannon.

"Yes?" asked Peter.

"What is the second most important question?" asked Rhiannon.

"One hesitates to say," said Peter.

"Tell the truth, my dear," said Rhiannon.

"Whether Cameron and I will have time to make love on the roof of the domed tower?" asked Peter.

"Rhiannon, my love, I take your point," I said.

"We will be up there anyway," said Peter. "It will be a beautiful dark night. It is the new moon."

"No, Peter," said Rhiannon.

"Why not?" asked Peter.

"Because you are more than a little vocal at such times," said Rhiannon. "And you will wake the entire town."

"I can be quiet," said Peter.

"And he might fall," said Rhiannon.

"I could tie him down," said Peter.

"No, Peter. Just no," said Rhiannon.

"Fine," said Peter. "Fine." But, yes, he did pout.

We woke the good professor from a sound sleep in the sunshine. She took my arm and we began our slow march out of the castle. Rhiannon and Peter ran ahead to take some time in the small, but excellent museum. After they were out of earshot, I stopped.

"You are such a faker," I said.

"Nonsense," said Traka.

"You heard every word, didn't you?" I asked.

She smiled a crooked grin.

"Plausible deniability, my child," she said. "Plausible deniability."

"I will report back to you," I said.

"Good boy," said Traka. "Because I could never look there on my own! And, Cameron?"

"Yes?" I asked.

"No sex on the ancient monuments," she said. "Seriously."

"Yes ma'am," I said.

CHAPTER EIGHT – THE ISLAND ADVENTURES

Kos, Greece

Megalou Alexandrou – the road, not the fellow who conquered much of the known world – runs up from the old harbor to end at a sort of traffic circle. I say sort of because even though six roads come together in a circle meant to be a traffic circle, everyone just drives straight through. This can be exciting.

On this circle is a small restaurant in an old, white two-story house. This is Aléxēs, the best souvlaki place on Kos. In the summer, the gravel front yard becomes a patio with white plastic chairs and tables covered with white and red checkered vinyl tablecloths. Lemon trees shade the tables. In the rainy season, one can eat upstairs or get takeout.

If you go there on a hot summer night, take your time to sit, relax, and chill out with an ice-cold 500 ml Malamatina Retsina with your meal. Watch the world go by. That is living.

That night, we got takeout. Three lamb on a pita with everything. Four chicken pitas with everything. Large village salad. Fries. Extra grilled pita. Extra tzatziki. Brilliant.

Later, after a short sleep, Peter dressed me for our excursion. Black jeans, black turtleneck, and a classic black blazer from Eddie Bauer.

As he straightened the lapels, he said, "Very sixties. Suits you just perfect."

"He does look most handsome," allowed Rhiannon. "Cameron, you should let Peter dress you more often."

I said nothing.

Peter had already dressed almost identically, but with a black windbreaker and grey fedora. He had also stowed our gear in my present, the white, 1983 Citroën Méhari.

"Do I not look very Felix Leiter?" asked Peter.

"You do, most handsome," I said.

Rhiannon tilted back his fedora and gave him a kiss. "Most handsome," she agreed.

Peter raised his arm and pulled back his sleeve, revealing his metallic 1957 Omega Speedmaster watch.

"We must depart," he said. "We need to be at the start line by one a.m."

"Why?" I asked.

He quickly kissed me. "Always so many questions. Have you no faith?"

Peter drove. This is always exciting, but even more so in the dark, along thin, twisting, stone-fenced, Greek country roads, with the stonework blurring by centimeters away at 80 kph. He slowed as we entered Kos town and in a few moments we were hugging the Mediterranean on Vasileos Georgiou, past the hard standing where sailboats and cruisers sat up high on their steel frames safe from the tossing waves, past the almost empty marina where a few lonely sailboats rocked easily in the most protected moorings, past the empty beaches, past the darkened shops, and past the police station to the castle.

He took the road to the right, heading to the ferry docks. Waves rolled in, smashing against the roadway, spewing showers of cold saltwater. Peter turned sharply into a parking spot on the left, putting the bonnet of the Citroën Méhari flush against the looming castle wall.

He checked his watch.

"Right on time," he said.

Bright spotlights illuminated the entire side of the castle facing the sea.

"Peter, did you notice that we are parked only a stone's throw from the police station?" I asked.

"You professed complete faith on the way here," said Peter.

"I do have complete faith, absolutely," I said.

"Oh, it is one!" he said, happily.

The lights went out, all of them. The entire town.

"Peter?" I asked.

"It happens all the time," said Peter. "They are used to it. Now, come on, we have at most two hours until they fix it."

"It?" I asked.

"The substation," said Peter. "Now, let's go."

He opened the door and headed for the rear of the vehicle. I followed. He opened the rear and removed a heavy pack.

"Come on," he said. "Turn around. You are carrying this one."

I presented my back and he helped me shoulder the pack.

"Good gods," I said. "What is in it?"

"This and that," he said.

He reached into the back, pulled out a small black backpack, and slipped it on.

"Why do you get the small one and I get the giant one?" I asked.

"Because I am an elegant leopard and you are a great lummox, a three-toed sloth," said Peter. He took a coiled rope from the vehicle, slipped it over his head and under his arm, and closed the hatch.

"I will climb up, tie off the rope, and lower it to you," said Peter. "Here there is only one wall and we will have direct access to the inner ward."

He gave me a quick kiss, crossed to the wall, and started free climbing. In the darkness, I could barely see him as a shadow, but I remembered from our daylight visit that the stones were large and rough, offering easy handholds for those who knew what they were doing, like our ninja. In a moment he was gone. I could still hear him scuffing against the stones as he climbed. Then, a few moments later, the end of the rope fell with a thud before me, followed by a pair of leather gloves.

I pulled on the gloves and drew the rope taut. Setting my feet against the wall, I leaned back and began to climb. The pack dragged me down and, as I climbed, I thought it would have been sensible to send it up first. I put it out of my mind and slowly walked and pulled myself upward. After about five minutes, I saw Peter's face peering over the battlements, and soon he was pulling me over the lip onto the parapet.

"Why didn't you let me pull the bag up first?" said Peter.

"Because you put it on me?" I asked.

"Idiot," said Peter. "Very manly, though. Now, watch your step, the stairs are this way. They are a tad rough."

Peter pulled up the rope and we slowly made our way along the top of the wall. Finally, my eyes started to adjust to the dark. I could see outlines of the stones, then the broad ramp of steps leading down into the inner ward.

Peter waited for me and took my hand.

"Slow and steady," he said.

We headed down the slope, then followed a dirt path through the long grass, across the ward, toward the gate and the domed tower. About halfway across the field, Peter froze, turned and motioned for me to crouch. I did so, fighting for balance against the weight of the pack.

I saw him silhouetted against the faint starlight of the night sky, turning slowly, listening.

"I could have sworn…" he whispered.

He extended his hand and pulled me up. As we moved ahead, my eyes continued to adjust, and movement became easier. We crossed the rest of the ward and climbed the broad stone ramp to the domed tower.

"You may set down the gear," said Peter.

I did so gladly, resting the pack on the same pillar Traka and I had used as a bench earlier that day.

"Good boy," said Peter. "Now lift me to the top of the tower, please."

I knelt and he stepped onto my shoulders, balancing with theatrical grace. To me, he weighed next to nothing. I stood and he pulled himself up onto the tower roof. His head poked over the side, looking down at me.

"Let me find a place to tie off the rope," he whispered and vanished.

I waited, still, in the darkness, listening, hearing only the sound of the waves crashing against the shore beyond the castle wall and the slight rustling of the breeze coming fresh with the scents of salt and seaweeds from the Aegean, across the grasses in the fortress meadows.

I waited. From above, only silence. I stood entirely still, closed my eyes and inhaled deeply, holding the air, then releasing it slowly. With my eyes closed, the scents of the night became more acute, more vibrant. How long had it been since I had slept in my forest, amongst the oaks and beech? Too long. I felt the need, a physical longing. Even here, in the heart of the fortress, a few trees stood. I heard their leaves clattering lightly in the moving air and smiled. Those roots went deep into rocky soil. Deep down.

"Cameron?" asked a voice.

"Puck?" I asked.

"No, love. Peter," said the voice.

I opened my eyes and looked up to see him silhouetted against the starlight, hands on his hips, looking down.

"With me now?" asked Peter.

"Yes, sorry," I said.

"That is alright. Here is the rope. Tie on the bag, please," said Peter.

I slipped the rope through the carry straps and tied it off with a simple reef knot.

"Ready," I said.

He hoisted it up, then lowered the rope again. Climbing without the pack seemed easy. In a moment I stood beside him. The smooth surface of the almost circular roof rose into a raised, flat, disk in the center of the tower.

"Peter, where did you tie off the rope?" I asked.

"I had to set three pitons in the center of tower," said Peter. "Sorry to take so long."

"Do not mention it to the good professor," I said. "You have defaced a monument."

"I will fix it before I go," said Peter. "I put premixed adhesive cement in the pack."

"Ah," I said.

He buckled a belt around my waist and handed me a coiled rope.

"Now, tie off," he said, and pointed to the center of the tower.

I felt in the darkness until my hand found the carabiner at the end of the rope, then carefully made my way to the center of the tower and clipped onto one of the pitons. Peter moved up silently and knelt beside me.

"Watch," he said.

He unclipped the carabiner, depressed the gate, twisted it until it slipped through the piton, and pulled the rope through. He then clipped it on the next piton.

"Always get at least two," he said. "Even at this low vertical."

"I understand," I said.

He took my hand and led me to the edge.

"The rope is just long enough to take you to the marble plaque, but it is a long way down to the rocky ground, so be careful," said Peter.

"And I am doing this because?" I asked.

"Three-toed sloths may be slow, but they are good climbers," said Peter.

"Peter, my love?" I asked.

"I am the better fighter if something goes amiss," said Peter. "So, I should stay in overwatch."

"Ah," I said. "And, what do I when I get there?"

"I will lower you a crowbar and two wires, both of which will be secured to a piton," said Peter. "Try to pry loose one end of the marble plaque and get a wire loop around it. Then do the same on the other end. The wires should support the plaque while you explore behind it. Easy."

"I see," I said.

"Then, when we are done, I will lower you the bucket of quick-setting cement to replace the plaque," said Peter. "After I open the bucket, you will have ten minutes to complete the work."

"I see," I said. "Is there a trowel?"

"I forgot the trowel," said Peter. "You may use your hands."

"This is the real reason I am doing it, isn't it?" I asked. "You don't want the curative agents on your hands?"

"It will damage my skin and get under my nails, even through the fabric of the gloves," said Peter. "You do not want my delicate hands to be ruined, do you?"

"Fine," I said.

"Good boy," he said. "Down you go."

And, down I went, walking backward down the side of the tower, step by cautious step, hand over hand on the rope. until I reached the plaque.

"Peter, I am at the coat-of-arms," I said.

"You are almost at the end of the rope," said Peter. "Drop another meter."

Two more steps took me to the end of the rope, dangling, directly opposite the marble plaque.

"It is set at least ten centimeters into the stone of the wall," I said.

"I am sending the crowbar down on a rope," said Peter. "Do not untie it in case you drop it."

A few moments later I felt a sharp pain on the top of my skull.

"Peter!" I said.

"Shush," he said. "We are burglaring."

Blood began to drip down across my forehead.

"Super," I whispered. I reached up and found the crowbar and, supported by the rope, walked sideways along the wall to the left side of the plaque. I felt with my left hand along the edge of the plaque.

"I think I can get the crowbar in along the edge," I said. "There is a gap of at least three centimeters."

"Take it slow," said Peter. "You don't want to pop it out before you get the wire around it."

I felt the cable drop onto my shoulder.

Everyone of a certain age has experienced that moment when they wonder how they got into a certain situation, whether it be waking up with someone inexplicable, waiting for the parachute to open, or patiently watching their child receive the scripture knowledge award at school. Dangling on a rope in near complete darkness, attempting to pry a marble plaque from the wall of a 13th century fortress was just such a moment for me.

What if I had never come to our Welsh valley? How had I fallen in love with The Rowan? What if I had not met Puck? What if I had fled or, worse, lost the sacred combat? What if we had not met Peter or the good professor? There were too many possible points of diversion.

I sighed.

"Yes?" asked Peter.

"Nothing," I said.

"Liar," said Peter. "Watch out for scorpions."

I sighed, again.

"And asps," said Peter.

"Seriously?" I asked.

"Yes," said Peter.

I worked the flat point of the crowbar into the crevice at the edge of the plaque and started wriggling it back and forth, trying to lever it out from its niche.

"It moves, but just a little," I said. "I can't get a good angle on it."

"Will your fingers fit in?" asked Peter.

"There would definitely be room for yours," I muttered.

"I beg your pardon, my love?" asked Peter.

"Nothing. I am letting go of the crowbar. Please pull it up," I said.

I released the bar and managed to get both sets of fingers into the hole behind the plaque. I pulled. It moved a centimeter or so with a sandy grating sound.

"The plaster has turned to dust," I said. "I think I can move it."

"Don't drop it," said Peter.

I pulled again, again moving it a bit. And again. And again, until it had pivoted out about six centimeters. I felt for the cable and found it. I rolled it between my forefinger and thumb -- multiple wires wound concentrically in a helix around a central core. A small carabiner marked the end of the wire.

"I am going to try to get the wire around the marble," I said. "Is it secured?"

"Proceed," said Peter.

I felt along the top and bottom of the plaque. It was tight, but the wire would fit. I slipped it slowly around the end of the marble and pulled the carabiner up in a loop to clip it to the cable above the plaque. I pulled it tight.

"I've got a good loop around it," I said. "Please send down the other cable."

It dropped beside me. I repeated to process until I had two loops of wire around the left end of the plague. Then it was a simple matter of slowly edging the plaque out, pivoting it on its right side, and with each few centimeters forward, sliding the righthand loop of wire toward the right. After about half an hour, one loop remained holding the left side and I had managed to slide the other to a point about two thirds down its one-meter length.

"Ready?" I asked.

"Ready aye ready," said Peter.

I pulled the left side of the plaque free of the niche, leaving the right end in the cavity, and felt the wire take the weight.

"Looks good," I said. I reached forward.

"Do not feel behind the plaque," said Peter.

I froze.

"You did, didn't you?" said Peter.

"A little," I admitted.

"Slowly pull your hand back," said Peter.

I did, ever so slowly.

"Take the flashlight from the left pocket of your stylish blazer and have a look," said Peter. "It shines red light."

I felt in my left pocket and found just such a light. I clicked it on and shone the light into the space behind the plaque. The red light provided enough light to see almost everything. Behind the plaque, a small cavity had been cut into the stone. Within the cavity sat a wooden box, perhaps a dozen centimeters square. Also, within the cavity numerous small, wiggly things twisted and wriggled around about the box.

"And?" asked Peter.

"A box and wiggly things," I said.

"How long are the wiggly things," asked Peter.

"Maybe ten centimeters?" I said.

"Asps," said Peter. "Keep your distance."

"Really?" I asked.

"Yes. Please wait," said Peter.

In a moment, he rappelled down the wall to my side.

"I brought my cooking tongs," said Peter. "Move away from the alcove, off to the left please. At least a meter from the edge of the plaque."

I skittered sideways along the wall.

"Clear," I said.

I watched Peter invert himself until he dangled head down above the alcove. He steadied himself against the wall with one hand and slowly reached into the hole with his tongs. Then, most cautiously, he withdrew the tongs.

"I have the box," he said. He shook it gently. "It is now asp free."

"Unless they are inside, too," I said.

"Good point, my love," said Peter. "Please wait."

He swung heads up and ascended the wall, vanishing into the night.

After a few minutes, I saw something being lowered slowly toward me.

"Peter?" I asked.

"The box is in my small pack," he said. "Do not open my pack. Something was definitely wiggling in there. Here is the cement. It is open."

The next steps went strangely well. I pushed the marble slab back into place, then tilted it forward on its bottom edge carefully avoiding the center of the piece, near the snakes. Then I poured the cement along the carving from the top and pushed the marble back into place. After ten minutes' curing time, Peter passed me wire cutters. I cut the cables and pulled them free of the cement. Ten minutes later we finished packing the large pack atop the tower.

Peter stepped close and kissed me.

"Good boy," he said. "I did bring my maid costume, but it is in a pocket of the little pack with the box and the poisonous snakes."

"Perhaps another night then," I said.

"Indeed," said Peter. "Shall we be on our way?"

We lowered the bag to the top of the wall above the gate, removed the pitons, repaired the holes with dabs of cement, and slipped off the tower to land next to the pack. Peter wore the small backpack with the box and the asps, and I carried the heavy pack with the gear. He took my hand and lead me down the broken ramp toward the field in the central ward.

Halfway down the ramp he stopped.

"Cameron, can you run with that pack?" he asked.

"In the dark? Not particularly," I said.

"We are not alone," said Peter.

"I do not want to go to prison," I said.

"Not the police," said Peter. "Our evil Nazi friends, perhaps?"

"We could try talking to them?" I suggested.

"You want to bargain with Nazis?" said Peter. "May I remind you of the Régime de Vichy?"

"We do not know they are Nazis," I said.

"Well… Perhaps it will be useful if you engage them in conversation," said Peter. "They are about three meters from the end of the ramp."

He released my hand. I peered into the darkness but could see nothing except the faint outline of the ramp.

"I see nothing," I said. "Peter?"

No answer. He was gone.

"Hello?" I called out.

No answer. I took a few more steps down the crumbling ramp.

"Hello?" I tried again.

I heard metal against leather, the sound of a knife leaving a sheath.

"Do we really need to fight, again?" I asked. I set down the pack. "Remember what happened to your friends."

"Did you find anything?" A heavily German accented male voice came from the darkness about four meters ahead.

"What?" I asked.

I heard them begin to move toward me, perhaps four or five of them.

"Asps. We found asps," I said.

The movement ceased. Silence.

"But we cemented most of them back in," I said. "They are poisonous, you know."

"And?" asked the same voice.

"Are you Nazis by any chance?" I asked.

A woman's laugh from my right.

"Must you be so cliché?" she said, her voice -- slightly accented, but recognizably German. "Why is that what people always expect?"

"Accents? Bad movies?" I asked.

I heard her sigh.

"So, who are you, then?" I asked.

"We could just as well ask you?" she said.

"I asked first," I said.

"What? Are you twelve?" said the first male voice.

"Emotionally? Pretty much," I allowed.

She chuckled in the dark.

"We are lay brothers and sisters from a religious order," she said. "Does that make a difference?"

"Well, I am kind of glad you aren't Nazis," I said.

"So, did you find anything?" said the male voice.

"Also," said the woman. "Where is your friend?"

I decided to spin things out.

"What do you seek?" I asked.

"I will answer," said the woman. "We seek the Grail."

"Why do you seek the Grail?" I asked.

"To restore the image of God in the minds of man," said the woman. "And return our civilization to the path of The Lord."

"Huh," I said. "That sounds rather Jungian. I admit my surprise."

"Literally," said the man.

"Oh," I said. "Well, we found nothing."

"You are a rotten liar," said the woman.

"That is rather rude," I said.

"I mean, you lie poorly," said the woman. "You are really not cut out for this, are you?"

I had learned to recognize a rhetorical question.

"Detain him. We can question him later," she said.

I dropped into a fighting stance.

To my right I heard a dead weight hit the earth. Then, ahead, a human gurgling sound. Two shapes appeared out of the darkness, charging toward me, then jerked suddenly backward into the gloom as if tugged by giant elastic bands.

"Peter?" I asked.

"Un instant s'il vous plait," sounded Peter's voice from the void.

A meaty tearing sound followed. Then, a high-pitched scream. Then another thud.

A small, lithe figure appeared before me.

"We may go now," said Peter.

"You didn't kill them, I trust?" I asked.

"Tut," he said.

"Thank you, Peter," I said.

"We should make haste," he said. "That scream…"

He helped me don the pack, took my hand, and led me across the field and back up the ramp to the wall. He dropped my pack over the edge of the wall, threw over the rope, and rappelled down to the car. I followed less cavalierly.

Peter drove slowly and cautiously, obeying all traffic laws as we passed the police station, heading out of town and up into the foothills. As he pulled into our garage, he turned to me.

"My love, you are bleeding again," he said. "I can see it by the dashboard light."

"My wound opened during our little projet de maçonnerie," I said. "That marble is heavy."

"First, thank you for your effort in French. You are sweet," he said. "Second, you should have told me."

"Perhaps you could bandage me before we go in?" I asked. "No reason to upset her."

"Of course," he said. "Please sit on the bonnet."

While I relocated, he got the first aid kit from the glove compartment, turned on the garage lights, and came around to where I sat on the vehicle's hood. The engine still radiated heat.

He unbuttoned my shirt, used some gauze to clean away the blood, and leaned in close to examine the wound.

"Cameron, it is only open a little, but it is not healing properly," he said. "And it is not a nutrition question. I am feeding you correctly."

"It does not hurt," I said. "And I am usually careful. Not tonight, though."

"No. Not tonight," he said.

His small hands moved with both sureness and gentleness as he poured alcohol over the wound and cleaned it again with more gauze. Then he bandaged it with tape and a rectangle of padding.

"You have been trained in this, haven't you?" I asked.

"I have," he said. He wagged his finger at me.

"I know," I said. "Questions are forbidden."

He smiled as he rebuttoned my shirt.

"Good boy," he said. "Let us shower and change. Then we can look at our new pets!"

Rhiannon looked up from behind the kitchen counter as we came through the front door.

"Okay, you are?" she asked.

"We are good," said Peter. He bounced over to her and kissed her. "Cameron is filthy, though. I should clean him up. I need the big pasta pot first though."

She looked at him quizzically but bent down beneath the counter and pulled out the stainless steel, glass-lidded pot and set it on the counter.

Peter lifted the lid and set his small pack in the pot, then resettled the lid.

"Best to be safe," said Peter.

"We found something," I said. "But it came with asps."

"Oh!" said Rhiannon.

"Do not touch the pot!" said Peter, and he took me by the hand and started to lead me upstairs.

"Rhiannon, my dear, could you please get the good professor?" I asked. "She may as well be here when we open it."

"She knows you went?" asked Rhiannon.

I did not answer as I followed Peter up the stairs.

Peter scrubbed my back in the shower, and I scrubbed his. The hot water and soap sluiced away the grit and grime of the fortress. Peter was right, my hands were raw and bright red from the chemicals in the quick-dry cement and stung in the heat of the water. He washed them gently with a soft cloth.

Afterward, Peter volunteered to dry me with a big, fluffy, white towel, but I pushed him gently away. The wooden box intrigued, so I dressed quickly into boxers and a t-shirt, though I did linger to watch him climb into his blue jammies.

By the time we returned to the kitchen, Rhiannon and the good professor had brewed a pot of tea and stood, cups in hand, at the counter. Traka wore a big, furry, black night robe.

"You dragged me out of bed," she said. "This better be good."

"I apologize," I said. "I thought you would be keen."

"Well, let's open it, then," said Traka. "We can all be disappointed together and head back to bed."

"No," said Peter. "First, we must tell of our adventures, then we will open the box. There is no point having adventures if you cannot tell the tale."

"Fine," said Traka.

So, Peter told the tale, quite eloquently – how we climbed the wall, removed the marble inset, retrieved the treasure, battled the foe, and made our escape. Throughout, I could see Traka's interest peak and Rhiannon's alarm flush her cheeks.

"So, monks, then?" asked Traka, when Peter ended his tale. "I do not suppose they named their order?"

"And nuns," I said. "And, no, they did not. They were not terribly forthcoming."

"I suppose they wouldn't be," said Traka. "Is the story complete, Peter?"

"Indeed," said Peter.

Traka reached for the lid to the pot. Peter stepped forward and gently took her hand, halting it.

"Curiosity killed the professor emeritus," said Peter. "Let us go slowly. Cameron, we need a big box."

"There are some big, grey plastic ones in the garage," I said. "I think they are for olives."

"Off you go," he said.

It took me a few minutes to run to the garage and get one of the larger boxes. When I returned, all three were peering intently into the pasta pot.

"Cameron," said Rhiannon. "I do not approve of you bringing home poisonous snakes."

"Three, at least," said Traka. She pointed into the pot.

I looked. Sure enough, three of the little, blackish, diamond-patterned beasts twisted and turned in the bottom of the pot near Peter's bag.

"They have them in Wales, as you know," I said.

"Not in my kitchen!" said Rhiannon.

"My kitchen," said Peter, under his breath, just quietly enough that Rhiannon would not hear.

"Also, it is a different kind of asp in Wales," said Traka.

I put the box on the counter. It could easily hold two large pasta pots. Peter lifted the pot and set it in the box off to one side. He then took cooking tongs from the utensil drawer and removed the pot lid, setting it aside.

"Please step back," said Peter.

We did so.

He used the tongs to slowly remove his bag from the pot and set it beside the pot. Two asps fell from the bag into the box as he did so, turning to strike angrily at the bag.

We all stared for a while as the snakes explored the bottom of the box.

"Gosh," said Peter.

"Indeed," I said.

"Are there likely more in the bag?" asked Rhiannon.

"Emm hmm. And in the box," said Peter.

He took a second pair of tongs from the drawer and, using both pairs, delicately opened the fabric flap of his bag. The wooden box lay within. Three more asps looked up at us.

"They do not blink," said Peter. "One would expect them to blink."

"Snakes have no eyelids," said Traka. "A transparent scale covers each eye to protect it and stop it from drying out."

"So, they sleep with their eyes open?" I asked.

"They do," said Traka. "Also, they are tasty."

This sparked a thought.

"Peter," I said. "Maybe you should use the barbeque tongs? They are much longer."

"Please," said Peter.

I got the longer tongs from the patio, washed them in the sink, dried them, and passed them to Peter. They were at least half-a-meter long.

Peter nodded at me. "Much better."

He reached the tongs into the pot and gently removed the three asps one at a time and placed them in the box. Then, he carefully removed the wooden box from the pack and set it in the pot.

We all stared at it for a while.

"It is pretty old," I observed.

"There is a hole," said Peter, pointing with the tongs. "Where the snakes went in and out."

"Small it is," said Rhiannon.

"They are small snakes," I said.

Peter used the tongs to turn the box over, revealing no obvious way into the thing.

"It may still be inhabited," I said.

"Obviously," said Traka. "Cameron, you should open the box."

"Why me?" I asked.

"You are the man," said Traka. "It is your duty to protect the gentle sex."

"The appalling logic and sexism of that aside, so is Peter," I said.

"I am through the male phase of the night," said Peter. "I am now firmly in the female phase."

"You are just making that up," I said.

"Also, your larger body mass will better absorb the snake venom," said Peter.

"Don't worry," said Traka. "I keep antivenom. Asps are not uncommon in the olive groves."

I looked at Rhiannon. She walked over to the sink and returned with a pair of yellow, rubber, dishwashing gloves and handed them to me.

"These are not thick enough to stop a snake bite," I said.

"They have tiny teeth," said Peter.

"Only four percent of even non-treated Vipera aspis bites are fatal," said Traka.

"Fine," I said. I put on the rubber gloves.

Peter used the two smaller tongs to remove the pot from the large box and set the pot on the counter, then set said box aside on the living room sofa.

"I think I will feel better if that is outside," said Rhiannon.

Peter moved it outside the front door.

I approached the pot and took a closer look at the box.

"It looks pretty fragile," I said. "I could probably break it open."

"It is an artifact!" snapped Traka.

"Fine," I said.

I reached in and poked the box with my finger. Nothing.

I picked it up, gave it a quick shake, and set it down. Nothing.

"If there is anything in there, you just made it angry, my love," said Peter.

"Super," I said.

We all looked at the box for a few more minutes.

"Cameron?" asked Rhiannon.

"Fine," I said.

I reached in with both hands and picked up the box. I saw no obvious hinges, clasps or locks. Then, I noticed that five sides showed rather nicely executed interlocking dovetail joins. The sixth side did not. It slid open with a little pressure.

"Nicely done, my love," said Rhiannon.

"My goodness," said Peter. "Are those eggs."

"I believe so," I said.

Inside the box, an even dozen small, pale eggs lay around and in what was clearly a gold cup: visible from the top it looked to be about ten centimeters in diameter.

Within the cup, a small asp looked up from underneath the eggs.

"There is also a cup and snake," I said.

"A cup you say?" said Traka, leaning in close. "Ah, take it out, Cameron. I must see it."

"Patience, please," I said. "Peter, could you please get me a large glass jar and a spoon?"

I set the box down in the pot, took the jar and spoon and gently removed the eggs, one-by-one, and put them in the jar. Only half out of its shell, the tiny snake came last.

I gave the jar to Peter. He placed it with the rest of the asps.

When he returned, I said, "Tomorrow we will find a place up the mountain for the snakes."

"Or eat them," said Traka.

"The symbol of new life from the Grail? When we are trying to have babies?" said Peter. "And you want to eat them? Bad karma."

"Oh, well thought out, boys," said Rhiannon.

"Give me the damn cup!" said Traka.

I gingerly removed the cup from the box and held it up to the light.

"Maybe it is a bowl?" I asked.

"It is beautiful," said Rhiannon.

The rim of this solid gold, bowl-shaped cup had been decorated with a Celtic-style, woven-knot pattern, beneath which large, roughly-cut emeralds had been set around the entire circumference, catching and refracting the light.

"Beauty," said Peter.

"Bah," said Traka. "It's a ringer. Tenth century Irish work. Not a day earlier. Del Carretto was setting a false trail."

"It seems warm," I observed.

"May I?" asked Peter.

I passed the cup to his tiny hands.

"It does. Perhaps from the warmth of the eggs?" asked Peter. He passed it to Rhiannon. She took it in both hands, brought it close to her face and inhaled.

"Smells sweet, it does," she said.

Peter and I both leaned forward to smell it.

"Sweet and musty," said Peter.

Traka exhaled. "No, I apologize, but it is not the Grail. It is way too new, by about a millennium at least."

"Really?" asked Peter.

"Sorry, Peter," said Traka.

He pouted.

"That pout cannot transform reality," said Traka.

"It can't?" I asked, somewhat startled.

"It can, I think," said Rhiannon.

"No," said Traka. "Even allowing for the fact that you three have, at best, a tenuous grip on reality, this cup is not old enough. Period."

"Alas," I said. "It certainly looks like it could play the role."

"Well, we should certainly have a sip of wine from it," said Peter. "Before we give it back."

"Give. It. Back." said Traka, oh so slowly.

"We did steal it," said Peter, "from the Greek people."

"Professor, your right eye is twitching," I said.

She held her hand to her face to stop the spasms.

"I can get twenty thousand euro for that ringer," said Traka. "Twenty thousand."

"That is a lot of euro," I observed.

"Cameron, my love," chastised Rhiannon.

"It is a lot," said Peter. "But it is not ours. To keep it would be wrong. Simple."

"Wrong? Peter, I was a successful, professional academic for more than forty years," said Traka. "Do you think I have one sliver of a morality left in my body? Do you?"

"I do not steal," said Peter. "Ever."

"You are stealing someone's husband, though, are you not?" said Traka.

"Tut. She left him to be found. Should I take him back?" said Peter. "And, professor, you cannot play false dichotomy with me."

"Ahem," I said.

They all turned to me.

"Peter is correct," I said. "It must be returned. Good professor, you can say it came from your collection and give it as a donation. You will get a tax receipt."

"Also, isn't anyone else interested in the note?" I added.

I pointed with my yellow-gloved finger to the bottom of the wooden box and enjoyed watching all three heads swivel to look down into the container. Life can be fun.

Traka reached slowly toward the box, a look of what can only be called intoxication on her wrinkled visage. But Peter's hand darted forward and snatched the box. He looked intently for a moment, then reached in and withdrew a folded, dark umber sheet of paper.

Traka scowled at him.

"Um, shouldn't we be using special tools and white gloves and stuff?" I asked.

Peter tilted his head and looked at me. "Me?" he asked.

"Never mind," I said.

Using both hands, he slowly unfolded the note.

"Tibi cordi immaculato concredimus nos ac consecramus," he read. "Cameron, that is… We consecrate to your immaculate heart and entrust to you for safekeeping. It is signed, Fabrizio del Carretto."

"The you in this context is generally understood to be Mary," said Traka.

She began to quiver. I grabbed one of the chairs from the dining table, set it behind her, and gently lowered her into it.

"Thank you, Cameron," she said. "Do you understand how significant this is?"

"Um, no," I said.

"It tells us that, whatever level of madness you three may carry about with you day-to-day, we were almost certainly correct," said Traka. "The knights did believe they possessed the Grail. And they did hide it here on the island. This is a sacred object and, yes Peter, we must return it."

"I am confused," I said. "I thought you said there was no way it was the Grail."

Rhiannon knelt before Traka and placed the cup in her hands, carefully closing both of Traka's hands about the vessel. Rhiannon stood.

"Cameron, the knights may well have believed this was the Grail as, for them, something five hundred years old was ancient, more than thirty generations ancient," said Rhiannon. "And, if they believed, then they used this object. They used it in the Grail ceremonies, in the processions, down through the generations. They *believed.*"

"So?" I asked.

"My love, a religious object venerated down through the generations has power. It becomes a thing, a sacred symbol of the people who believed," said Rhiannon. "For Christians this is just such a thing."

Traka began to rock back and forth, just a little, and started to weep.

"It is its own archetype, manifest," said Traka.

"But we are not Christian," I said.

"We are not," said Rhiannon.

"Fine," I said. "Well, I will leave it to you three. In truth, every muscle and bone in my body hurts. My hands are still burning. I am going to take a bubble bath and go to sleep."

Rhiannon smiled and touched my face. "I will take you up. You two have had a long day."

She took my hand, led me upstairs, and helped me run the bath, choosing Dr. Teal's Foaming Bath, lavender scented. I settled into the bubbles. Before returning to the others, she kissed me on the forehead. Heaven.

Later, as the water was just beginning to lose its heat, I opened my eyes. Peter knelt beside the tub in his Hello Kitty pajamas, holding the golden cup aloft with two hands.

"Peter?" I asked.

"I am Christian," he said. "So, for me this is a sacred thing."

He stood, then sat on the side of the tub.

"Drink from the cup, Cameron, that thou may knowest me," he said and brought the vessel to my lips. I sipped. He tilted the cup and tipped the whole contents into my mouth. I swallowed.

"Tomorrow," he said. "I will wake you and you will fulfill your duty."

He kissed me.

"No pressure."

Late the next morning, after I attempted to fulfill my duty, Peter made hamburgers and I headed outdoors into the bright sun by the pool to grill them over a charcoal bed in the raised fire pit. Peter put together a village salad and Rhiannon set the table by the pool – a heavy, black, wrought-iron affair Peter had imported from Albania. She set four places.

I raised an eyebrow at that, but she just smiled, knowingly.

Peter set a jug of fresh orange juice on the table.

"Peter, my love, it is a little cool to be wearing only an apron," said Rhiannon. "And the good professor will likely be here in a moment."

I heard a knock at the front door.

"Go put some clothes on, please," said Rhiannon.

For a moment, he looked like he might argue, but then he nodded and headed indoors.

"You watch the burgers," said Rhiannon. "I will get the door."

In a moment, she was back with the good professor.

"I could smell beef sizzling," said Traka.

"We already set a place," I said. "There are lots."

"Hamburgers!" she said.

Rhiannon pulled out a chair – also of heavy wrought iron – and Traka sat. In a moment, the beef was cooked rare and I used the barbeque tongs, now snake-free, to pile burgers on a platter. Peter, clothed in my former Abide hoodie and blue jeans, brought the hamburger buns to the table. We all sat.

"How lovely to sit outside for lunch this time of year," said Rhiannon.

"It is fifteen degrees," I said. "Warmer in the sun. Be a shame to waste it."

"But not warm enough for just an apron," said Rhiannon.

Peter stuck his tongue out at her.

We fell into silence as we assembled our burgers, acknowledged by all to be a deadly serious ritual -- bun, burger, dill relish, catchup, Dijon mustard, tomato slices, onion slices, lettuce leaves, black pepper, and spiced mayonnaise. Traka hummed as she worked. Peter, his construction defying gravity, wore a steely face of complete concentration. Rhiannon, who preferred only relish and catchup, waited patiently with her hands in her lap. For me, mayonnaise, pepper and tomato did the trick.

The good professor, flattened her burger with her palm, picked it up with two hands and took a proper bite.

"Ooh, Cameron. Perfect," said Traka.

"Peter made them, I just grilled them," I said. "He gets the credit."

"To both of you, thank you," said Traka. She took another bite, speaking around the edges of her food. "Oh, this morning I spoke with Director Zappides of the museum. He is so excited about my donation of the four Grails that he is going to work with me to create a special exhibit with a reception in my honor. He says it will get the punters in."

"So, no jail time?" I asked.

She laughed. "No Cameron, no jail time. I told him the truth about where it was found, just not when. He was circumspect enough not to ask so I told him about the note and I promised him he could write it up for a journal."

"Nice work, professor," said Rhiannon.

"Indeed," I said.

"I like to think that I am beyond the folly of seeking vainglorious academic fame," said Traka. "Passing time with you three is much more fun. After all, no one on this island is going to throw their seventy-five-year-old auntie into jail!"

"The Greeks are most respectful of age and wisdom," said Peter. He had not yet taken a bite of his artistically crafted burger. Instead, he slowly rotated his plate to admire his handiwork. He had blended, stacked, and arranged the ingredients by the seven wavelength ranges in the visible spectrum -- red, orange, yellow, green, blue, indigo, and violet.

"True, of course," said Traka. "But in this case, I know all the dirt. You have no idea the shenanigans people get up to on an island like this!"

"Peter, how did you make blue, for goodness' sake?" I asked.

"Secret," said Peter.

"But…" I started.

"Remember you are not blending color, you are blending ingredients which display as a color," said Peter. "So, combining different ingredients almost certainly produces a different hue than combining light of the same original colors."

"True…" I started.

"One must understand the underlying chemistry," said Peter.

"I see," I said. "You are really not going to tell me, are you?"

"Are you going to eat that?" asked Traka.

"All art is temporary," said Peter. He used two hands to lift his burger and took a formidable bite. The rainbow splashed across his cheeks.

Rhiannon picked up Peter's napkin and wiped his face.

"Good, Cameron," he said. "Just right."

"You are too kind," I said.

Traka began to construct another burger.

"We still have one more postcard to explore," said Traka. "The museum."

"I am keen to explore it," I said. "But we have no idea what we are looking for…"

"And, whatever it is, it is likely not even there anymore," said Peter.

"The questions are," said Traka. "What was there and when? And, of course, where is it now? The first question is the easiest. The postcard of the museum is from the Italian occupation. They opened the building in 1936 and the Germans occupied it in 1943 when the Italians switched sides."

"But the postcard could have been used during the German occupation, so up until 1945 then," said Peter.

"Between 1936 and 1945 is nine years," I said. "That does not narrow it down all that much."

"And the Ahnenerbe was not created until 1935," said Peter. "So, nine or ten years."

"Rhiannon? Do we know when SS Whatchamacallit was in the Ahnenerbe or when he was in Greece, 'cause those notes are all his?" I asked.

"Oh! Well done, Cameron! SS-Standarten Führe Wust," said Peter. "Obvious, of course, but still…"

"Alas, we do not," said Rhiannon. "At home, I have the hand-written notes. But they do not give the dates of travel."

"But the entries would have dates," I suggested.

"This is home," said Peter.

I looked over to see his eyes downcast, his hands folded silently in his lap. I looked to Rhiannon. Her eyes flicked between Peter and me. Her tongue wet her slightly open lips.

She made to speak, but I held up my right hand.

"One moment, please, my love," I said.

Life is such a minefield sometimes, isn't it? The most innocent word or deed can cause the deepest hurt to those we love. We all know this. If only I were a true god, able to see what is and what will be, Peter's pain could have been avoided. It is true that a dying god ultimately is responsible for the annual cycles of the seasons and, thus, all life on Earth. However, at that moment, as far as god-like powers go, apparently this dying god's powers ranked somewhere around the level of celestial pool boy.

"Peter, this is our home," I said. "This is where we will make love, get pregnant, and have our child. And, if you hurry and quicken, I may even meet that child. There is still time, after all."

"But this is true, mostly, for you and me. I will return to the valley only for the end game," I said. "This is my last home. But Rhiannon is tied to the valley. She is a Rowan. For her, the connection to the valley is absolute. Mandatory. It is her duty. She has no choice."

"Rhiannon and I have spoken of staying here, in this house, our home," said Peter. "Not to you, Cameron, that would have been cruel."

"Peter, our home this is," said Rhiannon. "I promise. It was a misspoken word, nothing more."

"Cameron, you have two daughters. The eldest, Morgan, is seven. At the end of the next cycle, she will be fourteen. Clarine, your wife, has many years as the Rowan ahead of her. There is me. And my mother is still going strong. That is four generations of Rowans. We only need three Rowans in the valley."

"There will be harsh words," I said.

"Let there be words then," said Peter.

"I should never have acquiesced to Clarine being your wife," said Rhiannon. "It was too much to ask. Now, I simply will not walk away from Peter. I will not. I cannot do it again."

"I have to say…" I began but trailed off.

"Cameron?" asked Rhiannon.

"I guess I am just cycling through my emotions," I said.

"Jealousy being one, I expect?" said Peter.

"Of whom?" asked Traka.

"Both of them, obviously," I said. "It is complicated. Did you know that in a group of three people, there are twelve different routes for emotions to move either partly or wholly around the triad?"

"Obviously," said Peter.

"But, in the end, I must say that this gives me joy," I said. "Good for you guys."

I saw Peter had once again hoisted his burger.

"Lunch here is always interesting," said Traka. "Even if we cannot follow through with but one line of inquiry."

"The entries!" said Rhiannon. "There are no dates. But in one entry, Wust does speak of not being able to return to Kos because of the start of the war. So, pre-1939."

"So, 1935 to 1939?" I said. "Four years. Much more manageable."

"Which leaves us with what and where?" said Peter.

"Indeed," I said.

"You know," said Traka. "We Greeks are quite covetous of our antiquities. Not just any visiting academic can get access to museum artifacts. And the note on that postcard did say check the museum collection for item. And the then Italian and now Greek bureaucracies being as they were and are, the records of SS-Standarten Führe Wust's request may still exist. I will ask the museum director, Diogenis Zappides. Maybe we can at least get an idea of what Wust sought."

Two weeks later, forty-eight large, dusty, moldy, leather-bound, hand-written journals arrived at Traka's villa. Two large men in white lab coats, both of whom showed Traka deep respect, carried the volumes from a white van into Traka's library with an excessive level of formality and solemnity.

And, while I admit the entries showed beautiful cursive penmanship, they were in Greek, Italian and occasionally Latin, so I left the mystery of SS-Standarten Führe Wust's quest to the anatomically feminine and focused on enjoying the improving weather.

By the second week of February, sunny days outnumbered rainy and bright, warm, humid days prevailed. My hikes up through the olive groves onto the lower, cypress-clad slopes of Mount Dikaios to the small, stone, barrel-vault chapel in the forest and beyond became wider ranging. I still made my offering of a one euro coin into a slot in the tin box and lit a thin taper to my predecessors, but spent less time sheltering in the chapel. I had long since completed Thoreau's *The Maine Woods* and now, when it drizzled, closed my eyes in the chapel's darkness and drifted, waiting for the sun.

Much of Mount Dikaios' slopes are barren, stripped by goats and humans. But, enough of the cypress forest remains to get happily lost. And I did get lost, contentedly so, wandering uphill alongside rushing streams, scrambling up beside frothing waterfalls, pricked bloody by thorns and brambles.

The streams are seasonal, fading with the summer heat. Average precipitation in the Dodecanese in July and August is three millimeters and the unirrigated land in summer turns desolate, brown and burnt beneath the sun. But in February, especially when it storms, the streams become thundering, rushing torrents. Immediately below the small chapel, one such stream tumbles, gurgling and frothing with considerable vigor over large, jagged rocks.

I remember that she first came in the last week of February, shortly before the vernal equinox. That day, late afternoon sunlight poked through breaking dark clouds, piercing the forest overstory. I sat on a large rock near the spring, having bathed my bramble-bloodied face in the fresh, chill water, catching the sunlight after an afternoon hiking in the dark woods, my mind drifting, my eyes opening and closing.

"She comes," said Puck's voice. "Careful boyo."

I jerked fully alert, looking around.

"What?" I asked.

"Just careful," said Puck.

I heard metal hinges creak and looked up to see the faded-blue metal door of the barrel-shaped, white-painted chapel swing slowly open. A woman, bent low so as not to rap her head on the low doorframe, emerged into the sunlight, blinking.

I cleared my throat. The stunningly beautiful woman with short, tightly curled black ringlets falling to either side of her face and a generous figure looked at me, straightened, and released a mesmerizing smile. A baggy black dress cascaded down below her knees.

"Hello," she said.

"Hello," I replied. "We have met before, I think."

"I think not," she said.

"In France," I said.

"I have never left this island," she said. "So, no."

"Hmmm," I said.

"I do have sisters…" she said. "Perhaps?"

"Perhaps," I allowed.

She walked over and looked down at me.

"Your face is bleeding," she said.

"A few scratches from thorns," I said. "Nothing to trouble about."

"There is a kit in the church" she said. "At least let me clean the cuts."

"I don't think we have permission," I said.

"I live nearby and mind the chapel for the Orthodox Church," she said. "I was just replenishing the candles. It is you, I suppose, who has been burning them away?"

"Indeed," I said.

"Well, then you have more than paid for a bit of disinfectant," she said, and smiled again.

She turned and ducked back into the chapel, appearing two minutes later with a white, metal box marked with a red cross. She removed a small, glass bottle of clear liquid and white, cotton balls that she moistened from the bottle.

"Be still," she said. "This will sting. Tilt your face up to me."

As I did so I heard Puck's voice whisper, "Careful. Careful."

"I will be gentle as can be," she said.

She took my chin in her left hand and began to wipe away the blood with the cotton balls in her right. I winced.

"I did say," she noted, her smile growing wider.

I sat completely and entirely still, my hands in my lap.

She bent, set the cotton balls aside, and took more from the kit. Twice more she cleaned my scratches, finally gathering up the bloodied cotton and returning the kit to the church. She returned with a large, black cloth bag.

"Are you hungry?" she asked.

"You have blood on your fingers," I said.

"I know," she said. "It is yours, of course. Are you hungry?"

"A little," I allowed.

"What would you like?" she asked. "We can share a late luncheon."

"Cucumber sandwiches?" I ventured.

"Ah, I just happen to have them," she said.

"I guessed you might," I said.

"Did you now?" she asked.

She reached into her large bag and removed a plastic container, then lifted the blue lid to reveal crustless, white bread sandwiches stacked three high. She licked the blood from her fingers, reached into the box and passed me a sandwich. I took it. And took a bite, never turning my eyes from hers.

"Nice," I said. "A little butter, spiced mayo; the bread is just baked?"

"Indeed," she said. "Indeed."

She took a sandwich for herself and nibbled at the edge.

"Not bad," she allowed.

I took another bite.

"You are one of the professor's friends," she said. "You live with your lover and companion. The one who is crazy to have your child."

I tilted my head at her, caution itself.

She laughed and her laugh was beauty itself as it slipped away into the cypress trees.

"It is a small island after all," she said. "And you three are quite gossip worthy."

"I would rather people did not gossip about my family," I said.

"I am lying," she said.

"I guessed," I said. "You just know things. It is your way."

"And yours, I dare say," she said.

I shook my head. "Usually, I am the last one to pick up on things, but this, this…"

"You and I are too similar indeed?" She asked it as a question, with a lilt at the end, but it was no question.

"Indeed," I agreed.

She removed a large, green glass, one-liter bottle of white wine and two wineglasses from her bag. The unlabeled bottle was half stoppered with a cork. An informally fermented local varietal.

"A glass?" she asked.

I nodded. She poured and I took the glass from her hand. I held it up to the sun. The wine shone yellow in the light, with faint bloody fingerprints on the side of the glass among the condensation dewing in the February air. I sipped to taste bitter fruitiness.

"An acquired taste," she said. And smiled again, sipping hers, watching my eyes.

She passed me another sandwich.

"Better with food," she said.

I nodded, feeling the wine enter my bloodstream.

"It is strong," I said.

"Indeed," she said, and laughed again – music.

"How long have you tended this chapel?" I asked.

"That is just another way of asking my age," she said, and frowned but with a spark in her eyes.

"I apologize," I said.

"I forgive you," she said. "You have special latitude."

"You are very pretty," I said.

"Even that much latitude," she said. "I have spent too much time by myself in recent times."

"I am sorry," I said. "But apparently I need to be careful of you."

"Not apparently," she said. "I can change your fate."

"Can you, then?" I asked.

"Mm-hmm," she said. "I can."

I said nothing, only watched her. She truly was beautiful, goddess-like in her natural, unadorned state: straight classical Greek nose, large open eyes the color of shifting storm clouds, smooth impossibly perfect skin, and a full, dramatic bouncy figure.

"You like what you see," she said.

"I do. I will not deny it," I said. "But my domestic situation is quite complicated enough, so it is strictly an aesthetic appreciation."

"Liar," she said. "You do get points for trying, though."

"Thank you," I said. "But back to the fate thing. You will understand that my immediate future preoccupies me somewhat. How can you change my fate? You understand the circumstances?"

"I do," she said.

"I have a responsibility," I said.

"Do you?" she said. "The cycle of the seasons has been broken before, you know. The earth does recover."

"Eventually," I said.

"Yes, eventually," she said. "And, if you came with me, just walked away from it all, you would see it return to its glory. With fewer people around, to be certain, but still..."

"To where?" I asked.

"I have a small, simple house in the forest, a few steps sideways from here," she said. "You would live with me and share my bed."

I smiled at that, despite myself. And she grinned back, her teeth perfect.

"And what of all those who would die? Of the civilizations that would fall?" I asked. "Have I no responsibility for them?"

"No one can make you take responsibility," she said. "What makes it all up to you? Why not turn away and look after yourself?"

"If one takes on a responsibility, then abandons it…" I started.

"So what?' she said. She bent and took my hands in hers. "Just come with me. Walk with me now and you will never need to return to all your cares."

"Or my loves," I said.

"You will lose them soon enough regardless," she said. "Can you deny it? Can you?"

"No, I cannot deny it," I said. "Nevertheless…"

"Nevertheless!" she shouted. She pulled me to my feet. "Do not be a fool, Cameron. I offer you eternity or close as, damn it. They offer you only death and darkness. Where do you think headless dying gods go anyway? And look at you. Your chest. You bleed again. Does that tell you nothing?"

I looked down. My wound had opened, staining my shirt with crimson.

"I must have pulled it open when I climbed up alongside the stream bed," I said. "It happens, but it heals."

She released my hands, stood back overdramatically, and pointed at me with an outstretched finger.

"You are a fool!" she said.

I smiled.

"I know," I said. "That may have been pointed out one or two times before. But in the end, a promise is a promise, an oath is an oath. And I love Peter and Rhiannon and must give them both a child. So, much as I would love to go with you and spend an age eating your perfect sandwiches, drinking your imperfect wine, and exploring your absolutely perfect body, I will stay with my lover and companion. And when the darkness comes, I will see where dying gods go when they lose their heads. Unless, of course, we find the Grail."

This seemed to take the fight out of her. Her face softened and she stepped forward to once again take my hands.

"You are a fool," she said, but this time she spoke the words softly, gently. "The Grail is not for you to find. You will never be healed by the Grail. Come, be my love. I will treat you with quiet kindness and sooth your troubled heart. I would treasure you beyond measure. We of the springs cannot take mortal men as lovers. It would be a kindness to me. Please. I will beg if that is what you desire."

I saw the tears begin to well in her eyes. I stepped forward and took her in my arms.

"I am sorry," I said. There was nothing more to say.

She held me for a minute or two, then stepped back still holding my hands.

"Ah, I knew it would play out thus," she said. She tried to manage a smile. "You are a dying god, after all, by now all caught up in the cycles, the trees, the lakes, the clouds."

"It is true," I said. "I do have trouble staying in the here and now."

"I think I like you," she said, giving me a quick kiss, so fast that I could not dodge it.

"Bye, dear one," she said. She turned and walked away, up the slope, into the cypress trees. She did not look back. She never said her name.

It was a long, thoughtful, walk home, down the slopes, out of the forests, through the olive groves to our home with its sparkling pool and my loves. I did not tell them of my encounter for three days. I needed time to consider.

When the time came, despite my planning, the conversation did not start with promise.

"When you came home from your hike three days ago, you smelled of another woman," said Peter. "I did not mention it then as you were bleeding again."

We sat, just the three of us, at dinner outside on the patio – fresh cucumber salad, pasta with ground pork in a light tomato sauce, fresh bread and a pleasant chianti. I looked up quickly. He was not pouting. He held his head tilted slightly to his right, watching me. I turned to Rhiannon. She watched me impassively. Clearly, this had been discussed.

"You are unharmed because you did not have sex with her," said Peter.

"True," said Rhiannon.

"I checked that night," said Peter.

"Also, true," said Rhiannon.

To say there was a degree of coolness at the table would be true, as well.

"I have been thinking about how to tell you," I said. "It is not what you think."

"Said every man ever," said Peter.

"No really," I said. "It was rather upsetting."

"Upsetting, was it?" said Peter. "Perhaps you should just give it to us in a nutshell, then? Just so we can put aside Rhiannon's notion of keeping you chained to the bedpost."

"With a cold, heavy, bronze chain," said Rhiannon. "And a shackle around your traitorous neck."

I put down my fork.

"In a nutshell, then," I said. "I met a Lady of the Well at the chapel in the forest. She offered to take me with her, to change my fate. I declined."

"E-lab-or-ate," said Peter.

"She offered to take me as her lover so I would not have to complete the final ceremony," I said.

"To where?" asked Peter.

"Just a few steps away, she said," I replied.

"Ah," said Rhiannon. "Cameron, you may pick up your fork."

I did so and swirled up a large forkful of spaghetti, shoving it in my mouth.

"Rhiannon?" asked Peter.

"If he had gone with her, even for a while, we would have never seen him again," said Rhiannon. "You know the stories as well as I do. Peter, pour him some more wine. He has been faithful."

Peter looked at me dubiously, but topped up my wineglass.

"And that upset you?" asked Rhiannon.

"Somewhat," I said. "She was so beautiful, but so lonely."

"Hmm," said Peter.

"Cameron, my love, best not to share how beautiful, I suggest," said Rhiannon.

"She looked almost exactly like the woman we met at the cliff top near the Benedictine Abbey of Ganagobie," I said. "Spookily so."

"And that was upsetting?" asked Rhiannon.

"Um, no," I said. "The upsetting part was that she said, and I quote: You are a fool. The Grail is not for you to find. You will never be healed by the Grail. It was a bit of a downer. She is a goddess after all."

"You do not know that," said Peter. "She might just have been the woman with the inappropriate off-shoulder blouse from the abbey. You do not know that she was a goddess. Did she do magic or something?"

"No," I said. "But, Peter, really?"

"You are so gullible," said Peter, looking to Rhiannon.

"She also asked me if I know where headless dying gods go," I said, quietly. "Rhiannon, where do headless dying gods go?"

Rhiannon reached across the table and took my hand. Peter watched with horror.

"It's fine. You don't have to answer," I said. "I guess I will find out soon enough. And, Peter?"

"Yes?" he said.

"Do not ruin your lovely meal with tears, please," I asked.

He nodded but left the table. From the kitchen we heard the pop of another bottle of wine being opened. I smiled at Rhiannon.

"A drunk Peter beats a crying Peter any day," I said.

She smiled at me and squeezed my hand.

"But he is going to take you violently to bed later," she said. "He will open your wound again."

"A small price to stop his tears," I said.

She nodded, slightly.

Peter returned to the table and thumped down the new bottle of chianti. He lathered butter on a slice of soft bread.

"By the way," he said. "We found what SS-Standarten Führe Wust was seeking. The request was correctly recorded by the Italians."

I cleared my throat. "Please do tell," I said.

"He wanted to examine the pre-Roman collection of tableware for a drinking cup or bowl," said Peter.

"Which doesn't really narrow it down a lot!" I said.

"Pre-Roman, helps," said Rhiannon. "And, he never got to look at the collection. His request was never approved. So…"

"It might still be there!" I said.

Peter smiled. "More wine, Cameron?"

He poured.

The small Kos Archaeological Museum is a newly renovated treasure in the heart of Kos town. Opened by the Italians in 1936 on Eleftherias Square, it shares the architectural style of the Italian colonial period, including a grand, stone façade with three tall arches housing the doorways opening onto the square. Inside, a naturally lit courtyard shows off exquisitely carved statues of a seated and wing-footed Hermes, Dionysus, Pan and a satyr, Artemis, Asclepius, and his daughter Hygeia, all set around a large tile mosaic of Asclepius bringing healing to the island. Other galleries touch on aspects of the island's ancient history, showcasing evocative artifacts in an open, accessible and elegant way.

The Kos Archaeological Museum is a work of art that casts a spell on even the casual visitor who enters its cool interior on a hot July day.

Alas, the Kos Archaeological Museum is not where the pre-Roman collection of tableware is gathered. This collection is hidden away in a rat infested, Italian-era warehouse on the outskirts of Kos town. High, poured-concrete walls, pockmarked with bullet holes from a World War II battle, and topped with corrugated metal roofing supported by steel girders, protect three thousand years of painstakingly recovered and hand-labelled metalware and pottery. Twelve rows of black wire shelves covered with clear plastic sheeting run the length of the warehouse. Pigeons flap overhead amongst the rafters, decorating the plastic sheeting with their excreta. A dust mask must be worn to keep the dried feces from one's lungs as one examines the artifacts.

The Greek government could no longer afford to supply electricity for the lights – this deprivation a gift from the avaricious French and German elites – so we worked by the light of kerosene lanterns, carefully examining broad-mouthed amphorae, flat platters showing only hints of once-bright painting, simple clay bowls and cups, carefully pieced together goblets and drinking horns, and countless small cup-like oil lamps.

This dust-filled, profanity-enhanced, relationship-testing dive into antiquity cost me every afternoon the first three weeks of March. If you are counting, that was roughly eight-and-one-half percent of the days remaining in my anticipated life span.

My mood soured. Peter and Rhiannon put on a brave face, but I watched as they started to begin considering the inevitable. Only Traka remained upbeat and positive, unwilling to quit until we had examined the last clay shard.

We found no hint of a Grail-like presence.

March 21, I awoke to hear Peter singing in French downstairs. Sunlight, broken into a shifting pattern of green leaf shapes, created a kaleidoscope of images on the wall opposite the foot of the bed. Rhiannon lay half across me, her leg thrown over my middle, her nightgown riding up above her bouncy behind.

I slid my hand across her back, over her bottom and between her legs.

"Shoo," she muttered. "Go find Peter."

She rolled over, presenting her back. I nodded silently and slipped quietly out of bed, heading downstairs, to find Peter barefoot in the kitchen wearing his Hello Kitty jammies and a white, cotton apron, pounding a large ball of dough on the counter. As I reached the bottom of the stairs, he looked up and smiled a profoundly happy smile.

"Morning, sleepy head," he said.

"You are baking," I observed.

"I am! Croissants!" he said.

"That is ambitious," I said. I came up behind him and gave him a kiss on the top of his head.

"You poke me, sir," he said. "Through your boxers."

"You are baking croissants," I said. "A most delicate process."

"It cannot be helped," he said. "I must set the dough to rise. Tonight, I am making a feast. And you love croissants."

"I do," I agreed. "I can wait."

I hugged him from behind and, again, kissed the top of this head, then stepped away.

"You poke me again, sir," said Peter. "Why do you not head back up those stairs to visit with Rhiannon?"

"She is sleepy," I observed. "I fear her."

"Very wise, my love," said Peter. He stopped pounding the dough and turned toward me, quickly slipping one of his flower-covered hands into my boxers and grabbing hold of me. He squeezed me tightly.

"You pulse, sir," he said. "You pulse in my hand."

"You tease, sir,' I countered.

He released me and returned to kneading the dough.

"I do," he said. "Croissants will come before you, today."

"Peter? Why are we having a feast this fine sunny day?" I asked.

"First day of spring, obviously," said Peter. "Also, we are finished in that wretched warehouse."

"Where we found nothing," I said.

"We found it wasn't there?" said Peter.

"Hmm," I said.

"Do we really need a reason for a feast?" asked Peter.

"Excellent point," I said, and kissed his head one more time. I headed back upstairs where I stopped in the bedroom door and watched Rhiannon sleep. I watched her back rise and fall with her even breathing.

"I know you are there," she said after a few minutes. She rolled over to face me, seeing me standing in the doorway.

"I am here," I said.

"Peter declined?" she asked. "I confess to being startled."

"He is kneading dough for croissants," I said. "It is a delicate process."

"Yet, somehow, you have flower all over your boxers?" said Rhiannon.

"He was bad," I said. "And I now have flower all over my genitalia."

"And you do love croissants," said Rhiannon.

"I do," I said.

"Well, then you better come back to bed," said Rhiannon. "I will clean you up."

That evening I was advised to dress formally for dinner. As they both knew I did not possess a dress coat, pique wing-collared shirt, white tie, gloves, a top hat or any of the other necessary paraphernalia, nor even a basic tuxedo and black tie, I resorted to my standard grey, pin-striped suit, white shirt and black cotton tie without fear.

Peter dressed snappily in his black tuxedo, white silk shirt and classic black bowtie, while Rhiannon looked beyond edible in a flowing, floor-length, off-the-shoulder, black gown and triple strand of pearls.

Peter imagined us dining alfresco, but a light, drifting, grey mist fell that evening. He had me set the table indoors, with a dark blue tablecloth and his 1950s French Navy dinnerware – white crockery with a small, blue fouled anchor design and a crisp blue nautical rope motif around the edges. Again, the tapered beeswax candles flipped and flickered in their silver candelabra.

Traka, as was her right due to advanced age, did not heed the dress code and arrived in a black, cotton sweater, knitted with a bizarre, bright yellow Grail, complete with radiant beams of light on the front, and grey trousers.

We three greeted her at the door with the traditional multifaceted kissing round. Peter took her arm and escorted her to the table.

She smiled broadly.

"Cameron, take note. This is how a gentleman behaves," said Traka.

I pulled out her chair and gently took her other arm as she sat.

"Not too bad," she allowed.

Rhiannon waited for me to pull out her chair. I did so. She rewarded me with a radiant smile. I felt the golden retriever pull in my heart.

"Cameron, you may seat me," said Peter. "You are serving tonight."

I nodded and assisted him into his chair, keeping my confusion to myself. Throughout the day, he had refused to let us see his dinner preparations, keeping the menu a strict secret.

"Some guidance, perhaps, good sir?" I suggested.

"The salad and appetizer tray are in the refrigerator, all else warms in the oven," said Peter. "You may toss the salad and serve it first, then bring the tray. Do not forget the feta."

I opened the refrigerator to see a lovely tomato-cucumber-basil salad in a large, flat white serving bowl. I removed it, set it on the counter, tossed it lightly and set it on the table by Rhiannon.

"Oh, Peter. It is beautiful," said Rhiannon.

He knew well her favorites.

I next set out the large tray of preserved duck foie gras with toasted country bread.

"Peter?" asked Rhiannon.

"Mais bien sûr," said Peter. "It is the same as I served you at the restaurant."

"How wonderful," I said.

"Cameron, I was hoping I would not have to say anything…" said Peter.

"All the gods!" I said. "I forgot the wine."

"You did," said Peter. "A lovely Bordeaux is decanted on the counter."

I poured four glasses, in each case pouring from the person's right with my left hand behind my back. I did not spill a drop.

"Thank you for not embarrassing me, Cameron," said Peter.

"Mais bien sûr," I said. "And, um, Peter, where are the croissants?"

"You weren't here when they came out of the oven," said Rhiannon.

"Seriously?" I asked.

"They were excellent," said Peter.

"Sorry," said Rhiannon.

"Me too," said Peter.

"You two," I said.

"Peter, would it be alright if Cameron brought the main course so we can all sit and relax?" asked Rhiannon.

He reached across the table and set his hand on hers.

"Only to make you happy, my love," he said.

Traka sighed.

"Cameron. Feta," she said.

"Sorry," I said and ran to get it from the refrigerator. I set it beside her, then returned to the oven.

First, I set out the baby, red, roasted potatoes in butter with chives. As I removed the lid from the serving dish, steam rose up carrying the scents toward the candles.

Second, the main course, Canard de Challans aux olives. An oval, white platter presented two golden, roast ducks on a bed of green olives. The smell of the crisped skin intoxicated.

"Oh. Wonderful," said Traka.

"Truly," I agreed. "Good professor, this is the meal that Peter served us the first time we met."

"How wonderful, indeed," said Rhiannon.

I sat. Peter carved the duck and served it directly onto our plates. Traka passed around the salad and potatoes. I quickly grabbed three toasts, rescuing them from Rhiannon. I saw her watching Peter closely.

"Cameron, could I have a glass of fresh, spring water," said Peter. "There is a pitcher in le réfrigérateur."

"Of course," I said. I rose and poured it immediately, setting it before him.

"Peter?" asked Rhiannon.

"Cameron, I beg a change of protocol this evening," said Peter. "May I give the toast?"

I nodded, transfixed. He stood, raising his glass of water. We raised our glasses of wine.

"Tonight, we arrive at a place in time and space that I had never dreamed I could attain before I met the two of you," said Peter. "I am so grateful that it cannot be expressed."

"At last!" said Traka.

Tears began to trickle down Peter cheeks.

"Yes," he said. "This toast is to the two parents of my child, Rhiannon and Cameron."

Traka stood and hugged him, wrapping him in her strange sweater. She kissed him on the cheeks, kissing away his tears.

"I am so happy for you, Peter," said Traka.

"The three parents, Peter," said Rhiannon. "You are actually the mother. You get most of the credit." She paused. "Or, the father, perhaps?"

She, too, rose and kissed him, fully on the lips.

"Pretty, pregnant, boy," she said. "You will be so beautiful."

I remained seated, twirling the wine in my glass.

"You are both going to be brilliant parents for my child. I am sure of it," I said. "Well done, Peter.

Peter beamed. I took his wineglass and set it before me.

"I know," he said. "I will stick with the regimen. And no more combat training."

He looked at me intently for a moment, bent to slip off his black brogues, stepped up on his chair, walked across the top to the table, carefully avoiding all the dishes and stepped into my lap, finally settling astride me with the elegance of a dancer. He wrapped his arms around me and set his head on my shoulder.

"Cameron," he said quietly. "Your child will want for nothing. I will be the most devoted mother and or father a child has ever had. I swear it. You need not worry about a thing."

I kissed him on his cheek.

"I know that you will be the absolute best," I said. "I am already so proud of you."

Rhiannon stood and wrapped her arms around both of us.

"As am I," she said. "And, Peter?"

"Yes?" he asked.

"Seriously, no wine," she said. "Seriously."

"I know," he said.

"I will kick your pretty little ass," said Rhiannon.

"I know," he said.

"And no climbing castle walls freestyle in the middle of the night, or fighting monks, or snapping people's arms," said Rhiannon.

"Really?" he asked.

"Really," she said.

"Peter, my love," I said. "We could not bear to see you lose this child."

"Ah, I am not sure I would be strong enough for that," said Peter.

I put my wine down on the table and hugged him tightly.

"You are going to be brilliant," I said.

"Brilliant," agreed Rhiannon.

I looked across the table to see tears on Traka's weather-worn face.

"Professor?" I asked.

"I must be the god-parent," said Traka.

Peter took my ear gently in his teeth.

"You must be," I said. "Clearly. Obviously."

Peter released my ear.

"The duck," said Rhiannon. "It will be getting cold."

Traka and Rhiannon resumed their seats. Peter stayed in my lap, hugging me.

"Peter," I said. "Today, you were barefoot, pregnant and in the kitchen."

"I was!" said Peter, delightedly.

Rhiannon and Traka sighed in unison.

"But still, somehow, most manly," I said. "And so handsome."

He kissed me fully and aggressively on my lips.

"God, how I love you," he said.

"He does have his occasional moments," said Rhiannon. "On a move ahead basis…"

"Yes?" asked Peter.

"I will be getting most of his sperm now," said Rhiannon.

"Of course," said Peter. "I can still get him started though."

"Oh, for God's sake!" said Traka. "We are at dinner."

"Thank you, professor," I said.

"And, Peter, get over here and eat," said Traka. "You need to feed your baby."

"Yes, ma'am," said Peter. He returned to his seat, this time walking around the table.

The duck was a culinary teenage dream of crisp and moist, the potatoes the perfect accompaniment, and the salad fresh and sweet.

"Peter, this is the perfect meal," I said. "You are perfect."

"Well, now that you are the father of my child, it is possible a few confessions may be in order," said Peter.

"A few?" asked Rhiannon. "Peter, my love, have you been fibbing to your mates?"

"Lies of omission, I fear," said Peter. "I hope you will forgive me."

"You are forgiven," I said, taking a deep draught of wine.

"Without hearing, first?" said Rhiannon.

"Indeed," I said. "How could I not?"

"Hmm," said Rhiannon. "Please do continue, Peter."

"Are you sure you want me here for this?" asked Traka. She looked, somewhat longingly at her food.

Peter set his hand on hers.

"You will be the godmother," he said. "You should know my dark past."

"Very well," said Traka.

"I did have an agricultural upbringing," said Peter. "But to say it was on a farm is a bit of an untruth. It was more of une domaine."

"An estate?" I queried around a tiny, red potato.

Peter nodded, reached for his wineglass partway across the table, then stopped himself.

"Merde," he said. "This no wine thing is going to be très difficile."

"Yes, but you are strong. Please do continue," I said.

"The D'Laurents are an old naval family," said Peter. "My father was an admiral, his father before him was an admiral, and his father before him. In fact, it is true that we have served France since the time of Le Roi Soleil. Cameron, that would be Louis XIV, the Sun King."

"I do know who Louis XIV is!" I said. "Everybody knows that."

"Very well," said Peter, clearly not convinced.

"Longest reigning European monarch," said Traka quietly. "From 1643 up to his demise in 1715."

"Any which way," said Rhiannon. "A long time."

"Indeed," I said.

"So, you are not a poor country boy?" said Rhiannon. "You are one of the oppressors?"

Peter hung his head. "I am so sorry."

"Peter, you bought me a car," I said.

"Pardon?" asked Peter.

"You bought me a car. Your tastes are refined and expensive," I said. "You, young man, are high maintenance. Surely you understand that Rhiannon and I have long since guessed that you grew up monied?"

"Really?" said Peter.

"This is hardly a dark secret, Peter," said Traka.

"No?" said Peter.

"Cameron, do you think he could possibly be cuter?" asked Rhiannon.

"Impossible," I allowed.

"There is more," said Peter.

"Please do continue," I said.

"You already know that I have my PhD. But I was also a serving officer, though it is not permitted to share the rank," said Peter. He pouted and looked across the table. "It is expected of all the men in my family."

"Obviously," I said. "It would be your duty."

"Truly?" asked Peter.

"Of course, dear," said Rhiannon. "No one could consider this a dark secret either."

"There is one more," said Peter.

"One shudders to imagine," said Traka, dryly.

"Le Cordon Bleu's Diplôme de Cuisine," said Peter.

"Oh!" I said. "Formally?"

"Of course," said Peter. "My father insisted. He said all good wives of naval officers should have the diploma. But, you understand, that was before… You know."

"My dear," said Rhiannon. "You are so accomplished."

"Peter, how is your relationship with your father now?" asked Traka.

"Mostly good," said Peter. "He was most happy with my naval career and the PhD. Less so with me working as a server, especially with my Diplôme de Cuisine. And, he was upset that I would probably not be giving him grandchildren, what with me being a man and all. He has wanted grandchildren terribly badly… Oh!"

"Exactly," said Traka. "Grandparents want to know."

"When do I tell him?" asked Peter. "What do I tell him?"

"Um," I said.

"Cameron. We must get married, immediately," said Peter.

"Peter, you will remember that I am already…" I began.

His head rotated to Rhiannon.

"Rhiannon. We must get married immediately," said Peter.

"Um," said Rhiannon.

"Perhaps," said Traka. "It will be good to start with an engagement and the marriage can wait until afterwards."

I looked to Rhiannon and she nodded, just slightly.

"That sounds like a fine notion," I said. "You know, Peter, you must ask her formally. Traditionally, with a ring. You never know the real answer until you ask, properly."

"That makes me a little nervous," said Peter. He looked at her with wide open eyes.

"That's rather the idea, dear," said Traka.

"And Peter, you will have to tell your parents about the engagement," I said. "Will they be ok with… everything?"

"My parents will adore Rhiannon!" said Peter. He looked down. "They would have adored you too."

"Cameron?" asked Rhiannon. "Are you okay?" She set her hand on my knee.

"Mixed emotions, certainly," I allowed. "But overall? Quite happy. Just save the wedding until afterwards. Is that okay, Peter?"

He nodded. "For you, yes," he said.

"And, if you find the Grail?" asked Traka. "And Cameron survives?"

"You imagine I have not researched this?" said Peter.

"Forgive me," said Traka.

"The Republic of Guin in Micronesia still allows traditional group marriages under the law," said Peter.

"Oh, do they?" asked Rhiannon.

"They do," said Peter. "And there is a French naval research vessel that visits there regularly. So, no challenge is insurmountable, you see?"

"Hmm," I said. "Look at you grin from ear to ear."

"I know, eh?" said Peter.

"So," said Traka. "The Grail."

"You both have such pretty eyes," I said, looking between Rhiannon and Peter. Rhiannon rested her head on my shoulder.

"Children!" said Traka, firmly. "The Grail. It is time for Cameron to dream in the sacred grove above the Asklepion. We have exhausted all other options."

"With the doggies," said Peter.

"Yes, obviously," said Traka. "My nephew in the police has been no help at all. Who knows if those foolish monks are still about?"

CHAPTER NINE – THE ISLAND
DREAMING

Kos, Greece

In truth, the next few days were a bit of a challenge, but I like to think that I did rather well. I managed to convince Peter that we all did not need to immediately fly to Paris to find an engagement ring for Rhiannon and that the countless jewelry shops on Kos could supply exactly what he wanted. I managed to convince Rhiannon that she did not need to get pregnant 'right now' so that she and Peter could have their babies at the same time and that, maybe, it would be better to separate the dates by a month or two. And I even managed to convince Traka that a raging, storm-tossed night was not the best night for mystic dreaming in the sacred grove.

Peter found a lovely, excessively sparkly, single diamond ring and arranged for Nikos to drive Rhiannon and him to Petrino Restaurant in Kos town for a formal date. After dinner, being truly traditional, Peter knelt as he proposed. Rhiannon accepted. Nephew Aris, the waiter, later advised Traka that there was not a dry eye in the restaurant.

That night, and for two more, I slept in the guest room at Traka's. I still caught no sight of Traka's elusive housekeeper, but she kept us both well fed and I was deeply grateful for the excellent wines she provided.

Via a rather static-confounded telephone connection, Admiral D'Laurent welcomed the news of Peter's pregnancy with unrepressed glee. Peter managed to convince the admiral that immediately deploying a small French fleet to the eastern Mediterranean was unnecessary.

Peter's mother advised she would be on a flight to Kos the next day, but the dear boy managed to calm her. To Rhiannon's dismay, his mother insisted she be on Kos for the birth. Of course, this is his mother's right and duty and the news gave me considerable comfort.

All families change when a child beckons and our ménage à trois was no different. Everything, even shared delusion, becomes more real, as serious as hockey. I painted the nursery in bright pastels – twice, as it turned out, as Peter changed his mind. Scandinavian nursery furniture arrived in many boxes. A crib, changing table, chest of drawers – on Rhiannon's instruction, I assembled them all.

We picked the night of April 3 – expected to be clear and pleasant with a bright full moon – for my night of dreaming. A simple, white plastic, folding beach bed and lightweight sleeping bag were to be my bower. Traka arranged special permission for us to be at the Asklepion.

On that night, the four of us gathered on our patio for a simple take-away dinner of village salad and lamb pita sandwiches. Traka brought a large bottle of unlabeled, local white wine – which was not horrible to drink. As she arrived, she plonked the bottle in the middle of the table.

"Are you all ready?' asked Traka, taking her seat beside Rhiannon.

Peter set a platter of sandwiches in the middle of the table and sat beside me.

"We are," said Rhiannon. "Bed and bag are in the car. The potion is mixed and ready."

"Outstanding," said Traka. "I am most excited."

"Then you do it," I said. "I am sure it would be most enlightening."

"No," said Rhiannon. "Just, no."

"Fine," I said.

"But I do have some Jungian pre-dream comments and suggestions," said Traka, as she selected a sandwich.

I uncorked the bottle and poured for all but Peter. I knew better than to argue, best to just let it all roll past.

"Cameron, don't pout," said Traka.

"I am not pouting," I said.

"Well, if you could, you would be," said Traka.

"Maybe," I allowed.

"You know, Carl Jung was a lot like you, Cameron," said Traka.

"Hmm. How so?" I asked.

"He lived much of his life as part of a romantic triad, with his wife Emma and his collaborator Toni Wolff," said Traka. "Sound familiar?"

"He was also a highly intelligent, innovative, classic 19th century Swiss intellectual," noted Peter.

"Oh, that sounds like me," I said.

"Peter, that was not helpful," said Traka.

"It is okay, professor, please do continue," I said. "I will be a good dog."

"Excellent. Thank you," said Traka. "So, you will already understand that dreaming is a doorway into the unconscious. It tells you things you know, but need to pay attention to in your own life. It is never literal. It communicates through symbols and archetypes."

"You know, professor, sometimes mine seem pretty darn literal," I said.

"That is just the surface meaning," said Traka. "The real value lies deeper."

"Truly, my love. Please listen," said Rhiannon.

"Your dreams point to things that you are not paying enough attention to consciously," said Traka. "This should all, theoretically, be especially true of mystic dreaming, with or without a spirit guide."

"Puck is not my..." I started. I sighed. "Never mind, please continue."

"So, good," said Traka. "I want you to try to pay attention to a few things when you are dreaming and immediately afterward. First, the people in your dreams are always part of you. All the characters in your dreams whether male or female represent you."

"Second, as soon as you wake up, ask yourself how you feel? Do this without thinking or analyzing your dream."

"Third write down your dream immediately."

"Fourth, try to think what you associate with the objects in your dream. Some things usually have a standard meaning. Water, for example, represents the deep unconscious. Babies represent creativity."

"These are all good suggestions, Cameron," said Rhiannon.

"Babies represent creativity," said Peter. He placed his hand on mine. "Good job, Cameron."

"That was a bad example for me to pick," said Traka. "But, Cameron, there is one more thing, and I mention it last as I want you to remember it."

"Okay," I said.

"Before you fall asleep, I want you to identify in your own mind the question you want answered," said Traka.

"Oh, I do that," I said.

"You do?" asked Peter.

"Yes, of course," I said. "Otherwise Puck wouldn't know what to prepare."

"I see," said Traka. "So, you believe he is real?"

"Ah. You've got me there. Maybe," I admitted.

Peter patted my hand and smiled broadly.

"Of course, he is real," said Peter. "Obviously."

Traka looked beside her, to Rhiannon. Rhiannon just smiled.

"A fine madness?" I asked.

Traka nodded.

"Never mind," I said. "Ya gotta be a little crazy to drink a potentially fatal potion and dive into the netherworld."

"And, Cameron, really good dreamers can interact with characters in the dream and ask them questions," said Traka.

"Oh, really?" I asked. "I do that, too!"

The climb up the three giant sets of steps to the upper level of the Asklepion, carrying my beach bed, mattress and sleeping bag, cast my mind fondly back to the perfection of Claude and his acolytes at hotel d'Pinus Nigra. Tonight, there would be no fine meal, no fine wine and, ideally, no wolves. There were, however, doggies, big ones at that – my old friend Chaney and his companion Jack accompanied us. Traka waited at the car to avoid the steps.

Peter, Rhiannon, the beasts and I reached the top level of the Asklepion and entered the grove as the sun started to set across the Mediterranean and the light began to die. We turned to watch the hazy tangerine ball touch the wavering, dark line of the horizon above the still, slate-grey sea.

"That," said Peter, "makes it worth the climb."

"Indeed," I said.

"Come," said Rhiannon. "We do not want Peter descending the steps after the light fails."

I nodded and we entered the cypress forest, quickly climbing to beyond the altar stone until we found an open, rocky, glade.

"This looks good," said Rhiannon.

I found a level area and set up the beach bed and mattress. Peter unrolled the sleeping bag atop the mattress.

"Looks fine," I said. "Very comfy."

Rhiannon reached into her bag and drew out the traditional simple, clay cup, then a small, glass vial. I knew it contained a bitter, thick, amber-colored liquid. She poured the entire contents of the vial into the cup, the last few sticky drops falling slowly into the vessel.

"Drink, my love," said Rhiannon.

I took the cup, tilted my head back, and poured the mixture down my throat. I quivered and shook my head.

"Goodness, can't you add sugar or something?" I said. I handed her the cup.

She smiled faintly and kissed me on the cheek.

"Dream well, my pretty one," she said.

"Hmm," I said.

Peter took my hand and kissed my other cheek.

"Just do not get hurt," said Peter. He took Rhiannon's hand and led her out of the clearing, turning once to look back and see me watching. I waved. He winked. And they were gone.

Chaney and Jack stood alert, heads up, watching me.

"Bedtime, boys," I said, and sat upon the bed. I removed my boots and settled, fully clothed, into the sleeping bag. Above, the blue sky faded to black. I lost sight of the dogs as they wandered in circles around the glade.

The moon, I knew, was up, though invisible behind the towering cypress trees.

Chaney returned and rested his head on my legs, looking at me.

"Fine," I said. "I think there is room."

He climbed up beside my legs, circled twice, settled into a curl, and closed his eyes. Jack had wandered away.

The slight wooziness that always foreshadows the dream state rose up.

"Here we go," I said.

Chaney stared, unblinking.

I shut my eyes to see only darkness.

"Puck?" I asked.

No response. I fell into a deep, untroubled sleep.

"Wake up," a woman's voice said.

Someone shook my shoulder and my eyes flickered open. Above, the full moon radiated brightly, sending the sun's lights back down upon the cypress forest. Stars shimmered through a slight haze.

To my right hovered a face. I blinked her into focus – stunningly beautiful with short, tightly curled black hair and ringlets falling to either side of her face.

"Ah, hello, well girl," I said.

"Well girl?" she asked. "That is the best you can manage?"

"Please forgive me, but I am somewhat sedated," I said.

"Yes, I know," she said.

"Are you with them?" I asked.

"Them?" she replied.

"Those German monks," I said.

"Do I look like a monk?" she said, crossly.

"Never," I said. "Nor like a nun."

"Fool," she said.

"Um, what's going on," I asked.

"Ah. Cameron, you are bleeding," she said. "I woke you to bind your wound."

I put my hand to my chest and closed my eyes.

"I must have stressed it carrying the bed up all those damn steps," I said.

"Well, Cameron, they were not likely to build an escalator, were they?" she said.

I opened my eyes to see her smiling.

"All the gods, you are beautiful," I said. My eyes wandered away from her face to see she wore a black hoodie and jeans. She held a small white box marked with a red cross in her hands.

"Shouldn't you be wearing shimmering robes or something?" I asked.

"Boy, this is not part of your dream state," she said, and began to unzip the sleeping bag.

I lay still as she raised my shirt and began bandaging my wound. As I looked to see her work, I noticed Chaney still in place, watching her intently.

"Have you met Chaney?" I asked.

"Of course, many times, up in the forest," she said. "We are great friends. I give him snacks you know."

"Super. So, basically, you could drive a dagger into my heart and he would be good with it?" I said.

"Mm. Not my style, though," she said. "There. All done."

She pulled my shirt back down and rezipped the sleeping bag, trapping my arms within.

"Thank you," I said.

"Aren't you going to ask how I happen to be here, just now?" she asked.

"This is a sacred grove, I was guessing. There is a sacred spring nearby. Where else would you be?" I said.

"Sometimes you really do follow along," she said. "Well done, Cameron."

She bent and kissed me lightly on the forehead.

"I will see you, in time," she said, and stepped back into the darkness of the trees.

"Thank you," I said, quietly. I closed my eyes, again, then opened them immediately. "Seriously, Chaney. Not even a growl as she approached?"

He closed his eyes.

A growl, lion-like, rumbled from the trees.

"Oh, give it up, Puck. I know it is you," I said.

"You know me too well, dear boy," said Puck.

"Finally," I said. "You took your time."

"She was lurking," said Puck. "Made me nervous."

He flew up and hovered above me, in classic sprite form. He looked over his shoulder.

"In fact, she still lurks. Watching. It is creepy."

"She is fine, relax," I said. "Let's get on with it."

"With what?" asked Puck.

"Oh, it's going to be one of those nights, is it?" I asked.

"What are you expecting, then?" asked Puck.

"And, why aren't you speaking in rhyme at all?" I asked.

"Two days after April Fools' Day?" asked Puck. "Do you have any idea how exhausted I am? It takes effort, you know?"

"Fine. But what I am expecting is… everything. The whole deal. The Asklepion in ancient times. The Grail ceremony in situ. To see the ritual. To see the thing itself – what it looks like – once and for all!" I said.

"To understand?" asked Puck.

"Yes!" I said. "Show me. Please."

"You seem to be confused as well as unnecessarily agitated," said Puck. "I don't create your dreams; I just accompany you through them."

"So, who does?" I asked.

"The gods? You? Who knows?" said Puck.

I closed my eyes, but it made no difference. I could still see him.

"Puck. I am exhausted. Worn out," I said. "And, I am running out of time."

"I know, dear boy," said Puck. "I am sorry, but there are rules."

"I know," I said. "And you can't tell me what they are."

He nodded his tiny head.

"Sorry for yelling," I said.

"I have some good news," said Puck.

"Okay," I said.

"Clarine's new boy has his dream guide," said Puck. He chuckled.

"Not you?" I asked.

"I don't like him," said Puck.

"So?" I asked.

"Titania," said Puck. "She likes her young, muscly, handsome boys. She will be all over him. Clarine will be furious."

"I don't see why that brings you joy," I said. "It is extremely immature."

Puck flew up and looked down at my face.

"Really?" he asked.

I smiled up at him.

"Got you," I said. "It is mildly hilarious.

"Bastard," said Puck.

"Puck, where are we going tonight, please?" I asked. "I really am done in."

He flew down to land, standing on my chin.

"Nowhere," he said. "As far as your quest goes, tonight we go to no place."

"Like a dark dimension or something?" I asked.

"No. We will take no journey of learning tonight," said Puck.

"Please explain," I said.

"You want to obtain the Grail," said Puck. "You do not need a mystic revelation. You already have all the pieces of the puzzle. And I am not allowed to give you the answer."

"I already know where it is?" I asked.

"No. But you have the knowledge to figure it out," said Puck.

"*You* plural, as in we? Or *you* singular, as in me?" I asked.

"Both," said Puck.

"Bloody hell," I said.

"Also, remember. If you find it, you only get to use it once," said Puck.

"I only need to use it once," I said.

"Just remember," said Puck. "I am trying to help."

"Okay, got it," I said. "Anything else?"

"So… Want to kill some time?" asked Puck.

"We have time to kill?" I asked.

"Enough," said Puck. "There is this place I want to show you. I want it to be a surprise. It will revive you."

"Okay," I said. "Wait. Are there goblins there?"

"No goblins. I promise," said Puck.

"Okay, then," I said.

I woke slowly to sunlight, the hectoring chirping of a rock partridge, a light breeze carrying the scent of the cypress and saltwater, and to see Rhiannon and Peter standing slightly bowed, looking down on me. Chaney and Jack stood close by, watching.

"He is smiling," said Peter.

"He is," said Rhiannon. "In that way."

"He is," said Peter.

"I… I was dreaming of you," I said.

They looked at each other.

Rhiannon reached down her hand.

"A worthy effort, Cameron," said Peter.

Rhiannon pulled me up, I unzipped the sleeping bag, swung my legs off the bed, and reached groggily for my boots.

"Be still, stoned one," said Peter. "I will do it."

He knelt and slipped my feet into the boots, then tied them.

"I do not think he is ready for those steps just yet," said Rhiannon.

"Indeed," I said. "I'm still a little dizzy."

"There is blood on his shirt," said Peter. He reached up and lifted it. He touched the bandage.

"But it is already bandaged, nicely, too."

"Oh, is it?" said Rhiannon.

"Um…" I said.

"Before you speak," said Peter. "Please be aware, this better be good."

"The Lady of Well woke me in the night," I said.

"Oh, did she?" said Rhiannon.

"And then she left," I said.

"She just woke you up, bound your wound, and left?" said Peter.

"Yes. That's it," I said.

Peter slid his hand down my stomach into my pants, feeling around.

"Seriously?" I said.

"He appears to speak the truth," said Peter.

"Of course, I am telling the truth," I said. "You guys have no faith."

"We have faith that you're a dog," said Peter, shoving his hand away.

"A well-trained dog, perhaps," said Rhiannon.

I gave up.

"Also, Chaney and Jack were useless," I said. "Apparently, they are old friends with well girl. They did not even growl. Oh, and don't call her that. Well girl. She doesn't like it."

"I would imagine," said Rhiannon.

"Seriously," said Peter.

"Puck didn't like her being here," I said. "He took forever to come."

"But he did come?" asked Rhiannon. "And?"

"Completely useless," I said.

She laughed at that.

"He can be, can he not?" she said.

"So, you did not travel. Anywhere?" asked Peter.

"No," I said. "He claimed we already have enough of the pieces of the puzzle to figure out where the stupid Grail is hidden."

"Ah!" said Peter. "How exciting."

"Were those his exact words?" asked Rhiannon.

"Um. No," I said.

"Try, Cameron," said Rhiannon.

"He said, You already have all the pieces of the puzzle. And I am not allowed to give you the answer. I asked if I know where it is and he replied, No. But you have the knowledge to figure it out. That is word for word," I said.

"Well done, Cameron," said Peter.

"I see. Nothing else?" asked Rhiannon.

"Not really," I said. "Except the part about remembering we can only use it once, if we find it. And, I said that I only need to use it once."

"Which rather does imply we can find it," said Peter.

"So, it does," said Rhiannon. "Cameron, can you stand?"

I stood.

"Shaky?" asked Peter.

"Pretty solid, I think," I said.

"Peter will hold your hand on the steps, and I will carry the beach bed," said Rhiannon. "You can carry the sleeping bag."

I nodded. Rhiannon rolled up the bag and handed it to me. She folded up the bed and mattress. I took Peter's hand and we began the descent. I had to sit at the bottom of the second set of stairs.

"Cameron?" asked Peter.

"That took more out of me than it usually does," I said. "I need to rest for a bit. Sorry."

"Ah," said Rhiannon. And she looked away to hide her face.

"Rhiannon?" asked Peter.

"It is near the end of the seven-year cycle," said Rhiannon without turning her face to us. "Sometimes this happens, for the more connected lords. It cannot be helped. But it will pass, soon."

"I am fine," I said. "No worries."

She turned back to face us. "That's my boy. It will all end well; I am sure of it."

After a few more moments, we headed downward. Peter held my left hand and kept casting glances to me, but we made the carpark without incident. Rhiannon threw the beach bed into the back of my lovely 1983 Citroën Méhari and climbed into the back seat. Peter took the driver's seat and I slipped in beside him.

He grinned at me.

"I have breakfast warming in the oven for when we get home," he said. "The good professor will join us. I am sure you will enjoy her debriefing!"

"Super," I said.

Peter set the plate of pancakes – stacked five high, buttered and decorated with swirls of maple syrup – in front of me. I admired them for a moment.

"Peter, you are spoiling me," I said.

"I am," said Peter. He nodded across the table to where Traka conscientiously assembled her own stack of flapjacks. "You are about to be interrogated, after all."

Peter took a seat to my right. Rhiannon stood in the kitchen, doing the washing up.

"You will not eat?" I asked.

"We ate earlier," said Rhiannon.

"It is bad to drive with low blood sugar," said Peter.

"Very wise," I agreed, and cut into the stack, creating a small wedge. I stabbed it and shoved it into my mouth.

"Very elegant," said Peter.

"It's so good," I said, around the mass of pancakes. "Outstanding."

"I forgive you, then," said Peter.

"Shall we begin?" asked Traka.

"Fine," I said.

"First, let us review: the people in your dreams are you. All the characters in your dreams represent you, male or female. Who was in your dream?"

"Only Puck and I," I said.

"That is not helpful," said Traka. "Second, the objects in your dream mean something. What objects were in your dream?"

"Only what was there in the grove, trees, rock, stuff like that," I said.

"Again, not helpful," said Traka. "Third, how did you feel when you woke up?"

"Groggy and tired," I said.

"You were smiling," said Peter.

"I was happy to see you," I said.

"You are such a liar," said Rhiannon. "Peter and I know that smile."

"Fourth, when you woke up, did you write down your dream?" asked Traka.

"No, but I told it to these doubters right away," I said.

"Good enough. Please tell it to me now," said Traka.

"To quote, Puck said, 'You already have all the pieces of the puzzle. And I am not allowed to give you the answer.' When I asked if I know where it is, he replied, 'No. But you have the knowledge to figure it out.' That is word for word," I said.

"And Puck said that we should remember we can only use it once, if we find it. And, Cameron said that he only needs to use it once," said Peter.

"Yes, that's right," I said.

"Hm. Before you fell asleep, did you to identify in your own mind the question you wanted answered?" said Traka.

"I did," I said. "I imagined exactly what I wanted to see, the Asklepion in the old times, the rite, all of it. For all the good it did."

"Sometimes Puck just wants to party," said Rhiannon. "We knew that before we started. We may have to just try again."

"Seriously?" asked Traka.

"It happens," I said. "He can be a lazy sprite."

"Well, there is not a lot to hang a Jungian analysis on," said Traka. "Is there, Peter?"

"Sainte Marie Mère de Dieu," said Peter. He turned to me, his right hand over his lower abdomen. "Pain."

The blood slowly drained from his face and he began to breathe in short, sharp breaths.

"Peter? What is happening?" asked Rhiannon. She slowly set down the dish cloth and dried her hands.

"Professor, please call your nephew, the doctor," I said.

Traka rose, stepped across the room and dialed the number from memory. She spoke in Greek, waited a moment and spoke again. I recognized the words moró (baby) and fóvos (fear). She hung up the phone.

"He says to come now," said Traka.

I stood. "I'll get the car," I said.

"No," said Rhiannon. "You are still drugged. And your car is too old."

"I'll get the Volvo," said Traka. "Please wait out front."

She hustled out the front door.

"I am going to lose the baby," said Peter, so quietly I could hardly understand his words.

"No," said Rhiannon. "You are not."

She took his right arm and I took his left. We helped him stand and he buckled over in pain. I put one arm around his back and one under his knees and lifted him. Rhiannon held the front door open as I carried him outside into the morning light.

Traka appeared almost immediately in her late-model, dark-green Volvo sedan. Rhiannon opened the rear door, I placed Peter in the back seat, and strapped him in with the seatbelt.

"I will sit in the back," I said.

"No," said Peter. "Cameron, I don't want you to experience this…"

"I am coming," I said.

"Please?" said Peter. I saw him crying, wincing in pain.

Rhiannon placed her hand on my arm.

"Stay," she said. "I will call you."

She ran around the car and jumped in the back. Traka pulled away in a swirl of gravel and dust.

I stood there and watched as the Volvo disappeared into the silver green of the olive trees. I stood there as the dust settled slowly to the driveway. Eventually, I went back inside our home, cleared the table, did the dishes, dusted and vacuumed the house, always listening for the telephone to ring. It did not.

I made tea. The length of the cable attaching the telephone to the wall outlet was long enough to let me put the telephone on the couch beside me as I drank the tea, three cups. The telephone did not ring.

Lunch time came and departed.

I sat, barely moving, as the afternoon stretched on, agonizingly slowly, all the sounds of the home overloud.

Dinner time came and departed, and the daylight began to fail.

Footsteps on the gravel outside the front door – one, single, slow set of footsteps. They stopped outside the front door. I waited for the knock, but it did not come.

I stood, picked up the telephone and put it back in the kitchen, then I opened the front door. Traka stood there, looking beaten.

"Cameron, I am sorry," she said. "They are gone. The island did not have the necessary medical skills or resources."

"Gone?" I asked. "Peter and the baby? Both dead?"

She stepped forward and took my arm in both hands.

"No, no, I am so sorry," she said. "Not dead. Gone from the island, all three."

"All three?" I asked.

"My nephew examined Peter and advised a specialist in Athens as soon as possible," said Traka. "Then, well, Peter called his father."

"Ah," I said.

"Coincidentally, there was a French Mistral class helicopter carrier nearby," said Traka.

"Coincidentally," I said.

"Yes. And they have a sixty-nine-bed hospital on board," said Traka. "To make a long story short, a helicopter picked him up at the football stadium near the hospital."

"I see," I said.

"They have good doctors, Cameron," said Traka.

"How long ago?" I asked.

"Two hours," she said. "Sorry for making you wait. But Peter said to wait until his examination aboard ship was complete."

"And is it?" I asked.

"Cameron, we should go inside," said Traka. "Your phone is going to ring in a few minutes."

I stared at her.

"Inside, Cameron," she said, and used my arm to guide me back indoors and sit me at the table.

Once inside, she set about making tea and cheddar cheese sandwiches. She set another cup of tea and two sandwiches in front of me.

"Eat," she said.

I ate, mechanically, using the bitter tea to wash down the dry bread. Traka could not make a decent sandwich.

The telephone rang. It rang again.

"Answer it, Cameron," said Traka.

I rose and lifted the receiver.

"Cameron?" Rhiannon's voice broke with static.

"Yes?" I asked.

"We are on some kind of aircraft with three beds and a doctor," said Rhiannon. "Everything is stable."

"Thank the gods," I said.

"But we are going to Zurich, to a private hospital," said Rhiannon.

"I see," I said.

"The doctor on the ship advised a specialist," said Rhiannon. "I am sorry that I made the decision without you."

"You made the right call," I said.

"You must have been worried to death," said Rhiannon.

I nodded, then remembered she could not see me.

"I was," I said.

"Poor dear," said Rhiannon. "I will call you after we see the doctors, likely tomorrow evening. Do not worry, he is in the best hands. His father must be someone."

I smiled at that.

"Please call when you can," I said.

"I will. Bye my love," said Rhiannon.

"Bye," I said.

She disconnected. I turned to face Traka.

"They are on a plane to Zurich," I said. "Peter is stable."

"Thank goodness," said Traka.

"How do I get to Zurich from here? Do I need to go via Athens?" I asked.

"Sit down and eat, Cameron," said Traka.

I stared at her.

"Sit," she ordered.

I sat and took another bite of the sandwich.

"Professor?" I asked.

"I have specific instructions from Rhiannon and Peter on this issue," said Traka. "You are not to follow them. You are to stay here and find the Grail."

"I am going, obviously," I said. "My place is with Peter. What if he loses the child for gods' sake?"

"Rhiannon is his wife-to-be. She is with him," said Traka. "She will look after him."

"But..." I began.

"Cameron, if you go, you will break their hearts," said Traka. "If you stop seeking the Grail, you will die in less than seven months. Peter adores you and does not want to lose the father to his child. Rhiannon cannot accept losing you. It is tearing her up inside. You must stay here with me and continue the search. Seriously, if you go to them, you will break their dear hearts."

"How long will they be there?" I asked.

"Do you want me to lie?" asked Traka. "Obviously, I have no idea."

I closed my eyes, my shoulders sagging.

"Professor?" I asked.

"Yes, dear boy?" said Traka.

"This is, perhaps, the worst cheddar cheese sandwich ever made," I said. "How does one mess up a cheese sandwich, for gods' sake?"

"Ingrate," said Traka. "From now on you make the sandwiches."

"I think that would be for the best," I said.

"Does this mean you will behave?" asked Traka. "You will do as they say?"

"When have I not?" I asked.

"Ha!" said Traka.

"Mostly, I do, you know," I said. "I don't like to make them sad."

"I know," said Traka. She stepped toward me and placed her wrinkled hand on my shoulder. "You can't bear being here without them, can you?"

"It is a challenge," I confessed.

"A challenge!" she said. "Cameron, you don't have to talk like that anymore."

"It is habit," I said. "Don't worry, I'll be fine."

"Nevertheless," she said. "You will eat at my place, at least for the time being. And, do not worry, I will not do the cooking. Mrs. Krillia will take care of us."

"The alleged Mrs. Krillia," I said.

The following day, I did not sit moping by the telephone during the morning or afternoon. In the morning, despite Peter's absence, I ran up through the olive orchards into the forest, following our usual route, stopping to douse my head with cool water from the spring. I pushed a little harder than normal and, by the time I reached our front door, I started bleeding again.

After a quick shower, I rebandaged myself, found my old Canon camera, grabbed a quick cheddar sandwich – made by me, not dry and with mayo and a light dusting of black pepper, quite tasty – and headed into Kos town in the Citroën Méhari, top open to the bright, early-April sky of cerulean blue and whispering, white clouds, with cool air rushing, and the sound of the wheels on tarmac whirring. I drove at half the speed of Peter's torturous careening. I smiled to myself. The boy was such a treasure in every way, but I took great joy in driving myself for a change.

Once more, I followed Vaileos Georgiou, past the hard standing where sailboats and cruisers sat up high on their steel frames, past the almost empty marina, past the empty beaches, past the shops, and past the police station to the castle.

I took the road to the right, heading to the ferry docks. To my right, the sea lay calm and still. At the docks, a huge Blue Star ferry moored stern in, giant ramps down, tractor trailers rumbling out of the hold, shrouded in purple diesel. Turning off before the docks, I parked in a spot on the left, putting the bonnet of the Citroën Méhari right up against the sunlit stone of the castle wall.

I looked carefully around the vehicle to see if any objects might tempt the lighter-fingered souls of the harbor, but, unless they were tempted by a Red Cross kit, all looked safe and I left the top down and the doors unlocked, then headed toward the castle gate, up the long ramp to Hippocrates' plane tree, over the bridge above the avenue and through the dark tunnel piercing the great wall, to emerge again into the light by the small, wooden ticket booth.

I paid the modest entrance fee and began my solo exploration of Castle Neratzia, seeking additional coats-of-arms of Grand Master Fabrizio del Carretto. I knew that he had been responsible for completing the outer walls and upgrading the inner, older fortress. And, I had seen the two crosses and slashy things carved and set into the outer wall of the huge, external bastion of Carretto. But, it seemed unlikely that the Grail would be hidden on the outer wall of the fortress, open to both thieves and cannon fire. Might he not have added an additional signature elsewhere in the fortifications?

I turned to the left and began a slow circumnavigation of the inside of the castle's massive outer wall. Strolling along the wall's base, through the yellow-flowered, bright green, uneven meadow between the inner and outer walls, scanning the faded pewter and cream of the monumental stones rising more than seven times my height to my left somehow did not feel at all quest-like. I smiled at my foolishness and found myself wondering why I had not brought, at the very least, a flask of tea.

Three quarters of an hour allowed me to complete my circumnavigation of the outer walls, returning to the main gate with at least a modicum of attention to my task. I found no hint of another signature from Fabrizio del Carretto. I decided to try again, but to modify my route to follow along the top of the wall. I headed toward the ramp to the top of the structure, waved to the woman in the ticket booth, and noticed a tall, thin man standing in the shadow of the entrance tunnel. He was watching me.

I waved to him, too. As he stepped out of the shadow, I noticed that he had taken the time to dress quite elegantly in a light, cream-colored linen suit, white shirt, and maroon tie. He nodded to me.

"Mister O'Donnel?" he asked.

"Yes, sir," I replied. Both his short beard and hair showed almost entirely grey.

"Join me for lunch," said the man.

"That does not sound like an invitation," I said.

"I suggest I have been quite patient thus far," he said.

"You have the advantage of me, sir," I said.

"Ah, forgive me. Please allow me to introduce myself," he said. He stepped forward, reached into an interior suit pocket, produced a gold-embossed business card, and handed it to me with a small bow.

"Diogenis Zappides, Director of Kos Archaeological Museum," I read. I looked up to see him smiling.

"You are wondering if old Carretto left a ringer, I am betting?" said Zappides.

"I was," I admitted. "And, yes you have been most understanding, sir. I would love to join you for lunch. I hope you will allow me to ask you to be my guest."

"Nonsense," said Zappides. "You will be my guest. But there will be no more digging behind the marble carvings, eh?"

"Yes, sir," I said.

He nodded.

"Good," he said. "Because I have already invoked a less intrusive solution."

I must have looked confused. He laughed.

"Let us discuss it over lunch," he said, and gestured toward the tunnel. "Shall we?"

I followed him back through the tunnel, across the bridge, under the ancient, widespread branches of Hippocrates' plane tree, down past the police station, and across the street to the sea. In silence, we walked another ten minutes to the four-story Kos Aktis Art Hotel, a bright, modern construction of cement, stone and blue-green colored glass. I held open the glass front door, then followed him through the minimalist lobby of white marble and dark wood paneling, and out onto a two-tier patio restaurant, which sat only a meter or so above the still, aqua hue of the sea.

"Nice," I said.

"Yes," he allowed. "Too new for some tastes, and I confess I do not understand modern style. But, I am told it is the bee's knees. And the food is good."

Only a few of the twenty odd tables were occupied. He waved toward a table right on the water.

"I like to come here this time of year," said Zappides. "In the summer, with the tourists, it is madness of course."

"I have never been here in the summer," I said, as we took our seats at the wooden slatted table.

"You will find it quite exciting," he said. "Oh, the Scandinavian women!"

Unfortunately, at this moment our server arrived. She examined us both with a stern face.

"Do you actually wish to be poisoned, professor?" the woman asked. A thin, fortyish, bespectacled, dark-haired beauty, she had her hair tied into a tight bun.

I thought for a moment of helping him out, but I confess I was curious to discover how deeply into the fire he had fallen.

"Kiki, my dear," said Zappides. "I am sure you understand that I was speaking only of a theoretical appreciation."

"As we Greek women are not enough to theoretically appreciate?" said the woman.

"Kiki, please forgive me. I misspoke," he said.

I smiled at that, and she saw. She looked at me over the top of her glasses.

"You are thinking he is wise to beg for forgiveness?" she asked.

"I confess. It is true," I said.

"And you are?" asked Kiki.

"Cameron O'Donnel," I said, offering her my hand. She shook it lightly.

"Then you are Professor Traka's friend," she said. "I am sorry about your friend. These things are always scary. You must be frightened."

I nodded. "Frightened. Worried. And they won't let me go to them."

She rested her hand on my shoulder.

"Once upon a time, the professor and I almost had a child, but…" she shrugged. "Sometimes it does not work out."

I tried not to cry, then. I really did. But she must have seen the water welling in my eyes. She took my cloth napkin from the table, wiped my eyes, then stood upright.

"Wine and lunch, professor?" said Kiki.

"Please, my dear," said Zappides.

"Tch," said Kiki. She departed.

"Obviously – on and off – we have been lovers," he said. "If she would have me, I would still be with her now."

"I am sorry," I said.

"No, no. It is for the best," said Zappides. "It ended when my wife stabbed me with a butcher's knife."

"Because of Kiki?" I asked.

"Possibly," allowed Zappides. "My wife was heavily pregnant at the time, so she may have just been angry that I was not sharing her discomfort."

"Was she charged?" I asked.

"For stabbing her husband? While pregnant? Is this not Greece?" asked Zappides. "She did not come close to any vital organs. So, no, I did not see any reason for it."

"So, I left him," said Kiki, who had just returned with a carafe of white wine. She placed her left arm behind her back and poured our wine with her right. "I told him that being stabbed by your wife was a perfectly acceptable reason to leave her, even if she was pregnant. But he pussied out."

"I did not pussy out!" said Zappides.

She ignored him.

"So, I realized that he never would and I left him," said Kiki.

"I understand," I said, once again resorting to the fallback safe response.

"I still love you, my dear," said Zappides.

"Tch," said Kiki. "You better or I will poison you."

She scowled at him, graced me with a smile, and departed.

"You are either frightfully brave or…" I stopped myself.

"Frightfully stupid?" asked Zappides. He laughed. "The latter, obviously. We men are frightful fools, are we not?"

"We are," I agreed. "Or, at least, I am."

He raised his glass. I lifted mine.

"Yiamas," said the director.

"Cheers," I returned.

We drank.

"Not bad," said Zappides.

"Indeed," I agreed.

I looked to my right, over the thin, stone beach to the sea. The water lapped quietly and softly onto the stones, rattling them gently when it receded. Beyond the shore, the sea lay clear and just touching still, revealing the yellow sand and dark tendrils of seaweed on the seabed. A school of dark fish flashing vertical yellow stripes slipped by, darting now toward, now away, from the shoreline. In the distance, the dark line of Asia Minor sat below an indigo sky laced with dark clouds sailing north, bypassing the islands. My mind slipped into the middle distance for a time.

"Mister O'Donnel?" Kiki's voice drew me back.

"Sorry, I was wandering," I said. I leaned back and she set a small, white plate before me.

She smiled again and set a platter of sliced meat and cheeses, pita, tzatziki, melitzanosalata, fava, and olives on the table between Zappides and me.

"Nice," I said.

She poured more wine, gave me a slight bow, another scowl to Zappides, and departed.

"So, you come here pretty much just to see her," I said.

"Not alone," said Zappides. "Thank you for being my wingman."

"Of course," I said.

We drank the chilled, dry wine and watched the waves.

"She will never come back to me, of course," he said. "But I still enjoy seeing her cute nose, hearing her sharp tongue, you understand."

"She obviously still loves you," I said.

"But one does have to be practical," he said. "I cannot blame her."

"Indeed," I said.

He reached for a slice of pita.

"I hope you do not mind our simple orektika or, as you say, appetizers, for lunch," said Zappides.

"It is perfect," I said. "I am eating supper at Professor Traka's for a while."

"I understand," he said. "It must be difficult for you, just now."

I took another sip of wine. He shrugged.

"You must understand, the French military helicopter landing in the football stadium caused a bit of a stir," said Zappides. "I doubt there is anyone on the island who does not know of your story."

"All of it?" I asked.

"This is Kos," he said. "By now the whole story is known in a dozen different versions, all only lightly moored to any version of reality. Also, there is a joke going about. Something about French helicopter parenting?"

"Super," I said.

He laughed and waved his finger at me.

"Tongues do tend to wag!" he said. "One must accept it. In Greece any truth is fair game, no matter how outlandish, especially now, in our time of troubles."

I gestured toward the Mediterranean.

"You have this," I said.

He poured me another glass of wine.

"And this," he said.

We drank.

"Sadly, what we do not have is your Grail, at least not at the castle," said Zappides. "Ah, I see I have your full attention, Mr. O'Donnel, at least for a while."

"You do," I said. "And I apologize, I do tend to drift away these days. Can you please explain?"

He reached across the table and patted my hand.

"Do not trouble yourself," he said. "And, I will explain. After your adventure in the dark of night at the castle…How exciting that must have been, I do so wish I had been there to see it! That Peter of yours must be a wonder!"

"He is a sacred treasure," I agreed.

Zappides nodded. "Any which way, after your adventure, I was forced to wonder what else lay behind those marble coats-of-arms. So, I took matters into my own hands!"

"You pried them off yourself?" I asked.

"Do I look like a savage?" he retorted. "Certainly not. I borrowed a radar imaging device from Athens and scanned each and every one!"

I looked at my hands, which still showed a little red from the quick-drying cement.

"I wish we had thought of that," I said.

He nodded. "I also wish you had, but that is yesterday's snow, as you say. Sadly, there is no Grail waiting behind the slabs."

I sighed. He went to pour me more wine, but the carafe was empty.

"Can you ask for some more?" he said. "She will not bring me more than one carafe. She fears a maudlin scene."

I took the carafe from his outstretched hand and held it aloft, successfully catching Kiki's eye. She frowned, but nodded.

"But," said Zappides. "We did find a tomb, a mummy-like soul buried behind one of the slabs. You will forgive me if I do not advise which one until I have funding for a proper excavation. As far as we could see, there are no grave goods, however. Alas, no Grail."

"You think I would be a grave robber?" I asked, a little hurt.

"Well, past behavior..." he said.

"Fair enough," I said. "I am glad you found something exciting."

"It is, isn't it?" he said. "I am frightfully keen. It could be almost anyone, could it not?"

Kiki brought the wine and poured. As she left, Zappides leaned forward, his cheeks rouged by the wine.

"It is frightfully cliché, I know, but she used to be one of my graduate students," he said.

"It is not for me to judge," I said, judging.

He raised both hands in surrender.

"I always promised myself it would never happen, then she came along," he said. "What a monstrous dog I am."

"Not at all," I said. "It is I who feel rather like a golden retriever these days."

He tilted his head and scanned my face. I changed the topic.

"We are, it seems, completely out of leads, as far as the Grail goes, I'm afraid," I said."

"But the good professor Traka, who slept with her share of grad students I assure you, says that your spirit guide advised you in a mystic dreaming session that you already know enough to find the wretched thing," said Zappides.

At that, I poured an entire glass of the white down my throat.

"Fine, my spirit guide," I muttered. "Where does that even come from?"

"Well..." began Zappides.

"No. Please. It was not a real question," I said. "I don't care from whence it fucking comes."

"I was going to say, it came to me from Traka," said Zappides.

"You see," I said. "That is how evil spreads."

He laughed, beginning a coughing fit as the wine attempted to enter his lungs. Kiki arrived promptly at his side, passed him a fresh napkin, and held him to steady his shaking frame.

"Mister O'Donnel, please be more careful," said Kiki.

"My error. I apologize," I said.

She continued to hold him as, wheezing, he regained his breath. As he steadied, she released him and stood straight. She examined Zappides, then me.

"Are either of you driving?" she asked.

"Certainly not," said Zappides.

"Um. I was," I said. "I quite forgot. Peter usually drives."

"Hmm," said Kiki. "It's like you are both children. You are not driving, obviously."

"Why is that a recurring theme?" I asked. "For goodness' sake."

"Perhaps you should dwell on that question yourself, oh Fertility God," said Kiki. "While you do, I will get you both some coffee and make a call."

She headed back to the kitchen.

"We should finish the wine before she takes it away," said Zappides.

I nodded and topped up our glasses.

"I don't usually drink coffee," I said.

"I suggest you drink this one," said Zappides.

"After the wine, then," I said, and took another sip.

"Now, as we were discussing before you tried to kill me," said Zappides. "You supposedly already know where the wretched thing hides."

"In theory," I said. "And why wretched thing? You have called it that twice."

"How many lives have been wasted by a fixation on the Grail? Countless, including Professor Traka's." said Zappides. "How many people have spent years writing Grail books?"

I recognized this as a rhetorical question.

"Think John Steinbeck. He was hypnotized. He lost almost three years of his life to *The Acts of King Arthur and His Noble Knights* and he never finished it," said Zappides.

"It's really more of a hobby, at least for me," I said.

"But not for your loved ones, I think," said Zappides.

"True," I said. "But if it were not for the Grail, I would never have visited this island. Never have sat here with you for this luncheon by the sea. Can that be a waste?"

"You keep dodging the question," said Zappides. "What do you know?"

Kiki approached the table with a small tray carrying two white, ceramic cups of coffee, American.

"You can discuss it tonight," said Kiki, setting the beverages on the table. "I have just spoken with Professor Traka. I will drive you both to her villa in Mr. O'Donnel's French thingy with the impossible gear box. Diogenis and I have been added to the guest list for dinner tonight. She suggests that two fresh viewpoints may assist in answering that very question."

"That very question?" I hazarded.

"My shift ends at five," said Kiki. "So, drink your coffee and find a spot to sober up. Because, really, you both are useless now."

She departed.

"The question being, what do you know?" said Zappides. "And thank you for letting her boss you about so, even though she and I are strangers to you."

"Well, you let me rob your castle and she scares me," I said.

"You are very wise," said Zappides. "My wife is not the only one to have stabbed me with a butcher knife."

He pushed up the right sleeve of his perfect suit to reveal a long, thin scar.

"In truth, I do not even remember why she became so angry," he said.

"Director Zappides, please permit me to observe that you live a dangerous life for the head of museum," I said.

He waved this away.

"Greek women are not cold fishes like British or German females. They embrace their deep and intense loves and hates without reservation," said Zappides. "It is only natural that they get a little excited at times. A Greek man must accept this without complaint."

It did not seem wise to argue. We drank the coffee. Zappides left euros, including an extravagant tip, on the table and we headed to the Kos Archaeological Museum. Entering, we walked past the exquisitely carved statues of a seated and wing-footed Hermes, past Dionysus, Pan and a satyr, past Artemis, Asclepius, and his daughter Hygeia, across the large, bright tile mosaic of Asclepius bringing healing to the island, to a dark wooden door. The Director opened it with a key, and we climbed the white marble stairs to his office.

The door lay open, revealing a small, cramped space lined with densely packed bookshelves. At the far end of the long, thin room, below an arched window, stood a pristine, completely barren desk. Two leather couches sat against the walls between the doorway and the desk.

"Oh, well thought, my good director," I said.

He hung his suitcoat on a hook behind the door, loosened his tie, and plopped into the righthand couch, stretching out with his feet on the arm rest.

"Kiki will find us here," he said. "The other one is yours, sir."

I sat, then stretched out.

"Nice," I said.

Shortly after five, a sharp rapping on the open door roused the director and me from a collective deep slumber. I blinked groggily at the door to see Kiki's wire-frame glasses sitting above her perfect, classic Greek nose. Her long, straight, black hair had been set free of its tidy bun to float down over her shoulders.

"Mister O'Donnel," she said. "You are smiling."

I cleared my throat. "And reasonably sober," I added.

"Well done," said Kiki. "And you Diogenis?"

He lay still, his eyes flickering open like butterfly wings.

"Director?" I asked, sitting up and setting my feet on the floor.

Kiki stepped into the tiny room and offered him her hand. He reached up and took it. She pulled him into a seated position.

"Ho!" he said. "As time passes it becomes harder to return to the light."

There followed a conversation in Greek wherein Kiki's voice modulated from concerned, to cross, back to concerned, finally settling on rather wistful. Zappides' voice remained that of a supplicant, with "I will love you forever, bowing before your infinite beauty" heavily implied. I stood and walked quietly over to the arched window. Outside, strolling couples and families wandered across Eleftherias Square in the late afternoon light. An invisible flock of pigeons cast fluttering shadows across the paving stones as the birds circled, just out of view.

Listening to the voices behind me continue in a gentle melody, I could not help but reflect in melancholy that the conversations of ex-lovers must be a sacred thing to the gods. Tinged with past lovemaking, tearful fights, abandoned and enduring love, and the phantom dreams of what might have been, they are a worshipful sonnet offering up our barely contained sorrow and lost hopes to our divine betters.

Staring out that window into the square, I realized that the slow progression stood complete. I no longer had any control over my emotions. Tears rushed down over my cheeks to dampen my chest, while my arms hung useless by my sides. This, then, was the final days of the Dying Gods: bare emotion, just like the wolf, the badger, the foolish squirrel, as all pretense of separateness slips away, all the barriers dissolve into fluttering leaves and water glittering over smooth stones in near imperceptible rapids.

Those families in the square, what invisible sorrows lay there? The low tones of the once and future lovers behind me... my family... Peter? And the baby, alive? Rhiannon? My little ones, Flora, Morgan and Andrew, how did they fare? Would I even see their wondrous faces again before the bright, bronze axe came down, inevitably, on my exposed jugular, sending me into darkness? It all rushed in, a wave of tumultuous saltwater on the shifting sands of an exposed Nova Scotia beach.

Such maudlin foolishness, yet it overwhelmed me. I started to tremble.

"Bloody hell," I whispered, still focused on the folk below.

"Mr. O'Donnel?" asked Zappides from the couch.

"I do believe I have at long last become untethered," I said. "I am entirely and ultimately embarrassed."

I felt a hand on my shoulder and turned to see Zappides, grey and serious, beside me.

"Young man," he said. "Stop being so Anglo-Saxon. You now live on an island in the Aegean, for God's sake. I can't count the tears I have seen in this very office."

"Including yours," said Kiki.

"Very true," said Zappides.

He rested his arm across my shoulders.

"All of us, we embrace both named and nameless sorrows. Can one escape this?" he said, shaking his head. "But, tonight, we will eat, drink, and talk of myth and legend and magic goblets. Just like the foolish mortals we will always be. And, in the end, fate will write the final stanza."

Kiki came forward and wiped tears from my face with a paper tissue. She nodded toward Zappides.

"This, of course, is why I love him so," said Kiki. "He is always there when the tears begin to fall, even if all ends in darkness."

I nodded but could say nothing.

Kiki took my hand and held it quietly for some minutes, until the tears began to ebb. Then she wiped my face again with the same somewhat sodden tissue.

"I am sorry. It is the only one I have," she said.

I took it from her and tossed it into the wastebasket beside Zappides' desk.

"Ah, the tears will dry in the wind," I said. "The top is down on the Méhari and the fresh air will help clear my head."

I reached into my pocket and tossed Kiki my car keys.

"Don't break it," I said. "It was a present from Peter."

"You love him so," said Kiki.

"I do," I said.

"You are going to make him cry, again," observed Zappides.

I cleared my throat. "I'm good," I said.

Kiki drove us with considerable élan from my parking space by the castle to Traka's villa, embracing enough velocity to make a mere mortal tremble. For those of us used to Peter's headlong plunge through the laws of physics, however, it seemed a calm and steady ride. I did not need to provide directions. She clearly knew the way. We arrived at Traka's in a swirl of dust and gravel, deposited Zappides, and I directed Kiki to my garage.

On the walk back to the villa, Kiki glanced at my family's house and said, "you have a lovely home."

"Peter fell in love with it," I said. "And we could not deny him."

"He is most fortunate," said Kiki.

"We are all most fortunate, would you not agree?" I asked.

"I would," she said and slipped her arm through mine.

"Room for one more?" said Kiki, mischievously.

I laughed out loud as we pushed open Traka's front door.

Dinner at the villa is always traditionally Greek. That night we feasted on moussaka -- sautéed eggplant, ground lamb, tomato, onion, garlic and potato, covered in béchamel sauce and cheese – charcoal-seared skewered pork, village salad, fluffed white rice and, inevitably, French-fried potatoes.

The dinner lay set on the dining room table when we arrived. No sign of the alleged Mrs. Krillia. The varietal Athiri white wine from Rhodes matched well the béchamel and the grilled pork.

As she opened a second bottle, Traka looked to me.

"You will pour, Cameron," said Traka.

I took the bottle and topped up our four glasses.

"The best Athiri grapes grow on the slopes of Mount Attavyros on Rodos at between 650 and 700 meters in altitude," said Traka. She looked around her table. "It has been a while since Director Zappides and Ms. Poole stopped by to enjoy my wine. Cameron, you do seem to collect people."

"Not at all," I said. "The good director was kind enough not to have me arrested at the castle. And he and Kiki are old friends. And then, you know, I forgot I was driving and may have had a little too much wine at lunch."

"Imagine that," said Traka. "And how nice that you and Ms. Poole are so quickly on a first name basis."

"You are being bad, professor," said Zappides. "The poor boy has had a long afternoon. Perhaps we should focus on the question at hand? What does this fellow..." he gestured toward me with a pork-cube-laden wooden skewer, "know about where the Grail might be?"

"You just want another example of a supposed Grail at your upcoming Grail exhibition," said Kiki.

"Oh, I most definitely do," said Zappides. "And, of course, to keep Mister O'Donnel's handsome head on his shoulders."

"Very well. Let us begin at the beginning, shall we?" said Traka. "Kiki, do you still carry your note pad? Can you take relevant notes?"

Kiki nodded and reached into her bag to pull out a medium-sized notepad and ballpoint pen.

"Cameron?"

"Eh?" I said.

"Puck said that you, both singular and plural, have the knowledge," said Traka. "The plural is you, me, Peter and Rhiannon. Cameron, you have the smaller sub-set of knowledge, so it makes sense to start with you, singular. This allows us to avoid things that I or Peter and Rhiannon know that you may not know. Understand?"

"And if I have forgotten or misunderstood?" I asked.

"Granted this approach assumes a capability that may be absent," allowed Traka. "But let's try it this way, shall we?"

"Yes, ma'am," I said.

An uncomfortable silence fell upon the table. I poured myself more wine.

"Begin at the beginning, child," said Traka.

"Well, I know the story of the Grail, more or less," I said.

"Which one?" asked Kiki. "There are so many."

"The central theme, so to speak. I will condense mightily," I said. "First, if we are to follow a linear progression..." I cleared my throat and took another sip of wine. "In ancient times, in the country of Logres, the following was true: in those days we lost the Song of the Wells and Girls who lived within them."

"In those days, travelers could arrive at one of these wells and ask for any food or drink they desired and two beautiful girls would come out of the well, one carrying cups of gold with drink and pastries, meats and bread, the other carrying a white napkin with the requested food."

"Sadly, Amangons, a new king, was crowned in Logres. He did not respect the old ways. This King Amangons raped one of the women of the wells and stole her gold cup. At this point, she would no longer emerge from the well, but the well still provided food to travelers."

"But then, the king's barons learned what he had done and did the same, raping the girls of the wells and stealing their golden cups. Then none of the girls would come out and no food or drink were provided."

"Then came the desolation. Trees lost their greenery. Meadows became wastes. Lakes evaporated. And, none could find the court of the rich fisherman."

"The Fisher King," said Zappides.

"Years later the tale of this woe came to the court of Arthur," I said. "The king decided that they should restore the wells and protect the girls. Many of Arthur's knights swore a sacred oath to do so and set out on the Grail Quest."

"In the stories, including those by Chrétien de Troyes, Wolfram von Eschenbach and Geoffrey of Monmouth, the hero -- Gawain, Perceval, Galahad, whomever -- seeks the Grail, embarking on a years-long search, sometimes, as in the case of Perceval, without even knowing it."

"Adventures are had. Again, in the case of Perceval, through the adventures, he grows from a boy into a knight. But all the adventures are stories of learning for the main characters."

"And all are completely compatible with the Jungian worldview, especially the Perceval story arc," said Traka. "Indeed, one can say that Gawain is Perceval's shadow self. Gawain is the sun hero and can be seen to embody the collective consciousness of the pagan times, while Perceval stumbles along in a much more modern, most human manner..."

"Good professor, please give me a fighting chance," I said. "You asked me to do it, remember?"

"Sorry," said Traka. "It is all just so..."

"Hypnotizing?" asked Zappides.

"Indeed," I said. "So, eventually, after a variety of trials that prove the character's worth, the seeker comes to the Grail Castle, home of the Fisher King."

Kiki paused in her note taking. "Alternately, the Rich Fisherman," she said.

"Indeed. And at the Fisher King's home, the seeker is welcomed by a well-dressed household to a lavish dinner," I said. "He meets the eternally wounded Fisher King, sees the Grail in procession, but fails -- through stupidity, lack of knowledge of the Grail, or even just an attempt to be polite – to ask the necessary question and heal the wasteland."

"But, do we even know the correct question?" asked Kiki. "According to Chrétien's version it is, 'Who is served by the grail?' Wolfram's story has it as, 'Why do you suffer so?' And Wagner's got it as a somewhat funky 'Who is the Grail?' How does one even begin to know?"

"It is a valid point, dear," said Traka. "But I suggest the key is that he fails to ask the question at all; he fails to act."

"So, anyway," I said. "He messes up. He fails to act, finishes his meal, is put to bed in a nice chamber, and wakes up in an empty castle. He doesn't even know how badly he has messed up, but does know something is off 'cause he is not a complete idiot."

"He leaves, has more adventures, meets more people, tells his tale, and they finally tell him how badly he has screwed the pooch."

"I am not familiar with that term," said Kiki.

"Ah," I said.

"Screwed you know, of course," said Traka. "Pooch is a North American slang term for dog."

"Ew," said Kiki.

"It means messed up badly," I said. "My apologies."

"From your perspective, dear, one might say Director Zappides was the pooch," said Traka.

"Shall we trot out some of your old Grail quest stories, my good professor?" I asked.

"Perhaps let's move along?" said Traka.

"So, our hero gets a reputation as the guy who failed to undo the desolation. He is shamed," I said. "More adventures happen, he wanders, sometimes he gets married, but he always does some growing up and, eventually, he ends up back at the Grail Castle."

"This time he asks the question, the question is answered, the Grail King is healed, and the land is restored, coming back to life in a spectacular fashion. Sometimes the seeker becomes the new Grail King, sometimes it is someone else. But, the old king always dies, happy to go to his Christian god."

"The End."

"I do believe that is strangely correct," said Traka. "If somewhat skeletal. And, missing essential Jungian context."

"Most skeletal," agreed Zappides.

Kiki held up her glass. "More wine, please."

I poured.

"I don't see how it helps," I said. "I mean pretty much every person on the whole freak'n planet knows the story. It hasn't helped them find the freak'n Grail. Has it?"

"Is he always like this?" asked Kiki.

"Not really," said Traka. "He appears to be migrating toward despondency now that his beloved are away. However, there is truth in what he says: this myth certainly is well known."

"*He* is right here," I said.

"So, what else do you know?" asked Traka.

"Characteristics of the Grail?" I asked.

"Please recall them as you are able," said Traka.

"Very well," I said. "This part is easy. To start, we don't know what it is. It could be a golden goblet or platter, a simple clay cup or a stone, a meteor fallen from heaven or a caldron."

"It provides food to taste. Whatever you want, it supplies it."

"It provides spiritual solace. It preserves youth and life and heals wounded knights."

"It emits light and a sweet fragrance, rejoices the heart – one cannot sin on the day one sees it. And it can tell good versus evil."

"Allegedly if you are unbaptized, then you cannot see it and the defender of the Grail can have only the one love prescribed by the Grail, but those might be considered a Christian overlay."

"Writing may appear on the Grail, letting the faithful know the will of God."

"Only those who are predestined can find it."

"And, based on the story Sir Gawain and the Green Knight, it may be possible for the Grail to reattach severed heads."

"Ooh, very good, Cameron," said Kiki. "Wait a moment please. Let me catch up!"

I could see her writing had become somewhat variable.

"My dear," said Zappides. "Perhaps a little water?"

"Say you?" asked Kiki. She poured more wine around the table. "Like you get to say anything."

"Perhaps this is not the time, my dear?" asked Zappides in a voice that can only be described as fearful.

"Kiki, no lovers' spats at the dinner table," said Traka.

"Ex-lovers' spats," said Kiki.

Zappides sighed and I watched as he surrendered, downing his glass of wine and refilling it.

"But, again, none of this is new," I said. "It is all known knowledge."

"It is best to lay the foundation before raising the walls," said Traka. "Now, perhaps we should focus on Grail knowledge gained during your little adventures? This is a sub-set of not widely known knowledge, as you put it."

Just then, the telephone in Traka's library shrilled a metallic ring.

"That will be for you, Cameron," said Traka. "Go and take your time. We will be fine at the table."

"And you know that how?" I asked.

She pointed toward the athenaeum with her Macbethian finger. I rose, bowed slightly to her and walked quickly to the library's double doors. The black, rotary telephone rang insistently on the large, wooden, book-laden table at the center of the room. I felt the tears start before I picked up the handset.

"Hello," I said. "Traka residence."

"Cameron?" said Rhiannon. The line sparked with static, but I would know her voice amongst millions.

"Yes," I said. "Tell me all is well."

Silence followed.

"Tell me," I said. "Please."

"Are you crying?" she asked.

"Yes," I said. "It is now quite common."

"Painful loss of control of the emotions?" asked Rhiannon.

"Yes," I said.

"It should last for only a month or so," said Rhiannon. "It is not uncommon at this time of the cycle."

"I guessed," I said. "Please tell me about Peter."

"They say it may be he was never meant to have children," said Rhiannon.

I felt a tug in my chest.

"Placental abruption," said Rhiannon. "His placenta has started to part from the uterine wall. If it gets too bad, the fetus will not get enough oxygen. There are lesser evils, but this is the main one."

"Placental abruption," I repeated.

"The doctors are calling it a moderate case," said Rhiannon. "He needs complete bed rest until it heals. It could be a month, my love, or more."

"But it will heal?" I asked.

"It should," said Rhiannon. "There is a risk, though…"

"Is he comfortable?" I asked. "Is he in pain?"

"We are in a private room at a private Swiss hospital," said Rhiannon. "I have never before seen such a thing. And he is fine."

I chose my next words carefully.

"May I please come?" I asked.

"Cameron, we miss you, but you must find the Grail, please," said Rhiannon. "I promise, if we have to stay too long, then I will book your ticket myself."

"Okay, then," I said. "Actually, we were reviewing what we know about the Grail over dinner when you called. Kind of touching on known knowns, so to speak."

"Good for you," said Rhiannon. "But who is we?"

"Professor Traka, Director Zappides, Kiki and I," I said.

"And who," said Peter's voice, somewhat distantly over the staticky line, "Is Kiki?"

"I should have mentioned that you are on a speaker phone," said Rhiannon. "This room has quite the set up."

"Peter, are you okay?" I asked.

"Do not dodge the question," said Peter. "Who is she? How old is she? And is she cute? Those are three specific questions which need three specific answers. Also, you are not supposed to upset me."

"I will not," I said. "She is Director Zappides' special lady friend. She appears to be in her early forties. And she is cute."

"She is his lover?" asked Rhiannon.

"They say ex-lover," I said. "But I would guess that once and future lover would be more correct."

I wanted to ask Rhiannon if she was sugar coating the truth about Peter and the baby, but thought not to do so in front of our dear companion. In fact, she may have been doing so for his sake.

"Promise you will not take her to bed," said Peter.

"I promise," I said.

"That was a little too fast," said Peter.

"Cameron, there is nothing you can say now to not be in trouble," said Rhiannon. "Even though you may be completely innocent. It is only logical for lovers to be instinctually jealous when their lover is married. There is a pre-established pattern of behavior, after all."

I opened and closed my mouth a few times, silently running possible responses through my mind. After a moment, I fell back on a proven approach.

"Will it help if I apologize?" I asked.

"For what?" asked Peter.

"I honestly don't know," I said.

I heard them both laugh, a distant, static-broken laughter. I smiled.

I heard rustling and clinking over the line.

"Cameron, our supper has arrived," said Rhiannon. "They are setting out the tableware. The chef here is quite good. Peter approves."

"Wow," I said. "When can we talk again?"

"I will call in a few days," said Rhiannon. "And I will telephone immediately if something goes amiss. So, do not fret, okay?"

"Bye, my love," called Peter from the background. "Do not worry. I am fine!"

"Be safe, Cameron," said Rhiannon. "And try not to lose yourself."

"No worries," I said. "All is good, my loves."

And the line went quiet. I took a few moments to wipe away the tears and compose myself, then returned to Traka's dining room. Three faces turned to me expectantly, one showing the shadowed face of a crone in the candlelight, another grey-bearded with wine-reddened cheeks, and a third, petite, pretty and strangely sober.

"They say the chef at the hospital is quite good," I said. "I have never heard the like."

"Cameron," said Traka, firmly.

"Placental abruption," I said. "Peter will need bed rest for at least a month and there is continued risk of losing the child."

"You will go, of course," said Kiki.

"I am to stay and find the grail," I said.

"Those are my instructions for you as well," said Traka.

"You have instructions for him?" asked Kiki, a little startled.

"Obviously," said Traka. "He cannot be left without a minder."

"Cameron, did they say anything else?"

I retook my place at the table. Someone had topped up my glass again. I sipped, then noticed I had also been served more moussaka. I took a forkful. The béchamel sauce really was excellent, buttery with a light, unpasteurized white cheese added for depth of flavor.

"Well, gosh, you know Peter. I had to promise not to take Kiki to bed," I said.

Traka cackled loudly. "The boy is flawless!" she said.

"Seriously?" asked Zappides, and I realized my error.

"And you, Director," I lied. "I also had to promise not to sleep with you. They are both extremely jealous types."

"I see," said Zappides.

"I am not some trollop to be discussed so," said Kiki, almost inaudibly.

Traka reached over and took Kiki's hand.

"No dear, of course not," said Traka. "There is a bit of a problem with Cameron being a dying god and all. Apparently, women who want to have babies are drawn to him."

"Really?" asked Zappides, now quite interested.

"And nobody told me about it for six years!" I said.

Traka cackled again, this time joined by Kiki.

"Good," said Kiki. "You men are all such dogs."

"True, true," said Zappides.

"But, babies?" asked Kiki.

"Cameron," said Traka. "Please get another bottle from the refrigerator, then we will continue our review."

I found another bottle of the white on the top shelf and opened it on the kitchen counter. I set it down beside Traka with a bit of a thud and resumed my seat.

"Where were we headed next, professor?" I asked.

"Grail knowledge gained during your wanderings," said Traka.

"It is unfortunate that Rhiannon is not here," I said. "Where should I start?"

"Rhiannon started with some documentation from the Ahnenerbe, did she not?" said Traka. "Acquired by her uncle?"

"There is that morally useful word again," I said.

"Pardon?" asked Kiki.

"Acquired," I said. "A useful word."

"Yes," said Zappides. "I fear I will have to use it in my new Grail exhibition, if you want to avoid cell time."

"Please," I said.

"Cameron!" said Traka, sharply.

"Very well," I said. "Yes, Rhiannon acquired a map and postcards from the Ahnenerbe's SS-Standarten Führe Wust. The map led us to the apparent Lady of the Wells sarcophagus at the Musée de Cluny, which led us to the Priory of Ganagobie, where we found the sarcophagus was really a ritual basin from an ancient temple in a sacred grove, wherein I dreamed and slept with wolves."

"In that dream, I learnt that the Grail was in Kos during the time of Roman Emperor Valentinian the Great. Backing this up, Rhiannon had some old postcards from the Ahnenerbe. So, we came to Kos."

"Which led us to the Hotel Starry Blue Skies and Yiani Papadopolous."

"Which is related to the Grail how?" asked Zappides.

"Oh! It isn't," I said. "I just really loved being there with Peter and Rhiannon."

"I see," said Zappides.

"And then, on recommendations, we met with Professor Traka, who lectured us sternly about the folly of seeking the Grail as an actual artifact, until Rhiannon sussed out her dark secret," I said.

"I have a reputation," said Traka.

"The good professor eventually confessed to her own quest and became our wise woman," I said. "She added her knowledge to ours after various promises of fealty were exchanged."

"Oh really, professor?" said Zappides. "After all these years you are sharing your secrets?"

"Time does pass," said Traka. "And Cameron's little family is so much fun to be around! Also, I am sharing my apocryphal grails with you, my good director."

"The key in all this being that you determined the Grail was here during Valentinian the First's time, from roughly 364 to 375," said Kiki. "In a dream?"

"Mystic dreaming, my dear," said Traka. "You have doubts?"

"Tomorrow, when I am hungover, I will have doubts," said Kiki. "For now, let's just go with the whole he's a god thing."

"Fair enough," allowed Traka.

"Anyway, despite following all the breadcrumbs left by Wust, and spending about a thousand years looking through the good director's nasty warehouse of pottery shards, and acquiring quite a nice grail from Grand Master Fabrizio del Carretto…" I said.

"Which may actually serve as a Grail-like relic for devout Christians," said Traka.

"Indeed," I said.

"I haven't heard much about this grail from del Carretto?" said Kiki. "That is new."

"They were bad," said Zappides. "But they have been forgiven. It is now in our possession. And we found a tomb hidden within the castle walls."

With this I saw a light come to Kiki's face.

"Any chance you would like to be on that little excavation, my dear?" asked Zappides. "I have applied for EU funding."

"You are shameless," said Traka. "You dangle shiny things before your ex-lover's eyes."

"He is," said Kiki. "And, yes, I will be there in a heartbeat."

"Thank you, my dear," said Zappides.

"Professor Traka, dinner at your villa is always interesting," said Kiki. "Thank you."

"It is even more fun when Cameron's lover and companion are here," said Traka. "I hope you will meet them both."

"And Peter's baby," said Kiki.

"Thank you," I said. "I appreciate any support you will be able to offer."

"Young man," said Zappides. "I think you missed a few things?"

I thought for a moment.

"We were attacked by overzealous German monks and nuns seeking the Grail?" I asked.

"Oh!" said Kiki.

"I know, eh?" I said. I pointed to my chest. "The bastards cut me here and the darn thing opens if I push myself too hard. It's good now, though. They seemed to be shadowing us."

"Where are they now?" asked Kiki.

"Peter hurt them during our last encounter at the castle," I said. "It was dark and I couldn't see, but there were unpleasant snapping and ripping sounds. I believe, like Snagglepus, they have exited stage left."

"I know not this Snagglepus," said Zappides. "An obscure ancient myth?"

"Um, sort of," I said, sheepishly.

"Moving along," said Traka.

"Yes, moving right along, I met your Lady of the Well a few times," I said.

At that, both Kiki and Zappides first froze, then turned their faces slowly toward me.

"Ah, that you did not yet hear," said Traka. "Interesting is it not?"

"Professor, you know well that she is of interest to the director and me," said Kiki. "Please do elaborate, Cameron."

"The first time, by the spring in the forest, she cleaned small wounds on my face. We had a lovely lunch of cucumber sandwiches and she suggested I go with her," I said. "She also said, and this is still a bit of a downer, You are a fool. The Grail is not for you to find. You will never be healed by the Grail. Can't say I enjoyed hearing that. She also reminded me that it can only be used once."

"She offered to take you with her?" said Kiki. She and Zappides exchanged glances.

"Are you sure she was the Lady of the Well?" asked Zappides. "How do you know?"

"We met her twin at the Abbey of Ganagobie, though we did not know it at the time," I said.

"I see," said Zappides. "Please continue."

"I met her again in the glade above the Asklepion," I said. "She bandaged my wound. I had stressed it climbing those wretched steps."

"And?" asked Kiki.

"She left, saying she would see me again, in time. Then Puck came," I said.

"His spirit guide," said Traka.

I sighed, but said nothing.

"And Puck said that Cameron already knew enough to find the Grail," said Traka. "And here we are."

"It is a wonderful meal," I said. "Please pass my thanks to Mrs. Krillia." Traka nodded.

"I would like to point out the insanely obvious," said Kiki.

"Please do," I said.

"The Lady told you three things," said Kiki. "First, you are a fool."

"Well, sadly, everyone tells me that." I said.

"The wise and sacred fool who reveals the truth," said Kiki. "It is an archetype, of course."

"Well done, girl," said Traka.

"Seems rather unlikely," I suggested, thinking again that she seemed strangely sober.

"Second, she said the Grail is not for you to find," said Kiki. "*That* you might have been singular, only you Cameron, but what about Rhiannon, Peter, Professor Traka, Diogenis, me? Could one of us not find the Grail?"

"And, third, *you* will never be healed by the Grail," she said. "Perhaps it is not meant for you? Perhaps it is meant for someone else?"

Zappides nodded. "It is all fate," he said. "Kiki, me, the Grail. All fate."

His head sagged slowly and majestically to rest on the table, his beard in his plate.

"Perhaps we have had enough wine?" asked Traka.

"He has," said Kiki. "Professor, can I put him in the guest room?"

"Of course," said Traka. "Cameron, help her."

Kiki took one arm. I took the other. We raised him to his feet. I carried him like a baby and laid him on the bed I had shared with Chaney. He snored, deeply. Kiki smiled down at him, then took my hand and led me back to the table.

As we sat, she looked to Traka. "He is so cute when he is asleep, your nephew."

"Good gods, not him too?" I asked.

"Obviously," said Traka. "Do you think I would have allowed your shenanigans otherwise?"

Kiki giggled. "Cameron, seriously? You would so be in jail."

"Speaking of following along," I said. "You are saying that maybe one of you lot can find the Grail, and that it will do me no good, but may be meant for someone else? That rather makes finding the darn thing moot for the dying god, doesn't it?"

"But, not for me," said Traka. She rubbed her lower back. "At my age, I live in pain, you know."

"I apologize," I said. "Of course, you deserve the Grail. I am inherently selfish."

"Aren't we all, mister fertility god," said Kiki. She stood, lifted the wine bottle with two hands and carefully filled my glass, then hers and Traka's.

"Still, that axe is starting to feel grimly inevitable," I said. "I am glad Rhiannon and Peter are not here for this discussion."

"There would be more tears, certainly," said Traka.

I raised my glass in salute, first to Traka, then to Kiki.

"Thank goodness for wine," I said.

"Indeed," said Traka.

We all took respectful sips from our glasses.

"Is there anything else in what we have just reviewed?" asked Traka. She looked up to her left, gazing into the distance. "Cameron, perhaps there is something in one of the more obscure Grail stories you have studied? Or something you remember that Rhiannon, Peter or I have said?"

"In fairness, Rhiannon is correct when she notes that reading the Graham's Notes one-hundred-and-seventy-five-page book for high schoolers entitled '*The Quick Grail*' is not really making a study of anything," I said. "And, truthfully, I really wasn't listening a lot of the time when they rattled on…"

"You really are just a muscle-bound head-chopper," said Traka. "It is amazing they put up with you."

"He is very cute, though," said Kiki.

Traka ignored her. "Cameron, let us try one more approach, sort of an informal connect the dots. I apologize if it gets a little Jungian."

"Go for it, professor," I said.

"I am going to ask questions. Just say the first thing that comes to mind," said Traka. "No filtering."

"I'm pretty sure that is not a good idea," I said.

"Cameron be good," said Traka.

"Fine," I said.

"The first thing, remember? Now close your eyes," said Traka.

I closed them. I could see the candles flickering dimly through my eyelids.

"What is the most important thing you have discovered on this quest?" asked Traka.

"I miss my children more than I would have thought possible," I said.

"Okay, fair enough, the second most important thing?" asked Traka.

"Peter," I said.

"And, third?" she asked.

"Our baby," I said.

"None of these things are Grail related," said Kiki. "But I like your answers."

"I will make it more specific," said Traka. "Cameron, what is the most sacred Grail-related thing you have discovered on this quest?"

"The Lady by the Well," I said.

"Next?" she asked.

"The not-sarcophagus," I said.

"Next?" she asked.

"The well in the forest and the grove above the Asklepion," I said.

"And how do you know this, that they are all sacred?" she asked.

"I can sense it, almost like a warmth," I said.

"And where did Puck take you the night of your last mystic dreaming?" she asked.

"To party with the dryads," I said. I opened my eyes. "Oh, you witch!"

"I knew it!" said Traka. "You are such a liar."

"There was no reason to upset anyone," I said. "That part of the story was not relevant."

"Kiki and I will keep your little secret," said Traka. "Won't we, dear?"

A closer look at Kiki revealed her shaking with silent laughter, her mouth hidden behind her wineglass, but she nodded.

"But you must share," said Traka.

"Not much to say, really," I said. "Imagine a beautiful, mature forest of towering oak, a cool pool surrounded by moss, four shapely dryads with hair a mass of leaves and skin of smooth bark, and wine from wild grapes, strong and dry."

"Seriously?" asked Kiki. "Talk about a dive into the subconscious. Professor, what is your take on this mundane male fantasy?"

But I saw her writing it all down.

"Well, at a basic level he is himself, Puck and the dryads," said Traka. "Which are essentially a mobile mini-forest."

"Oh, nicely done, professor," said Kiki. "So, he is leading himself to screw himself, while he is a forest?"

"But remember Kiki in Jungian dreams everything is a symbol or metaphor," said Traka. "So, we need to ask ourselves, what do Puck, the dryads, and the trees represent from Cameron's point of view? Does sex in this context represent a joining or harmony or is it because his sexuality has been suppressed?"

"Suppressed? Around Peter and Rhiannon?" I asked. I stood. "Professor, thank you for dinner. I will let you two continue this discussion. I hope our discussion was useful to you, but I fear I may have had a drop too much wine to follow any further."

"You are welcome, but you sway, sir," said Traka.

"A little," I confessed.

"Kiki, obviously you are staying here tonight," said Traka. "But you may walk Cameron to his home."

"Thank you, professor," said Kiki.

"I could just lie down in your garden, by the pool," I said. "The house seems so far away."

"No, Cameron," said Traka. "Let Kiki take you."

I nodded. Kiki came around the table, slipped her arm through mine, and led me from the room toward the villa doors. As we left, I thought I caught a glimpse of a shadow entering the room.

"Thank you, Mrs. Krillia," I called out over my shoulder.

Outside Traka's villa, the night air lay still and heavy with nary the slightest hint of breeze. Cicadas sang shrilly from the olive trees as Kiki and I crunched slowly up the gravel drive arm-in-arm toward my home.

"Cicada's have represented insouciance since classical times, Cameron," said Kiki. She gave me a small smile. I could just see it in the light from the gibbous moon.

"I don't understand what that means," I said. "You must avoid big words with me."

"Playing the fool, still?" said Kiki.

"Um, not really," I said.

"Liar," she said. "Insouciance means heedlessness, carelessness or even frivolousness. Are you feeling careless tonight, Cameron?"

"Are you flirting with me, young lady?" I asked.

"Young lady? I am older than you!" she said.

"Ah, you seem younger," I said. "I feel old these days, you know. Worn out."

"I know," said Kiki. "Diogenis and I have both remarked upon it. Not your face or body, of course, but in your eyes. You have weary eyes, my dear."

"I think you just told me I look old and flirted with me in the same breath," I said. "I am not sure that works."

She laughed. "Fair enough."

"Also, I did specifically promise Peter that I would not sleep with you," I said. "I promised Pregnant Peter who is in hospital putting his life at risk to have my child."

"You make assumptions of both my desires and morals," said Kiki. "I am offended."

"Really?" I asked.

"No, not really," she said. "But I take your point. It would pretty much make both of us scum."

"Indeed," I said.

"However," she began.

"I am not sure that you can *however* this one," I said.

"However, technically, you only promised not to take me to bed," said Kiki. "Ergo if, say, I, completely naked, wrapped my legs around you on the sofa, and thrashed up and down like a feral cat, you would not be breaking your promise, technically."

"Interesting image and technically true. But we would both still be trailer-park trash," I said.

"Still, I am experiencing insouciance," she said.

"How can you be experiencing something I cannot even pronounce?" I asked.

"Specifically, heedlessness or not-give-a-fuckedness," said Kiki. "I will be scum for one night, then. You do totally have the fertility god thing going on and I want you. I am at the end of my fertility, after all."

"No," I said.

"You said that firmly," said Kiki, but she held me close as we approached my front door. I opened it and stopped.

"Good night," I said. "Thank you for walking me home."

"Goodness, how many times have I said that?" said Kiki. "I do believe I will be forced to respect your wishes, you clever bastard. And I was going to suggest a swim?"

"Kiki, I am tired," I said. "We will, no doubt, be getting together again soon. And I am flattered by your attentions, so please?"

She reached up and kissed me on the cheek.

"Alright, Cameron. I will mail a summary of my notes from the evening to Peter and Rhiannon to see if they can add anything," she said. "I will omit this part. And the dryads."

She smiled and turned to go.

I watched as she vanished into the gloom. I turned into my home and flicked on the overhead light as I entered. All lay just as it had when I left. The clean dishes in the kitchen dishrack beside the sink, the half-empty bottle of Valpolicella on the counter, the graphic novel, *Demons of Sherwood*, half-read on the sofa. All unchanged. A heavy emptiness held the scene. I could not bear it. I turned and exited back into the night.

Instinctively, I turned right and headed uphill into the progressively greater darkness of the olive orchard and then the forest. Finally, the cypress closed in above the trail and the moonlight ended, caught up, diffracted, in the canopy above. In the pure forest darkness, the still air of the night held heavy the sweet acid aroma of the conifers all around me. Sounds muted; distant traffic on the road below, the light music of goat bells up on the mountain, the slight, almost imperceptible crunch of cypress needles beneath my feet.

I stopped, sucked in the light-free air, tasted it: the forest. I exhaled, slowly. I felt the tension begin to ease.

"That's it then," I said aloud.

Blind, I followed the path higher and deeper into the darkened woods. I knew the path well, so did not stumble. The twisted roots were old friends from a hundred hikes and runs; the exposed rock, old neighbors. I heard the running water before I saw the moonlight on the glade, so I knew the chapel lay near even before I broke into the open light. After the darkness, the white, half-barrel-shaped chapel glowed bright in the moonlight. I could still hear the stream – lesser now as the rainy season turned toward summer – running in the blackness behind the chapel and see the glint of water from the basin beside the spring. Then, movement.

I froze, then sank to my knees. A large stag stepped out into the moonlight, a seeming aureole about its shape as its delicate steps brought it toward the spring, small fires flickering across the twelve points of its antlers.

"So," I said. "This is what madness looks like."

"Wondrous, is he not?" said voice behind me.

I did not turn.

"Hello, well girl," I said, still watching as the stag approached the spring and dipped his head to drink. "You know, of course, that there are no deer on Kos. None. Zero."

"That is true, admittedly," she said.

I felt her hand on my shoulder.

"At least in a conventional sense," she said.

"So, what am I seeing?" I asked. "Is it real? Or, have I moved on to visual hallucinations?"

"As real as the hand on your shoulder," she said.

"Not entirely comforting," I admitted. "So, I have lost my mind, then."

We watched in silence as the stag repeatedly dipped his long, pink tongue into the basin, the faint lap-lap sound clearly heard across the glade.

"I guess the aureole is a clue," I said. "It is a touch mystic."

"Indeed," she said. And she laughed. Music.

We watched as the deer raised his head and moved regally across the open space of the glade, step by cautious step, turning his head just once to look at us before disappearing into the black of the forest.

"I brought a basket," said she.

I stood and turned. And there she stood, the stunningly beautiful woman with short, tightly curled black hair with ringlets falling to either side of her face, and a generous figure, her perfect face radiating a mesmerizing smile. A light fabric of white samite floated around her form.

"Ah, how mystic," I said. 'Wonderful."

"Thank you, Cameron," she said. "I thought I would make an effort."

"But I did just eat," I said. "And drank too much wine."

"I think you will find that was some time ago," said she. "Are you not hungry, just a little?'

"Odd, but, yes," I said. And I was, too. A little peckish. "What do you have?"

"Cucumber sandwiches?" she asked.

"That, too, would be wondrous," I said.

She took my hand and led me to a weathered stone bench next to the chapel door. I sat and she sat next to me, pressing against my thigh. She set her wicker basket on a large, upright, ancient Doric white-marble capital next to the bench and opened it, removing a plastic container. She lifted the lid and offered me a cucumber sandwich on white bread. I took it.

Next, she removed two wineglasses from the basket, followed by a stoppered bottle of her nameless white wine. She set the glasses on the capital, removed the stopper and poured. She offered me a glass. I took it.

I sipped to taste bitter fruitiness.

"It is an acquired taste," she said. And smiled again, sipping hers, watching my eyes.

"You did well, tonight," she said. "Keeping your promise."

"You were watching?" I asked.

She laughed. "Foolish boy."

I shrugged and took a bite of the sandwich -- fresh bread, butter, fresh cucumber, pepper, mayonnaise.

"It is good," I said.

"Thank you," she said.

"Truth be told, it was not hard to keep the promise," I said. "For all the right reasons, of course, but also, 'cause I am so freak'n tired. When Peter left, it just sucked away my energy."

"I understand," she said. "But I must say, it is odd to see it so almost seven months before the end of your cycle. No matter what Rhiannon tells you, you are ahead of the curve, so to speak."

"Super," I said, taking another bite of the sandwich and another sip of wine. We sat quietly, listening to the sound of water running. I finished the sandwich and the wine. She poured me more and handed me another sandwich. I took both.

"You will come with me tonight, Cameron," she said, stoppering the wine. "You understand that you belonged to me as soon as you ate my sandwiches."

"I ate your sandwiches before," I noted.

"That is when you belonged to me," she said. "But I am a gentle creature. I knew you would need time to come around to the idea. I do not wish to upset you."

"I see," I said. "You know I am tempted, but will not go with you to your house in the forest, as much as I might find love and contentment there, with you. I will go back to Peter and Rhiannon. And, in the end, I will go to meet the contender. Promises were made. Oaths were taken. And, I do love them."

"I am sure you will respect this."

She watched me for a short while, sipping her wine, before replying, "Very well. But, in time, you will come to me, at least for a while. I have foreseen it."

I closed my eyes for a moment.

"Not you, as well?" I said. "You witches and your foreseeing. Seriously."

She offered me more wine, another sandwich. I declined with a slight shake of my head and a slight smile.

She returned the smile. It held only kindness. She sealed away the remaining sandwiches with the plastic lid, took my wineglass from my hand, wrapped it in a cloth napkin, and placed it back in the wicker basket. Hers remained half full.

She slid away from me to the far end of the bench and patted her lap.

"You are worn out, Cameron. Weary," she said. "Rest your head here and sleep, dream."

"I am, but just for a bit," I said. "I will sleep at home, tonight."

I stretched out on the hard, stone bench, lying on my right side, and set my head on her lap, the back of my head against her stomach. The fabric of her garment slid, silky white against her thighs and I could feel the warmth of her skin. She rested one hand on my head and sipped her wine.

"Sleep, dear one. Sleep," she said.

I slept. I dreamt.

In this dream, I wandered the forests at night, up through ravines rushing with cold, clear water, up to the top of Kos' mountain, to look down the sheer cliff to the still Aegean far below. I sat there, on the edge, my feet dangling into the abyss. Up there on the clifftop, I watched the rainy season end, and hot, dry, brutal summer begin. Green fled the fields and meadows turned first to thorns, then to burnt, ochre desert. Below, the sea flicked from aquamarine, to dark black, to icy clarity. The hot scent of dry conifers blended with salt sea air, creating an intoxicating perfume.

"I wonder," I said. "If I could fly? It is a dream, after all."

"You can't," said Puck, from behind me. "Don't be an asshole. It is a long way down. Mount Dikaios is 846 meters high. When you fall you will hit limestone, marble, or plutonite, all of which are most hard."

"Hello, Puck," I said. "How long have you been there?"

"That is a good question," said Puck. "Time is all messed up here. Now, come away from the edge. You are freaking me out."

"Really?" I asked. "But you can fly."

"As previously noted, *you* cannot," said Puck.

I carefully brought my dangling legs up from the cliff's edge, inched back from the abys on my bottom, and stood. I turned to see Puck standing before me, human-sized, delicate, cute and completely naked.

"Puck, you are a girl," I said. "And you are naked."

"You have seen me naked before," said Puck.

"As a boy," I noted.

"True," said Puck. "It was hard to get here. Males cannot come to this place without invitation, it seems; so I had to be flexible."

"I have no idea what you are talking about," I said. "This is just my dream."

"Yes and no," said Puck. "You went with her, didn't you?"

"I did not," I said. "She asked, but I declined. Politely, of course."

"Of course," said Puck. "So, please tell me what happened?"

"We had wine and cucumber sandwiches," I said. "And, by-the-way, why didn't anyone tell me about the food thing before? She says it made me hers, or something stupid like that."

"Because it was too late, you idiot," said Puck. "And, who doesn't know not to eat the food of the fey? Moron."

"I did know that," I said. "I forgot. Also, cucumber sandwiches?"

"You are too easily led astray," said Puck. "Something else happened, though, did it not? You had sex with her. I will bet good gold on it."

"I most certainly did not," I said. "I did rest my head on her lap, though."

"Fool," said Puck.

"I was really worn out," I said. "And she is stunningly beautiful and makes wonderful cucumber sandwiches?"

Puck looked at me with a gaze that heavily implied that, even though I lacked intellect, he loved me dearly. It was a look I had seen before from others. He held out his hand.

"Come on, then," said Puck. "Peter is waiting by the chapel. He is heavily pregnant and rather cranky."

"Heavily pregnant, you say?" I asked. "A heavily pregnant Peter sent you? How much time has passed?"

"You really are not following along, are you?" said Puck. "Yes, he is heavily pregnant. And cranky. When he called me, I toyed with not appearing, but then he threatened to pluck off my wings if I could not find you."

"That's our boy," I said. "And the time?"

"It is late July," said Puck. "And it is hot as Hades, let me tell you."

"July," I said. Had four months slipped away?

"Puck, tell me truly, is this real or have I descended into madness?" I asked.

"Does it matter?" asked Puck. "Either way, just take my hand and come back with me. Please?"

I nodded and took his hand.

"Puck?" I asked.

"Yes, boyo?" said Puck.

"You are rather pretty as a girl," I observed, clinically and with no wistfulness.

"Forget it," said Puck. "Now close your eyes."

I awoke slowly. The dry, acid sweet scent of cypress trees came to me first. Next, something hard poked me in the back. I rolled onto my side and opened my eyes. I was not resting my head on a beautiful woman's lap. I lay beneath a cypress tree amidst a litter of twigs, stones and conifer needles.

Rhiannon stood, bent over, looking down at me.

"Crap," I said.

Rhiannon smiled down at me.

"We have been looking for you for a long time," she said. "Thank all the gods."

She stood straight.

"Here," she called. "He is here."

Kiki appeared, slipping through the trees with skill. Nikos followed more cautiously, then even more slowly, Zappides.

"Cameron, can you stand?" asked Rhiannon.

"Of course," I said.

But, of course, I could not. Rhiannon and Nikos helped me to my feet. Together, step-by-tortuous-step, they guided me back through the forest to the chapel clearing. It lay fewer than thirty meters away. Peter waited on the bench by the chapel with Traka by his side holding his hand. They both stood as I entered the light of the clearing.

Peter strode toward me, Traka trailing behind. Even blinking in the sunlight, I could see the tears starting. He stopped one pace away and slapped me, hard.

"You have a bump, sir," I said. "You look lovely."

Traka grabbed him from behind as he collapsed into tears. I fainted. I remember Nikos catching me from behind.

Perception-wise, the next few days were touch and go. I slipped in and out of consciousness, moving between dream and reality with uncomfortable ease. I had sustained no serious injuries during my time on the mountain, but countless thorns, sharp rocks and several asps had opened countless small wounds. My skin had been flayed by the summer sun. Everything hurt.

I returned to full consciousness on the first of August, Lughnasadh, the harvest festival in honor of the god Lugh. In the valley, on that date we would climb into the mountains to the sacred wells.

That day, I blinked my eyes open to see Peter sitting in a wingback chair beside the bed. He lay back, his head flung to the side, fast asleep. The top of his blue Hello Kitty pajamas had ridden up to show his four-month pregnant belly. In his lap lay a closed hardcover French novel by someone named Christine Delphy, titled *L'Ennemi principal 1*. I guessed it was another French romance. Overhead, a ceiling fan swept in continuous slow motion.

"That's new," I said, my voice hoarse and croaky.

Peter opened his eyes, instantly fully awake. He leaned forward and took hold of my right hand with both of his.

"I formally apologize for slapping you," he said. "I should not have done so. Please forgive me."

"Zappides' wife stabbed him when she was pregnant and he forgave her immediately," I said. "So, I guess you are well within your rights to slap me when you are upset. There is nothing to forgive."

"Are you certain?" he asked.

"Mais bien sûr," I said.

He smiled, straightened, reached behind the chair and presented a glass of water.

"Drink," he said and held the glass to my mouth.

I gulped it down, the cold eased the burning in my throat.

"Enough for now," he said and pulled the glass away.

"Peter, please tell me, you, the baby?" I asked.

"I think that can wait until you feel better," said Peter.

"My love, that will only make me think the worst," I said.

He nodded. "Very well. They say the immediate danger has passed, but my chances are only fifty-fifty to bring the little one to term."

"Ah," I said. I felt the overwhelming sadness begin to rise again.

"But, fear not," said Peter. "For unto you this day on the island of Kos I will bring a solution."

"You will? Just like that?" I asked.

"Yes, mon Seigneur," he said. "But first, you really need a bath."

I nodded. I looked at my arms and could see they had given me sponge baths, but a thin layer of grime still covered my skin.

"Please," I said. "And, Peter?"

"Yes?" he replied.

"Could it be a bubble bath?" I asked.

He smiled, bent and kissed me on the lips. I took that to mean yes.

"Let me get Rhiannon to help," he said.

He walked to the bedroom door and called down the stairs.

"He is finally awake, the layabout."

I heard hurried footsteps on the marble stairs and Rhiannon appeared in the door, she paused, dashed across the room, and threw her arms around me.

"Idiot," she said.

"I know," I agreed. "Sorry."

"I will run the bath," said Peter.

He exited into the en-suite bathroom and a moment later I heard the water begin to flow into the tub. A minute later, I caught the scent of lavender. He reappeared and returned to his wingback chair.

"The ceiling fan is new," I said. "Good idea."

"It is as hot as the devil's backside here in the summer," said Peter. "And electricity for the AC costs the earth."

Rhiannon held me and said nothing.

"Can you at least give me a hint?" I asked.

"About what?" asked Rhiannon, looking up.

"About your solution to Peter's health issue," I said.

She turned to Peter.

"I thought we agreed we were going to wait," she said.

"He was getting upset," said Peter. "I caved."

Rhiannon sighed.

"After your bath," she said. "You really are quite ripe."

She pulled back the sheets to expose my naked form. I saw that I had lost a little weight, but nothing to be worried about. I sat up, took a moment or two to steady myself, then stood. Rhiannon took my hand and walked me to the large, oval tub and Peter followed. I stepped cautiously into the mass of white bubbles and sank gratefully into the hot water. My scratches burned briefly, then the pain eased.

"Ah," I said. "Thank you."

"Perhaps you should slip in behind him," said Peter. "He might faint again."

Rhiannon nodded, slipped off her jeans, underthings and t-shirt and eased herself in behind me wrapping her legs around me and beneath my knees.

"Hi pretty one," I said.

She rested her chin on my shoulder.

"Idiot," she said.

"In know," I said.

"Why do you not scrub him clean while I get Traka?" asked Peter. "We can do it now."

"Because naked I am?" said Rhiannon. "And so is he?"

"There are lots of bubbles," said Peter. "And Traka will be tickled pink."

He exited, not waiting for a reply.

"Anxious he is," said Rhiannon. "We cannot upset him."

"Whatever you think best," I said.

I slid down in the water, resting the back of my head against her breasts.

"Hey. You are really comfortable," I said. "Why haven't we done this before?"

She laughed.

"Because you were too frisky," said Rhiannon. "Now sit up straight so I can clean you."

She reached for the soap and a facecloth, then, ever so gently, cleansed every nook and cranny of my body. By the time she finished her task I felt exhausted. I, again, lay back against her.

"Now I will be your pillow," said Rhiannon. "Mind I do not."

She put her arms around my chest and held me.

"You may come in now," said Rhiannon.

Peter poked his head into the doorway, nodded, then entered. Traka followed him.

"Good heavens," she said.

"He was filthy," said Rhiannon.

"Hello, professor," I said. "Sorry to have been a bother."

She waved this away.

"Now, can anyone please explain?" I asked.

Traka lowered the lid of the toilet and sat. Peter lowered himself slowly and sat cross-legged on the tile floor.

"Shall I?" asked Traka.

Both Rhiannon and Peter nodded.

"The day after our last supper together, Kiki went to get you for lunch at my place and could not find you," said Traka. "At first, we were not alarmed because, well, you do have a habit of wandering. But, after a few days, I called my nephew in the police service and we searched. Couldn't find you anywhere. You are a pain in the ass."

"Sorry," I said.

"I called Rhiannon, but she and Peter could not yet come as he was not stable. Here, the police figured you had gotten bored and done a runner. So they stopped looking. But Zappides, Ms. Poole, Nikos and I kept at it. Eventually, we guessed that you were stupid enough to go with the Lady of the Well and gave it up. It's not that big an island, after all. In the meantime, Ms. Poole typed up her notes from our last get together and mailed them to Rhiannon,"

"In my defense," I said. "I did not go with the lady. I just had a little rest. I was wiped."

"Moving along," said Traka. "Peter and Rhiannon reviewed Kiki's notes and, after mulling for a few days, Peter figured it out. After Peter finally stabilized, they came immediately back to Kos and Peter persuaded Puck to find you."

"Figured what out?" I asked.

"Cameron, love," said Rhiannon, hugging me from behind. "Please try to follow along."

"Where to find the Grail," said Peter. "And, yes, I figured it out, on my own."

"He did," said Rhiannon. "He is a clever boy."

"But how?" I asked. "Just from the notes?"

"The notes helped me focus on the issue," said Peter. "Everything was there. Your Kiki is a good scribe."

"She is not my Kiki," I said.

"Hmm," said Peter.

"Please explain," I said.

Peter looked to Rhiannon.

"Cameron, my love," said Rhiannon. "First you need to know that this is one of those horrible good news, bad news things."

"I rather guessed," I said.

"So, you need to be prepared to be disappointed," said Rhiannon.

"Fine," I said.

"Cameron, the Lady of the Wells is correct," said Peter. "The Grail is not for you to find. You will never be healed by the Grail. My love, you are not the seeker, I am. It is for me to find, not you. It is for me to be healed, not you."

I thought for a moment.

"Peter, I am good with that, obviously," I said. "But why?"

"Cameron, this is his story, not yours," said Rhiannon. "My love, this is his quest."

"Mon Seigneur," said Peter. "You are the lord. You have the wound that will not heal. You have the Grail. It is for you to give to me."

"I am the Fisher King?" I asked. "That is just not possible. What do I have that could be the Grail... Crap."

"Sorry, my love," said Rhiannon.

"One moment, please," said Peter.

He stood, exited the bathroom and returned a moment later. Then, there in the bathroom, beside the bathtub, in his blue-flannel, Hello Kitty pajamas, he knelt and raised both of his hands above his head. In his hands he held Rhiannon's simple clay cup, the same cup I had used dozens of times to drink her bitter, thick amber liquid and enter the dreamlands.

"Mon Seigneur," said Peter. "Why do you suffer so?"

Rhiannon squeezed me tight from behind with both her arms and legs. I swallowed.

"My love," I said. "My greatest suffering is that you and the baby are in danger. This is my most manifest sorrow."

Rhiannon squeezed me again and I saw Traka nodding slowly.

"Take the cup, mon Seigneur," said Peter. "And fill it."

He handed me the clay vessel.

"Um?" I said.

"The bathwater," said Rhiannon.

"It is filthy," I said. "It will make him sick."

"Just do it, my love," said Rhiannon.

So, I did, dipping the cup below the lavender-scented bubbles and scooping out grey bathwater. Peter took it from my hand, examined it, smiled and showed it to Traka. She kissed him on the forehead.

Peter turned and showed the contents of the cup to Rhiannon and me. The water swirled there in the clay, perfectly clean and clear.

Peter raised the cup to his mouth with both hands and drank. It did not take long for him to empty the small cup, seconds really. Then he sat back, cross-legged on the floor.

"Do you feel anything?" asked Traka, leaning forward, intent.

Peter began rubbing his belly with his right hand.

"I do," he said. "A kind of warmth. A gentle internal glow, almost."

"Fascinating," said Traka.

"Peter are you okay?" asked Rhiannon. "Really?"

He stood quickly, doing one little bounce.

"Oh my God," he said. "I totally am!"

"My love, perhaps we should be cautious until we are sure?" suggested Rhiannon.

"It changed the water," said Peter.

"Perhaps it settled." I said.

"No, it is the Grail and that, my loves, was a bonafide miracle," said Peter. "And now…"

Peter stepped forward toward the bath and dipped the clay cup into the bathwater. He raised it and examined the contents, swirled the water, then looked again. He showed it to Traka.

"It was worth a try," said Traka.

"Sorry, Cameron," said Peter. "It is still disgusting."

"I guessed," I said. "Peter, it is alright. It is expected."

"But it means you have only three months left!" said Peter.

"Well, then, you had best make the most of it, hadn't you?" said Traka.

"Thank you, professor," I said. "My thoughts exactly."

"Fine," said Peter. "I will not burst into tears. I will, instead, go for a swim."

He handed the Grail to Rhiannon and turned to exit, but stopped in the bathroom doorway.

"Oh, Rhiannon," he said. "I think we should freeze our beloved's sperm. That would be the practical approach to multiple children."

He exited.

"Professor, could you please keep an eye on him?" asked Rhiannon. "I will rinse Cameron off and put him back to bed."

Traka stood and looked down at us in the bath.

"Cameron, Rhiannon, thank you both for letting me see that," she said. "It means the world to me. I never imagined that I would ever see it, nevermind witness it in action."

"I was kind of expecting holy lights and celestial singers," I said. "Don't you think it was a little underwhelming?"

Rhiannon hugged me from behind.

"Cameron, love, it is always the quiet magic that changes the world," she said.

Traka stood and headed after Peter. Through the open window, we could hear splashing from the pool.

"I think he is right, though," said Rhiannon. "We should freeze your sperm."

"Seriously?" I asked.

"Seriously," she said. "That way, after we marry, we can have as many of your children as we choose."

"Do I get a say?" I asked.

"Did you ever?" asked Rhiannon.

She handed me the Grail and reached around me to pull out the bathtub plug.

"Be a dear and hold the Grail while I rinse you off," said Rhiannon.

I held the Grail close to my face, turning it, investigating it.

"I can't believe we had the darn thing the entire time," I said.

Rhiannon began to hose me down with the shower nozzle. The steady, warm water felt good against my scalp.

"I couldn't believe that you are the Fisher King," said Rhiannon. "But it totally makes sense, you being the dying god and all."

"You just said totally," I said.

She laughed. "Peter it is. Between the two of you I will lose the ability to speak proper English."

"I can see Peter as the real hero of our quest, though," I said. "That is not hard. He really is the purest soul amongst us."

"He is, in truth, a fair and noble knight," said Rhiannon. "Stand please."

I did, carefully, making certain not to slip in the soapy tub. Rhiannon stood beside me, her legs slightly apart. She moved the showerhead, washing all the soap from my body.

"Look at me, you do," she said.

"I do," I said.

I watched as she rinsed herself, moving the shower head about her body, occasionally splashing water on the bathroom floor. When she finished, she stepped out of the bath, took my hand and steadied me as I stepped out to join her.

"I has been a long time," I said.

"You need to rest," said Rhiannon.

I reached out to touch her face with my fingertips.

"Well, perhaps if you lie still," she said. She stepped forward against me.

"As always," I said.

"As always?" she asked, then kissed my shoulder.

"As always, you take my breath away," I said.

"Of course, I do," said Rhiannon. "I am one third of a sacred witch queen."

She took my right hand and led me from the bathroom to our bed. We lay down together, she took the Grail from my left hand and tossed it to the bottom of the bed. She then pushed me onto my back and climbed onto me, settling herself upon me, her back straight and her arms akimbo.

"You have perfect posture," I noted.

"You are ogling my breasts," said Rhiannon.

And I was, too. They bounced there in manifest perfection.

"You have the most perfect body," I said. "Naturally, I am ogling your breasts."

"That is the correct attitude," she said as she began to grind herself against me. "For the man who is going to give me a child today."

CHAPTER TEN – THE ISLAND
SUMMER ISLE

Kos, Greece

August in the Aegean. Cloudless, yet hazy skies, perfect blue tainted white by wisps from Asia Minor. Tourist-packed sunbeds on endless beaches; striped, multihued umbrellas holding back a merciless sun. Tall, strong, drinks of ice and blended fruit, fortified by impossible intoxicants. At night, barely clad bodies writhing, jumping, twisting on bar street to improbable Europop noise machines. Fireworks low over the harbor. Quiet, almost empty beaches below stern cliff faces. And everywhere, all around, the perfect Aegean, clear, calm and aquamarine, the gift of the ancient Greek gods to a bewildered humanity.

Kos in summertime.

Everyone who spends any time on Kos finds two favorite beaches. The first is a quiet, seldom frequented beach, maybe a little rough, with stones or weathered rock leaving only thin strips of sand for the placement of one's foolishly decorated beach towels. The second is a beach bed beach. This might be in Kos town or out in one of the smaller beachside communities, such as Tigaki or Kefalos; but it always comes with a simple, affiliated beachside restaurant, umbrellas and a fresh-water shower.

We were no different. Our favorite is almost in town, but not quite downtown. It hides behind a row of restaurants east of the marina, protected on one side by the hard standing for boats and, on the other, by a long, jumbled-rock breakwater and is, thus, good for a pregnant Peter on even wave tossed days. This sheltered bay is home to colonies of grass-like seaweed, bending with the currents and hosting small schools of fish who do not seem to mind the flip of a snorkeler's fins. The beach is white sand and holds about thirty double beach beds with blue, vinyl mattresses and umbrellas. Immediately behind the beach a thin lawn of vibrant green grass separates the sand from perhaps fifteen tables and a walkup bar.

The food is simple, but fresh and tasty. The wine is cold and endless. You may wish to try the improbably named Texas Burger.

All of it together? A small slice of heaven.

One cannot spend every day at the beach, but on August 15, a Sunday, we gathered. Rhiannon, Peter and I arrived early, before lunch. Later Traka, Zappides and Kiki presented themselves towels in hand, walking in single file along the thin, wooden-slat pathway that leads to the beach beds and preserves tender, tourist feet from the burning sands.

Kiki lead the procession in a black, thong bikini bottom below and a semi-transparent, white shirt. Zappides followed in boxer-style swim trunks and an excessively floral loose shirt. Traka ended the procession in a knee-length black dress and wide-brimmed straw hat.

Rhiannon, Peter and I had lunched, and I admit to consuming wine both with, and after, said lunch. I lay in the shade of one of our beach umbrellas – we had reserved six beds for our party – and may have been ogling Kiki's toplessness through the thin fabric of her blouse when I felt a sharp stab of pain in my right leg. I looked down to see Peter's hand withdrawing from where a small penknife stuck in my thigh.

Wearing only a white bikini bottom, Peter sat on the beach bed next to me, lovely and pregnant, his breasts beginning to swell with milk. I watched as he reclined on the bed and returned to his novel, *Hart of Darkness*.

"I understand, based on our previous conversations," he said, without raising his eyes from the print. "That it is entirely legal on this fine island to stab the father of your child, whilst pregnant."

I watched the blood ooze from the wound.

"Indeed," I said.

Kiki walked by smiling. Zappides followed her, examined the wound carefully, shrugged slightly and continued to his bed. Traka stopped and looked down.

"You bring these things on yourself, Cameron," she said. "You really should know better by now."

I looked up to see Rhiannon rising from the water, tossing back her hair, flinging droplets out to catch the sun. She bounced delightfully in her relatively modest classic white bikini.

"She is one of the two you may watch, Cameron," said Peter, all-seeing, without lifting his eyes from his classic novel of good versus evil.

Rhiannon jogged, bouncing up from the sea, looked down to see the small knife sticking out of my leg and sighed.

"I leave for a few moments and this?" she said. "Bad boys."

"He was ogling Kiki," said Peter.

"Did he say anything? Did he touch?" asked Rhiannon.

"He was thinking about doing one or the other," said Peter, pouting.

"It is fine," I said. "Please do not chastise a pregnant, pouting Peter."

She looked at him and smiled a crooked smile.

"Pregnant, pouting Peter?" she asked.

He looked up. She pouted back at him.

"Be still my heart," I said.

"Give me strength, oh Lord," said Traka.

"He is not even going to need stitches," said Peter. "I avoided major veins and arteries."

"Does anyone have a bandage?" I asked.

Rhiannon pulled out the knife and bandaged my wound with an Elastoplast from her bag. The bandage slowly turned red, but the bleeding stopped quite quickly. Peter knew his knife play.

Kiki and Zappides shared a twinned beach bed and umbrella. Traka rolled out her towel on the blue, plastic mattress beside Rhiannon's, lay on her back, covered her face with her straw hat and began to snore.

Kiki watched her fondly. "Nap time," she whispered.

"Let's go swimming," whispered Peter. "Not Cameron, of course. His blood might attract sharks."

"I just got out," said Rhiannon. But Peter rose took her hand and led her toward the water. Zappides nodded, removed his shirt to reveal a swimmer's torso, and followed. Kiki winked at me, removed her shirt and bounced after him, perfectly and evenly tanned.

"Gosh," I said to no one in particular, and lay back in the shade, eyes closed.

The sound of small waves lapping on the sand merged with Swedish voices from the bar and children's laughter. I drifted away, settling into sleep.

"Mister O'Donnel?" asked a woman's voice, strongly accented with German vowels.

I kept my eyes closed and pretended to be asleep.

She shook my shoulder.

"Go away," I said, keeping my eyes closed. "I don't want to get stabbed again. I want to nap."

"Why would you get stabbed?" asked the voice.

"I believe I saw you watching us earlier," I said. "Are you wearing a cast on your right wrist, a fluorescent green bikini bottom and nothing else?"

"That is correct," she said.

"You have beautiful, big German, um, aspects and if I open my eyes, I, wrapped up in a shallow and unworthy male fantasy, will not be able to take my eyes off them," I said. "My companion will see and stab me, again. Ergo, go away."

"North Americans are always this way," she said. "Can't you grow up?"

"It will take time," I said. "I am working on it."

"Very well," she said. "Just a minute."

Silence followed. I kept my eyes closed.

"I am back," she said. "I put on a blouse."

I opened my eyes to see her perched on the edge of Peter's beach bed, not more than a hand's breadth away. She still wore the fluorescent green bottom, but now with a bright, paisley blouse of some satiny material that clung tightly. She seemed to be about thirty-five years of age.

"I am not sure that helps," I said. "Also, and let's get this out of the way immediately, I am not going to give you babies."

"Pardon?" she said, but leaned in closer, almost touching me.

"Um, never mind," I said. "Can I help you in some way? If Peter comes back your life may be at risk."

She leaned in even closer and whispered. "I am a nun," she said. "Your boyfriend broke my arm at the castle. He is really scary."

"So, you waited for them all to leave before speaking with me?" I asked.

"Obviously," she said.

"And?" I asked.

"Well, the others went home to Munich and left me to negotiate with you," she said. "I am the least damaged."

"That was one reason," I said.

She flushed, her cheeks turning bright pink.

"And, yes, they said I was the prettiest," she said. "But I am a nun, you know."

"That doesn't really help, either, image-wise," I said.

She leaned even closer. I could feel the heat from her body. I froze.

"I am Sister Frieda," she said. "And you are the dying god who has stopped looking for the Grail. Did you find it?"

"Ah," I said.

"Ah?" she whispered. "Cameron?"

A dark shadow loomed over us. We looked sideways to see Traka in her black dress and wide-brimmed straw hat.

"Sister Frieda," said Traka. "How nice that you are speaking with Cameron, but you should really be talking to one of the women."

"Hey!" I said.

Sister Frieda stood, placing her hand on my chest to push herself up.

"Very well, professor," she said. "Did you find it?"

Traka smiled. "We did," she said. "We found it. And used it. And it worked."

Sister Frieda stared at Traka, completely entranced.

"And then, sister..." said Traka.

"Yes?" whispered Sister Frieda.

"Then, we gave it away," said Traka.

"Gave it away?" asked Frieda. "Just like that?"

"Yup," I said. "Just like that."

"When?" asked Sister Frieda.

"Yesterday morning, wasn't it, professor?" I asked.

"That is correct, young man," said Traka.

Sister Frieda sat back down with thump, landing right on my stomach.

"Oof," I said.

She ignored me but looked up at Traka. "I was hungover in bed yesterday morning. I should have spoken with you earlier."

"It would have made no difference," said Traka. "And, to forestall your query, no we will not tell you who has it. In fact, this monkey, your divine divan, if you will, does not even know who currently possesses the thing, so you are wasting your efforts."

"Hungover?" I asked, focusing on the obvious, most salient point.

She looked down at me.

"It is hard to be a nun on Kos in the summer," she said. "Very hard."

"Especially with those aspects, one would think," said Traka.

"So true," said Sister Frieda. She sighed, deeply. "Well, they gave me funds to stay until the end of month..."

"Or 'til the end of September, if you stay at my villa," said Traka. "The price would be silence, of course."

Sister Frieda pondered this for, from an ethical perspective, an astonishingly short time. She stood and reached out her hand to Traka.

"Deal," she said.

Traka cackled, shook the sister's hand, and pointed to her own beach bed.

"You may take mine," Traka said. "I am going to visit with my nephew at the bar."

Sister Frieda nodded. "Any chance you can bring me back a Blue Hawaiian milk shake?"

Traka cackled again, turned and headed toward the shade of the bar.

"And, Cameron?" said Sister Frieda, quietly. "What was that about babies?"

"May I please nap?" I asked. "I had wine at lunch and you contribute to excessively cliché thought processes."

She smiled down at me. I closed my eyes and slept.

The two remaining weeks of August slipped by astonishingly quickly. Beaches, outdoor cafés, marinated lamb cubes on skewers, chips and ketchup, retsina, bright, scorching sun, Peter in the pool looking round and healthy, Rhiannon in our bed looking round and lovely, wonderous meals on the back patio in the evenings. All slipped by, tinged ever so slightly with the sorrow of time's passage.

They say, those clever men and women of science who speak the mystic language of numbers, that time is not linear. They say we only experience time that way by some quirk of evolution: there is no straight arrow of time. They say that all of time exists always, past, present and future. All that is always was. All that was always is. All that will be is. How wonderful if true, for all those days in Paris, in Alpes-de-Haute-Provence, on Kos, will then have always existed and will always exist until time herself ends.

But, for those of us bound to the turn of the seasons, this frozen eternity is hard to see, harder still to live.

Sister Frieda did move into Traka's villa. Kiki followed not long after raising Traka's spirits immensely. Amongst those who would have access to my now frozen sperm, there was talk of the sister and Kiki sharing nanny responsibilities, post-Cameron. This seemed to me a fine notion.

Rhiannon and Peter began to drift closer together. They still showed me the utmost kindness and affection, of course, but, well, it is only human nature, isn't it? There was no further talk of strangulation with hempen ropes. Peter stopped stabbing me. They no longer let me see them cry.

I began to spend more nights in the forest, never alone, always with either Peter or Rhiannon, as they feared I might wander away to the well. This, too, suited me as I found it more and more difficult to match up to the short cycles of the day. Sometimes an hour passed in a moment, or a moment in an age. Sometimes in the cypress forest, time froze just for an instant, as my point of view became free, no longer linked to my line of sight or place of being, all touched with crystal clarity, all locked in amber.

I still trained, running up and down the mountain every day and sparring against a hired local, the psycho killer who ran a local Kungfu studio. I came to believe this relentless, muscled behemoth, chosen by Peter, was really a killer robot sent from the future. Peter always supervised, watching from the sideline, fanning himself with an ōgi – his contribution remained mainly limited to shouting again, faster, or fool.

My wound did not open again. Peter remained healthy. And the baby within continued to grow as it should. The intense heat of August bled into the mere summer of September. The Scandinavians and Germans began to slip away to their northern fastness.

September 3, another beach day, this time at the far, southwestern end of the island, in Kefalos, a small, traditional, beach town both surrounded by, and perched upon, tall cliffs and rocky hills. One of the less crowded occupied beaches on Kos, Kefalos' beach is a mix of low-density sunbeds and open sand running for a little more than two kilometers alongside a shallow bay of pristine, clear, warm waters. In the mid-distance, about a dozen kilometers away, the barren volcanic island of Nisyros rises in a classic truncated, flat-top cone.

That day, Peter, having projected the cost of a university education roughly two decades into the future, decided we would forgo renting beach beds. Nor would we be eating at a restaurant. Our multi-hued quilts from Peter's trousseau chest were spread out over the sand within a few meters of the gently lapping sea. A large, wicker basket lay open on the quilts, revealing, at first glance, fresh baguettes, raw milk Mont d'Or cheese in its thin wooden wrap, olives from Traka's trees, fresh butter, thinly sliced beef carpaccio, and a lone 500 ml bottle of Malamatina Retsina.

I decided not to query Peter's idea of fiscal restraint. I just looked at him and smiled as he slowly removed the delicacies from his basket. He knelt beside it, deeply tanned and wearing only his white bikini bottom. At five months pregnant on his slight frame, his belly seemed about to burst, an illusion certainly. He saw me watching him.

"You watch me, sir," he said.

"I do. You are most beautiful," I said.

"You are kind to say so," said Peter. "I am a narwhale."

"You are not, sir," I said. "You are perfect in every way."

"Ha! You are flattering me in the hope of larger portions," said Peter.

"Not so, young man," I said. "Come sit in my lap and I will show you the truth behind my words."

At that he glanced about the beach.

"Well, there are no children about, and the beach is very nearly ours..." he said. "Where is Rhiannon?"

I pointed out into the placid Mediterranean.

"You can see her head," I said. "I think she is returning."

Rhiannon stood, rising out of the water and waved. Even though she was more than fifty meters from shore, the water came only to her waist revealing her white bikini top. She began to walk toward us.

"This is a good place for children," said Peter.

"It is," I said.

"Glad we froze your stuff?" said Peter.

"I am," I said. "I can imagine you all here."

I wagged my finger at him.

"Make sure you use waterproof sunscreen on the little monsters."

"I promise," he said. He looked away, but just for a moment.

I felt water droplets on my arm and looked to see Rhiannon beside the quilts, shaking her hair, a broad, happy smile showing on her tanned face.

"I am interrupting something," said Rhiannon.

"Not at all," said Peter. "I was considering the viability of Cameron's lap vis-à-vis a quick shag."

Rhiannon closed her eyes.

"With a towel wrapped around us, obviously," said Peter.

"Peter," said Rhiannon, opening her eyes. "You need to practice being a good role model."

"Not yet," said Peter, grinning.

He rose and started toward me. She stepped forward onto the quilts and stopped him with her hands.

"No," said Rhiannon. "I wish to talk to both of you over lunch."

"To us, or with us," asked Peter.

"To," said Rhiannon. "At least at first."

He nodded to her and stepped back.

"Very well, first I will serve," he said.

Peter returned to kneel by the basket and set out our luncheon. White crockery plates, wineglasses, cutlery sets wrapped in oakleaf-patterned napkins, all were set out in place settings with each setting at the point of a small triangle. He laid out the lunch in the middle of the trinity.

"Please take your places," said Peter.

We sat. Rhiannon dripped sea water onto her plate. Peter regarded her with an arched eyebrow and tossed her a beach towel. She began to dab herself distractedly.

"Peter, perhaps you should put on a shirt?" asked Rhiannon.

"This is as good as my tiny breasts are ever going to look," said Peter. "Pregnant and pre-breastfeeding. And I would hide them away?"

"And wonderful they are, but think of the sun, my love," I said. "Helios, they say, ages skin dreadfully."

"Fine, then give me yours," he said.

I peeled off my short-sleeved, white-cotton button up and handed it to him. He slipped it over his head.

"I rather float in this," he said.

"It does the job," I said. "Please pass the retsina, young sir."

He removed the old-style bottle cap with this thumb and fingers and passed the bottle to me. I filled my glass, but Rhiannon waved me away when I leaned in to pour hers.

"There are three things we need to discuss today," she said.

"Oh dear," I said. "No good news ever follows the phrase 'need to discuss', does it?"

I took a strong sip of the retsina and served myself some carpaccio and sliced each of us a piece from the baguette.

"First, and I am sorry, Cameron, to mention her at lunch," said Rhiannon. "I received a letter from your wife, my daughter. She wants to know when you will return and adds, by-the-way, that she is pregnant."

"Ah," I said.

"Slut," said Peter.

"He will be her next husband," I said.

"Tramp, harlot, hussy," said Peter. "And do not tell me I am not allowed to take sides."

"May I continue?" asked Rhiannon.

Peter stabbed several rolls of carpaccio with his fork and stuffed them into his mouth.

"So, when are we going back?" asked Rhiannon. "We have a little less than two months until Samhain. And, we, by-the-way Cameron, would be you and me, not Peter."

"Why would that be so?" I asked.

"You need to ask?" said Rhiannon.

"Because, obviously, I would hunt down this new challenger, Roland Hamstead, and use spikes to nail him to an oak," said Peter.

"Ah, obviously. My error. I apologize," I said. "And, in that case, I would like to wait until the last moment to return. I would like to spend as much time as possible with Peter and you. That is, unless I can see my children?"

"You cannot," said Rhiannon. "It is forbidden."

"Worth a try," I said. "So, a few days before then. That is when we should return."

Peter reached over and placed his hand on mine.

"Thank you, my dear," he said.

"Mais bien sûr," I said.

"Which leads to the second topic," said Rhiannon. "I will write back to your wife and advise her of our return date and of Peter's pregnancy."

"Also, advise her I shall, of her mother's pregnancy."

Peter removed his hand from mine, reached across the presented luncheon and, quite delicately took Rhiannon's wineglass by the stem and put it back in hamper.

"Well done," he said, and leaned across the carpaccio to kiss her.

"Well done, indeed," I said. I closed my eyes and tried to envision Rhiannon with my child, but all I could see were the dark boles of oak trees in a forest at night. I felt Rhiannon's arm around my waist.

"Cameron, love, now is not the time to drift away," she said.

I opened my eyes.

"It was not my intent," I said. "I tried to imagine the baby."

"I know," said Rhiannon. She kissed me on the cheek. "I have foreseen it, the child will be a girl, healthy and well. Peter and I will raise her here on this island. Good with that, are you?"

I nodded. "I am. I am. It all makes me extraordinarily pleased."

"Happy?" said Rhiannon. "Please tell me it makes you happy?"

"It does," I said. "Both children, you and Peter together here on this sacred island. It all brings me nothing but joy."

"I will be the best father for your child," said Peter. "I swear it."

"I know you will," I said. "Even I can foresee that."

"You smile, sir," said Peter. "Yet it is an evil smile."

"Not at all," I said. "I just realized I get all the wine."

"You dog, sir!" said Peter. He reached to take my glass, but I dodged him.

Rhiannon rested her wet head on my shoulder.

"Let him have his wine," she said.

"What was the third thing?" asked Peter. "You said there were three things?"

"Oh, that was it," said Rhiannon. "Clarine's pregnancy, our date of return, and my pregnancy. I think. Am I forgetting something? I am not thinking clearly."

"And, Cameron, you may place your hand on my belly and tell us you love us," said Rhiannon.

I set my hand gently on her stomach.

"I love you," I said.

"Well done, Cameron," said Peter. "Now she must be spoiled. At least for today. I will prepare tasty morsels and you must feed her, by hand."

"Really?" I asked.

"Oh, like this I do," said Rhiannon.

So that is what I did. And Peter watched me watching Rhiannon's perfect mouth take snippets of carpaccio, olives, morsels of bread, and white cheese from my fingertips. And, there, in the early September sun, a few steps from the aquamarine clarity of Kefalos bay, with the slight rush of wavelets upon the sand, a sense of perfect wonderment settled down upon me.

I remained there, in that moment, and it was good. This was, perhaps, the most perfect instant in my life.

CHAPTER ELEVEN – AVALON

A Meadow, Wales

I watched it all that night, from beginning to the inevitable end. I know my duty well and I did love the man.

I followed the pathway in, flitting through the thick darkness of the embankment tunnel, through the young forest that lay to either side of the path, across glades of cool night air. To either side, the sheer faces of the quarry rose almost vertically in four giant steps. The bright moon lay behind me, illuminating the entire workings the quarrying had cut three-hundred meters into the mountain. The glitter of rippled water lay perhaps fifty human paces ahead. I flew toward it, past the sign reading, "Danger. Abandoned Mine Works. Absolutely No Trespassing." It said it in Welsh, too. I looked to either side. The path, or rather a reduced form of the path, moved off to the right, paralleling the fence. I followed it, came to the inevitable gap in the wire, and passed through. The trail led straight to a stone ramp that extended down into the sacred lake.

I flew out over the water. Looking down I saw it showed black and dark in the night. The rectangular lake filled the old mine pit that occupied about half of the quarry's floor, its stygian waters licking gently against the smooth-cut slate that formed its shores. Looking out I could see half-way down the two hundred meter-long lake. There, another ramp rose up out of the pit to a level stone platform set against the far quarry wall. The lake surrounded this platform on its other three sides. And on that platform, torches.

A small barge loaded with a rectangular pyre lay alongside.

I flitted up and up, above it all, looking down at the witnesses with their circle of torches. Every fourth person held a torch – thirty lights for the killing ground. It was enough. Clarine, Anna and Rhiannon, all clustered together in green robes by the cliff, near the cave mouth; Celyn, Cameron's friend, stood behind them honing the blade of an axe.

The new challenger, Roland Hamstead, stood across the lawn from the Rowans, shirtless, stretching, calm. The torchlight caught his well-muscled frame, a thin, chiseled masterpiece. He twirled a large, steel, two-handed axe easily with one hand. A dark-purple scarf embroidered with leaves in every hue of green, lay lightly around his neck, held fast with a simple knot. I saw the women in the crowd watching, eager as is their way.

How cliché, I thought, but had to acknowledge that the bastard was born and bred for this night.

I watched as Cameron appeared to step out of the cliff face – from where I hovered, the narrow cave entrance could not be seen. He looked good, I had to admit it, bronzed and in good shape. He wore a light t-shirt in the chill of the early November air, with a pair of boxers and leather sandals. He held the steel axe easily with both hands. He smiled across the glade, the smile of a lord. Hamstead stopped his twirling and knelt, as if to begin a race.

Then, it unfolded as it always does. The chanting began, starting with The Rowans and circling the field, round and round, twelve times in all. The words of indistinct Welsh rose and fell, echoing round the quarry, two beats after the chanting, creating a swirling whirl of sound. An invitation.

And, as the echoes died, I watched Cameron step forward three paces. Hamstead remained frozen in his crouch. A light wind rustled through the oak leaves and fluttered the torches.

"Boy. Come!" commanded Cameron.

And the boy came, launching himself across the glade at speed, his axe a blur in the torchlight. Cameron blocked the first swing easily and countered, cutting low toward Hamstead's legs. The axe cut through air as Hamstead sprung up, a Jack-in-the-Box with a deadly toy.

Cameron's head fell to the grass, rolling three times, ending face up toward the stars, blood black in the torchlight, pooling from the neck. One eye twitched shut. His mouth was still locked in that damn smile.

Rhiannon collapsed. They carried her away.

Three seconds it took. Poor Cameron, our last-minute stand in for Lord of Summer.

I lingered to watch as they poured the olive oil, three barrels of it, onto the stacked wood of the pyre. Clarine, his wife, lay daisies on the coffin. Even from my vantagepoint, up in the sky, I could see she shed no tears in the torch light.

Celyn used a long pole to push the barge away from the shore. Clarine tossed a burning brand across the water, toward the pyre. She missed, the torch falling into the water with a hiss. The barge drifted away.

I sighed and spoke some quiet words. At once, the barge burst into flame.

They sang, a sweet beautiful song in Welsh that floated up above the lake like morning mist. The flashing flames of the blazing pyre grew and grew, until they lit the entire quarry, illuminating even the highest reaches of the shear, slate cliffs. And the woodsmoke carried the scent of cedar.

Too late, I swept down toward Cameron's body. I cursed my foolish sentiment. He had already moved on.

I know what you are thinking: Foolish sprite, how hard is it to find the soul of a dying god? But, please remember, it is Cameron O'Donnel we are talking about. It wasn't my fault, really. First, I searched the woods nearby, slipping among the branches, searching about for a bright spark. Then, up and up soaring well above the valley, looking down upon the bright lights of the village, the headlights on the twisting highway, the quiet darkness of the mountaintops. Nothing. The bastard had slipped away without so much as a thought for making my life easier.

Typical.

I dodged a long-eared owl – the beasts are always after an easy meal, but the rush of air across their meter-wide wings makes them easy to avoid – and I slipped sideways into the void. There, in the formless grey, I took a moment to think. The void is good for that.

The boy was raised a Christian and later adopted Rhiannon's pagan ways. He loved her, after all. But I never knew what he really believed. Did he even believe anything at all, in the end?

I slipped sideways again, emerging high up in the air above the Elysian Fields, where, as Homer says 'life is easiest for men. No snow is there, nor heavy storm, nor ever rain, but ever does Ocean send up blasts of the shrill-blowing West Wind that they may give cooling to men'. I quickly scanned the groves, the glades, the orchards, the pools and the streams, all glorious and verdant under the bright sunlight. He was not there.

Where next?

The darker parts of Hades? The dying gods are forgiven all sins.

Valhalla? Well, he did die in battle, but all that shouting didn't really seem like his gig. The drinking did, though. I slipped in, materializing high up in the oak rafters of the that colossal drinking hall. Below, all was just as one would expect: drinking and shouting, fornicating on the tables. The usual. Then, alarming stillness as all eyes turned upwards.

Too late, I recalled some highly amusing pranks I may or may not have played on these dear, departed Vikings in the past.

The drinking horns began flying my way immediately, rising toward me in an alarming number at demigod-like velocity. I managed to quickly scan this tiny world before fleeing. He was not there.

I really needed to make up with them some day. The mead in Valhalla is brilliant.

The Summerland? Even though a decidedly new Wiccan thing, I

thought I should check. I popped in at medium height above a peach orchard and was immediately surrounded by winged fairies. One flew closer and held out a small silver tray piled with white squares.

"Tofu?" she asked.

"Um, no thank you," I said. "But could you tell me please, has Cameron O'Donnel been this way?"

She shook her tiny head.

"The Summer Lord?" she said. "Have you lost him?"

A disapproving growl rose from the surrounding fairies as the collective exposed their fangs.

I fled, again. The Summerland is scary.

Next, Kos.

I materialized in their kitchen. Below me, Rhiannon, now visibly pregnant, in a loose, white t-shirt and blue jeans, warmed a baby bottle in a double saucepan. In the living room nearby, a similarly dressed Peter held – and I am not at all biased – an alarmingly beautiful young boy in his arms, rocking in a simple, Quaker-style rocker. He read aloud, so I waited, politely, so as not to have my wings plucked.

"Thus, we may know that there are five essentials for victory: One, He will win who knows when to fight and when not to fight. Two, He will win who knows how to handle both superior and inferior forces. Three, He will win whose army is animated by the same spirit throughout all its ranks. Four, He will win who, prepared himself, waits to take the enemy unprepared. Five, He will win who has military capacity and is not interfered with by the sovereign," said Peter.

"Peter, my love," said Rhiannon. "Perhaps the *Art of War* is a touch heavy for an infant?"

"Really?" said Peter. "It is traditional in my family."

"You know best, I am sure," said Rhiannon.

"No, no," said Peter. "If you are concerned, perhaps some Clausewitz? And, also, I think Puck is here."

"He is?" asked Rhiannon.

"I am here," I said.

"He says he is here," said Peter. "Puck, why are you here?"

"Just coming to see the baby," I said. "He is amazing."

"Thank you," said Peter. "We named him Cameron Junior, obviously. We've been calling him CJ."

I flew toward Peter and the child and hovered in front of them.

"Can you see me at all?" I asked.

"Just a slight distortion in the air," said Peter.

The baby reached out toward me with both hands.

"Ack!" said CJ.

"I do believe he can," I said.

"Hmm," said Peter.

"Forgive me, but can I ask a question?" I asked.

He nodded.

"Anything weird happening lately? Any ghosts or spirit visitations?" I asked.

"No," said Peter.

"I see," I said.

"Puck, I am guessing, but you were supposed to meet our beloved Cameron and lead him somewhere, were you not?" said Peter. "And you lost him?"

"You always were too darn quick," I muttered.

"Rhiannon, my love, Puck has lost Cameron," said Peter.

"What!" said Rhiannon.

"It was a mere moment of inattention, caused by a sentimental desire to watch his funeral," I said.

"Now he is making excuses," said Peter.

"Puck!" yelled Rhiannon.

"I will find him, I swear!" I said and stepped sideways.

The last thing I heard was Peter's voice. "If you do not, I will..."

The House of Peter is scary.

There are countless worlds, dimensions, and realities. I lost track of how many of these I searched. Then, though I am not a brave sprite, I began searching the dark spaces in between.

It is easy to lose track of time in those, formless, colorless places. And I did. Eventually, though, in time, I found him, just standing there in the chill of the formless, swirling, shapeless mist, dressed as he was on that last day, in a light t-shirt, and a pair of boxers in the Cameron plaid, and leather sandals.

He stood there, holding his head under his arm, still dripping blood.

"Hello Cameron," I said. "Waiting long?"

"Hi Puck," said Cameron. "It is hard to tell. Have I been?"

"I think so," said Puck. "My fault, I fear."

"I was beginning to believe this might be it," said Cameron. "I was starting to despair."

"I apologize," said Puck. "I missed you at the glade."

"Well, that is ok," said Cameron. He held up his head with two hands. "But, Puck, I can't seem to put my head back on."

I saw tears forming in his eyes.

"Cameron, I really am sorry, you have been through so much," I said. "This place will not allow you to mend, but will you come with me now?"

He moved his head up and down, as if to nod. I flew forward to touch his shoulder, then we stepped sideways. We appeared together in a deep fiord, on a beach of small grey stones surrounded by steep cliffs. A deep sea lay before us. And, on that sea, a short distance from shore, in the gentle, grey waves, bobbed a small, open sailing ship in the Viking style. Three stunningly beautiful women stood upon that ship, all clad in gold-laced white samite. All three wore gold circlets upon their short, tightly curled black hair with ringlets falling to either side of theirs faces. I knew they had been waiting, but not for how long. I also knew they would not mention it, not them. As one, they released their mesmerizing smiles.

"Cameron, please put your head back on now," I said.

He did so, lifting his head with two hands and setting it upon the stump of his neck. A sharp, bright golden light forced me to look away. When I looked back, he was turning his head from side to side. I could see no wound.

"Seems good," said Cameron. "Thank you, Puck."

He looked around.

"This is much better," he said. "Thanks."

"No worries," I said. "Again, sorry for the delay."

He nodded, properly this time.

"Am I to go with them?" he asked.

"You are," I said. "To the Isle of the Blessed. You have earned it, boyo."

"Thanks," said Cameron. "Will they be coming in?"

"You just walk out to them," I said.

He started toward them, then stopped.

"Puck, I am walking on water," he said.

"Obviously," I said. "Else you would drown."

"Huh," said Cameron. "Are you coming?"

I flew toward him and hovered in front of his face.

"It is not permitted," I said. "Sorry."

"So, this is goodbye then?" he said.

"Yes," I said.

"Well, thanks for all your help," said Cameron. "And for your friendship."

I nodded. "And yours, my dear. Now get going, boyo," I said. "It is time for you to heal. And, it will take a while."

He turned and walked out across the gentle swells of that dark water to the ship. The three took his hands and helped him over the side. I saw as each in turn embraced him and kissed his forehead.

The great sail, dark green and emblazoned with a bright, golden sun, unfurled and filled with wind, and the ship turned out to sea, leaving a sharp wake in the waters behind it. Cameron waved as the craft became haze upon the waters.

"Fuck," I said to the stillness.

I waited a while in that quiet place. I had loved him so. And the dying gods give so much, becoming in the end mere reflections of forest and meadow.

I stepped sideways.

Their kitchen lay dark when I materialized. I heard not the slightest sound. I shifted, rematerializing high above their home into a hot, cloudless summer night. A halfmoon hung amongst pinpoint stars. The sounds of cicadas rose, shrill and strident from the silver-green olive groves below. I hovered, turning about, seeking. In the distance, up in the hills I spied the glow of a large bonfire. I headed that way.

I flew up, past the olive trees, up, over the cypress, and into a small, forested valley in the side of the mountain. The bonfire leapt bright and angry within a ring of large standing stones. Clearly some time had passed since my last visit.

A circle of people sat watching the fire. I saw Rhiannon, a toddler asleep in her lap. The Rowans only ever have girl children. And, next to Rhiannon, Peter with a boy jumping up and down in his lap, pointing up toward me.

"Pretty!" cried CJ.

And I, shallow sprite that I am, loved him immediately.

All of them, Rhiannon, Peter, Traka, Kiki, Zappides, Sister Frieda and Nikos looked up toward me. I flew down toward Peter.

CJ clapped his hands.

"Pretty fairy!" he said.

"I found him," I said quietly. "I sent him on his way. He will be safe now on the Isle of the Blessed. But do not tell them that last part, I should not have mentioned it. My mind is a little muddled."

"Thank you, Puck," said Peter. He turned to Rhiannon.

"Puck found our beloved," he said. "He is now in a good place."

"Thank you, Puck," said Rhiannon. "Where is he?"

"Puck is not permitted to say," said Peter.

"Ah," said Rhiannon. She looked down at her daughter.

"Puck, you seem sad," said Peter. "Is it because of what I did to Hamstead?"

"What did you do to our new Lord of Summer?" I asked.

"Nothing, really," said Peter. "It was rather biblical, though, seeing him nailed spread eagle on the beech tree like that, with spikes through his hands."

"You did not do that, did you?" I asked.

"I am sure he will heal, in time," said Peter. "Almost certainly. But you really do seem upset."

"I am merely weary," I said. "It was hard to see Cameron so. Do not tell Rhiannon. She, too, has suffered enough."

Peter nodded.

"Puck, stay with us a while, will you?" he asked. "CJ would you like to play with the pretty fairy?"

The boy leapt from his lap to the ground, landing on his tiny legs.

"Yes, please!" he cried.

"Would you please, Puck?" said Peter. "It would be a kindness."

I flitted down and hovered before the boy, just out of hands' reach.

"Can you catch me?" I asked.

He squealed with delight and charged toward me. I dodged and fled, at first too quickly, then more slowly as I lead him in a dance, at first between and around the standing stones, then out into the cypress forest.

"Ten minutes, Puck!" called Peter.

I swore, then, to all the deities, that CJ would never be a dying god and that I would watch over his family until the close of time. Adding the caveat of allowance, of course: I am an unreliable sprite, and somewhat prone to meandering.

The End.

Dramatis Personae:

Cameron O'Donnel – The Lord of Summer, Rhiannon's Love
Rhiannon Rowan – A former Rowan, Cameron's Love
Anna Rowan – A former Rowan, Rhiannon's Mother
Clarine Rowan – The Rowan, Cameron's Wife, Rhiannon's Daughter
Flora Rowan – Daughter of Clarine and Cameron
Morgan Rowan – Daughter of Clarine and Cameron
Andrew Stone-Horvath – Son of Cameron and Judge Angeline Stone-Horvath
Peter D'Laurent – A waiter
Puck – A spirit or illusion
Nikos – A taxi driver
Vassilia Traka – Professor emeritus of the University of Alban in Scotland, a Wise Woman
Diogenis Zappides -- Director of Kos Archaeological Museum
Kiki Poole – A waitress
Sister Frieda – A nun

The Yearly Cycle (exact dates vary):

Yule: 20-23 December
Imbolc: 2 February
Ostara: 19-22 March
Beltane: 1 May
Midsummer: 19-23 June
Lughnasadh: 1 August
Mabon: September 21-24
Samhain: November 1

ACKNOWLEDGEMENTS

Down through the years, I have enjoyed countless books on the Grail and Arthurian lore. One of the best is the Folio Society's three-book-set, *Legends of King Arthur*. This set includes *Arthur, Tristan* and *The Holy Grail*. Edited and introduced by Richard Barber, it includes translations of most of the original Arthurian works by Geoffrey of Monmouth, Gottfried Von Strassburg, Chretien de Troyes, and Wolfram von Eschenbach. Barber has cleverly edited the narratives into a single voice so the progression through the stories does not throw off the modern reader. If you are interested in pursuing the Arthurian saga, I would recommend this set – though you may have to search for it a bit.

If you are interested in the Jungian interpretation of the Grail saga, then, in my mind, there is only one place to go, *The Grail Legend* by Emma Jung and Marie-Louise von Franz. Originally published in German in 1960 as Die Graalslegend in psychologischer Sicht, it is the culmination and synthesis of Emma Jung's life's work. This book, too, can be a challenge to find. My rather beat up paperback version came to me as a gift.

The images accompanying the text are from various sources. The floorplan of Musée de Cluny is from 1901. Source unknown (author's collection). The sketch of mosaics at Ganagobie Abbey was provided by my excessively tolerant spouse. All the postcards are based on actual cards in the author's collection. Sadly, the images shown in this text are recreations of the original postcards based on modern photographs. The Asklepion image (figure 3) was provided by the Wikimedia.org – the original photo (now altered) by Mickapr. The museum image (figure 4) and the castle image (figure 5) were both provided by Wikimedia.org – both original photos (now altered) by Tedmek. All Wikimedia photos are used under the Attribution/ShareAlike licenses.

My eternal thanks go out to both Ginevra Saylor and Béa González, both of whom are kind enough to provide necessary correction to my errant thoughts and prose. If only I were wise enough to listen.

As always, I am responsible for all errors.

ABOUT THE AUTHOR

Patrick Boal was born in Montreal, Quebec, Canada and moved to Southern Ontario, Canada just in time to enter kindergarten. Raised by two ex-RCAF parents, he learned how to make a bed properly at an early age.

Patrick has written, lived and explored in numerous landscapes, including Northwestern Ontario, Canada; Philadelphia, USA; Kos, Greece; and Wales, United Kingdom. He has an abiding interest in myth and legend, which inspires and informs his written work.

He currently lives in Toronto, Canada with his wife and daughter, his dog Cosmos and is possessed by demons.

Made in the USA
Monee, IL
20 July 2020